# Never Becomes Now

*Zachary Zander Series*

*Book II*

**by**

**Larry J. Kachik, M.D.**

This book is a work of fiction. Names, characters, places and incidents are either the product of the author's imagination or are used fictitiously, and any resemblance to actual persons, living or dead, events, or locales is entirely coincidental.

Copyright 2024 by *Larry J. Kachik, MD*

All rights reserved.

# Table of Contents

# Author's Note

This book and all future works are first dedicated to my departed wife, Kathy. She inspired me, encouraged me, and made me better.

In addition to Kathy, this book is dedicated to a very special group of people who had profound impacts on my career.

These are the amazing people with which I worked. The group begins with the brothers and sisters in the emergency department. ER, doctors, consultants, physician's assistants, nurse practitioners, nurses, secretaries, aids, technicians, and technologists such as radiology, laboratory, pulmonary, security officers, pharmacists, social workers, housekeepers, administrators, maintenance staff, registration staff, secretaries, and last but not least prehospital care providers such as EMT's and paramedics. There were very few things that I did in the ER that I did alone. Emergency Medicine is a great team sport, and I worked with incredible teammates. Much like my wife Kathy, they made me better.

Likewise, when I joined The Joint Commission, I rarely functioned independently. I was part of a team, and I benefitted greatly from the expertise of my teams and a large staff at the central office.

I will leave it up to others to decide how successful I was as an ER physician, ER medical director, hospital medical director, and a physician surveyor for The Joint Commission. I was just a small part of an amazing group of professionals.

This book is dedicated to the awesome army of people who assisted me in my career.

# Chapter 1

## *Office of Terrence Carrington, Governor of New Jersey*

"Dr. Zander, it is so good to see you."

"Please, governor, call me ZZ."

"Only if you call me Terry."

"Deal, Governor Terry"

Here, I am meeting with the governor of NJ. He is a good friend. I did a small favor for him years ago that he never forgot. He helped me get my dad out of jail on a fraudulent conviction. It's nice to have connections.

OK, you know who the governor is, but who the hell am I? That is a pretty astute question. I am Zachary Zander, MD. I am an emergency medicine physician. Some people say that I am an irreverent smartass. They could be right. In my spare time, I am also a harness racing driver. I have a rather disfiguring scar on my face courtesy of the back right hoof of a 1000-pound equine athlete. More on me later. I hate to keep the governor waiting.

"ZZ, I need your help again."

"How can I help? Someone need an enema?"

"Ha, most of the legislature. They are so full of shit."

"Good diagnosis, Governor Terry. Tell me what I can do."

"In the wake of the conviction of the administrator and his partner, owner of Supreme Medical Center in Krenshaw, it has become public knowledge that the hospital was propped up by money laundering and other illegal acts."

"Yes, I enjoyed every minute of their trials. I can't believe it took so long to get them to face justice. I hope they rot. Those pricks tried to frame my father for a homicide by a vehicle that he did not commit. They parlayed that with an attempt to ruin my career, and then they attempted to have me killed. Rat bastards. To top that off, they then tried to ruin our school for special needs children and take our farm and our best horses. They finally got what they deserved, and I hope they rot some more."

The governor nodded sympathetically. "I understand that, but here is something that you might not know.  That hospital is insolvent, and there are no bidders. Now, I can finagle some funds to float the hospital for a short period of time until it can recover. But it does need to recover."

"Why is that, Governor? I hope I can speak candidly but hospitals open and close all the time. This one was built on crap, and maybe we should let it go down the drain."

"All other things aside, I might agree. But the closure of this hospital could spell grave consequences for Miracle Mile Racetrack in particular, and harness racing in general."

"Terry, now you have my full attention." (I was so flummoxed that I forgot the governor part.)

"The contract with Miracle Mile Racetrack requires that there is an accredited hospital within five miles. Other than Supreme Medical Center, the next closest hospital is twenty-five miles away. If Supreme Medical Center closes it voids the contract. Are you familiar with the Horse Racing Support Act?"

I had to think for a minute; then it came to me. "Of course, that diverts a portion of casino profits to support racing purses and sire's stakes programs in the state. Without its passage seven years ago, horse racing as we know it would not exist."

"Correct. Because of the number of jobs created and the economic impact of horse racing, the legislature was smart enough to make repeal almost impossible. It's not that groups have not tried, but so far, the bill has stood up".

I was getting nervous. "Why do I sense impending doom?"

"Well, the bill contains a clause that allows the bill to be 'reevaluated' if any track in the state, either harness or thoroughbred, closes. Closure of Miracle Mile would allow the bill to be amended or even repealed."

"Is that likely?"

"It's certainly possible. Ever since the original bill got passed, the teacher's unions have been squawking about the money not going to education. I also heard a rumor that the thoroughbred interests in the state would love nothing better than to relegate harness racing to state and county fairs only."

"Can they do that?" I was very nervous now.

"Hopefully not. But let's face it. The money bet on harness races dropped significantly after you and your friends revealed that the top harness stable at the time was drugging most of their horses."

"Well, it needed to be revealed. Deuce and Knuckles had to be stopped."

Deuce was the CEO of Supreme Medical Center and Supreme Stables. Knuckles was his ruthless partner and assistant. They had found a way to drug their racehorses without detection. They almost ruined harness racing.

The governor pondered my response. "Of course, they did. But that hit to the integrity of harness racing weakened its position versus thoroughbred racing. I know for a fact that three of the board members of Miracle Casino and Racetrack would love to dump harness racing and race thoroughbreds exclusively there. They don't have the hospital rule that harness does. It gets worse. I also got wind that the teacher's union and the thoroughbred interests are working on a deal. If they can dump harness racing from any future subsidies, the teacher's unions will get the share from the casinos that used to go to the harness interests. They will use that to increase salaries and pay off school loans for teachers. The thoroughbred interests will still get the same share. But with harness racing gone, they figure to vastly expand thoroughbred racing wagering throughout the state and country. It would be a big win with them, and it makes the deal with the teachers very lucrative."

"What can I do?" Obviously, the governor brought me here for more than coffee, although the coffee was excellent.

"For now, everything depends on the hospital in Krenshaw staying open. The name will need to be changed. Maybe it's just me, but I always hated the name Supreme Medical Center. I hate hospitals with catchy names that make you think they are great. But that's small potatoes compared to the work that needs to be done there. My people have spoken with trusted parties in the hospital. We all want you to be the Chief Medical Officer (CMO)."

We were finally getting to the reason I was summoned to Trenton. "I already am."

The governor shook his head. "No, not just the ER, chief medical officer for the hospital. A large part of the problem in Krenshaw is that there are about a dozen members of the medical staff who are bad actors. Either impaired, incompetent or just plain belligerent. Half of the staff has no respect for any rules or regulations."

"You got that right. But why me?"

"Two board members demanded that you be appointed. Mr. Upton and Dr. Morehead. You might know him as I Need." (The governor chuckled.)

Here I go again, getting myself into trouble with my nicknames. I give a lot of people nicknames, some people that I like, and especially the ones that I dislike. Dr. Morehead is an outstanding orthopedic surgeon at Krenshaw. He helped to save my career there. I had, on one occasion in the ER, referred to him as I Need. As in "I Need More Head." The perverted ER staff fully adopted it. Lucky for me, Dr.

Morehead thought it was funny. Now the governor knows. When will I grow up?

The governor wanted an answer. "Well, are you up for this?"

Other than my parents and my sister, no one has done more for me than the governor and harness racing. "No guts, no glory."

That's what I usually say when I embark on some crazy scheme.

# Chapter 2

## *Juicy Lucy's Apartment*
## *Krenshaw, NJ*

I'll let you in on a secret. I have a potty mouth. I had a job as a busboy when I was in high school. In that restaurant, like many restaurants, every other word out of your mouth better start with an F, or you were sure to be abused. I never liked being abused, so I learned; in fact, I excelled. In my current capacity as the Director of the ER and Chief Medical Officer at Krenshaw Medical Center, I have plenty of occasions to exercise my foul mouth. Sometimes I just can't help myself. I never slip up with patients or families, but the doctors on the staff are a different matter. Some of the physicians really get my goat, and they often get an earful. But you, good reader, can feel free to skip over my verbal indiscretions. They are not directed at you.

I'll explain more about myself as we go, but I must get some rest. It's 4:30 AM, and my ER shift starts at 7 AM. Up until a few minutes ago I was paying off a debt, so I haven't gotten any sleep. Who could sleep with all the noise coming out of Juicy Lucy? She's the babe lying next to me. When she wasn't screaming like a banshee, she was purring like a kitten.

Juicy Lucy is the medical staff secretary at Krenshaw Medical Center. It used to be Supreme Medical Center until the governor asked us to change it. Up until a few months ago there were two Lucy's in the medical staff office. The lead secretary was an old, dried-out maggot. I named her Not Too Juicy Lucy. That witch conspired with the previous and now rotting-in-prison administrator and some incompetent physicians to try to ruin me. It was my pleasure to boot her dehydrated carcass into the world of unemployment.

Her young and bodacious assistant is also named Lucy. She has fiery red hair. She worked behind the scenes to help me save my career and license. I named her Juicy Lucy. I am a man of principles. I pay my bills in full. In return for Juicy Lucy's help, she requested a complete physical prior to her first attempted wedding. I reluctantly (I hope you didn't believe that) paid off my debt. Unfortunately, before the big day, her fiancé ran off with his boyfriend. What a mess!

Now she has a new fiancé and a new wedding date. She claims that her physical was outdated, and she demanded a new one prior to this wedding. With her being young and healthy, I thought it was a technicality, but again she convinced me. Ok, fine, I have very little willpower. If she wasn't so sound asleep, she would tell you that I fulfilled my promise.

Damn. My phone is ringing. I immediately recognized the ringtone. It was "Bad Medicine" by Bon Jovi. That meant it was the hospital calling. That was ominous, but it could have been worse. It could have been Juicy Lucy's new fiancé telling me he was in the living room with a shotgun.

Thanks to two board members and my friend, the governor, who convinced me to take the job, I am in charge of all physician-related matters at the hospital. It's like running an adult daycare center. We don't have to change diapers too often, but other than that, it is like most pediatric daycare centers. There was always something happening. Most of the time, you didn't know about it until you smelled it.

I answered the phone. The operator said that Dr. Maliterna requested that I come immediately to the Obstetrics department. Dr. Maliterna would call me when she could, but she wanted me on my way. I kissed Juicy Lucy on her comatose forehead and threw on my scrubs. I penciled a note for the sleeping beauty and slipped out the front door.

I needed coffee but knew I didn't have time to look around for someplace open. I passed a coffee shop, but I didn't want a macchiato-guava bean espresso covered in whipped cream flavored with elephant dung. Plus, they didn't have a drive-through. I continued to the hospital with dangerously low caffeine levels.

Dr. Maliterna was the head of Ob-Gyn. She had been an attending physician at Jefferson Medical College in Philadelphia. That was its name when I went there, so that's what it is to me. They changed the name later, no doubt due to a significant donation. Nobody donated anything to me. So, I still call it Jefferson. As a third-year medical student, I did an OB rotation with Dr. Maliterna.

She testified on my behalf at my attempted medical lynching. I also owed her, but she did not request a physical. That's good for two reasons. I have some integrity, albeit not too much. I don't do physicals on married women outside of the healthcare setting. Engaged isn't married. The second reason is that Dr. Maliterna's husband is a linebacker for the NY Giants. I like my neck intact, thank you.

My family runs Fired Up Farms, which is the primo harness racing stable in North America. It was initially named FU Farms. My dad came up with that. He got away with it until he named a filly FU Too. That woke up somebody at The United States Trotting Association. He reluctantly changed the name to Fired Up Farms. Owners are permitted to name horses that they breed or buy before they have raced. All of our horses in that category are given the Fired Up moniker. I drive my family's horses when I can, and I seem to have a knack for it. What does all that have to do with Dr. Maliterna? A lot.

In addition to being a world-class OB-GYN physician, Dr. Maliterna is a harness horse nut. After my appointment as chief medical officer, I convinced her to leave the city of brotherly murder. She and her husband were happy to relocate to Krenshaw, NJ. With my urging and board connections, she was named chairperson of the department of OB-GYN. In her spare time, she hangs out at our farm and is learning the fine art of harness racing from the bottom up. Nothing like mucking out stalls to open your sinuses.

My phone rang again. The ringtone was "Rio" by Duran Duran. Fired Up Rio is one of our best horses and Dr. Celeste Maliterna's favorite. It was a logical choice for her ringtone if I do say so myself.

"Hey Celeste, what's up?"

"That asshole Buster is tuned to the gills and malpracticing his brains out."

Buster was the nickname I gave Dr. Hyman. He's an OB-GYN physician around the age of 60. Yeah, I thought that was funny too. A gynecologist named Hyman. It got even better when I christened him "Buster Hyman."

He was the medical staff president who tried to end my career with the help of the previous administrator. After the truth about the witch hunt that ensnared me surfaced, the board of directors removed all the medical staff officers. Buster is now just a drunk old doctor. I haven't had the grounds to remove him from the staff yet, but it sounds like I may just get my chance.

"Celeste, what the hell is going on?"

"I came in for a patient in labor and opened Buster's locker by mistake. I found a ¾ empty fifth of Stoli vodka in there. I didn't touch anything. I closed the locker and put my combo lock on it so he couldn't get rid of the bottle."

"Great thinking! Did you see him drinking?"

"No, but let me finish. So, I check on my patient, and I hear a lot of commotion coming from the recovery area. He and the nurses were in a shouting match. The long and short of it was that both the scrub and circulating nurses claimed a sponge was missing from the c-section they just performed. They told Buster before he closed the peritoneum. He ignored them and continued to close the patient. When they asked for a final sponge count, he insisted the patient be taken immediately to recovery. When I walked into recovery, he screamed at me. 'Get the hell out of here, you bitch.'"

"Always the charmer," I lamented.

Celeste continued. "Well, now I have two problems. A drunken ignorant doctor and a patient with a possible retained foreign body."

"What a mess. I will be there in about fifteen minutes. What is your plan?" I still needed some coffee. This was going to be a fiasco.

"As the chief of his department, I had the right to request he submit to an exam in the ER. I informed him that the exam would include testing for alcohol usage. He refused, and now I was called an f-ing c-word."

"You moved up in the world, and you got an adjective and the c-word both together!" I tried to lighten the moment. Celeste was seriously pissed.

"That won't be the first or last time that I was referred to in that manner. But I need to be brief. My patient is five cm and ready for her epidural. I need to evaluate the patient with the possible retained foreign body. I need to take her back to surgery. As chair of the department, I am permitted to assume her care if I feel she is in danger. But I want your approval."

"Of course, you have my approval. Do whatever you need to do for the patient." I was adding up the malpractice verdict in my head as I spoke.

Celeste then gave me some good news. "After Buster refused the blood alcohol level, I had security, and your buddy Amos restrain him. I knew he would try to leave to avoid any testing. That Amos is smart. He got a nice video of Buster slurring his speech while calling him the "N" word. That should help. I asked them to lock him in a storeroom until you got here. So, he's in the room outside of Obstetrics recovery. With that much vodka onboard, he will eventually have to empty his bladder. I had Amos let two urinals out in plain sight. One way or another, I think we will get some type of alcohol sample."

"Urine alcohol levels are tricky to interpret. However, it might be the best evidence we can get. We may not be able to prove a certain level, but anything other than zero will be damning. I will be there in five minutes or less now. Please have the nurses call me if you need anything else from me."

"I get to jog Rio!!"

Now Fired Up Rio, Rio for short, was our best world-class trotter. She was worth three or four million. Celeste had only two months under her belt in the stable. She stuck her neck out for me, and I liked to reward good behavior. Somehow, I will have to explain to Dad why one of our least experienced grooms should get to jog our best horse.

"You drive a hard bargain, but I owe. You get to jog Rio."

"Good deal. Talk to you later." Celeste hung up.

Celeste had mentioned Amos. Amos worked two jobs. During the day, he was a paramedic with the local ambulance service. At night, he was a patient care tech in our emergency department. When I first joined the hospital, I worked permanent night shift. That is where I befriended Amos.

Amos is an astute medic and a workhorse. He can smell bullshit two miles away. He was wise to the fact that the previous nurse manager of the ER was involved in nefarious deeds before her involvement became obvious. He also figured out I was boffing her before that became common knowledge.

Don't get the wrong idea. I am not some kind of Don Juan. The truth is that I don't get very much. You just happened to hear about two of my trysts. I wish there was more to tell.

I asked the operator to connect me to I Need.

"Hellllllllloo," the voice got softer and softer and then I heard snoring.

I screamed, "I Need, I need you to come in."

The phone was filled with static as millions of neurons in I Need's brain focused on the magic phrase. He had a habit of not wanting to come in at night and falling asleep when called. As part of his talking me into the Chief Medical Officer job, we made an agreement. If I required his help, I had simply to use the magic phrase that I just used. It worked. His next words were clear.

"Dr. Morehead here, what do you need, ZZ?"

"Here are the short strokes. Celeste Maliterna thinks Buster is drunk and may have left a sponge in a patient during a c-section. Maliterna is his chief of department, but she is tied up delivering one of her own patients and treating the mom with the extra sponge in her. Buster refused her request for a blood alcohol level. Both you and I also have the authority to request one, but considering my previous history with Buster, I think it would be better if both of us were there to make the request.

"You know I hate to come in at night, but that damn drunk must go, and now is the time. See you in twenty minutes."

# Chapter 3

## *Krenshaw Medical Center*

I entered through the ER entrance because I knew I could score some coffee there. I also decided that I had better get someone to cover my morning shift. I knew that I was walking into a shit-storm, and they never end in a timely fashion. As I gave instructions to Wanda, the ward secretary, as to which physicians were likely to be interested in my shift, Amos handed me a freshly brewed cup of coffee. See what I mean about this dude? The man always had what you need when you needed it.

"Thanks Amos. You are a lifesaver. Dr. Maliterna really appreciated your help. I understand you have a nice video for me."

"You are welcome, Doc ZZ. Buster is blitzed out of his gourd. His eyes are glassy, his speech is slurred, and he about fell trying to get down the hall. Lucky for us, he got the "N" word out clearly!"

"Sorry you had to get that treatment, Amos."

"Thanks, Doc, comes with the territory sometimes."

I sipped my coffee. "Is he still locked in the supply room?"

"Yeah, Frank from security is parked outside the door. The last I heard, he was asleep in the storeroom. Not sure if he took the bait on the urinals, but knowing him, he might just go on the floor."

"Hopefully, he can be convinced to submit to a blood test. You never know."

"You know where I am if you need me. The video has been sent to your email."

**Obstetrics Department.**

Sabrina, the night shift charge nurse, met me at the door. She was not one of my favorite people. Every time Buster acted out of line, she seemed to take his side. She downplayed what we all thought might be significant incidents. I had her investigated for ties to Buster, but it looks like she was only loyal to what had once been a good physician. In some ways, I had to applaud that. I wondered if anyone would stick up for me when I lost it.

"Dr. Zander, sorry you had to wait."

"No problem, Sabrina. Can you give me an update?"

"Dr. Maliterna has been tied up with her own patient, so she hasn't seen Dr Hyman's patient yet. She should be free in a few minutes. Dr. Hyman is asleep in the storage room."

Before she could come out with another word she broke down in tears. "Dr. Zander, I am so sorry. I saw Dr. Hyman do so many amazing things in his younger years. Those memories made me blind to just how impaired he had gotten. I know that I soft-peddled some of his past indiscretions. But tonight, I saw a drunk operate, and I almost vomited. Then he left a sponge in and refused to listen to me and the staff tell him of his mistake. I assure you that I will testify to exactly what I saw. Please make sure he never hurts another patient."

"Why didn't someone call me or Dr. Maliterna when he showed up drunk? We might have been able to avoid this mess."

"That's just it, Dr. Zander, his patient has been in labor for eight to ten hours. I swear Dr. Hyman was stone-cold sober at 11 PM when he arrived. No one really noticed that he was impaired until he was in the middle of the c-section. We tried to get Dr. Hyman to stop after he delivered the baby, but he refused. Dr. Maliterna took over after we were in recovery."

"Is the baby ok?" Things were bad enough. I didn't need any further problems.

"The baby's fine. It was after the baby was born that Dr. Hyman really decompensated."

I found Frank at his post outside the storeroom. In a few minutes, I was joined by I Need. We entered the room and woke up Buster. He had curled up in a fetal position on the floor. How appropriate.

"Waaaa fuuuuck you." He sounded exactly like an addict who had been given Narcan.

I Need got into his face and said "Dr. Hyman, Sam, we got a real problem here. Can you help us?"

"Fuck you both." Came the reply, badly slurred. Followed by a wad of spit that narrowly missed I Need's face.

I Need was unfazed. "Sorry, you have that attitude. You appear drunk to me. As the president of the medical staff, I hereby request that you submit to a blood alcohol test."

"Fuck you both again," Buster uttered, a little more clearly this time.

"Does that mean no?" I Need quickly retorted.

"Fuck you both thrice."

I couldn't help but think. *Who in the hell uses the word thrice*? Assholes like Buster, I guessed.

Just as I Need and I were pondering our next move, I noticed the urinal in the corner of the room was nearly full of Buster's urine. We had what we needed. A Chain of Evidence form was initiated, and the specimen went to the lab. I also collected the hocker that Buster had just spit with a swab that I labeled and sealed.

I Need, and I both went to the lab to watch the tech run the urine sample. We also videotaped the placement of the saliva sample in the forensics safe. Incriminating specimens had a way of disappearing at Krenshaw Medical Center. We were taking no chances that the tech might be a friend of Buster.

Once that was accomplished, we took Buster to his locker and removed the lock. In severely slurred speech, he denied any knowledge of the Stoli bottle. He claimed someone had put it there to frame him. I Need, and I witnessed as the chief of hospital security bagged and tagged the bottle while wearing gloves. We submitted the bottle to have the contents verified and fingerprints taken.

Buster's wife was called to pick him up. The alcohol level we got from the urine was 305. It's not always easy to convert a urine result to the equivalent blood alcohol concentration. But we didn't need to. Any alcohol in his urine was proof he had been drinking.

# Chapter 4

## *Obstetrics Unit*
## *Krenshaw Medical Center*

Celeste had not initially told Mr. Campbell about the probable retained foreign body. She told him that Dr. Hyman was ill and that the nurses had asked her to reevaluate his wife. She hadn't totally lied. Buster was a sick bastard. After obtaining their permission, she examined Mrs. Campbell.

Her exam didn't reveal much. The patient was still under the effects of the spinal anesthesia. Her belly was soft. Celeste pondered whether to get a CT scan to confirm that a sponge had been left behind. But she was worried that Buster may have been so drunk that he made other, and potentially more serious, errors.

Her decision-making was further influenced by the nursing staff. Sponge counts being off was not uncommon. Sometimes, two were stuck together and counted as one. Sometimes, the missing culprit was found in the trash or the laundry. In this case, the nursing staff tore the room apart and one sponge was still missing.

I arrived outside the room as Celeste finished her exam. She met me in the hall.

"I think I should explore her. The nurses are 99.9% certain that our missing sponge is in her abdomen. I also want to be sure that Buster Putz didn't do anything else wrong."

I agreed. "Sounds appropriate."

Celeste had a raised eyebrow. "How much of this do we tell the Campbells? There is most definitely a lawsuit here."

I was sure she wasn't expecting my response. "Tell them exactly what you are thinking and why. Stick to the facts, but be as honest as possible."

We disclosed everything. That included that we suspected Buster of being drunk and that he had left a sponge in during the c-section. Celeste offered to prove it with a CT scan first, but she also told them that she would feel better if she got a look around under the hood, so to speak.

The Campbells were shocked. They asked a few intelligent questions and consented to the abdominal exploration. I met with the nursing staff to be certain they were calm enough to continue working. If need be, I could call down another crew from the operating room to assist Celeste.

They appeared fine and were eager to make this case right. I elected to seek out Mr. Campbell and remain with him during the operation. He finished a conversation on his cell phone as I walked into the waiting area. I offered him a coffee, and he accepted. I was happy to be able to escort him to the nurse manager's office. I knew he might want to vent. The people in the waiting room did not need to know our business. The next thirty minutes were quite painful for me.

"You think you can trust doctors and hospitals. Lives are on the line. You assume that people will do the right thing. Then you find out that the doctor who just delivered your wife was blitzed and that he left a sponge in. This sucks. You know we are going to sue. We have retained MEP Legal Associates. I am sure you have heard of them," stated the seriously perturbed husband.

I always hated it when people threatened to sue. After all, any dipshit can you sue for just about anything. The big question wasn't if they could sue. The question was, could they win? In this case, I knew they could win. They should win. I want them to win.

MEP stood for McPherson, Epstein, and Prinzmetal. They were big, and they were ruthless. They spent more on their advertising budget than the entire payroll of my ER. Billboards, radio, TV ads, and internet pop-ups inundated you 24/7. I had nicknamed the firm Make Em' Pay.

I replied, "The legal proceedings are your right. We have done nothing to hide what has gone on here. When we are prepared to settle, we will make you an appropriate offer for the hospital's involvement.

You will still be free to pursue an action against Dr. Hyman." (Hint to Mr. Campbell to sue that drunk prick!)

He was taken aback. "I expected a cover-up and double talk. That's what MEP told me would happen."

I was proud to have disappointed MEP.

**Nurse Manager's Office, Obstetrics**

Celeste poked her head in the door. Mr. Campbell immediately jumped up.

"Is she ok?" He demanded to know. But his voice and demeanor were considerably less hostile than just an hour before.

Celeste shook her head. "Please sit. She is in recovery now. As soon as she is fully awake, we will get you in there to see her."

I couldn't wait any longer. "What did you find?"

Celeste ignored me and addressed Mr. Campbell. "We found the sponge and removed it. This may sound strange, but it was a stroke of good luck that it had been left behind. During this operation I found two different errors that had been committed in the first operation. Your wife had a perforation of her bladder, and her abdomen was not properly closed. Eventually, she would have deteriorated, and we would have had to operate. I guess you can call it good news that we were able to fix those things before they became more serious."

"Will she be ok?" Tears ran down Mr. Campbell's face. He made no attempt to wipe them away.

Celeste grabbed some tissues from the manager's desk and handed them to him. "I believe so. The next few days are critical. She is young and healthy. I am cautiously optimistic."

Celeste answered every question Mr. Campbell could think of. We promised him that we would sit down with him and his wife tomorrow and bring her up to speed. He thanked Dr. Maliterna. I think he meant it.

# Chapter 5

## *Office of the Chief Medical Officer*
## *Krenshaw Medical Center*

I told Celeste I would meet her in the medical staff office to complete the tons of paperwork that would be required to document today's cluster. Her own patient was now ready to push. She headed back to the OB suite as I entered my office. I had hardly settled in when I heard a knock on my door.

"Come in."

The door slowly opened and there stood Juicy Lucy in a yellow sun dress with red flowers. The color of the flowers matched her flaming red hair. She was simply stunning. She had a satisfied look on her face that I hoped I helped to create.

"Dr. Zander. I cancelled the wedding."

I almost filled my drawers. "You what?"

"After last night, I know that you are the only person that can ring my bell. I wasn't sure after our previous encounter, but now, I am positive. I called Michael this morning and called it all off. I am yours."

"Juicy Lucy, be serious. You can't just call off a wedding like that!"

"ZZ last night was incredible. It changed me forever!"

I started to stutter as I was searching for a way out. I had a great time last night, but I wasn't ready to buy the cow. Before I could say another word, Juicy Lucy spoke up.

"April fools, you goof. Got your ass good, didn't I? I mean, you were great last night, but that changes nothing. You closed a chapter in my life with a bang. (She giggled.) Now, I am ready for the next chapter. Are you coming to the wedding? You didn't respond to the RSVP."

I would be lying if I told you I wasn't relieved. I was always the jokester. Well, this one beat most things I ever pulled.

"Juicy Lucy, you scared me. Do we have any fresh Depends here? You really had me going, and I think I might have gone."

With what you have been through since you left my place, I thought you could use a little humor. Sit down and relax. I will bring you some coffee. Please review the suspension letter that I prepared for Buster. Once you finalize it, I will have a courier deliver it to his home."

"So, you know all about it?"

"While you were meeting with the husband, I Need came in to do his documentation. He gave me a brief synopsis and asked me to prepare a summary suspension letter."

"I will be at the wedding."

"Who are you bringing?" (Even though she was getting married, she still wanted to know who I might be entertaining.)

"One of my horses. Can I get the coffee now?"

Celeste joined me after the delivery. It was almost 11 AM by the time we completed the paperwork documenting the conversation with the Campbells. I was dead beat, and I looked like it. It was after 12:30 when we finished the novel we had written describing Buster's actions. Now Celeste had less sleep than me, but she looked totally fresh. How in the hell do those obstetricians do that?

She declined my offer for lunch as she had a full afternoon ahead of her in her office. She had not forgotten her request.

"As to me jogging Rio?"

I smiled. "Dad is ok with you jogging her. But you know she is retiring soon, so you need to schedule it before she does. Dad wants you and Stephanie to go a few laps in the two-seated jog cart. If Stephanie thinks Rio is behaving and you can handle her, she will let you go the last laps alone."

"Wowww, I can't wait. That has been a dream of mine since I saw my first race twenty years ago. Thank you." Before I could say another word, she was out the door. I guess she didn't want me to change my mind.

Some of you may not know much about harness racing. It's horseracing with the horses that pull the carts. They are called sulkies, and the people sitting in them are called drivers, not jockeys. Harness horses have to maintain a certain gait when they race. Either they pace or they trot.

When they trot, they look like your cat. They move their front left and back right legs at the same time. It's a diagonal gait. The ones that pace move their front left and back left legs at the same time. They waddle. The successful ones waddle fast. They don't go quite as fast as a thoroughbred, but they still move about 35 mph. That may not seem that fast, but considering that in a race, there is a 1,000 pound horse in front of you and usually another one that big breathing down your neck, it gets a little interesting. Plus, the seat on a race bike is about 12-14 inches square. My ass is bigger than that. It doesn't give you a lot of confidence. Yes, I did fall off a few times, but I have gotten much better at holding on.

I don't think Celeste's butt is as big as mine. But I also don't think her husband, the all-pro linebacker, would appreciate me measuring it. Fortunately, we won't have to worry about that. When the horses are jogging for exercise as opposed to training or racing, we use a jog cart. It has a much bigger seat. The one we use to train rookie grooms has a seat that can hold two people. That is what we will use for Celeste. That way, Stephanie can go with her until she feels comfortable letting Celeste solo with Rio.

# Chapter 6

## *Office of the Chief Medical Officer*
## *Krenshaw Medical Center*

Juicy Lucy brought fresh coffee and handed me a call slip. Attorney Samuel Issacs was representing Buster and wanted to talk to me as soon as possible. One of my friends had tried to retain Sam Issacs to represent me during my medical staff lynching. He was supposedly the best at defending physicians in medical staff issues. He was overbooked at the time and had to decline. He reluctantly gave us the name of an attorney whom he disliked but who he thought was competent in medical staff affairs.

That is how I came to be represented by Dan Santucci. Dan was, and still is, a wizard. He proved my innocence, restored my license, and helped secure funding in perpetuity for the Always Hope School. More on the school later. Dan became one of the family and I was instrumental in getting Krenshsaw Medical Center to hire him as our CEO. I knew that days like today would be a frequent stop on our long journey to turn this hospital into a respectable medical institution. I decided to call Dan before returning the call to Issacs.

"Dan, how the hell are you?"

"Up to my ass in spiders and alligators, and I hear that you threw a rattlesnake into my pit this morning. Don't you ever take a rest?"

"No rest for the wicked. I take it you heard about Buster?"

"Just that he was drunk and botched a c-section."

"Word travels fast."

I briefed Dan on the bottle in the locker, the retained sponge, and the feelings of all involved that Buster was drunk. When that was done, I filled him in on how we obtained a urine alcohol level and Buster's suspension. He seemed impressed that we followed procedure and may have preserved valuable evidence.

I had to know. "Will the urine alcohol hold up?"

Dan thought for a minute. "Of course, a blood alcohol would have been better. If this was a DUI case, I would be skeptical. But we only need to prove that he had been drinking while practicing. I think we can do that with the urine result. No judge in their right mind would throw that out on a technicality when a woman's life and the life of her child were on the line."

I asked. "Can we also get DNA testing from the top of the bottle in case he was drinking from the bottle?"

Dan quickly responded. "It would make sense, but without a sample of Dr. Hyman's DNA, what good would it do? From what I hear, there isn't a lot of DNA in a urine sample, and what is there degrades quickly."

I grinned. "But there is plenty of DNA in saliva. Dr. Hyman gave us a nice sample when he attempted to spit on I Need. We bagged and tagged it. It's in the forensics locker."

Dan laughed. "We might have some difficulty getting it into evidence since he didn't consent to the testing. But let's cross that bridge later. Get the testing done."

He then continued to praise Dr. Maliterna. "I heard via the grapevine that she might have a good video and still picture evidence of Buster's c-section mistakes."

"Per our policies, Celeste and I already disclosed the information we have with the husband and wife. We are to meet with him and his wife again tomorrow. Do you want to be there?"

Dan surprised me. "Believe it or not, I don't. Our process is based on full disclosure and transparency. You and Celeste have a rapport with them. Bringing an attorney CEO to sit in smells of conditional answers and cover-up. Just stick to the known facts, avoid conjecture, and you two will do fine."

"Ok, thanks for your confidence. Buster has already engaged counsel, and his attorney wants me to call him."

"Ok, who's the stooge?" Dan inquired.

"Sam Issacs."

"That's no stooge. Sam is the best in the business of defending doctors in medical staff matters."

"Number two in my book." I quickly added.

"Thanks, but he is a formidable opponent. Let me call him to see what he wants. Buster must be paying him a fortuna to find a technicality. We aren't going to give him one."

A fortuna was Dan-speak for a fortune.

**CEO's Office**

"Sam, this is Dan Santucci. I understand that you requested Dr. Zander return a call. I thought it might be more productive for me to return your call."

"Of course, Dan. Thank you for getting back to me so quickly."

Sam continued. "I was delighted when you were appointed CEO. That place needs a strong leader. How do you run it while you also wear the hat of the in-house counsel?"

Dan chuckled. "I have a kick-ass COO. She takes care of the day-to-day stuff. I am just a figurehead."

It was Sam's turn to laugh. "I don't believe a word of that. We better get down to business. I don't have a kick-ass COO to do my work."

"What can I help you with today?"

"As you know, I represent Dr. Hyman. He was issued a summary suspension, and I need as much information as you can provide me."

"That would be little to none. Counselor, you know we are in the infancy of our investigation. You and I both know that anything that I, or Dr. Zander, or any hospital official says is on the record. So, we chose to say nothing until the hearing."

"When is the hearing?"

"It hasn't been scheduled, but without disclosing insider information, I think next Wednesday is a likely day." Dan knew from past experience that Wednesday evenings were the best time to schedule meetings involving the medical staff.

Sam made his pitch. "Would it be possible to meet with you and appropriate hospital staff a few days before the hearing to review the evidence that you have?"

"In the past, that would have been out of the question. Both sides held their cards tight until the hearing, and then they unloaded. Being on your side of the fence, I always hated that. But I can grant your request. We are all about fairness, full disclosure, and due process. We will share with you the facts that we have."

"That's amazing. I applaud the honesty and openness. But I do have to caution you that I will attack, nitpick, and generally try to destroy any evidence that you have."

"For the benefit of your client, I would expect nothing else. We only intend to bring forward rock solid evidence with appropriate legal foundation."

Sam inquired. "When can we meet?"

"Will your client be there?"

"He has the right."

Dan was receptive but laid down the ground rules. "Yes, he does, but this meeting is a courtesy and doesn't need to happen. He can only come if you personally vouch for his behavior. Your word is good for me."

"He will come if he meets my conditions."

# Chapter 7

***Fired Up Farms***
***Krenshaw, NJ***

"Good morning, Celeste. How is Mrs. Campbell doing?" I was worried.

"She doesn't have a fever, and her abdomen is soft. She passed some gas this morning. So far so good."

Isn't medicine wonderful? Nothing like a good fart to put a smile on your doctor's face, provided they aren't examining you at the time. In this case that welcome flatulence means that Mrs. Campbell is not developing an ileus. Her bowels aren't shutting down, which could be a symptom of complications.

"What time are we meeting with them today?"

She smiled. "We aren't. They had a lot of questions for me, and we had a good conversation. They did not feel another meeting was necessary."

Standing beside Dr. Maliterna was a chiseled statue of a man. Six feet four inches and 245 pounds of almost pure muscle. He was wearing shorts that exposed his intensely defined legs and a NY Giants tee shirt.

"ZZ, I would like you to meet Adrian Burns, my husband," Celeste added.

"Adrian, it's my pleasure. I really enjoy watching you play for the Giants. It's nice to see them have a stout defense again. You are a big part of it."

Adrian shook and almost broke my hand with his firm grip. I was glad I wasn't a running back. I was really happy I hadn't asked to measure Celeste's ass.

"Dr. Zander."

"Please ZZ."

"OK, ZZ, I can't thank you enough for what you are doing for Celeste. Ever since I met her, she has talked incessantly about horses, harness in particular. I know how long I dreamt of playing in the NFL. Every week, I thank God for the opportunity. Jogging a world-class horse has been her dream. Thank you for allowing her to fulfill it."

"Adrian, I know you are a tough dude, but I have seen your wife kick some serious ass in the hospital when needed. She's all pro in my book. The way she handled Dr. Hyman and saved his patient was deserving of everything I could do."

"Just the same, ZZ, I want to show our appreciation. I would like to visit the school later. I brought some jerseys and footballs to autograph for those incredible kids. Celeste tells me that the work you folks make possible there is awesome."

Adrian was referring to The Always Hope School. It's a school for special needs kids of all types, although their specialty is autism spectrum disorder. There are 50 children enrolled there of all races, creeds, and sizes. They range in age from 3 years to 25 years. Their families are not charged to send them here. I was always happy to talk about it.

Before Celeste departed to join Stephanie in the barn, I handed her a small present. She opened it and began to laugh. It was a tee shirt. On the front was a picture of Fired Up Rio. Under her picture, it read, "Piloted today by Dr. Celeste Maliterna." What she and Adrian liked the best was the inscription on the back. "There's nothing like 1,000 pounds of excitement between your legs."

Adrian and I headed toward the finish line of the training track. If Rio is behaving and Celeste is ready, Dad said she could open Rio up down the stretch of her last lap. I knew Celeste was going to go for it. The best view would be at the finish line. On the walk over there, Adrian wanted to know more about the school.

"Our successes with the kids have been extensively published. There are many keys to those gains. The first is that all therapy is worked around the track and the horses. Most kids bond well with animals if taught early how to interact with them. We have found that autistic children of all forms do exceptionally well with horses. The therapy also uses dogs, hamsters, parakeets, and even snakes. Any animal can sometimes break down the walls that are constructed around some of these kid's minds.

The second key is the therapy itself. Each child has an attendant 24/7. For 16 hours a day, their attendant is a psychologist, physical therapist, occupational therapist, or speech therapist. We rotate them around. But, each child gets 16 hours of individual therapy a day. We encourage the therapists to go far beyond their standard approach, and it works. Think about it, even in the best of institutions, the kids get a couple of hours of therapy a day. Our kids get 16 a day, and to them, it doesn't seem like therapy. But that much therapy has a significant cost. Fortunately, we don't have to worry about that."

Adrian was intrigued. "Why not?"

"The school was the brainchild of Justin McGregor. He was an entrepreneur who owned horses with our stable. He owned Always Hope. Hope was the name of Justin's wife, who passed away in her 30s of breast cancer. Justin named Always Hope after her. Always Hope was a world record trotter, which I had the privilege to drive. She won over $2 million in her racing career. That's her in the first paddock near the barn. She's the dam of Fired Up Rio. She's owned by the school.

Justin was visiting her at the farm one day when my parents brought Stephanie for a visit. At that time, Stephanie was an orphaned child of a harness race driver. He was killed in a tragic racing accident. Her mother became an alcoholic. After her mother's liver died and took her mother with it, Stephanie went from institution to institution. She was felt to have some form of autism and had never spoken. My mom and dad visited her as often as possible. By chance, they brought her to the farm one day when Justin was here.

Justin was feeding Always Hope some peppermint candies. (They are her favorite). Stephanie wandered over and rubbed Always Hope on her chest. Always Hope nudged Stephanie lovingly with her nose, and it happened. Stephanie spoke. "Nice fucking horse, nice fucking horse."

Those were the first words anyone had ever heard Stephanie speak. Justin broke down in tears, and then he broke out his checkbook. He requested that Mom and Dad try to keep her at the farm and have therapists work with her around the clock.

Over the next few months, Stephanie made incredible gains. She spoke more and more but with a few minor wrinkles. Most sentences contained significant vulgarity. It was surmised that they were probably the only things she ever learned in the homes. The therapists felt that any speech was progress. After they got her to speak freely, they would work on decreasing the profanity. Dad and Mom adopted her, and she became my sister. I am proud to be her big brother.

Justin had a business that took off beyond his wildest dreams. You can trust me; this guy was a dreamer. Anyway, he conceived of and built the Always Hope School that you see near the ¾ pole. He funded it with a large endowment. Unfortunately, that was cleaned out by unscrupulous venture capitalists. They preyed upon the school after Justin's untimely death from an amebic brain abscess."

"He died?" Adrian asked.

"Yeah, he had been swimming in a pond a few days before he developed a severe headache. He happened to be in Boston and was cared for in a very prestigious hospital. But he lapsed into a coma and was dead within a few days of admission."

Adrian nodded and then asked, "Smart dudes like him usually have great attorneys and wills. How did the venture capitalists get money that he had endowed to the school?"

"Long story short, Justin was a talker. Apparently, at an investor meeting, he told them that he would continue to help them promote the company after they purchased it. He died a short time later, and that cut the value of the company by 90%. The investors sued with the idea being that if Justin was alive and able to promote the company, they would not have lost their shirts. They won, and temporarily, the school lost."

Adrian wanted to know more. "Temporarily lost?"

Although it looked like the school might have to close due to lack of funding, fate smiled upon us. Azzie Huggins (a dear friend and the CEO of Exquisite Evolutions) invested five dollars in a national lottery ticket. She won a prize of $934 million and donated it all to the school."

Adrian seemed to enjoy the story. We arrived at the bench near the finish line of the training track.

Adrian wanted to know more about Stephanie. "So, Stephanie went from being non-verbal to a successful harness race driver?"

I beamed when I talked about Stephanie. "Her therapists saw her attraction to horses and capitalized on that. Most of her therapy centered around the horses. She first learned how to groom. Then she started to jog them, and eventually, she began to train them. She was fearless. She appeared to be able to communicate with them on a different level. She tamed our most rambunctious horses. Some of them I was even afraid to drive. That's why I convinced her to get her harness driver's license."

Celeste had told Adrian about Stephanie. "Didn't she win the Millions Mile once?"

"Yes, she did. It's a long story, but my dad wanted her to drive that race, and she drove a great race. This year, the hospital has been taking up more of my time, and she is driving more of our horses. Her driving average is better than mine."

Adrian laughed. "She is also very pretty."

I agreed. "She is now. Well, she always was, but it was hidden. My good friend Azzie Huggins, who I mentioned a short time ago, showed Stephanie how to look and act a little more ladylike. It took a while to get rid of the manure smell and even longer to teach her how to use a little makeup and work a comb. But Azzie uncovered the beautiful woman that she was the whole time."

Adrian nodded his head. "She is a knockout. Celeste told me that Stephanie is also making progress with her speech."

She speaks with reasonable grammar and sentence structure. When she is very happy or mad, she still uses a lot of profanity, primarily F-bombs. The therapists are working on decreasing that, but slowly. They want her to speak without worrying about it. Over time they have considerably cleaned up her language, but she still has a way to go. Everyone who knows and loves Stephanie understands. It's a little embarrassing when she says some things, but we tolerate it. This is a long process, and she is making amazing gains."

Adrian and I sat down, and he turned toward me. "ZZ, here's some tickets to the opener against the Steelers. I hope you can use them."

"I was thinking about going to the museum that day, but I'll consider it." I quickly snatched the tickets from his firm grasp.

# Chapter 8

*Fired Up Farms*

*Krenshaw, NJ*

"I hardly slept last night," Celeste said to Stephanie as she arrived at Rio's stall.

"Dr. Celeste, this is your lucky day. The big girl seems calm. You just might get back home in one fucking piece."

Stephanie hooked up the two seated jog cart after she and Celeste donned their helmets. I wanted Celeste to wear a flak jacket like drivers are required to wear in races, but she told me to eat shit. Women just don't respect me sometimes.

I clued Adrian in. "The plan is for the two of them to go three laps with Celeste holding the lines. If all is well, Stephanie will jump off, and Celeste will go the final three laps alone with Rio."

"How old is Rio, and how long has she been racing?" Adrian asked.

"Rio is now five years old. She raced at ages three, four, and five. In those three years she is undefeated in 34 lifetime starts and has banked $7.75 million in purses."

That brought a whistle out of Adrian.

"Last year, she was the harness horse of the year. Her final race comes up in ten days. As a broodmare, she is worth around three million. She can win two million in that last race. So, your wife is driving $5 mill around the track. Do you have a credit card that I can hold as collateral?"

Adrian gave me a funny look. I just laughed. Stephanie didn't have a care in the world, but I was a little nervous. My dad was crapping large bricks.

It was clear from the start that Celeste had this under control. Stephanie sat back in the cart and relaxed after the first lap. She took the opportunity to talk privately.

"Dr. Celeste. I need a favor."

"Shoot Stephanie. I always imagined doing this, but jogging a world class trotter is too much. I owe you."

"Good, I want to breed with my boyfriend, but I don't want to get in foal."

Celeste knew that you had to be ready for Stephanie to say just about anything, but she wasn't ready for that. "Just to be sure I got this right. You wish to have intercourse with your boyfriend, and you want some birth control."

"Isn't that what I said?"

"Stephanie, I can help you, but I need to see you in the office. When we are done, text me your cell number, and I will have my office set up an appointment."

"Soon?" Stephanie was anxious. "And you can't tell ZZ."

"Sure, soon, and you are right. Whatever you and I discuss about your health is confidential!"

Their last lap together was uneventful. Stephanie seemed relieved that she would get what she wanted, and Rio was in competent hands. Stephanie asked Celeste about a club that her boyfriend was taking her to. Celeste said she never heard of it, but she should ask me about it.

I could see Adrian was a little nervous. "Adrian, she looks good out there. She's a natural."

"Thanks ZZ. Just the same. I will feel better when she's done."

Rio got a little feisty when the kids from the school gathered outside the fence at the top of the stretch. The kids loved her, and she loved them. She always dug in when she saw them. To her credit, Celeste knew this and was ready. Coming out of the last turn, Celeste kicked out the earplugs, shook the lines and spoke to Rio. It was like watching a rocket take off. Celeste leaned back in the seat. They were flying at the wire.

Adrian and I hurried back to the barn area. Celeste was beaming. She was breathing harder than Rio. Adrian brought a spray of roses that he placed on Rio's neck. He took pictures of Celeste and Rio and then we got pictures of him and Celeste and Rio.

Celeste insisted on cooling Rio out and doing her up in the wraps that she wore in the stall. That was a two-hour project. I offered to take Adrian over to the school while Celeste finished her labor of love. He went to the car to retrieve the goodies he brought for the kids.

Stephanie was all smiles as she approached me. "The big girl was good for Dr. Celeste, and Dr. Celeste was really good with her."

"I agree. I will see you later, Steph. I must take Adrian to the school."

"Before you go, Dr. Celeste said you might know something about the new club that PC wants to take me to."

PC was one of my best friends. PC stands for Pisscatcher. During college and up until a short time ago, he collected equine urine samples at the track. He did it for the money when he was in college. After that he did it because he liked to hang out at the track. He also likes to bet, and he claims to get great tips.

He caught his samples with a cup on the end of a stick. Hence the nickname Pisscatcher. He was also a distinguished CPA with his own firm. He was instrumental in helping my family and other friends expose a horse race doping scandal and saving my medical career. Prior to Azzie's help, Stephanie had no significant female role models. My mom, and most of the women at the track were tomboys. PC was immediately smitten when Azzie showed Stephanie how to showcase her beauty. He has been dating Stephanie for the past six months.

"What new club?"

"He said he wanted to take me to the sixty-nine club."

Now I was worried. "What exactly did he say?" Stephanie sometimes used different speech and got words confused. Some people took this as Stephanie not being intelligent. Boy were they wrong! Her IQ is higher than mine. Significantly. She is a very high-functioning autistic, although, on some subjects, she is very naïve. She just sees and hears things differently, and she says some things differently. In this case, I was hoping for the best.

She thought for a minute and then replied. "He said we were going to go sixty-nine tonight. That's a club, right?"

"Ask your mother."

# Chapter 9

## *Krenshaw Medical Center*

It's not nice to have a heart attack. But it is good when you try to die doing it, and someone intervenes. The poor little old lady was hurting badly. The medics had done an EKG that they sent to me via telemetry. So, I knew she was infarcting before she arrived. Fortunately, they gave her some morphine and nitroglycerine, which she liked. She was much more comfortable on arrival.

But myocardial infarction patients can never be trusted to behave themselves, and grandma was no exception. Just as I was listening to her troubled heart, she went into ventricular fibrillation. That rhythm is as useless as the rhythms I created on my trumpet when I was a kid. The heart just kind of quivers, and it doesn't pump the blood it needs to survive.

We, of course, had a defibrillator immediately available. You know, the paddles they always use on TV. But since I was right there, and the paddles needed to be charged, I gave her a precordial thump. Yeah, I whacked her in the chest with my fist. Boom! She went back into a normal sinus rhythm. I was at first immensely pleased with myself.

Next time, I will just wait a few seconds for the paddles to charge. It will save me from having to explain to granny why I punched her in the chest. I thought she was out for the count, but I guess she wasn't. I got an earful. She got some drugs to hopefully prevent her from fibrillating again and a cocktail of drugs to get her ready for the cardiac catheterization lab. With luck she will be eating her lunch with a new lease on life.

She was followed by two drug seekers, and they weren't the sharpest tools in the shed. They usually showed up together, although they claimed not to know each other. Their stories were bogus and not even well thought out. They took their shots, but they did not score. They left with none of the precious narcotics that they so craved!

Believe it or not, I have a special place in my heart for addicts. I work hard to encourage them to get meaningful help, but I won't be a party to their addiction. I sometimes am sure my name is motherf'er. I am called that quite often.

The seven-year-old with belly pain turned out to have appendicitis. He was nice enough to provide us with a textbook ultrasound diagnosis. I like a patient who cooperates. After all, it's the patient's job to make the physician look good!

I topped that off with a wrist fracture that I reduced and splinted. He got something for pain and a referral to I Need's office for casting in a few days. While I was patting myself on the back for a successful morning, Wanda, the ward secretary, wanted to know if I had a few minutes to talk with the Campbells.

"Sure, I'll call them in their room."

"No need. They are in the family room."

I wandered over to the family room, and the three of them were waiting for me. Mom, Dad, and now four-day-old son, Blaze. Mrs. Campbell spoke first.

"Dr. Zander, we wanted to thank you. Dr. Maliterna discharged us. I feel pretty good, and the baby is fine. We are happy to put this behind us. You and Dr. Maliterna really impressed us with your honesty. Most of the time, when a doctor makes a mistake, it gets buried. But patients aren't stupid. We know. We really appreciated that you treated us with care and respect."

I was humbled. "I have a lot to learn as a medical administrator. I know I will make mistakes along the way. But I assure you that I will never make the error of deceiving a patient or family. We are very fortunate to have Dr. Maliterna on staff. She's incredible. I'm glad she was able to help you. I really appreciate your taking the time to say goodbye and to meet your son."

I rubbed Blaze's head and laughed. "Look at all that hair. He needs a trim."

Mr. Campbell laughed, too, as he rubbed his own sparsely populated head. "Honey, you are sure that is MY son? Doesn't our mailman have a good head of hair?"

Mrs. Campbell smacked him affectionately on the arm. Mr. Campbell composed himself and went on.

"We also wanted you to know that we asked MEP Legal Associates not to represent us against the hospital. We all know that the hospital has some liability. We view that as significantly less than Dr. Hyman. Therefore, we have engaged West & Smallins to handle the hospital matter for us."

I was relieved. "I appreciate that. We've worked well with West & Smallins. They appear to be fair and aboveboard. Once they feel enough time has passed that the extent of your injuries is fully known, have them contact us. We will do our very best to settle out of court and reduce any legal expenses."

Blaze, crying temporarily, interrupted the conversation. No doubt the little goober needed to be fed. Mrs. Campbell put the final touches on the conversation.

"We think we may want one more child. We will be following with Dr. Maliterna for our future needs. We still have employed MEP to pursue a separate action against Dr. Hyman. He deserves the very worst, and they appear to be able to deliver just that."

I shook their hands, patted the baby on the head and wished them well. I wanted to talk a little longer, but Wanda's voice blared out of the intercom.

"Dr. Zander, Exam 12 stat, Dr. Zander Exam 12 stat."

I ran to room 12 and was greeted by an unmistakable odor. There are certain smells that are common and sometimes diagnostic in the ER. A lower gastrointestinal bleed has a distinctive smell. Many nurses claim they can smell C. difficile diarrhea. I can't. All diarrhea smells bad to me. Sometimes, urinary tract infections are sniffable from the door to the exam room. The odor emanating from room 12 was highly suspicious of gangrene.

Unfortunately, my crooked nose was right. The nurses were busy removing the clothes from the patient as I entered the room. On the gurney was a somewhat obese patient who was lethargic. His blood pressure was low at 80, and his heart rate was 140. He appeared to be conscious but would not respond to verbal stimuli. His blood sugar was greater than 450. That's as high as the glucometer went. This dude was in shock. Even a bottom-of-the-class medical student could have figured that out.

Once his pajama bottoms were cut away, the diagnosis became obvious. The odor in the room was emanating from his blackened penis, scrotum, and perineum. Since the patient was Caucasian, this was gangrene. It was one of those rare cases that I had read about but had never seen. Immediately, I made the diagnosis of Fournier's gangrene. Don't be too impressed. The diagnosis was easy, much easier than the treatment. I will explain more later, but if I don't start resuscitating, this dude is going to cash his chips.

"Dawn, try to get a 16 (a large bore IV catheter) in his right arm and get two liters of normal saline in him as soon as possible. Gerry, get cultures from a couple areas of his groin, both aerobic and anerobic. Ken, draw a trauma panel and add blood cultures x3."

They responded like the seasoned professionals that they were. Assignments were accomplished in record time. We were looking for infections that grow well with and without oxygen and we were checking to see if his infection had reached his bloodstream. That was called sepsis, and I was pretty sure he had it.

I did a brief exam including a quick listen to his heart and lungs. The lungs were clear. His heart sounded like Fired Up Rio thundering down the stretch. His heart rate may be the only thing on this planet faster than her. I asked for someone to bring the ultrasound machine. I wanted to insert a central line. While I waited, I placed a call to CC Medical Center. The phone was answered on the first ring.

"CC Medical Center Stat Referral Service. How can we help?"

I was familiar with their process. I would give them a brief synopsis of my patient's issues, and they would have the appropriate specialist call me back. They were quick and effective.

"60-year-old male patient with Fournier Gangrene."

That's all I had to say. CC Medical was the best at necrotizing fasciitis. Fournier gangrene is a type of necrotizing fasciitis. You might know it better as flesh-eating bacteria. Fournier's is the name for the type that eats away at the groin and genitalia. This patient was the poster child for Fournier's. He was a diabetic, alcoholic, and was on a medicine for his diabetes known as an SGLT2 inhibitor. (FYI, Jardiance, for example, is in that class). All of those were risk factors for this disease. How did I know that from my exam? Even though I am an astute physician, there are no physical clues to those bits of history. I'll let you in on my secret. I walked out into the hall and talked with his sister, who brought him in. How she got him into the car, I'll never know.

I got back into the room just as the lab called a critical value of his blood sugar being 961. Normal is about 100 fasting. His potassium was high at 6.2, but that was mostly due to his blood sugar being so far out of whack. He will likely need potassium replacement at some point in this process. His blood pressure increased to 84 systolic after Dawn got in two liters of saline before her line blew.

As best I could, I created a sterile field around the patient's neck. Under the guidance of ultrasound, I located the large vein I was looking for and placed a triple-lumen catheter. That's a big honking catheter with three lines. I flushed out each line and it was working perfectly. With it in place we could give fluids, antibiotics, and other drugs at the same time.

I ordered an insulin drip after a small loading dose of insulin had been given. You would think that I would need a whopping insulin dose with his blood sugar that high. Score no points for that guess. I wanted his sugar to come down, but I didn't want it to crash like the stock market in 1929. Slow and steady was the goal.

I also ordered two different antibiotics, Cipro and Clindamycin. I needed to cover a lot of bad bugs. Finally, I ordered tetanus and hypertet. We had no way of knowing this guy's vaccination status. The hypertet would give him immediate protection from tetanus, while the tetanus shot itself would give him longer-term immunity.

Frank Scarlotta, the chief of surgery at CCMC, called and was placed on the speakerphone in room 12. I had never met him, but I recognized his name. He was world-renowned for his knowledge of necrotizing fasciitis. I gave him a full report, including our latest vital signs, which had improved. The BP was 90 and his heart rate was 118. The surgeon was happy with our stabilization efforts. He appreciated the choice of antibiotics and the tetanus treatment.

"Did you give any IVIG?"

I remembered reading something about its use in necrotizing fasciitis, but I had forgotten what it was. He prompted my memory. IVIG was intravenous immunoglobulin. There was good proof that it helped shut down the infection.

"The helicopter just landed. I will either get it into him here or give it to the helicopter crew to administer."

"Good job, nice work."

He then told me that the patient would likely be taken directly to the OR to remove any gangrenous tissue. They would put a catheter in his bladder through the skin. He might lose his penis, and therefore putting a catheter in there was not wise. They would also give him a colostomy to divert stool away from his anus until that area could be stabilized. If he survived it would be a miracle, but our ER team gave him every possible chance.

When the helicopter crew wheeled our patient out the door, it was only 11:30 am. I was tired. Those tough cases are rewarding, but they take a lot out of you. As I walked to the nurse's station, I spied Juicy Lucy waiting for me. She was gorgeous, and it was always good to see her. Unfortunately, it usually meant some kind of trouble.

"ZZ, do you have a minute?"

"Who blabbed that I am only good for a minute? For you, I can go an hour."

She laughed. Either she thought it was funny, or she knew it would help a future sexual harassment case. I wasn't too worried. "Dan called. He is meeting with Sam Issacs tomorrow. He thinks it would be better if you and Dr. Maliterna were not present."

"My lucky day." The sarcasm dripped from my mouth. "I was so looking forward to seeing my old buddy and colleague, Buster. Damn, what will I do to console myself?"

"You can console yourself by stopping in the office when your shift is over. Dan wants you and Celeste to review your documentation one last time. He wants no errors or ambiguities. He plans on sharing everything with Issacs."

"Ok, I'll get to it."

I finished in the ER at 7:30 PM. They just kept coming and coming all afternoon. I had a cardiac arrest patient at 6:45 PM who unfortunately didn't make it. It took until 7:30 to finish the chart and talk with the family. That wasn't something I could pass off to the next doctor coming on duty.

I finally got to the medical staff office where I found Dr. Maliterna busy at work reviewing her documentation. Juicy Lucy had made us each a pile to review. She left a note indicating that she was coming in at 6 AM, just in case anything needed to be corrected or reprinted.

"Celeste, you're here late."

"Actually, I just came back to the hospital. I have two in early labor, so I figured now was as good a time as any to finish this."

"I just finished in the ER, but at least when I get done with this, I can go home. Did you see Stephanie in the office? What did she want?"

"Yes, I did. She is transitioning her gender to male, and I gave her some of the medications she needs now." She said calmly without looking up from her reading.

I spit my coffee over the top document in my pile. There's one for Juicy Lucy to reprint.

"You HAVE to be shitting me!!!" I was incredulous and scared.

"ZZ, for someone so smart, you can be a real asshole. Stephanie did come to the office. Why she came and what we discussed are none of your business. You know better. She may look 16, but she IS 22. Back off. Sit down and do your review."

"I'm going to have a hard time sitting without an ass. You just chewed most of it off. Of course, you are right. I just love her so much. I know I'm too protective."

Celeste shook her head. "Ok, I guess I can share one item we discussed."

"What is that?"

"I told her how to drive Fired Up Frat Boy in the Millions Mile so she can beat you and Rio." She chuckled.

I was quick to reply. "Speaking of Rio. What the hell did you do to her? She's dead lame after the way you jogged her."

Celeste flipped me off. I returned the salute. We both laughed and finished our work.

# Chapter 10

*Administrative Offices*
*Krenshaw Medical Center*

Dan stood and extended his hand to Sam Issacs.

"Sam, nice to see you. Will Dr. Hyman being joining us?"

"Dan, I really appreciate the courtesy of this meeting. Dr. Hyman is a little under the weather today, so I came alone. Will Drs. Zander and Maliterna be coming?"

"No, I didn't want any negative interactions with Dr. Hyman. They have carefully prepared their documentation, which covers the facts. You can question them next week at the hearing if you like."

"Probably better that we are here alone. I don't know if you agree, but I find doctors can be a real pain in the ass during legal meetings and proceedings."

"Dan let out a large laugh. Tell me about it. But where would we be without them?"

"Probably chasing ambulances!"

Dan started passing out his pile of materials. The first folder was Dr. Hyman's credential file. He was duly licensed, board certified in his specialty, and had the privileges to perform c-sections. There were no reports of disciplinary actions in the file.

Issacs liked what he saw. "Looks like a model citizen. Not a blemish on this record."

Dan replied. "Can I speak candidly and off the record?"

Issacs was agreeable. "I guess we didn't officially set the ground rules. Because of the courtesy of this meeting, everything we discuss will be off the record."

Dan was pleased. "That works for me. Since we are off the record, I want to caution you that Dr. Hyman's file appears more spotless than is probably true. He had been chief of his department for twenty years, and he was the medical staff president for the last four years."

Issacs smiled. "Admirable service."

Dan responded. "And very convenient. We have affidavits from three employees who lodged complaints against Dr. Hyman over the years. They allege various misconducts, but all involved some question of impairment while practicing."

Issacs questioned, "Why are those not in the file?"

"The bylaws required that any allegations that were unfounded be removed from the file."

"So, he was cleared."

Dan nodded. "Yes, he was. Neither Dr. Zander nor I were here at the time. Dr. Hyman was very close friends with the previous administrator, who is now imprisoned."

"So?"

Dan sat back in his chair. "The rumor is that Deuce, I mean that Thomas Hofecker II, the previous administrator, used hearing officers and coercion of witnesses to clear Hyman. Hyman then owed him favors. Mr. Hofecker made a career and fortune out of people owing him favors. There is an allegation that Mr. Hofecker had a blood alcohol specimen that had been taken from Dr. Hyman switched. Hyman was allegedly drunk when he hit and killed an elderly pedestrian in a crosswalk. Medics and ER staff swear he was under the influence. But his blood alcohol was under the legal limit. Mr. Hofecker's niece was the charge nurse on the night shift. Hofecker allegedly blackmailed her to switch specimens for friends of his and people he wanted to be indebted to him."

"That's a nice tale, but can you prove it?"

"The niece can testify that she was blackmailed and did switch a tube of Dr. Hyman's. Unfortunately, she discarded the original, so she can't testify to his true blood alcohol concentration."

Issacs thought for a minute and then responded. "So, you won't try to introduce any of that at the hearing?"

"No, I am only providing that as background."

Issacs was pleased. "Ok, let's get to the night in question."

Dan agreed. "Let's start with Dr. Maliterna's report."

Issacs took his time to fully peruse the information. He was skeptical. "Do you expect anyone to believe that she accidentally opened his locker? Sounds a little fishy. Plus, even if there was a bottle of vodka in there, no one can prove that it was his. He could easily have been set up. Did anyone see him drinking from the bottle?"

Dan knew where this was leading. "I believe Dr. Maliterna. Regardless of how she came to find it, she did see a bottle of vodka in his locker. There is DNA evidence from the top of the bottle that matches Dr. Hyman's DNA. There were fingerprints on the bottle, but Dr. Hyman refused to allow us to fingerprint him, so we cannot identify the source of the prints.

"Did Dr. Hyman consent to provide a comparative sample for DNA testing?"

"No, he attempted to spit on the medical staff president. Dr. Zander collected the saliva sample with Dr. Morehead as a witness."

Issacs was ready to earn his fee. "Dan, Dr. Hyman was locked in a room without a bathroom. He had refused Dr. Maliterna's and Dr. Morehead's request for a blood alcohol sample. He relieved himself into a urinal he found in the room, and you illegally tested it. Then, you compounded that by collecting a saliva sample for DNA testing. Both of those were obtained without proper consent."

Dan tapped his pencil on the table. "Well, Sam, this is where I am going to respectfully disagree. I stipulate that Hyman refused testing and that we did it against his will. But, we did not forcibly obtain any samples. He voluntarily put the urine in the container and the saliva we got after he willfully parted with it to spit on Dr. Morehead."

"He did not authorize any testing!!"

Dan took a deep breath to stay calm. "Yes, I know. However, with the circumstances of the treatment he provided to Mrs. Campbell, I feel confident that I can get a judge to admit that evidence. The bylaws required that he submit to testing, and we committed no assault and battery to obtain it. We'll take our chances in court on that one. He left a sponge behind despite nursing personnel screaming at him to stop his closure. He did a rectal exam on the patient when attempting to do a vaginal exam. The video and still pictures Dr. Maliterna took of the botched repair he did after the c-section are damning. I will be glad to let you see them if you like. Any judge or jury in their right mind will rule in the favor of the injured patient over a doctor's right to refuse testing on samples he provided. Especially when the urine alcohol concentration equates to a blood alcohol of 305!!!"

Issacs made no comment. He remained silent as he watched Dr. Maliterna's video and reviewed the still photos. Dan was happy that he had remembered to have the Campbell's authorize sharing them. When he was finished, Issacs summarized his thoughts.

"Dan, Off the record I will admit that Dr. Hyman left a sponge behind. If our experts agree with Dr. Maliterna, it appears that he may have made additional errors during the C-section. But his past malpractice history is benign. Doctors are human, they make mistakes. In spite of your "evidence," I am not convinced that Dr. Hyman was under the influence. Urine alcohol levels are easily challenged. Just because his DNA was on the bottle means only that his lips touched it. You have nothing to prove that he drank from it."

Dan was ready. "Although I am comfortable that we can get the urine alcohol and DNA admitted as evidence, I have another video to show you."

Dan played the video that Amos recorded. Dr. Hyman was slurring his speech. His eyes were bloodshot, and his gait was wobbly at best. When they let him stand alone, he almost fell. But the most damning part of the recording was the clearly heard berating he gave Amos, including calling him a fucking dumb-ass N-word medic.

Issacs appeared visibly shaken as he slowly removed his glasses and put them in his coat pocket. "Dan, what is your bottom line in terms of Dr. Hyman continuing to practice?"

"Steep price. First, he goes to inpatient alcohol treatment in one of those places that specializes in physicians. If he meets all inpatient goals, he then agrees to a monitored outpatient program. He undergoes full cognitive and functional testing to ascertain that he can make critical decisions and that he has the physical capabilities to carry them out. Last, he agrees to enter our medical staff's impaired physician program and meet all rules in terms of supervision, testing etc. All of that can only happen if he satisfies whatever gauntlet the State Licensing Board puts him through."

"Tough bargain. I will pass this along. Dan, I thank you again. I will meet with my client later, and we will see you on Wednesday."

# Chapter 11

*Fired Up Farms*
*Krenshaw, NJ*
*Sunday of Millions Week*

"ZZ, great driving last night. Sorry you got beat in the last race, but your post position hurt you."

"Thanks, Dad. As you know, Stephanie drew inside me. She parked my ass out, and the rest is history. If I had her horse and her post position, I would have done the same thing. She really can drive."

"Yes, she can. She learned from watching you. You are her idol." Dad was smiling.

I was smiling, too, until I realized that many of you readers are new to harness racing. I explained earlier about the gait of the horses and the difference between a jog cart and race sulky. Now, to understand a race. What a dufus I can be.

Most races are one mile, but there are a few at different distances. The starter sits in an enclosure on the back of a car, facing the horses following the car. The car has a folding gate attached. The horses gather behind the gate about ¼ mile from the start line. The vehicle gradually picks up speed and is going around 35 mph at the start. When they reach the start line, the car pulls away.

The horses leave from post positions 1-8 at our track. The 1 is closest to the inside pylons, and the 8 is on the outside. When the gate pulls away, the horses try to get a good position. The horse in the lead at the pylons is "on the engine." The horse behind the leader is in the two-hole, etc. The first horse racing on the outside (one position away from the pylons) is called the "first over" horse.

It's a little bit like a Nascar race. Drafting behind the horse in front of you can cut the wind and save a little energy. But being on the front allows you to control the pace. Lot's of options and a lot of split-second decisions to make.

A horse that wants to get to the pylons but can't find a position is known as "parked out." That's what happened to me last night. I tried to get to the pylons, and Stephanie was inside me. She blocked me from getting there. She parked me out. The problem with that is that the parked-out horse has to travel around 45 feet more for each turn that they are parked out for. At our track, we have three turns.

Stephanie made my horse go an extra 135 feet last night. We finished last, and it cost me an additional $100. I have a bad habit. When someone does something on the track that I don't like, I salute them. OK, I only use one finger. But it has been nicknamed the Zander salute. Harness race judges can be sticks in the mud. Each time I express my inner feelings, they fine me $100. Stephanie got saluted last night.

More racing education later. Keep reading.

"Great sunrise mass today until the rainstorm." I was still wet.

Dad shook his head. "At least we got everyone in safely. What an amazing story that Father Jonathan told."

Our family believed in many things, but friends and traditions were top on the list. Although Millions Week officially started last night, our family's traditional luncheon was scheduled for the Sunday of Millions Week.

Million's Week is the epitome of harness racing. The best harness horses in the world go head-to-head on Miracle Mile Racetrack for incredible purses. Rules were relaxed (or ignored), and some unusual types of races occurred. Champions would be crowned. Every driver, trainer, owner, and horse wanted a piece of the spotlight and, of course, the money!

Our Sunday started with a sunrise mass for any children and caretakers from The Always Hope School that wanted to attend. Not all our gathered friends and family were Catholic, but none of them wanted to miss Father Jonathan's sermon. We had set up an altar and chairs at the start line of the training track. It was dark as we walked out and got in our seats.

Luckily, we had more than enough adults present when our phones blared out a severe thunderstorm alert. We had rehearsed scenarios like this. Every time a child left the building, their handler had to sign them out on the computer.

Jenny was the first in the building. She checked off each child and handler as they arrived and directed them to proceed to the internal gym. That was the safest area of the building to ride out a severe storm.

All doors and windows in the school were secured. Heads were counted as a double check, and the mass continued. Father Jonathan held everyone spellbound, enunciating the power of the Lord as flashes of lightning and crashes of thunder accentuated his delivery. By the time we sang the last hymn, the sky had cleared, and the sun was glowing brightly.

The men were left behind to put things in the school back in order while the womenfolk headed to the kitchen. I offered to help the women, but I was told in no uncertain terms that I was not welcome. Stephanie accentuated the feeling of the group by flipping me a Zander salute. A few years ago, things were looser, but I was caught in the kitchen sampling foods with my bare fingers. Hence, the testosterone banishment.

As I put the last chair back into place, I looked up to see two of my closest friends talking and standing side by side. What a contrast. Father Jonathan was six feet six inches tall. Joe was almost a foot shorter. Father Jonathan was a Catholic priest, and Joe was the president of his own construction company, Crinelli Construction. Father Jonathan was an orphan raised by his grandmother. Joe Crinelli was the grandson of Aldo Crinelli, aka Razor. Aldo was connected. He was the connection, a godfather figure both literally and figuratively.

I met these two lugs when we were freshmen in college. The three of us and our other friend, Azquela Huggins, shared an apartment. Unfortunately, we also shared heroin that we first snorted and then eventually got to injecting. One night, we scored some wicked stuff. I answered a knock on the door while the other three shot up. After I dispatched one of our pesty neighbors I turned around to see my three friends blue and not breathing. This was before naloxone was available for use outside of hospitals. Even then, it was only able to be used with an IV.

I called 911 and then went from person to person, administering two breaths. I continued this for fifteen minutes until the medics arrived. Four hours later, in the emergency department, we reunited. Vows were made that were never broken. Together, we went into inpatient rehab and, from there, to an outpatient program. We swore on each other's souls that we would never use again. We promised to immediately come to support any member of our little group if requested.

We adopted the code phrase "Dying Was Easy." They should have died. After all, they were in the express lane to Exit 666, Gehenna, known to most as Hell. But dying may have been easier than going on living and battling narcotic addiction for the rest of our lives.

If anyone of us uttered, emailed, or texted the magic phrase, the other three dropped everything and immediately supported the person. The result was that none of us ever used heroin again. There were plenty of occasions when we each needed help, but those diminished over time.

I finished my pre-med requirements and was accepted to Jefferson Medical college in Philadelphia. Joe completed his engineering degree and took control of his grandfather's construction business. The clean part of the business. Aldo made sure that Joe was never involved in anything illegal or even shady. Supposedly.

Father Jonathan got his degree in political science. He had been a star tight end in college. There were many pro scouts that felt he could be a high NFL draft pick. That was until he developed a blood clot in his leg. Testing showed that he had an inherited coagulation disorder requiring anticoagulants for the rest of his life. Football and all contact sports were out of the question. He struggled with the loss of a promising career that he was eagerly anticipating. He sounded the "Dying Was Easy" alarm many times. We all responded to each one.

That was before it happened. He was called. Not to the NFL but to the priesthood. He found great peace in his religion. Six years later he was ordained a Roman Catholic priest. We were so proud. Plus, we figured we would get a break on penance when we went to confession.

Azquela outperformed anyone's dreams. As an African American woman raised by a single mom in public housing, she broke all stereotypes and glass ceilings. The only affirmative action she benefitted from was the affirmative action that she took on her own behalf. She was brilliant, and she was determined. Of the four of us, she was the only one never tempted to use heroin again. She just walked away from it while the rest of us crawled.

It was no surprise to any of us that she graduated Summa Cum Laude with a degree in marketing. She only lasted one year in her first job when she left to start her own company. Like any start-up, she began with a small shop. Within five years, she had a chain of cosmetic stores called "Exquisite Evolutions."

After her initial public stock offering, she was set for life financially. That changed absolutely nothing. She worked just as hard and was just as determined. She built her mother a house in a great neighborhood, but money meant little to her. That was good news for The Always Hope School.

Azzie (that is what Joe called her, and we all adopted it) wasn't much of a gambler. One day, on a lark, she invested $5 in a lottery ticket. She won $934 million, and she gave it all to the school. The school was set financially. She refused to keep a dime. "I have so much, and these kids need so much help. What else could I do?" What a class act she was and is.

It was great to see the four of us together, successful, clean, and happy. Sometimes, Joe and Azzie were happier than Father and me.

They were an on-again, off-again item. Those two were made for each other. But each one was so into their work that they occasionally grew apart. Then, they would grow back together. They were engaged, unengaged, on, off. This week, it looks like they are on. They better be. We're short of bedrooms, and Mom put them in the same one. They didn't object.

# Chapter 12

## *Fired Up Farms*

There were three others attending the luncheon today. Dear friends, one and all. The first is Jenny. I mentioned that she was helpful in checking in kids this morning. Jenny is an ER nurse who I met when I began working at Supreme Medical Center. Even though I knew workplace relationships were fraught with danger, I got into a torrid love affair with Jenny. More like a lust affair, but I was a happy camper. Everything was fine until Jenny attempted to murder me. No, she didn't try to hump me to death. The bitch drugged me and attempted to kill me by injecting me with an overdose of fentanyl. How rude!

In the end, we discovered that Jenny was blackmailed into doing that by her uncle, Thomas "Deuce" Hofecker. I mentioned him before. He was the hospital administrator who is now wearing an orange jumpsuit with a number on it. Prick, I hope he rots. He tried to get me underground.

Although it took a while, I forgave Jenny. I consider her a friend, but there will never be another "us." She was helpful in setting up nursing procedures at the school.

The second person is Billie "cha-ching" Browner. Billie is the most talented harness race driver I know, other than Stephanie and Dave Dunstan. His fans nicknamed him "cha-ching" to simulate the sound of them making money betting on his horses. He and horses are one. I drive my horses on a very high cerebral level. I study the program's every detail. I think about the race, and my monster brain determines what I do. Billie just gets in the bike and drives. Like all hall of fame drivers, he has an internal stopwatch that helps him rate his horses. I must look at a timer or a stopwatch in my hand. He looks for good-looking women in the crowd. At least, he did before he hooked up with Jenny. They seem to get along well. She hasn't tried to kill him yet, so maybe they have a future.

Billie was given his start in harness racing by none other than my dad, Carl Zander. He quickly realized that Billie had great talent and used him exclusively to drive our horses. That was before I learned how to drive. Well, as soon as Billie got to the top of the driver's standings at the track, he forgot who my dad was. He also teamed up with Thomas "Deuce" Hofecker. They were a team made in hell. Deuce was shrewd, and Billie was clueless about anything other than driving horses. Deuce waved a wad of cash, and Billie did what he was told.

I am not so sure that Billie was the dullest tool in the shed, but he didn't ask a lot of questions. Part of the reason for that was that he had a terrible stuttering problem. It took so long for Billie to ask a question that the listener lost interest. So, Billie gave up asking.

Eventually Deuce and Billie had a falling out. Billie ended up coming back to my dad to apologize. He then helped us get ready to win the Miracle Millions a few years back, which helped us save the school. Billie's coaching and advice helped me win a few big races that week that I would not have won without his help. Stephanie won the biggest race, and we made over $6 million dollars that night to save the school temporarily. That was before Azzie won the lottery.

Billie met Jenny somewhere in the weeks leading up to the big races. They have been an item since. It was Jenny who got Billie to work with a speech therapist. He still stuttered, but it was a lot less. People started to listen to him. Although Billie is staying at the farm, Stephanie and I will have to contend with him on the track this week. He has many promising drives this week, and we know he will want to win them all. Hopefully, we can spoil his week.

The last guest is just arriving now. He just piloted his beautiful blue Toyota Tundra into the area in front of the barn. He is pulling a large horse trailer containing six horses from the Dunstan stable. Tim jumped out of the cab and almost broke my hand with a handshake. Between Timmy and Adrian Burns, my hand is taking a beating.

Tim is one of our blacksmiths. He would be our only one, except he won't relocate to New Jersey. But we fly him out once a month or so, and he works his magic. Tim never had much luck with women, but he could select and create the perfect shoe and pad for any trotter or pacer. He is the best blacksmith in the business. He's not a large man, but he's solid. He reminds me of a smaller version of Adrian Burns.  His hands are like steel, and his arms are pure muscle. He could have posed for an anatomy class. Every muscle was well-defined and easy to locate.

Once the horses were unloaded and bedded down, Tim and I headed to the house to dive into the feast.

# Chapter 13

## *Route 28 Krenshaw, NJ*
## *Monday of Millions Week*

I only had two meetings scheduled this morning. Neither of which was exciting. But Buster's hearing later this week would give me my required adrenaline rush. I punched a button on my phone, and Bachman Turner Overdrive blared out of the truck's speakers at least 10 decibels higher than what was safe for my hearing. *Roll on Down the Highway* seemed appropriate as I was rolling. I continued for a mile or so until bright red and blue flashing lights appeared in my rear-view mirror. Shit.

"License and registration," said the officer as he peered in the window. I couldn't make out his name badge due to the sun's glare. I didn't recognize the voice either. So, I decided to be cordial instead of offering up a lame or smart-ass protest about being pulled over.

"Yes, sir." I leaned right to access the glove compartment to retrieve the documents. I turned back to my left to hand them to the officer when I noticed that he had his taser out and pointed at my crotch. I was terrified.

"Got ya, ZZ," laughed the cop.

I finally recognized Mika Washington, an asshole buddy of Amos. I had met him on two or three occasions, but I couldn't previously make out his identity due to the sun.

"Mika, what are you doing stopping hard-working, law-abiding citizens on their way to work?"

"I ought to taze your ass for the way you drove that horse last Saturday. Your sister made you look like a wussy. Parking you out and all. Cost me $50."

"That's why you stopped me?"

"That and going 67 in a 45 zone."

"Ooops. How about a warning?"

"Sure, I warn you that I will fry your balls off if you screw me on a bet like that again." Then, he busted up laughing and holstered his taser.

"You did have me going there for a while," I said as I put my documents back in place.

"I thought it was your truck. So, I neglected to tell dispatch why I stopped you. If I told them I stopped someone for doing 67 in a 45, they would expect a big ticket. I will tell them that you had a taillight out. But ZZ, be careful. This road is due for what they call 'enhanced enforcement' for the next few weeks. Slow down or find another route."

"You got it, Mika. Bet me in the Millions Finale. I won't let you down again."

I thought that encounter was a sign of good luck. Hopefully, this will be the beginning of a great week. My phone beeped as I pulled back out on the road. Being a good boy, I used the hands-free feature. I might not know the next cop around the block.

"This is ZZ."

"ZZ, it's Dan. Got good and bad news."

"Please give me the good first."

"Ok, you don't have to worry about Buster's hearing this week."

I smiled. "That is great news. Did his liver explode, or did he get a job in a distillery as a quality control engineer?"

Dan laughed. "Well, now here is the bad news. Sam is no longer representing Buster. That means only one thing. Buster is refusing to follow Sam's advice. Sam won't represent anyone that he doesn't believe in. That's one of the reasons his record is so good. If Sam doesn't believe you, he figures no judge or jury will."

"But isn't that good news? I mean, you and Sam are the best. Buster will be going to the bullpen now. Our job should be getting easier."

Dan didn't share my joy. "I am sure we will prevail, but some of these lower-tier guys need the work. So, they drag things out, fight over the tiniest details, and generally gum up the works. He hired a third-stringer, Desmond Howard. He is low on the legal totem pole, and he has started the delay tactics already. He wants Buster reinstated immediately because of his past fine record."

I was livid. "People in hell want ice water, too. You didn't give in to him, did you?"

"I told him that Buster shouldn't practice Ob-Gyn, but I hired him to work in the ER. You will be side by side with your best bud!"

"Screw you, Dan."

"ZZ, you insult me. I told Desmond that his proposal was a nonstarter. That's legalese for 'eat shit.' I gave him another week, but I refused to allow Buster to practice."

"Sorry, Dan, I know you have this under control. I can live with another week if Buster is on the sidelines."

"OK, good deal. ZZ, Juicy Lucy just stuck her head in the door and wants you to call her ASAP."

I took a sip of coffee and commanded my phone to call Juicy Lucy.

"Juicy Lucy, this is ZZ, what's up?"

"We have visitors on the way."

"Who?"

"Joint Commission. I just checked the website, and our triennial survey starts today."

"Ah damn, this week of all weeks. I was hoping to take a few days off to spend more time at the track."

"Guess again."

"Did you get the CVs of the assigned surveyors?"

"Yep, we have an engineer for two days and a physician and nurse for five days.

"What's the background of the physician?" I had my fingers crossed.

"Let's see. Oh my, he's a physician from a mentally challenged specialty. He's an ER doc." Juicy Lucy giggled.

"I am going to spank you and wash out your mouth!"

She sighed. "Promises, promises. Will you be here for the opening conference? It starts at 9 AM "

"I will. Did you alert all the appropriate department heads?"

"Yep, they already came and took my doorstop and gave me a card saying what I should do in case of a fire."

"Good job, Juicy Lucy. I will be there in twenty minutes."

Hospitals that receive Licensure Board reimbursement (they almost all do) are required to be evaluated every three years. They are surveyed to assess their compliance with what the Licensure Board calls "Conditions of Participation." Our hospital elects to pay The Joint Commission to perform our assessment. They are the largest accreditor in the world.

Some people really worry about Joint Commission (JC) surveys. I hear that in some for-profit hospitals, a bad JC report can be your first leg out the door. In my new position, I have a different perspective. I want them to find stuff, provided it's real. I don't want any nitpicking. I know this place hasn't been run right, and any help I can get cleaning it up is a plus.

I arrived at 0830. Juicy Lucy had my coffee ready.

"ZZ, just to be sure, what are you going to call me this week?"

"What do you mean?" I was clueless.

Juicy Lucy laughed and said, "I don't think you want to call me Juicy Lucy in front of our company."

"You got that right. I will call you Lucy."

"OK, just remember that. Or maybe JL if you want."

"Good thinking, JL."

"Great. They are setting up the war room in the café conference room. Our consultant will be at the opening conference."

"What war room and what consultant?"

"You really are lost sometimes. The war room is set up to help us reduce or eliminate any findings JC comes up with. They are the people that already ran through the hospital collecting doorstops and distributing the cards with the information on fires."

I tried to comprehend why people had doorstops where they weren't permitted and why it was acceptable to remove them only when inspectors came around. And why doesn't everyone in the hospital know what to do in the event of a fire? Maybe one of the wise guys in the war room could enlighten me. JL interrupted my thoughts.

"The consultant will tell us how to act with the surveyors and how to get them to drop findings. They have profiles on the surveyors from previous surveys, and they know the things each of them is interested in."

"Whose crazy assed idea is that?"

"Deuce set it up. It works well. We usually get great reports."

I wasn't here to play games. I was here to make this hospital function normally and pay its bills. I needed it to succeed to keep the track open. Unlike my predecessors, I had the naive impression that success came in the form of better patient outcomes and little or no significant safety errors. My plan was to drive that horse to victory.

# Chapter 14

## *Krenshaw Medical Center*
## *Joint Commission War Room*

I entered the room. There were around twenty people there. Banks of phone lines had been set up, and at least ten laptops were operational. They even had an espresso machine. Tons of sugar-laden snacks filled bowls on a refreshment table. Other bowls contained fresh fruit for the health conscious. This was a war room. The problem was I didn't think we were at war with The Joint Commission.

I attempted to get their attention. "I really appreciate all of you being here and your dedication."

People were fussing with their computers or texting on their phones, and they ignored me.

"Yo, Yo, please listen up."

There was still considerable noise in the room. The loud splat from the mango that I tossed at the chalkboard focused them.

I screamed. "The next person that makes a sound is fired."

Huh. That brought some peace and quiet.

"Thank you for your attention. There are some new ground rules for this survey."

I was interrupted by a voice from the back of the room.

"Excuse me, sir. No one discussed any new ground rules with me."

"And you are?"

"Sam Michaelson, I oversee all things related to Joint Commission," replied the gaunt, cocky consultant. He had a squeaky voice and was wearing a pink bowtie. I generally disliked people who wore bowties.

I was fresh out of mangos, so I had to assault him verbally. "Good for you, and now you are gone. Get your stuff and get the hell out of here!"

He looked at me defiantly as the rest of the assembled staff cowered.

He screamed. "You must be kidding me. This place sucks, and you need me to get you through this survey. Your reimbursement depends on me. With a 'Never Episode' on your Licensure Board scorecard, you need all the help you can get. These people will be gunning for you."

He had some facts behind him. Never Episodes were just that. According to Licensure Board they were things that should never occur in a hospital. A retained foreign object after a surgical procedure was a Never Episode. Buster had succeeded in putting us on the Licensure Board shit list. I could go along with the consultant and employ mushroom management for the surveyors. Cover them with crap and keep them in the dark, or I could take the riskier route, the high road. That was to find our weaknesses and fix them. No guts, no glory.

I addressed the highly-paid consultant standing with his hands on his hips. "Kiss my ass. This isn't Supreme Medical Center, and I'm not Deuce Hofecker. Hit the trail."

He flipped me a Zander salute as he stormed out.

The room was in shock. I took that opportunity to explain myself.

"Anyone not sharing my vision is free to resign and head out the door. I am telling you all that I welcome the input from Joint Commission. Does that mean that I want you to sit back and take a beating? Far from it. If the surveyors find something they think is important, I expect you to be certain they got their facts right.

When they are clearly wrong, and we are right, I want to challenge them. I will lead that challenge. However, when they have us cold in noncompliance, I want the conversation to be about how we get back into compliance. Ask them to steer us to best practices or other information to benefit us. I want us to be better when we are done, that is all."

No one else resigned. The remainder of the first day was reasonable. The engineer racked us up when he found tons of holes in our smoke and firewalls. He exposed significant problems with tests of our backup generators. He wrote a ton of deficiencies for things stored in our fire exit stairwells.

I called Joe Crinelli, who knew the Life Safety Code like the back of his hand. That's the fire code used to judge hospitals and other occupancies.

He told me, "Kiss that surveyor's ass. Everything he found makes you vulnerable to a fire disaster. A generator failure can be catastrophic. Exit stairwells are for exit only, not storage. I know someone who can help you fix those things, but trust me, this guy did you some major favors."

The clinical survey process was intriguing. Instead of just reading charts, they picked some live patients to trace their care from start to finish. They would meet the patient and talk to various staff members who took care of the patient. Then, they would go anywhere in the hospital where the patient had been. It was customary for a hospital staff member to accompany each surveyor.

I went with the physician. We started in the ICU with a gentleman who had a myocardial infarction (heart attack) the night before. He spoke with the patient, his wife, and the ICU nurse. From there, he went to the ER to review the care he received with the staff.

When he finished in the ER, we went to the cath lab and looked over their documentation. He watched the set-up for another patient, and we got an RFI (Requirement for Improvement) for labeling issues. That was a serious finding that would be in our report.

There were very specific procedures to be followed when placing medications onto an operative field. We didn't come close to meeting the standard. The surveyor very carefully and in an uncondescending tone, explained the standard to the staff. He followed that up with a true-life example of a patient error that had occurred due to poor medication labeling practices. A patient had his coronary artery injected with liquid soap instead of a blood thinner. Both solutions were on the table, and neither one was labeled. That patient died. The cath lab staff made a quick transition from being defensive to wanting to do better. No one in healthcare comes to work to hurt a patient. At least, so I thought.

# Chapter 15

## *Krenshaw Medical Center*

On Tuesday I got much more than what I wanted from this survey. The nurse surveyor picked an outpatient carpal tunnel surgery to follow. She met the patient and his wife in the holding area for the operating room. She reviewed the history and physical, surgical consent form, and other required paperwork. She asked permission to observe site marking and the time-out in the OR.

Site marking is a process whereby the surgeon marks the operative site to be certain the correct side (usually right or left) was operated on. That usually occurred in the surgery holding area. Our policies require that the surgeon mark the site with his/her initials if anatomically possible. For a carpal tunnel surgery, it was certainly possible and required. For something like a hemorrhoidectomy, we used a different process. Kind of tough to initial that site. I digress.

Time-outs were done in the operating room prior to the start of the case. Everyone in the OR was required to stop what they were doing and verify that they had the correct patient and they were ready to perform the correct procedure.

I had read about some cases that caused these procedures to be put into place. One patient had the wrong leg amputated. Another patient had his normal kidney removed instead of the one with cancer. Another patient had the wrong side of his brain operated on. That made me cringe. Sickening outcomes but totally preventable.

In a stroke of bad luck for us the nurse surveyor had picked one of Dr. Bator's patients. Roy Bator is a neurosurgeon. He is brilliant beyond belief and very talented surgically. But Roy is also an arrogant pain in the ass. I nicknamed him Master when I first arrived in the ER. Master Bator. He was a jagoff, so it fits perfectly.

Roy attended college and medical school at a prestigious Ivy League institution. Everyone knew it because he told anyone who would listen. I remember when he first informed me. I congratulated him and then asked him, "Is it true that the last sentence on the diplomas read: 'Go forth this day knowing that thy arse will forever be a gold mine and that thy stools will never again emit odors.'" He didn't seem to like me after that.

I should have shown him my Jefferson diploma. The dean had written a personal note at the bottom. "Get out of here before we change our minds." I digress.

Master came to the surgical holding area and insisted the nurse surveyor leave as he talked to the patient. When Master was finished, the nurse surveyor returned. She requested the patient show her the site mark. The patient told her the doctor hadn't done one. The nurse pulled out her notebook and recorded the information she needed to write us up. The OR nurse manager texted me.

"RFI coming. Nurse tracing patient of Master's (I guess most of the hospital adopted my nickname) due to undergo left carpal tunnel surgery. Nurse asked to see the site mark. Master doesn't believe in site marking. So, there was no site mark, and we get an RFI. We are on our way into OR to watch the time out. The problem is that Master doesn't do those either."

Screw me, I never knew that Master didn't site mark nor do time outs. It's part of the accepted protocol to prevent wrong-site surgery. That dickhead thinks he doesn't have to follow the rules made for mere mortals. I am going to have my hands full after this survey is over.

A few minutes later, the physician surveyor and I were reviewing some credential files when JL pounded on the door. I was a little miffed. She knew better than to disturb me unless there was a fire or an earthquake. I opened the door just wide enough to glare at her.

"JL, you know we didn't want to be disturbed." She wasn't deterred.

"ZZ, get your ass to the OR. Master and the nurse surveyor are going at it in the hallway."

Did she just call me ZZ instead of Dr. Zander, say Master instead of Dr. Bator, and did she tell me to get my ass to the OR? I think that is what I heard.

The physician and I sprinted to the OR and hurriedly changed into scrubs. The sound of Master screaming at the nurse surveyor made us move a little faster. JL was right to interrupt. There was an earthquake in progress. In the hallway outside of his operating rooms, we found Master berating the nurse surveyor. I asked him to back off, but he persisted. I stepped in between Master and the nurse. The physician surveyor took that opportunity to escort his nurse to the safety of the nurse manager's office. That left Master and me in the hallway.

"Zander, you damn moron. How dare you let these people run amuck in my OR."

"Roy (I didn't call him Master to his face), please calm down and lower your voice."

Instead, he took it up a few decibels. "You are the biggest fucking mistake this hospital ever made." (He could have been right about that. But I had to shut him down for the sake of anyone operating or being operated upon.)

I hadn't noticed that I Need had arrived on scene. He had just finished a joint replacement and heard the commotion. Like a lot of orthopedic surgeons, he was a jock. Even though he was in his sixties, he was in excellent shape. He put one arm on each of Master's shoulders and whispered in his ear.

"You shut the hell up and do it now. I swear if you don't, you will never work again in this state, and you might not walk either."

Master opened his mouth but closed it promptly. I Need was infamous. He was fair, but not someone who you messed with. He then grabbed Master by the hand while motioning for me to join them with his other hand. The three of us walked into the surgeon's lounge. There were two or three surgeons and their assistants in there. I Need never said a word to them. He just pointed at the door, and they scattered. The three of us were alone.

I Need lit up a cigarette and sat down. He motioned for Master and me to sit. Our hospital was a nonsmoking facility. Smoking was not permitted in the building nor on the grounds. But I didn't think that now was a good time to remind I Need of anything. So, I kept my mouth shut.

I Need exhaled a large cloud of blue smoke and addressed Master.

"Now, slowly, calmly, and quietly, I want to know what happened out there." He pointed to the hallway.

Master started to scream. I Need put his hand over Master's mouth and said, "Slowly, calmly, and quietly. This is your last warning."

Master took a deep breath and began playing with his glasses. He often did that when he was stressed. But when he spoke, his voice was quiet, and he began to speak slowly and calmly.

"You both know that I am a world-class neurosurgeon."

I wanted to vomit.

"That stupid JC Nurse bullied her way into my operating theater."

He liked to throw in some old medical jargon like "operating theater" when he could to make himself sound even smarter than he was. But in this instance, he was right. What happened today was theater.

I Need questioned him. "What did she want to do?

"She said she wanted to observe the time out. I asked her to get out."

I jumped into the fray. "Did the patient give permission for her to observe?"

"What difference does that make? It's my operating room. You aren't a surgeon, so you have little clue. Mr. Hofecker and I have a contract that stipulates that I have total control over everything that goes on in those rooms. If I chose not to allow JC to snoop around, it is my option and my decision. I see it as an infection control issue to have needless traffic in my operating rooms."

I Need was the first to react. "ZZ, I wouldn't doubt there is a contract. All the surgeons knew there was something strange about how his rooms ran. But if it didn't affect the rest of the department, we all ignored it."

Master had a smug look on his face that I quickly erased.

"I wouldn't doubt that Deuce got into some contract with you. Those surveyors can go anywhere the hospital license covers. Your OR is no exception unless you have a lease for the space and a separate license from the State. Do YOU?"

Master just glared at me.

I Need nodded. "I don't know about those things, but what you say sounds right. Roy, is your patient still in the OR?"

"They took him back to holding. He's my last case today."

"Are you calm enough to do the case?"

"Yes."

I Need turned towards me. "ZZ, I have a closed reduction coming up. I think it would be best that we avoid Roy's room today. The nurse is free to observe anything she wants in my room."

# Chapter 16

## *Krenshaw Medical Center*

I knocked on the door to the surveyor's room. I was greeted by the physician.

"I was just about to call you ZZ. We've got a real mess here."

I nodded my head in agreement, then I walked past him and sat beside the nurse surveyor.

"M'am, I can't apologize enough. There is no excuse for Dr. Bator to have treated you the way he did. Plus, it is unfathomable that he would create chaos in an active operating suite."

"Thank you, Dr. Zander. I'm a retired OR nurse so I am used to surgeon's shenanigans. But this was off the charts. Did I do anything to cause such an incident?"

"Absolutely not. I spoke with the OR manager. She told me that you followed all survey rules and were very respectful of the patient and his privacy. Dr. Bator will be dealt with. He has no more cases this week, so he shouldn't further interfere with the survey."

The physician interrupted me. "The survey may be over now anyway."

"What? This is day two. Isn't this a five-day survey?"

"It was, but I just spoke with the Field Director on call. That's our boss in the field. They have to report this to the Licensure Board, and they may terminate this survey."

I went to the war room to explain to the group what had happened in the OR and that the survey was on a temporary hold. The mood in the room was somber. JL scared me as she suddenly showed up at my side.

"The nurse surveyor would like to speak with you."

JL walked back to their room with me, but neither of us spoke. I invited JL to come in with me. I felt I might need some support.

The nurse stood to address us. "Dr. Zander. Thank you for your help today and during the survey. Is there any way that I could speak with the surgical patient, Mr. Quincy? He was very uptight about the surgery, and I want to apologize if I caused him any further anxiety or problems."

"You owe no one an apology."

"I appreciate that, but I still would like to speak with the patient. If he will speak with me, provided Dr. Bator is not in the area."

I called the OR manager. When she called back, she told me that the patient really wanted to see the nurse surveyor. He credited her with his not backing out of the surgery. The nurse manager further reported that Dr. Bator left in a huff as soon as he finished his last case. He claimed to be late for a lecture he was giving at the medical school.

I called security and verified that he beat feet out of the parking lot ten minutes ago. I asked them to notify me immediately if he returned in the next hour. I accompanied the nurse to outpatient surgery. We quickly located the patient. I verified with him that he was happy to see her, and we sat down. He introduced his wife.

The nurse surveyor began. "I want to apologize if my presence today caused any increased anxiety. I had an unfortunate encounter with your surgeon. I hope that you didn't hear it or get more worried because of it."

The patient shook his head no. "I was really uptight about having surgery. Someone cutting on you and all. I almost called to cancel. When they asked me if you could observe my case, I jumped at the chance. Why not have a guardian angel look over everything?"

The nurse pointed to her left wrist and asked. "Are you having much pain in your left wrist?"

Both of his wrists were under the sheet. He pulled out his left wrist and held it in the air as he laughed. "None at all. They operated on the right wrist." He then held up a bandaged right wrist.

I know my colors. I knew them before I went to kindergarten. That knowledge was now very useful. That nurse's face was pure white before she heard that. Then it turned bright red.

She talked hurriedly. "Your history and physical and consent both said the surgery was to be on your left. The nerve conduction study documenting that you had severe carpal tunnel syndrome indicated that it was on the left!"

The patient calmly nodded his head signaling he understood. "I had some light sedation to settle me down when they started the procedure. But I was wide awake when it was over. I was happy as hell that it didn't hurt as bad as I thought it would. Anyway, while I was still in the OR, Dr. Bator explained that he had examined me again after I received some sedation, so I may not remember it. He felt that my right arm was worse than my left, and he went ahead and did the right arm."

"Were you having any symptoms in the right hand? Before today, did you have any tests on that hand or wrist?"

"No, that's the funny part. I had no symptoms. But Dr. Bator said that sometimes the carpal tunnel syndrome is so bad that you don't have symptoms. He said that's when it's possible for it to suddenly get worse and cause paralysis. That's why he did the right today. When that heals up, he will bring me back and do the left. He wants me to come to his office this afternoon to check the wound and to schedule the next procedure, probably a month from now."

The nurse shook his left hand and we returned to the surveyor conference room. I slumped in a chair and wanted to cry. Before she could relay her story to the physician surveyor, I jumped in.

"Nancy, thank you for the professional manner that you used with the patient. I saw your face changing colors as he told his tale. I think you and I both strongly suspect that Dr. Bator performed wrong site surgery today. I think Dr. Bator, in his haste and anger, operated on the wrong side and then concocted the story he told Mr. Quincy."

"Dr. Zander, thank you for your candor. I wasn't buying it, but I surely did not have enough information to tell the patient for certain. Furthermore, any discussion of the appropriateness of a particular procedure is beyond our scope."

The physician surveyor chimed in. "We will treat this as a possible Sentinel Event on site. We will do no further investigation of that here. Our rule is that we turn it over to our Sentinel Event specialists, and they work with you to resolve any standard deficiencies. However, please be aware that they will report this to Licensure Board. This may be considered a Licensure Board Never Episode."

# Chapter 17

## *Krenshaw Medical Center*

What a cluster this was. The phone call with JC management confirmed that it was even worse than I thought. This survey was now terminated. We will have another survey in a few months if we are still open. The Licensure Board was informed of the survey failure and a probable Never Episode. The Joint Commission surveyors candidly told us to expect an army of Licensure Board surveyors and inspectors to descend upon us in the next few weeks.

Once the call was concluded and the surveyors departed, I Need, Dan, Mr. Upton, our Board Chairman, and I pondered our options.

Mr. Upton began the discussion. "Why don't we just close for a month or two? In the Air Force we called it Standing Down. We shut things down until we could get a handle on what needed to be fixed. Sometimes, it's too hard to do that when running normal operations. It's like repairing a running motor."

I Need disagreed. "Closing the ER would be a death sentence for the community. Surgeons would have no place to operate, and many would think about leaving. Their patients needing surgery would have to go elsewhere. We may never recover the volume we would lose."

I did not say it, but Dan and I both knew that any closure of the hospital would screw harness racing and open the potential for the teacher's unions and thoroughbred interests to plow us under.

Mr. Upton relented. "OK, we stay open. But we are barely breaking even now. I would assume that it will take a lot of capital to get the building back in order and to appease the inspectors."

Dan reluctantly informed him that his assumptions were right but that our fiscal woes were even deeper. "The Licensure Board likes to fine hospitals. They do it as a punishment. With Never Episodes, the fines are steep to start with, and they double with each subsequent one in a single fiscal year. We are likely looking at a $50,000 fine for Buster's retained sponge. If it is determined that Roy did wrong site surgery, that fine will be $100,000."

**Master's office 4 PM**

Master was always pleased with himself when he looked at his work. Even work that was done on the wrong side.

"Mr. Quincy. Nice to see you. Are you having much pain in your wrist?"

"Not too much pain. But I just took a pill."

"The wound looks just perfect. You are lucky that I decided to examine your right arm. It was so much worse than the left."

Mr. Quincy wasn't buying it. "How about we knock off the bullshit. You promised me $25,000. Do you have it?"

Master was unfazed. "Yes, I do. Do you know what you are to say?"

"Yeah, yeah. I had tests on both arms. You and I both got a little confused. We thought you were doing the left today. But after you examined me and noticed how flat the muscle in my right hand was, you did the right side and told me after the case."

Master was pleased. "Good. Say little else. Make it sound like it's no big deal."

"Got that right." Quincy's eyes lit up as Master laid a large envelope pregnant with cash on the table.

"Come back in two weeks, and my physician assistant will remove the stitches. No lifting with the right hand until then."

Mr. Quincy did not follow directions well. He grabbed the envelope filled with $100 bills with his right hand and scurried out the door.

# Chapter 18

## *Krenshaw Medical Center*
## *Wednesday, Millions Week*

I lost out on three live drives last night. I cancelled all my racing Tuesday through Thursday so I could accompany our surveyors. This being Millions Week meant that there was some serious money to be made. But Stephanie and Billie were more than willing to pick up my slack.

Stephanie won with one of the Dunstan two-year-olds. Billie banked the big check in the third race that I missed. It was a $150,000 race, so Billie got $3750. Good for him. He didn't drive him the way I expected, but he got the horse home anyway.

It might have been better that I hadn't driven last night. I was home early and got some sleep. With my calendar today, I will need it. I moved my meeting with Master to 4 PM. Dan and I decided to do the root cause analysis (RCA) with the OR staff without Buster. We might change our findings after we met with him, but we both knew he would intimidate everyone in the room. A good root cause analysis depended upon people being able to speak.

An RCA was about trying to get to the root cause of a problem. It's just the opposite of a congressional hearing. The purpose of a hearing is to try to fix blame, hopefully on the other party. A properly conducted RCA is done to fix a problem and to fix it as permanently as possible.

We liked to use the "five why" approach. For any problem, you can ask five whys, and that might get you to the root cause.

The staff provided us with some valuable information about the Quincy case. After Master's battle with the surveyor, he was in an incredible hurry. He took the patient himself from the surgical holding area back to the operating room. That was something he had never done before today. The operating room that Quincy was in was small. Staff reported that they usually pushed the stretchers in and then they turned them around. It made it easier to get out of the room when the case was done.

Master apparently did not know that. He demanded to start the case immediately after he pushed Quincy in. Therefore, the patient was never turned. His right arm was in the location where the left arm should have been. Staff did not see Master examine the right arm. But he was f-bombing everyone to get going, so they might not have noticed.

The staff was pretty sure that halfway through the case Master realized his error. They said he launched into a diatribe about carpal tunnel surgery, including the part about it sometimes being painless and without symptoms. He went on to spew the garbage about it potentially causing paralysis. The staff said that he never spoke during cases except to ask for something or to bitch at someone.

So even though we had five whys, we only needed to use one.

Why was wrong site surgery done?

Because Master is an asshole.

Dan found the contract that Deuce had made with Master. It was exactly as Master said. Dan felt that it was not a valid contract, and he would ask him to agree to terminate it. Because those operating rooms were under the hospital license, Deuce could not permit Master to totally control them.

I Need joined Dan and me for lunch. He wasn't surprised that the contract was not legal. Deuce did anything he could to keep Master happy. It was clear in retrospect that Deuce only wanted the hospital as a vehicle to launder his money from his other operations. So, he made sure that most troublemakers were kept happy. It was a lot less work for him.

I asked, "Is that why he never pursued any action against Buster? Obstetrics staff said he often smelled of alcohol when working. He was reported numerous times, but none of the allegations were ever proven. We are pretty sure they were never investigated."

I Need nodded. "Buster was Deuce's ace in the hole. As president of the staff, he did Deuce's bidding. In return, Deuce protected Buster. Deuce also looked the other way with Master's antics, but I heard he didn't like him much. No one does."

Dan wanted to know. "Then why did Deuce put up with Master's crap?"

I Need smiled. "Buster and Master were best buddies outside the hospital. Buster went to bat for him with Deuce. It gave Deuce further leverage with Buster and the medical staff. That's how Master got to have two operating rooms."

"What's the big deal about two rooms? I mean, you can only operate in one at a time?" I asked.

I Need laughed. "ZZ, you have a ton to learn about things outside the ER. You need to spend a day or two in the operating room with me. There are two things you don't cost a surgeon: time or money. For most surgeons, those are one and the same. Do you know how long it takes to turn over an operating room? That is to clean up after a case and get it ready for the next case."

I guessed. "Ten minutes?"

"Ha. You are thinking about wiping down an ER stretcher and putting a new sheet on for the next patient. That's possible in ten minutes. It takes anywhere from 30 minutes to one hour to go from case to case. When I finish a case, I do my operative dictation and talk with the family. That takes about 15 minutes. Then I sit there and smoke a couple cigarettes while I wait for the next case to start."

"You aren't allowed to smoke in the hospital!" I was proud that I found the balls to tell him.

"OK, I chew a couple candy cigarettes, happy??" I Need sounded seriously annoyed.

I decided not to pursue the smoking subject further. I Need seemed pleased to move on with his explanation.

"Not only is it bad for my health, but it takes me six hours to finish most days even though I only operate for three. I waste about three hours here, and then I must go to the office. What Master had was the surgeon's dream. While he was doing one case, they were turning the other room over for his next case. When he finished in room one, he went immediately to room two. He did that all day long. He got twice as many cases done in the same amount of time."

I was beginning to understand. "Very efficient. When did he do his dictations?" Surgeons were required to do an in-depth dictation describing all aspects of the surgeries they performed.

I Need responded, "They say he did them all at the end of the day."

"Wouldn't that be hard to do without mixing cases up?"

"I do mine after each case, but Buster made his process work."

"What's the difference between a dictation and an operative note?" I was trying to bone up on OR jargon.

I Need lit up a cigarette, and it wasn't candy so much for my lecture. "Our rules require that the dictation describing the operative procedure and any complications be done within 24 hours of the case. But until that dictation hits the chart there would be no record of the case. Caregivers taking care of the patient in the immediate post operative period needed to know certain things. Therefore, surgeons are required to enter an immediate post-op note that names the procedure done, lists complications, blood loss, etc."

I had to ask. "What did his immediate post-operative note say?"

Dan answered. "He didn't do one. I pulled several charts from different days he operated, and he never recorded an immediate post-operative note."

I Need exploded. "That prick! He knows the rules and openly flaunts them. I ride herd on everyone else to do what is required. I have no idea how he was able to avoid detection, but I will find out!"

Dan nodded. "There is more. I pulled two dictations from the Quincy case. The first one he dictated indicated that he operated on the left wrist. He did not mention examining or operating on the right wrist or hand. There is a second one dictated last night that documents the exam and surgery on the right."

I Need wrinkled his brow and crushed his cigarette out in his coffee cup. If anyone asks, I will blame the cigarette smoke on Juicy Lucy. She doesn't smoke, but she'll take the hit for me, I think. Who knows what that is going to cost me.

Dan continued, "I spoke with the head of transcription. I think I know how this happened. He dictated all his operative notes at the end of his operating day. But the way he did it was a royal pain in the ass for the transcriptionists. The surgeon was supposed to enter the patient's medical record number into the system and, then do his dictation, and hang up. One number, one dictation. Master refused to hang up the phone. He insisted on getting into the system and doing all six or eight or whatever number of dictations he had at once. He would give the medical record number and patient name, but he did his dictations in a single call. The transcriptionists had to pause the system each time they finished a transcription. Then they had to manually enter the name and number for the next one and so on."

I was disgusted. "So, Master got his work done faster, and the transcriptionists had to do more work. Sounds typical for him."

"That bastard," screamed I Need.

Now I was interested. "What? Master inconveniencing everyone for his own good isn't news."

I Need wanted to fire up another cancer stick, but his pack was empty. He crushed the empty pack and threw it across the room, making a three-pointer into the trash can. True jock. He was livid. "No, it's not, but I think I know what he is doing. I disciplined him for it about five years ago."

Dan pleaded, "Please go on."

"That son of a bitch is doing his operative notes before the surgery. The night before, he dictates the note of a perfect operation for each case. But since the transcriptions are time-stamped, he can't dictate them into the system. So, he makes a tape of all the dictations. When he finishes for the day, he logs into the system and plays the tape. That is why he doesn't enter the system separately for each one. He just gets in his car and takes off while the tape plays. He picks up another half hour a day with that trick."

I had to give the dude credit for his ingenuity, but the whole thing stunk. "That would explain the fact that he indicated that he operated on Mr. Quincy's left wrist. He used the previously recorded tape that he had done the night before. But later in the day, he realized the original note would implicate him in doing wrong site surgery and did the second one."

I Need was livid. "That cuts it. He's gone. I want him off the staff permanently."

I had called security to see when Master blew out of the parking lot yesterday. At the time he left, only two of six of his dictations were done. So, they were being dictated as he was going down the road. But the call to transcription did not come from an outside line. It came from x5681, and that happened to be the phone in Buster's private OR lounge. Yeah, that asshole had his own lounge. But we had proof that he did not do the dictations live. Master was busted!

# Chapter 19

*Krenshaw Medical Center*

*Friday, Millions Week*

The big hand on my watch hitting 12 while the little one landed on the 4 came much faster than I expected or wanted. I still had a ton of research to do on Master's behavior, but we had to have the meeting today. The longer we delayed, the more problems he would cause. The bookies made it odds-on that this was going to be a fiasco. You could get 2:1 betting on a debacle. A catastrophe was paying 3:1.

JL had the documents in order. She told me that Master was bringing his attorney. We had the right to exclude him, but Dan and I figured we had nothing to hide. The message we wanted to send was clear. Your man is out. We have the proof we need, and we are not giving in.

Master and his attorney arrived right on time. Master was dressed in a tennis outfit. He had a sweater tied around his neck and oversized, bright rose-colored, Elton John-type sunglasses on. He was carrying a black briefcase. Most people in tennis outfits don't carry a briefcase. He looked like a goof, so at least he was in character.

His attorney was in a dark blue pantsuit. She was the poster child for a professional woman. Every hair was in place. Her makeup was perfect, and her nails were tastefully done. Although she was attractive, her appearance downplayed that. She was here to represent a client, not to make a fashion statement. I was hoping for an arrogant but incompetent attorney. No early Christmas for me.

Master glared at me as his attorney walked past him and introduced herself to Dan and me with a firm handshake. She handed each of us her card, which I studied. Jasmine Disimone JD. JD stood for Juris Doctor. So, her initials were JDJD. That was now her name, at least in my pea brain.

We walked into the medical staff conference room. I introduced her to I Need, Dr. Hiram Goldstein, our chief of surgery, and Dr. Beatrice Worthington, our chief of anesthesia. Master set his briefcase at his assigned seat and then just pranced around the conference room like he was a peacock observer.

I called the meeting to order. He sat down to the left of JDJD. They were on the other side of the table from me. She pulled out a legal pad and a very expensive-looking pen. Dan asked permission to video record the meeting. He wanted no misunderstandings. JDJD wasn't thrilled but acquiesced after Dan agreed that she would leave with her own copy and that she would get a copy of the transcription.

Now that that tape was running, I had to introduce myself. "Good afternoon. I am Dr. Zachary Zander." (See how professional I could be? It was Dr. Zander, not ZZ.) "I have researched the contract that Dr. Bator has with the hospital concerning the operating rooms that he utilizes. I have also investigated Dr. Bator's compliance with hospital policies and, rules, and regulations of the surgical department. Finally, I have investigated Dr. Bator's handling of the Quincy case."

Master pulled off his glasses and pointed them at me. "You are in no position to judge anything I do. Only a fellow board-certified neurosurgeon with equal experience could come close to understanding my work. You certainly are not in my league. You have been after me since you narrowly avoided being thrown off staff. This is nothing but a vendetta."

Dr. Goldstein introduced himself to the tape and jumped into the ring. "As the chief of your department, I am required to review your work in the hospital and your compliance with hospital rules. I have provided my information to Dr. Zander. He is also speaking for myself, Dr. Worthington, and Dr. Morehead."

Master was unfazed. "Am I to be impressed with the biased opinions of four community hospital hacks? You know I am on the faculty of the most prestigious medical school in the state. I have published more articles than all of you have ever read combined!"

I Need quietly used only the middle finger of his right hand to slide his glasses further up the bridge of his nose. We had planned for this. If Master came into the meeting with respect and decorum, we would ask him to invalidate the contract. If he was agreeable to that we would give him a reprimand for lack of site marking, time outs, and dictation irregularities. That was provided he agreed to follow the rules and regulations from here on out.

If he presented like the true butthead we knew he was, we would go for the throat. I Need was to make the call. When I Need subtly flipped him off, we got the green light.

Dan interrupted Dr. Bator and laid out the ground rules for the meeting. JDJD nodded her head in agreement. Master stared out the window. Dan recognized me, and the fiasco-debacle commenced.

"Dr. Bator. I hereby inform you that your privileges to practice at Krenshaw Medical Center are suspended as of this moment."

Master got out a loud "fuck you" before JDJD put her hand on his arm. She spoke softly and slowly.

"I apologize for Dr. Bator. We will follow the rules."

I continued. "I will recite the reasons for the suspension. These are abbreviated summaries of the infractions. Full information will be presented at the medical executive committee meeting in two weeks. 1. Failure to follow hospital policies and Department of Surgery rules and regulations requiring site marking of surgical sites. 2. Failure to follow the universal protocol as it pertains to a time-out being conducted prior to any invasive surgical procedure. 3. Falsification of records. Dictating operative notes before cases have been completed violates the integrity of the record. 4. Failure to complete medical records. Specifically, failure to document a brief operative note when required."

JDJD sat very quietly. She made notes but didn't appear phased or flustered. Remind me never to play poker with her unless it's strip poker. She tries to hide it, but I think she's hot.

I composed myself and went on. "5. We reserve the right to bring charges based on the Quincy case. An investigation of that case is ongoing."

That got JDJD a little more animated. She raised her hand, and Dan recognized her.

"What are your concerns with that case?"

I answered, "Possible wrong site surgery with an attempt to cover up same with lies to the patient and falsification of documents."

JDJD said nothing. The only noise in the room was the barely audible squeak of her pen on her paper. Dan nodded for me to continue.

"Furthermore, please be informed that the contract that Dr. Bator has concerning operating rooms one and two is hereby terminated."

JDJD raised her hand and was recognized.

"What is the basis for terminating the contract?"

I took a sip of water as Dan answered. "In your packet of information is a copy of the contract with appropriate citing of state and federal statutes that we feel it violates."

JDJD said nothing, so I continued.

"Lastly, we intend to petition the medical executive committee for a full and permanent revocation of Dr. Bator's privileges to practice here at Krenshaw, in addition to his removal from the medical staff. We feel he is a disruptive influence that compromises the mission of this hospital."

I looked up from my notes to see the reaction on Master's face. I had waited for this moment all day. Unfortunately, he was searching for something in his briefcase, and his face was obscured by the open briefcase lid. When the lid closed, it was clear that Master was pointing a .44 Magnum in my direction.

I Need screamed, "NOOOOOOO!"

I thought about diving under the table as I heard a thud. The .44 Magnum suddenly flew in the air and landed on a chair at the end of the table. JDJD had Karate chopped it from his right arm with her left hand. I couldn't wait to see the video replay. It was like a lightning bolt.

I Need jumped over the table and got Buster in a headlock. JDJD calmly walked over and retrieved the weapon. She expertly held it up, verified it for herself and then demonstrated to everyone that it was not loaded. She then handed it to Dan. JDJD knew how to handle a firearm.

Her voice was as calm as before the gun appeared. "I imagine you will want the gun for the hearing. Too bad I will miss it."

I Need let loose of his hold and assisted Master into a chair. He then stood looking down at Master. JDJD walked over and addressed Master.

"I officially inform you that our firm will no longer represent you. In addition, I will cooperate with the officials from Krenshaw as they pursue criminal charges for today's events."

"Cunt," Master uttered.

SMACK. It was a sickening sound but a welcome one. She slapped his face so hard that he fell from the chair. I Need grinned as he helped him back up. Two of our bigger security guards arrived and took up positions on either side of Master. Both had their tasers drawn.

Shortly thereafter a few of Krenshaw's finest police officers arrived and took control of the scene. Because a weapon was involved, they handcuffed Master and perp walked him out the door. I was dying to watch the video tape. I hoped we could find some popcorn. You couldn't invent stuff like this.

After Master was escorted to jail, Dan and the physicians bade JDJD farewell after thanking her for disarming Master. I excused myself to go to my office. I needed a flash drive to copy JDJD's video onto for her records. When I returned, she was alone in the conference room. She was gathering her notepads and pens. I must have startled her.

"Oh my, you scared me." She blushed.

"I doubt that. From what I saw today, you don't scare easily, if at all."

"I hide it well. Can I ask you a favor?"

"Shoot. Whoops I guess that was not a good word choice. Please, ask away."

I couldn't believe what happened next. She pointed at the Stoli Vodka bottle that was on the bookcase at the end of the room. It was the evidence we had against Buster. The forensics lab had returned it, and we were saving it for his hearings.

She quietly said. "I could sure use a shot of that. How about you?"

I locked the door to the conference room and poured out a couple of shots. She retrieved a deck of cards from her briefcase and our poker game commenced. I was thinking the same thought I had a few minutes ago; you can't invent stuff like this. The sound of the conference room door closing as JDJD exited brought me back from fantasy land to reality. That sucked.

# Chapter 20

## *Fired Up Farms*

It was a long and way to exciting week. I was supposed to drive two horses tonight. We only had three horses racing. Stephanie was more than happy to take them when I called her this afternoon. I was just too tired to think I could perform effectively on the track, so I just headed home. I wasn't sure I should be driving a car, let alone a racehorse.

We would have a full house tonight. Everyone was coming in for the big race tomorrow. The house was empty when I arrived as everyone else had gone to the track. I went to get a beer and found the note that Mom had written on the fridge.

"Zachary, there are some sandwiches in the crisper drawer and some meatloaf left over from last night. We will bring pizza home after the races. Get some rest. Love, Mom"

My first beer just evaporated. I heard some of those IPAs did that. You open them, and boom they are empty. I went to the kitchen and retrieved a second one. I was conducting a scientific experiment designed to see if another one would behave the same way. I was distracted by the front door opening as I returned to the living room.

"Peace be with you, my brother," I said to the ultra large, bald man with a full beard. He was dressed like a priest.

"Stuff it, ZZ," said the priest as he pulled off his collar and flopped down into my favorite lounge chair. When I went over to protest, he grabbed the beer from my hand and downed it in a couple gulps.

He let out a forceful burp. "Sorry," he giggled. "Can you get me another beer? This one seems to have evaporated."

See, I was right about the beer.

If it was anyone else, I would have responded with a slew of profanity. But this was Father Jonathan, one of my best friends and a charter member of the Dying Was Easy gang. So, believe it not, I shut my mouth. I wandered back to the kitchen and grabbed two more cold ones and some sandwiches. I handed him a beer and a sandwich and took up residence on the couch.

"Little John, you look beat. I thought I had a tough week, but you make me look good." Little John was our nickname for Father Jonathan.

His speech was initially garbled by the massive bite of roast beef sandwich that filled his mouth. It improved when he washed the obstruction down with half of his second beer.

"ZZ, sorry to bust your balls. I spent the morning at the school trying to get ready for the admission committee meeting. I had a question about one of the applications, so I phoned the parents. Mom gave me the information that I needed. Then her husband asked to speak to me. He made it clear that he expected his daughter to be accepted. I started to explain our process when he interrupted me. He then went on to say that we admitted way too many kids that weren't white. He faced the same crap at work, and he wouldn't tolerate it for his daughter."

I shook my head. "Wow, I never heard that one before. Everyone knows we have an open and aboveboard process. We take the kids that will benefit the most. Period!"

Father Jonathan agreed. "We both know it! But it really pissed me off to hear that garbage. I should have just hung up. Maybe it's being around you and Joe too much, but I just had to tell the jerk off. So, I did. I may have used the f word a few times."

I pressed him for some clarity. "May have? A few times?"

"OK, I ripped him a new asshole in no uncertain words. The dude called the bishop, and I had to go to the diocesan office. After he heard my confession, the bishop unloaded on me. He felt I had so much potential, but he has little patience left with me."

"It sounds like you are back in the bishop's doghouse, just like before."

He nodded. "Worse than that. I am going to Rome. I leave on Monday. I will be gone for at least three or four months."

"That doesn't sound like punishment. Don't you guys (priests) love going there?"

"I would if I was on a sabbatical or a special assignment. But I am going to Arbitrium Arbor."

I had no idea what that was. "And that is?"

"Latin for Decision Tree."

"And that means?"

"It's a place they send bad priests. It's months of intense prayer, penance, and counseling. At any time during the process if I am determined to be beyond hope, I will be asked to leave the priesthood for good. If I complete the process, I still must pass a review board and get a favorable rating from them. My bishop will come there and participate in the review board. If they rate me positively, I can return to the States and will be on a probationary status. If they rate me negatively, I am banished."

"Father Jonathan, can I do anything? Half of the reason that you ended up sideways with the bishop before was that you walked out on the diocese when I sounded the Dying Was Easy alarm. Your help in proving that Deuce and Knuckles were running an operation to facilitate the use of performance enhancing drugs in sports and harness racing was invaluable. The bishop ended up forgiving you, but it must still be sticking in his craw."

"Thanks ZZ. I am pretty sure that he only forgave me because we were able to save The Always Hope School. He just adores those kids, and that helped me avoid a more serious punishment."

I protested, "But we never would have been able to do that without your help. That must count for something."

He went on after another swig of beer. "You, Azzie, and Joe have saved my life and career on numerous occasions. I would never turn you down. But I do have to face the fact that there are occasions, like today, when I don't live up to my vows."

I was sympathetic. "There are plenty of races that I don't win when I should have. To err is human."

"True, but if I am going to continue as a priest I must do better, much better. Maybe this trip to Rome will be exactly what I need. ZZ, can I ask one favor?"

"Sure, name it."

"Don't tell anyone why I am going. The bishop has allowed me to imply that I am going on a sabbatical. This whole Decision Tree concept is a secret. No one is to know. I was not supposed to talk to you about it."

"No wonder you are going there. You tell me something that two hours ago you promised the bishop you wouldn't. Nice move."

The big priest flipped me a Zander salute. I returned it. We both laughed.

We might have been a little tipsy when the rest of the gang arrived. They were so busy hooting and hollering about the night Stephanie had that they didn't notice. She won three races and put three lifetime marks on the horses. PC was grinning from ear to ear.

I tried to be gracious. "I guess I might as well retire from racing. Queen Stephanie is now in charge."

"You may need to after I pummel your ass tomorrow," Stephanie said as she combed her hair.

For someone who always smelled like a stable, and whose hair was more knotted than the pine in our living room, she had become a grooming perfection. That damn Azzie did amazing work. I secretly wondered if she had anything in her beauty bag that could make my scar less noticeable.

It was midnight when we finished reviewing the races and discussing the news from the hospital. Father Jonathan informed the group of his good fortune to get a sabbatical in Rome, and we called it a night.

# Chapter 21

## *Miracle Mile Racetrack and Casino*
## *Krenshaw, NJ*

After a great night's sleep, I really couldn't wait to get to the track. Something different to keep my mind off the problems at the hospital. I loved working at the hospital until the governor and I Need conned me into being the Chief Medical Officer. Up to that point, the ER was running smoothly, and I was winning more than my share of races. I had to cancel all my drives this week, the most important racing week of the season. At least I would get some racing in today.

The hospital was really getting me down. I couldn't help but think about what could have happened if Master had remembered to load his gun. I had to put all that aside. Stephanie and I were racing against each other for a $10 million purse. I had better be focused, or she would never let me hear the end of it.

As soon as the star-spangled banner finished, the announcer, Gabe Vatter, appeared on the track televisions.

"Welcome race fans to the final card of the Miracle Millions Week. And what a week it has been. Six new track records and scores of personal records. I have some news for you. We saved the best for last. Today's $10 million finale features two undefeated horses from the same stable. Each are scheduled to retire from racing after the race.

Fired Up Farms did the unthinkable this week when they entered them to race against each other. Fired Up Frat Boy logically belongs in the big race. But they could have entered Fired Up Rio in the Filly and Mare Invitational for a purse of $3 million as they did last year. She dominated that race last year, and it appears that she could have done the same thing this year. It looks like they turned down an easy $1.5 million to race against one of their own horses. I caught up with Carl

Zander earlier this week and asked him to shed some light on this. Here's the tape:

"Carl, can you explain why you entered these horses to race against each other? They are both undefeated, and each likely could end their careers undefeated. People are scratching their heads."

"Sure, Gabe, it's easy. I tend to indulge my children. The two of them were instrumental in getting my legal troubles turned around and in securing funding for The Always Hope School. A short time ago, I saw my daughter Stephanie chasing my son ZZ with a pitchfork. That's not an uncommon site. But she was screaming at him about how she could drive Fired Up Frat Boy and beat Fired Up Rio if ZZ was driving her. One thing led to another, and they planned to settle the argument by racing them at the farm.

I didn't want to see an all-out race of two of the best horses I ever had at a farm for no purse. No one would see, so they would remain officially undefeated. But I still couldn't get my head around that. So, I agreed to allow them both to be entered in the Millions Finale. Stephanie will sit behind Fired Up Frat Boy, and ZZ will drive Fired Up Rio."

"But Carl, you are pretty much allowing only one of your horses to remain undefeated? Does that make economic sense?"

"No, it doesn't, but it made sense to my kids, and it is great for the sport. Harness racing took it on the chin after those drugging escapades became public a couple years ago. We have been blessed to train and own two of the finest horses ever. I think we owe it to the sport to see which one is the best and to do our part to restore integrity and true competition to harness racing."

"C'mon Carl, you are not really going to race these horses flat out? They both stand out over everyone else in the field. I see them leaving the gate, controlling the front end, and then jogging home. Maybe they race only the last sixteenth of a mile. Am I wrong?"

"Gabe, you couldn't be further off course. ZZ drove both horses until our stakes schedule made it difficult for him to be with both.

Stephanie took over the reins of Fired Up Frat Boy and has maneuvered him to ten straight victories and put three new lifetime marks on him. She reminds ZZ of this daily. This will be a race like no other. Plus, this year's field is awesome. I appreciate your thinking that our horses stand out over the field. But any one of the other seven horses in the race could step up. It ain't over till the finish line."

"Ok Carl, Let's talk about the horses. Frat Boy is a little on the small side. He makes up for it with malignant speed and a brush that no one has been able to match. Fired up Rio is a monster. Her legs are so long that she covers much more ground in a single stride. How do you see them in this race and what kind of shape are they in? Neither one raced last week."

"Gabe you are correct. But first, they are both in excellent shape. A few nicks and bruises, but considering how hard they have been raced they are great. They each got a needed week off last week and played around in the field. We put a light workout in them last Saturday and turned them out. They both trained on Wednesday but not together. After that they went back to the field after the kids from The Always Hope School groomed both of them.

Rio is freakishly big. Seventeen hands. But for that size she is amazingly coordinated. Some big horses are just not great athletes. She is the exception. She has speed, but not as quick a brush as Frat Boy. It takes her a little while to get into gear. Plus, with her size ZZ must be careful in the turns. She almost trots off her feet in the turns at high speeds.

Frat Boy is just a speed demon. He can leave the gate like a rocket, but he can also be put in a hole with just two fingers. When he makes his move, he does it so fast that no one can react quickly enough."

"Carl, are you sure Stephanie is up to the task of driving Frat Boy in this race? I know she has won ten straight. But this is the biggest race of all, and she is the least experienced driver?"

"I hope she didn't hear you say that. Stephanie is special, but she can get irritated quickly. That said, I have never seen anyone so chilly in the race bike. Nothing phases her. She has uncanny instincts, and she is fearless. Do you remember the big race two years ago? The one where you said she made a mistake when she pulled and was hung out?"

Gabe shook his head. "Oh, do I ever. People still remind me. I was so into the race that I just called what I saw. She was getting the perfect trip behind the best horse in the race. She had no business pulling. So, I thought. What did she win by? Ten lengths."

Carl laughed. "Sometimes experience brings its own baggage. Other than ZZ, there is no one I'd rather have drive him in this race."

"Speaking of ZZ and Stephanie, who is the better driver?"

"Are you nuts? I wouldn't answer that question if I knew the answer. I have got to live with them both and my wife."

Vatter missed on the big question, so he moved on. "Carl, what is your strategy for this race?"

"We normally have a plan. But that plan is subject to change at the whim of the drivers. I never second guess what they do on the track. That's one of the reasons they are both successful. My guess is that Stephanie will put Frat Boy on the lead. ZZ will follow her if he can. But if there are a lot of horses leaving, he will duck for position and come first over and take his chances in the stretch. As you know he sometimes likes to sit on the outside of the leading horse in the first over position. Looking over at big Rio can be intimidating to both the horse and driver at the pylons. It should be an interesting race."

"It already is. Good luck and a safe trip to both."

# Chapter 22

*Master's House*
*Blueberry Fields Estates*
*Krenshaw, NJ*

Master was in a very surly mood. Hanging out in jail last night was an unnerving experience. It took him hours to engage new counsel and the rest of the night to arrange bail. He got home at 5 AM and got to sleep two hours and three glasses of scotch later. He was awakened at noon by his cell phone buzzing.

"What the hell do you want? I told you I don't want to be disturbed." Master screamed into the phone.

His answering service was used to his abuse. They charged him double their normal rate, but this was below their economically lowered threshold for acceptable behavior. The voice presented her case. "Your patient, Vernon Quincy, demands to see you immediately. He says his wound is badly infected, and he is in a lot of pain."

Master was in no mood. "You damn well know my protocol for that kind of complaint. You send him to the ER and have them call me after they evaluate it."

The voice persisted. "I advised him of that, but he refused to go. He demanded your number, which I did not provide him. But he did state that if you did not call him back in the next ten minutes his next call would be to Dr. Zander."

The voice from the answering service was expecting another profanity laden tirade. Master surprised her.

"Tell him to meet me at my office in 30 minutes."

He hung up before she could repeat back the order as was their procedure.

## OFFICE OF ROY BATOR

Master did his best to control himself. "When did you notice the infection?"

"There is no infection."

Master's worst fears were coming to fruition. "Well, then what the hell do you want?"

"$200,000," Quincy said without blinking.

"Out of the question."

"Oh really. We both know you operated on the wrong arm."

"But we agreed on $25,000." Buster reminded him.

"Yeah, but now I am un-agreeing. When I looked around on the internet, I saw that those cases are worth a lot more. Plus, I know that you are in deep shit with the hospital. Your incident from yesterday was on the front page of the paper. Nice booking photo! $200,000 and I tell the tale you told me to anyone who wants to listen. Hospital, judge, television anchor, I could care less. You need me to pull your ass out of the fire, and I don't come cheap."

The redness of Master's face quickly faded. His scowl turned into a wry smile. He looked pensive. No one spoke for a minute before he answered Vernon Quincy.

"Sorry to have reacted negatively. I have never been involved in anything like this before. I know you are right. You are entitled to more compensation. But it's not in my best interest to turn this over to my malpractice insurance carrier. They will raise my rates, notify the state medical board, and give the hospital even more ammunition. Can we work something out?"

"I ain't unreasonable. I want more money. If you can come up with $150,000 that is untraceable, we can put this to bed."

"I will need time to raise the cash. Would next Wednesday be ok?"

Quincy wasn't sure how to play this. "I was hoping for a little sooner."

"I might be able to have it by Monday. I have most of my liquid assets tied up in my bail arrangement. I need some time to move money around, but I think I can borrow what I need from a close friend. Let me see if I can reach him."

Master faked a conversation with his mythical close friend. It sounded more like a conversation with a loan shark.

"Just like the last time: a short-term loan. Yes, I understand the terms. Sunday night, 11 PM, usual spot. Got it."

Master ended the imaginary conversation. He decided to sweeten the offer to lock in Quincy's cooperation.

"I'm sorry I can't pay you today, but maybe I can help you pass the time until I can. I can arrange for you to stay in a luxury suite tonight at the Borgata. All your room charges, food and drinks will be comped. Deal?"

Quincy smelled blood in the water. "Ok, but how about a little cash today. I used the $25,000 you gave me to pay off bills. $5,000 today sounds right. It will make the trip more interesting."

Quincy had most of the $25,000 hidden at his house. He lied to shake a few more dollars out of Master. It worked.

Master peeled $5,000 in $100 bills from his money roll and handed them to Quincy. "Come back to the office Monday at 4 AM. Park in the back lot, and I will come to your car. We don't need any witnesses."

"Great. 4 AM Monday in your parking lot."

Master tried to sound sincere. "Good luck this weekend, have fun."

Master watched Quincy exit the parking lot. Master locked the office and drove to Serene Pines Memorial Gardens. It wasn't difficult to find his late wife's grave. The monument was enormous and pretentious. It read Veronica Bator 1980-2020. He got out of his car to pay his lack of respect.

"Hey bitch. How's the view down there?" He laughed as he continued. "Too bad you committed suicide. I would have loved choking the life out of you. Oh well, I am enjoying the life insurance money. It was great to get the ten million, but it was even better when that drunk Hyman turned me on to that new IUD company. The old bastard is pretty burnt, but he had that one right. I put five million in and got twenty-five million back out. Thanks for dying to get me started."

Satisfied that he had defiled his dead wife's grave enough, he carefully opened the glass chamber that contained her picture. He pulled out one of the slips of paper hidden behind the picture and pocketed it. He spat on the headstone and walked back to his car.

The coffee shop was not too crowded. He took out one of his burner smartphones and accessed the internet. After consulting the paper he had retrieved from the grave, he found his way to the sparsely used email site and made a draft of a message. The nefarious people he was dealing with liked to communicate via the use of drafts. They never were sent over the net. Once the recipient read it, he would erase 90% of the message and then delete it. In addition, the message was encrypted using a onetime pad like the Russians used to use. It was a safe and effective way to communicate with people who specialized in the type of services he required.

He encrypted and slowly typed his message. "Megabrain requests two new players to join wife. 100k with 50k bonus for prompt service."

He signed out and went into the chatroom that he had used before. He left a note for B4.

After waiting 30 minutes he found his reply. "Acceptable. Names and address? Usual payment process."

In a new encrypted email draft he typed in the Quincy's name and address, and he added the information about the Borgata. Provided he got the payment on its way in time, he would never hear from B4 again.

A few minutes later the instructions were on their way to his bank in the Caymans. They would send $200,000 in crypto on a journey around the world. The crypto would be turned into diamonds and then gold and back to crypto etc. The money would be transformed fifteen times at a total cost of $50,000. B4 would pick up $150,000 at the end of the complicated and impossible to trace line. He smiled as he arrived home.

"That asshole wants to blackmail me? Fuck him and his wife."

# Chapter 23

## *Miracle Mile Racetrack and Casino*

In the paddock, the trash-talking between Stephanie and me was in full form. Stephanie asked me to come to Frat Boy's stall to look at his face. She sounded worried. I fell for it and began to examine his head when she screamed, "You might want to look at his face now because once the race starts, all you will ever see is his ass."

I had used that trick a few times to intimidate other drivers. Stephanie did it as a prank. She knew I wasn't going to be intimidated. I fished a small bottle of Exquisite Evolutions face cream out of my pocket and tossed it to Stephanie.

"You might want to put some of that on, to prevent windburn when I rocket past you in the stretch." I giggled as she flipped me a Zander salute. I must admit that I was a tad nervous, but she wasn't, or at least I didn't see it. Speaking of nervous, Dad checked both horses' equipment for the millionth time.

"ZZ, we can still scratch her. No one would blame us."

"I would. I need to show Stephanie her place, and we need to see who the best is. Best driver and best horse."

The paddock judge called for the horses to be brought to the racetrack. Stephanie gave me a big hug and whispered, "I love you ZZ, safe trip."

I kissed her softly on the cheek and said, "You too sweetie, you too."

I felt a tear start down my cheek, but I was able to wipe it off before Stephanie saw it. Mom led Rio out into the bright sun. That made the diamonds in her ears and all four hoofs sparkle. That was $3 million of sparkle lent to us by Azzie.

I followed holding the reins. Right behind us was Dad leading Frat Boy with Stephanie in a similar trailing position. Almost in unison Mom and Dad snapped the overchecks into position. Stephanie and I hopped into our race bikes. No more trash talk.

I did a radio check with Stephanie, and all was good. Rio was a little on the bit. She had every right to be excited. The stands were packed. People were bunched at the fences to get a glimpse of the horses parading to post. The Army was in its usual position at the top of the stretch. The flag for The Always Hope School was flying proudly.

Gabe jabbered on about the conditions and purse for the race. He sounded like he had just finished a dozen Red Bulls. Rat tat tat. He took a breath and his speech slowed as he introduced the field for this year's Millions Race.

"Number one is Heaven Eleven. He's a four-year-old owned by Roll Em' Stables of Buffalo, New York. He has won 27 out of 38 races, banking $2,580,000. He has a lifetime mark of 1:48:3 on a mile track. He is trained by hall-of-fame trainer Gus Foster and is driven by Tony Spinelli.

Number two is That's All Folks. He's a seven-year-old owned by Stanley Cupferman and Felix Klein of New York. He has won 52 of 81 races banking $4,953,000. He has a lifetime mark of 1:48. He is trained by Jackie Stevenson and is driven by Lester Queensbury.

Number three is Abitibi. He's a six-year-old owned by Thompson, Jenkins, Plessinger and Grinnel. He has won 28 of 37 races banking $6,258,000. Two million of that came when he won this race three years ago. He took a lifetime mark that year of 1:46:3 and is currently tied for the track record for colts and geldings with Fired Up Frat Boy. He is trained by the hall of fame trainer Gus Foster, with Sammy 'The Hammy' Molinero in the sulky.

Number four is Fired Up Rio. She's a five-year-old owned by Fired Up Farms of NJ. She is undefeated in 34 lifetime starts with earnings of $7,755,000. The mare has a lifetime mark of 1:46. That is the current track record for trotters of all ages and sexes here at Millions Mile and everywhere else on the planet. She is the undisputed world record holder. She set that record in The Millions Finale two years ago. She is trained by Carl Zander, with Zachary "ZZ" Zander driving.

Number five is Fired Up Frat Boy. He's a four-year-old, also owned by Fired Up Farms of NJ. He is undefeated in 41 lifetime starts with earnings of $7,302,000. His lifetime mark is 1:46:3, which ties Abitibi's record. He is trained by Carl Zander with Stephanie Zander in the bike today. She has driven him to victories in his last ten starts, including the race where he took his lifetime mark. This is her second appearance in this race. She won her first appearance with Fired Up Rio.

Number six is Trottin Rocket. He's a five-year-old owned by the Deliver Us From Evil Stable of Boca Raton Florida. He has won 25 of 27 starts with earnings of $2,138,000. His lifetime mark is 1:47:0. He is trained by Cynthia Vimco, with Derrick Stone driving.

Number Seven is Hurricane Force. He's a five-year-old owned by the Hurricane Force Syndicate of Clarksburg,PA. He has won 37 of 55 with earnings of $2,980,00. He has a lifetime mark of 1:46:4. He is trained by Sonny Destefano, with Billie "Cha-ching" Browner driving.

Number eight is Sitdownandshutup. He's a four-year-old owned by A Little Old Lady Stable from Passedena, CA. He has won 18/20 starts with earnings of $1,999,000. His only two losses were to the five horse, Fired Up Frat Boy. He holds a lifetime mark of 1:46:4. He is trained by Andy Thurston with Dominic Giordano in the sulky.

Rounding out the field is number nine Yodel. He's the oldest horse in the race at age eight. He is owned by Millie Christopherson of Xenia Ohio. He has won 54 of 100 lifetime starts with earnings of $10,311,000. Most of that came from Million's Miles competition including last year's win on a very sloppy track. The old guy seems to get up for this race every year. His lifetime mark of 1:47:2 was set here four years ago. He is trained by another hall of fame trainer, Frances "Frannie" Jones with Phil Westwood driving.

There is your field for 27$^{th}$ running of the Millions Mile. Never has such a field been assembled. Make your wagers now to avoid being shut out.

# Chapter 24

## *Miracle Mile Racetrack and Casino*

I had Rio under better control, and she was starting to relax. I saluted The Army as we passed the top of the stretch. The kids went crazy. They had baseball caps on that proclaimed their membership in "The Army." They wore tee shirts with Rio and me on the front and Stephanie and Frat Boy's pictures on the back. What a sight.

Amid the pack, I spied PC talking with Father Jonathan and Bishop Carlucci. Joe was nervous. I saw him inspecting and reinspecting the fencing that protected the kids from the racetrack. I finally caught a glimpse of Azzie. She was brushing the hair of one of the children. She never stopped.

Rio got a little feisty when she saw the kids, but once we got to the back stretch, she settled back down. We passed Stephanie and Frat Boy who turned in front of us. They were cool as cucumbers. Not a word was said. There were none left to say. I turned and followed her to the gate. The starter was dragging his feet a little. A record handle of $150,000,000 had already been bet on this race, and the cash was pouring in. Frat boy was the favorite at 4/5 and Rio was even-money. The closest horse to them was Yodel at 7:1. The rest were greater than 10:1.

We got behind the gate and the starter sped up the car. I looked at Stephanie, but she never glanced at me. Her eyes were on the horses up and down the line. She took a better grip of her reins, dropped her visor into position, and sat back in the sulky.

The starter got up to speed and began to pull the car away. I heard Stephanie yell "duck,duck,duck." That was our signal to pull our horses off the gate. We both grabbed leather and pulled back. It was a great call on her part. That's All Folks had fired out from the two-hole. The old guy, Yodel, sprinted from the nine-hole. Abitibi to my left, rocketed out of the gate. Sammy 'The Hammy' Molinero had the throttle wide open.

Stephanie got away eighth, and I was dead last. But in front of us was one of the most viscous starts of all times to a harness race. I heard Gabe call it in my headset.

"Great balls of fire, we are seeing nothing less than an equine explosion. Sammy 'The Hammy' has Abitibi on the front. He is being severely challenged by Hurricane Force on the outside. Phil Westwood placed Yodel in the three hole. It looks like he's not letting anyone in. He is followed by Trottin Rocket at the pylons. That's All Folks is parked out fifth. Sitdownandshutup is three wide. Dom Giordano is praying for a hole to open. Heaven Eleven is seventh. The favorite, Fired Up Frat Boy, is eighth, Fired Up Rio and ZZ Zander can see them all.

Phil Westwood quickly closes the hole with Yodel and that seals the fate of That's All Folks. He will be going the long mile from here. Hurricane Force finally gets to the front under intense urging by Billie "cha-ching" Browner. Sammy Molinero is having none of it. He brushes Abitibi back to the front. First quarter in a blistering 25:1. No first quarter has ever been faster."

I was still trying to figure out how Stephanie knew to avoid leaving the gate. We were 8th and 9th in the field but we were fresh. The fractions and action on the front were murder. As sometimes happens when there are heavy favorites, a lot of horses left the gate. They were hoping to take the lead and give it up to one of the favorites. They would then suck along in the two-hole and try to get lucky in the stretch.

Fortunately, Stephanie sniffed it out, and we ducked. The first quarter went in 25:1. Rio had enough of eating everyone's dust in last place. She pulled to the outside and put it into overdrive. I wish I could take credit for the move, but I was just a passenger. Rio was on autopilot. Stephanie appeared shocked, but she followed in behind.

"Oh My God," screamed Gabe as he saw us. "Two scud missiles have been launched from the back of the pack. Team Z is rolling."

We cruised three wide down the stretch to avoid some parked out horses. Gabe was going absolutely nuts.

"Team Z firing three wide down the stretch for the first time. These horses are serious and trying to end this race here and now!!"

Before the second turn we had gained the lead and opened three lengths on the field. Gabe really lost control when he screamed.

"Horses don't go…..". He paused. He almost let the f bomb fly. He almost said, "horses don't go this f 'ing fast." Two years ago, he let it slip and it almost cost him his job. He caught himself in time. "Horses don't go this freaking fast!!! Half time in 52 seconds. That's the fastest first half ever trotted."

Satisfied that he might have a job tomorrow, he continued his call.

"Fired Up Rio is rolling on the front end with Fired Up Frat Boy chewing on ZZ's helmet."

I wasn't totally happy with the wicked fast fractions and was thinking about backing down the third quarter. Stephanie had a different idea.

"Let's roll these guys and see who's the best."

I couldn't resist. "See you in the winner's circle," I screamed into the mic and kicked my left leg to pull Rio's earplugs.

The announcer kept up his bumbling, babbling, and shrieking. "Holy crap, team Z have popped their plugs and are rolling down the back side. They have opened five lengths on the field. Rio continues to cut it out, and Frat Boy appears comfortable in the pocket. As the trotters near the ¾ mile pole it certainly appears that a world record is within reach."

Just when you thought he was running out of gas Gabe found another octave. "OH MY GOD!!!! Stephanie Zander just pulled Frat boy. That could be a big mistake. She was getting the perfect trip. I said the same stupid thing the last time she won this race!!"

I knew it was the right move on her part. I had to be patient with Rio in the last turn and that was Stephanie's opportunity to get past me. She cut him loose and quickly was even with me. I gave her a thumbs up. I would have done the same thing if I was driving Frat Boy. I had to hope she didn't clear me before we hit the top of the stretch.

Gabe must have inserted a spare set of vocal cords. His previously hoarse voice was now clear and thunderous. "They pass the ¾ pole in 1:18. No trotter has ever gotten to the ¾'s, that fast. Both Zanders look chilly in their bikes. Stephanie has Frat Boy just about ready to clear Rio and she is working the lines to encourage him to take the lead. ZZ is past chilly. He appears frozen. He looks like an Amish guy on a ride to the feed store. Not a care in the world! They are nearing the top of the stretch and Frat Boy has just about passed Rio. ZZ gives Rio a right wrist flip of the reins and the big mare reengages as they enter the stretch. They are passing The Army who appear to be in a total frenzy."

Somewhere in the middle of the Army, Azzie pulled out her phone and screamed, "Fly the drones, fly the drones!"

Gabe passionately described the stretch drive. "The battle is on. The horses are neck and neck, and the drivers are working feverishly. Neither Zander will carry a whip, so there is no whipping. But there is one whole hell of a lot of driving. Both drivers are asking for everything their horses can give. The horses are head-to-head, toe to toe. They are approaching the finish line and there isn't a clear leader. Both Zanders are lying flat back in their bikes as they continue to work the lines. Here's the wire! Mile in 145:3, a new world's record. But I have no idea who won, none whatsoever. Hold all tickets for the photo."

I screamed into my mic. "Stephanie, you drove a brilliant race. I hope you won."

Stephanie quickly responded. "Of course, I did big brother, but I think I came up short to the master. You're the best. I love you so much."

The outrider signaled for us to return to the stands. They wanted both of us in in front of the stands until the winner was determined. We turned the horses and jogged back to the finish line. As we passed the other horses who competed in the race, we were amazed to see each driver raise their whip in their left hand as a salute. They were led by

Billie. He was standing in his race bike and bowed to us each as we passed. Billy was a great competitor and a showboat!

In the sky behind the tote board some numbers were being painted in the sky. The drones were at work. As we got back to the front of the stands, we got a standing ovation from the crowd and a screaming ovation from The Army. Half of them were shouting ZZ, and the other half Stephanie. Too bad someone was likely to be disappointed.

I looked over at the tote board and was shocked to see a final time of 1:45.3. I knew we were motoring, but I was concentrating more on winning the race as opposed to the time. Neither Rio nor Frat boy were breathing all that hard. I don't think I was breathing at all when I saw flashing lights beside numbers 4 and 5 on the tote board. Could it be?

In my headset I swore I heard Stephanie crying like a baby. It was hard to hear because I heard wailing coming from my bike too. Rio wasn't crying, so it must have been me! It was a dead heat for win! We tied for win in a world record time!

My parents gave each other a hug. They unhooked the overchecks and slowly walked the horses toward the winner's circle. The next thing I knew, I was on the ground. Stephanie had jumped on my back and knocked me down. After we helped each other up she hugged me so hard that I could hardly breathe.

Our parents called for us to return to our bikes. They were ready to take the picture and present the trophy. It was a sight. There was a table with the large Million's trophy in the middle. On the left of the table, my father had Rio's head as I stood behind the sulky. On the right, my mother held Frat Boy's head while Stephanie stood behind her bike. Other than the sizes of the horses, we were mirror images. And in the sky behind them was written 1:45:3!! In bright pink numbering, that was Azzie's trademark color. That Azzie was too much. Always the marketing guru.

Next, a sea of children and their handlers invaded the winner's circle. They were led by Father Jonathan and the bishop. Joe brought up the rear. He quickly reunited with Azzie. Pure unadulterated bedlam was on display for the world to see. It took a while for Gabe to gather everyone's attention.

"Ladies and gentlemen, never have two horses and drivers put on such an exhibition. It's most appropriate that it ended up in a dead heat. It is fitting to honor both horses and drivers in the world's most prestigious winner's circle. It is our pleasure to present them with the largest purse ever won in a harness race. $5,000,000, and of course the second-place purse of $2,500,000. Each horse will receive $3,750,000!!!!

Once the presentation was complete, Gabe continued.

"We are now honored to have Tim Dunstan arrive in the winner's circle. Tim is one of the preeminent blacksmiths in the business. Tonight, his job is a little different. Go ahead Tim, as I explain to the fans."

The race bikes and harnesses had been removed from each horse. Tim put on his chaps and went over to Rio. Gabe explained. "Tim is pulling the racing shoes from Rio as this is her last race. When he is done with her, he will do the same for Frat Boy, who is also retiring."

In a few minutes Tim had the shoes off both horses.

Gabe continued. "Ladies and gentleman, Fired Up Rio is retiring with a perfect record of 35 starts and 35 wins. She took her lifetime mark tonight with a world record performance in 1:45:3 Her lifetime earnings are $11,505,000. She is owned by the Fired Up Farms for the benefit of The Always Hope School. She is trained by Carl Zander and has been driven almost exclusively in her career by Zachary "ZZ" Zander.

Fired Up Frat Boy finishes his career with a perfect record of 42 starts and 42 wins with earnings of $11,052,000. He shares the world record for trotters with Rio. He is owned by the Fired Up Farms and also trained by Carl Zander. Tonight, he was expertly guided to a dead heat win by the spitfire, Stephanie Zander. I promise to never again say that she made a mistake on the track. I'm 0 for 2 in that area, and I quit!

One shoe from each horse will be placed above the entrance to The Always Hope School for good luck. The others will be sold at auction with the proceeds to benefit the Standardbred Retirement Foundation. These horses will be returning to the Fired Up Farm to begin their second careers. That's right, Fired up Rio will be bred to Fired Up Frat Boy this February. Can you imagine the pedigree of that foal?"

Stephanie looked at me and smiled. "Frat Boy better bring a big damn ladder if he thinks he can get in there." She pointed at Rio's tall back side. I could have sworn the bishop even had a smile on his face. Stephanie has special dispensation.

The horses were led away to be properly cooled out and watered. Gabe asked that everyone else remain. "At this time, I want to introduce Johnson Stevens, a longtime employee, and friend of Miracle Mile Racetrack. We affectionally call him PC. PC the mic is yours."

At the finish line stood PC with a chair beside him. He opened the mic and thanked everyone for their attention. He then invited Stephanie to come and sit in the chair. He got on one knee in front of her and pulled a ring from his pocket.

"Stephanie Zander, I love you with my whole heart and soul. Please allow me the honor to remove your racing shoes, at least temporarily. I want to marry you and breed you in the spring, if not before then." Stephanie kicked off her shoes and jumped into his arms. Unfortunately, the mic was still on as she screamed. "Yes, take me home and ride me you fucking cowboy." Special dispensation. Nothing like it.

# Chapter 25

*Route 17*

*Krenshaw, NJ*

It's Monday morning, and I have a hell of a headache. One too many shots of Crown Royal yesterday. It was probably five too many. But it was an amazing day. Not only did we throw a few back while watching reruns of the race, but we also celebrated Stephanie's engagement to PC. Life was good.

I was happy that I had my hands-free phone working on the way to the hospital. As I turned the bend near the school, I saw one of Kresnshaw's finest parked along the berm. She was just waiting for someone to go by yacking on their phone. At the same time, Dan called.

"Hello, Dan. Be gentle. My head is trying to explode."

"I thought you might be slightly incapacitated today. That Crown Royal can sneak up on you. But I have some good news that may help you get through the morning."

"Good news and a couple of Tylenol would be welcome."

Dan continued. "We may have caught a break. Buster's current attorney called me. He convinced Buster to retire and revise his license to retired status. With what we had on him the state was going to rake him over the coals and probably take his license anyway. His attorney is offering to have Buster permanently give up all privileges here. He did request that Buster not be removed from the medical staff. He will request Emeritus status. Without privileges he will not be able to practice at all. Buster will go into retirement without having been thrown off staff. He gets to save face."

I wasn't happy. "As an Emeritus he would be permitted to attend medical staff meetings. I would prefer that he never enter the building again unless he is on a stretcher."

Dan was sympathetic. "I understand your concerns, but this arrangement will save us a lot of litigation. If he becomes a disruptive force at staff meetings, we can always remove him then. His attorney seems to feel that he will fade into the woodwork."

I was satisfied. "Beautiful. Get the package together, and we will present it to the board. Any thoughts as to how his attorney convinced him to give in? That cost him a chunk of fees that he could have bled out of Buster."

"As it turns out I think Desmond Howard is a pretty good egg. He confidentially told me that he met with Buster on three occasions. Desmond was pretty sure he was drunk all three times. The last was a breakfast meeting. The kid wanted the money, but in the end, he did not think Buster should drive let alone take care of patients."

I was happy. "Well, that is good news for us. I hope the shithead gets some help. His liver has to be sucking wind not to mention his pickled brain. Dan, do you know the location of a phone booth?"

"WTF? There aren't many of them around since cell phones started to be widely used. Why?"

"I am looking for one to host Buster's farewell party."

I stopped in the ER on arrival to the hospital and scored some coffee and a couple Tylenol. I spied Angela in the conference room. Her shift ended an hour ago. I knocked on the door and went in to find out why she was still here.

"Good morning, Dr. Zander."

"Angela, why can't you bring yourself to call me ZZ?"

"I just can't. You were one of my most influential instructors. You will always be known as Dr. Zander, or that asshole Dr. Zander."

I just adored Angela from the minute I met her. She was a third-year resident whom I worked with as an attending. She was smart, she was fast, and she was funny. She told some of the dirtiest jokes. She even got me to blush once or twice. I hired her right out of residency, and she is one of my strongest players.

I liked to pull her chain. "Are you here for a reason or are you just padding your overtime?"

That got me a Zander salute.

"Actually, I just finished a chart that I am sure will end up in court."

"Who would sue you?"

She shook her head. "Nah, not a malpractice thing, but a police matter. I am glad you stopped in. You saved me having to call you later. But before I forget, I also have a note for you from Bella. I pulled a shift at Surfside last week, and she asked me to give it to you."

She handed me the note after sniffing it. She teased me. "A perfumed note, someone in Atlantic City is horny. No, I guess a text message would mean horny. A perfumed note means uber-horny."

The note did smell good. I opened it and turned beet red. I did consider that Angela had been known to play pranks, but I recognized Bella's handwriting. "Are you mad at me? Come on down to AC and we'll play Pearl Harbor."

I knew what that meant. It was naughty, even for Bella. Bella is an RN whom I got hooked up with when I was doing some work in Atlantic City. We periodically get together to get together if you know what I mean. I pocketed the incriminating evidence and quickly changed the subject.

"You were going to call me later about something else?"

"Yeah, do you remember a patient named Quincy? Vernon Quincy?"

Oh, did I remember Vernon Quincy, our poster child for wrong site surgery. I could imagine a picture of him holding up his right arm with a caption that read. 'Don't let this happen to you.' "Yeah, why?"

Angela looked serious. "He and his wife were killed in a probable road rage incident last night. I am here late because I was buffing up his chart. I am sure I will have to testify when they find the guy who did it."

I took a sip from my coffee. "I heard about that on the radio this morning. They didn't release the names of the victims, so I didn't know it was the Quincys. They said some whack job ran them off the side of a bridge."

Angela nodded. "You know the bridge over Beaver Creek? That's where it happened. She died at the scene, and he died here. The wreck was so close to the hospital that they just carted him here. I was hoping to stabilize him and send him on to the trauma center, but he cooled." (That was ER slang for the patient expiring and assuming room temperature.) "He was in extremis on arrival, but he said something with one of his last breaths that I didn't understand."

"What did he say?" I was anxious to hear.

Angela continued the story. "I was preparing to intubate him when he grabbed my arm."

She slowly read the words verbatim from her notes. Before she did, she added that Amos also heard it. "Tell Zander wrong side. Paid 25 shut up, wanted more."

She let that sink in, and then she finished her report. "Then he coded. His mediastinum was wider than Route 30. I am sure he tore his aorta. Amos and I were shocked to hear your name, but we didn't understand the message. Does it mean anything to you?"

I kissed her on the cheek. "More than I can tell you, but thanks. I can't discuss it, but I owe you, big time."

"Good, approve that vacation request I turned in last week."

# Chapter 26

## *Krenshaw Medical Center*

I got to my office, and my headache got worse. I was asking my hungover brain to process the information I was given, and my brain was resisting. Vernon Quincy and his wife were dead. They seemed like nice people. But if they were that nice, why did they agree to lie to collect a big paycheck? Regardless, they didn't deserve what they ended up getting.

In addition to regretting the unnecessary loss of life, I had to face the fact that they took with them any chance of proving Master operated on the wrong side. Can you believe it? A doctor who we are in the process of throwing off staff for wrong site surgery is spared by the untimely death of the only witnesses that could prove he did it. What a coincidence. I hate coincidences.

I had to nail that bastard. With Buster down the drain and out the door I could totally focus on Master. I called Dan to see if Master was still incarcerated. I hoped that he was and that he had been raped repeatedly.

"Dan, is Master still residing at the jail?"

"No ZZ. He made bail. He was out early Saturday morning. The DA just called me. He reviewed our tape from the meeting. He felt that Master's gun waving episode was simple assault and a violation of hospital policy. It wasn't clear from the tape that he pointed the gun at you."

I protested. "I know when a gun was pointed in my direction. Loaded or unloaded that prick was aiming at me, and at a very delicate part of me."

"He'd have to be a pretty good shot to hit that small of a target." Dan laughed.

"Ha Ha." I wasn't amused.

Dan got down to business. "He has no previous record, and the gun wasn't loaded." I could tell that Dan was trying to get me to agree to back things down.

I had to know. "I guess, based upon our conversation, that he isn't looking at any jail time."

"Probably just a fine ZZ, maybe some community service too, but I wouldn't hold my breath."

I sipped my coffee after I hung up. That wasn't what I wanted to hear. I tried to focus on what I could control and what I might be able to prove. I was frustrated for a while then the light went on, that little one in your brain that suddenly lights up when enough neurons sing the same song, the ones that escaped the Crown Royal drowning.

I knew that when Master, or any surgeon, scheduled a case involving laterality, (a side, right or left), that information was included on the scheduling request. I contacted our head of computing and asked him to create a special search. I asked him to go back five years and compare the scheduling diagnosis with the final operative report for Master's cases. I wondered if there were any instances where those did not agree as to which side was operated upon. Just to be fair I asked him to do the same search on I Need's cases for the same period.

Low and behold there were four cases in the last five years. The Quincy case was the most recent, but there were three others. All four belonged to Master. I Need had zero. I spent the rest of the afternoon reading those charts. The noose was tightening.

# Chapter 27

## *Administrative Conference Room*
## *Krenshaw Medical Center*

The Tylenol kicked in, and I was looking forward to a great lunch. Our chef was amazing. Tina had other ideas. Tina was Dan's kick-ass COO. She ran the day-to-day while Dan tended to the legal stuff and provided overall direction. They made a good team. Tina recently came up with a new policy that the administrative staff ate what was being served to the patients. She further brought her point home by ordering for us. Dan got the low-fat cardiac diet. Tina sat down to the no added salt tray, and I licked my chops as I stared at the clear liquid diet lunch. Today's fare for me included beef broth, green Jello, and ginger ale. I attempted to look pleased.

Tina crunched on some unsalted celery and asked, "Where do we stand with Dr Bator?"

"He's an asshole," I added as I wiggled my Jello. It was more fun than eating it.

"I agree," Dan echoed.

Tina nodded. "He may be an asshole, but that asshole makes us a lot of money."

I took a spoonful of broth. It was awful. I didn't like what I swallowed and what I just heard. "We can do without him."

Tina answered. "I spent the past few days analyzing our financial health. We are on life support as it is. The neurosurgery program generates about $4mil a year in revenue. If we lose that, we will be in financial hospice. We got a $50,000 fine from the Licensing Board for Buster's sponge. Dan feels we need to self-report Master's wrong site surgery. That will bring a fine of $100,000. The next incident would cost

$200,000. We are barely keeping up with our accounts payable now. We can't afford fines and loss of services."

I took the lead. I might as well. My lunch wasn't cutting it. Remind me to try not to meet with Tina over any mealtime in the future.

"What do you have up your sleeve?" I inquired.

She shocked us. "I propose that we give Dr. Bator a break."

I reacted. "Break his freaking neck? Both legs? Gladly!"

Tina persisted with her case. "No, reinstate him."

My jaw dropped, and my underwear prepared for an assault as she continued.

"I know he is a loose cannon. But I know that I can work with him. With our help he will be able get ARD for the gun and assault charges. I know I can convince him to play ball, do time outs, and generally be a good doobie."

Dan started sputtering legalese objections. I cut him off.

"Tina. You are an amazing person, and you certainly know more about running a hospital than I would ever care to know."

She took a bite of her bland mashed potatoes before she responded. "I sense there is a but coming."

I unloaded. "You bet. But I know doctors. I know good doctors from evil doctors. Master is an evil doctor. He says the right things to the right people, but his only mission is to serve himself. His colleagues and patients are fodder. I hate to get down to the lowest common denominator, but he is a piece of shit."

Tina persisted. "I am not naïve enough to think he is a saint. But he is a neurosurgeon, they are different."

I wasn't giving in. "Why should they be allowed to be different? Because they pull in four mil?"

She pleaded. "Can't we work this out. The neurosurgery program is the linchpin to my recovery efforts. Dr. Bator really changed after his wife committed suicide. I think the man needs help and with our encouragement, he just might get it as a condition of reinstatement."

I pounded the table. "Tina, please take this as a promise and not a threat, but I will resign as the Chief Medical Officer before I would ever let Master on staff again."

She laughed. That pissed me off until she explained herself. "Ok, screw him. I just wanted to see how firm you were in your convictions. Sorry to challenge you. Where do we go from here?"

I wiped my brow. "You had me scared."

Dan just laughed and continued the briefing. "We will oppose any efforts on Dr. Bator's part to regain his staff privileges."

Tina wanted to meet again in a few days. She had some ideas about how to make up for some of the revenue we were going to lose when neurosurgery folded. She needed a little more time to refine them. She proposed a breakfast meeting. I was quick to recommend something around 10 AM. My schedule was open, but I wasn't chancing another liquid meal.

Tina agreed. She added that appointment to the calendar in her phone, stood, and excused herself. As soon as she exited, I headed for the door, but Dan stopped me.

"Where are you going? I thought we were going to finalize Dr Bator's hearing agenda."

"McDonald's! Can I bring you anything?"

# Chapter 28

## *Executive Boardroom*
## *Krenshaw Medical Center*

It took a full three days for Dan and me to prepare for Master's hearing with the executive committee. We were ready. As we waited for the meeting to start, Dan filled me in on the status of Master's assault charges. The judge had called Dan. He asked that we not further pursue the gun-waving episode in hospital proceedings. With Master's lack of any past criminal history, he felt that it would be double jeopardy if we pursued the incident in a hospital punishment. He felt that Master's agreement to the ARD arrangement was sufficient to end the matter.

"You didn't agree to that, did you?"

Dan had his head down. "I finally gave in. I am confident that we can keep him off the staff with what we have clinically. Now in the court's eye we have given him a second chance. It smells, but I had to agree."

Dan was ready for an argument that did not come. "OK, you da man. I trust you."

At the appointed time the Executive Committee arrived and took their seats. Many of them would learn about the charges for the first time. They all had heard scuttlebutt in the hospital, but Dan and I had done our best not to discuss anything with the staff, especially the committee who would be judging. When possible, we provided documentation to Master's attorneys. That proved difficult as he fired two more of them the week before the hearing. We weren't sure who would be representing him tonight. The attorneys at the assault hearing were strictly criminal defense, so they would not be here.

After Master cleared the metal detector, (we weren't taking any more chances of his being armed), security escorted him to the conference room. I was shocked when he showed up alone. He wasn't in his tennis outfit, but this was even worse. He had a bright blue suit with a yellow shirt and a matching blue bowtie. He might have looked OK as a cheerleader for the LA Rams, but for a doctor defending his reputation, he looked like a jerk.

I always distrusted people who wore bowties. My old nemesis, Deuce Hofecker, was famous for his. I wondered if he wore a bowtie with his prison uniform. That made me smile. I think Master thought I was smiling at him. Dan asked when his attorney was coming. Dan didn't want any delays.

Master bellowed, "I am appearing pro se."

I had no idea what that meant. "Oh say can you see," I sung.

Juicy Lucy giggled. Dan gave me the evil eye and then informed the group that pro se meant that Master was representing himself. He was appearing without counsel. That was his right.

At exactly 7 PM Dan rapped a gavel. Dan sat to my left and JL to my right. The executive committee sat across the table from us. Master took his assigned seat at the end of the table.

Dan looked at Master. "Can you please tell us what you have in your right hand?"

"Just a tennis ball. I use it to keep calm. I squeeze it, and that helps me deal with stress." He opened his hand exposing a yellow tennis ball.

Dan just nodded. My guess was that it was a tennis ball full of C-4 explosive that he would use to kill us all. That dude worried me. The ridiculously smart ones were always a problem.

Dan read the rules for the hearing, including the right to appeal the decision to the board. There were no questions, so he proceeded to the charges. "1. Failure to follow hospital policies, and surgery rules and regulations, requiring site marking of appropriate surgical sites while the patient is in surgical holding. Since this case involved laterality a site mark was required. 2. Failure to follow the universal protocol as it pertains to a time-out to be conducted prior to any invasive surgical procedure. 3. Falsification of records. Operative notes are meant to be a detailed description of procedures performed. Dictating operative notes before cases have been completed violates the integrity of the record. 4. Failure to cooperate with duly licensed and authorized surveyors from The Joint Commission in the completion of their survey."

Dan paused. Master was squeezing the tennis ball harder and more rapidly, but he stayed seated and made no attempt to speak. Dan let the bombshell go. "5. Commission of wrong side surgery on a patient, Mr. Vernon Quincy. 6. Giving false information to the patient after the procedure indicating that he had reexamined the patient prior to the surgery. Staff have testified that no such reexamination occurred. 7. Paying the patient the sum of $25,000 to keep the patient from cooperating with any investigation."

Dan took a drink of water before he continued. "Your information packet includes documentation of two previous reprimands given to Dr. Bator by then chief of surgery, Dr. Morehead. The reprimands were due to falsification issues involving medical records. Based upon the seriousness of today's charges and the obvious fact that Dr. Bator has continued to falsify records despite previous agreements not to do so, Dr. Zander and I recommend that Dr. Bator's privileges to practice at Krenshaw be terminated permanently, without recourse for him to reapply."

There were questions from members of the Executive Committee about the survey, the dictations, and his interaction with the surveyors. Dan answered them.

A full hour was devoted to a review of the facts that we had concerning the Quincy case. Dan laid out everything. Witness statements, copies of operative dictations, and the Dying Declaration as documented by Angela. Master just stared at me and squeezed his ball. When the committee had asked their final questions of Dan and me,

Master requested to speak. Dan agreed. Master stood, but he still was working over that tennis ball. That relieved me. If it was any type of explosive, it would have gone off by now.

"Throughout the course of history many a genius in their field have been ostracized."

*Shit, I thought. This is going to be a long stemwinder.* Both of my middle fingers were extended, but they were under the table. JL looked down and grinned. Master droned on.

"Such is the case here. Many in this room are jealous of me. My accomplishments significantly out shadow their meager contribution to medical care in this community. These charges are ridiculous, and I vehemently deny most of them.

I am guilty of not following the universal protocol. I refuse to follow something that is not effective. I have provided for you a list of wrong site surgeries that occurred throughout the world despite site marking and time outs.

I deny falsifying records. Yes, I did my dictations prior to the surgeries. But in every case when I identified significant deviation from what I knew I dictated, I redid the dictation after the case.

I am sorry for the interaction that occurred with the Joint Commission surveyor."

Finally, the prick was admitting to something. Oh, was I wrong.

"The way that Dr. Zander permitted them to run amuck in a highly functioning operating theater was abominable. Their presence was not necessary and was extremely disruptive to OR operations. My negative interaction with them was only me trying to protect my patients from infection and harm."

He pounded the table.

"Distraction in an OR is unacceptable." He let that sink in for a few seconds before he continued his verbal assault. His face was beyond red. It clashed with his yellow and blue ensemble.

"There is no question that this a witch hunt and a vendetta promulgated by Zander and Santucci. Even a brilliant and talented physician such as I, should be open to review. Hell, if you people spent more time reviewing my work, you might learn something about how to provide effective and efficient medical care. But, but, but."

He slammed the table three times, once for each but.

"The baseless claim that I would perform wrong site surgery and then lie about it to the patient is too much to bear. Accusing me of bribing the patient to cover up the incident is ludicrous and quite damaging to my reputation."

He shoved an envelope down the beautifully polished table in my direction.

"This is a notice of intent to sue. I am bringing action against Krenshaw Medical Center and individually against Drs. Zander, Morehead, and attorney Dan Santucci. You will see numerous charges elicited, but the most damning, and the one that will ultimately be the most expensive, is the defamation. My reputation should be praised and not pissed upon. I reserve the right to add any members of the Executive Committee who support this witch hunt to the suit."

I attempted to speak, but he interrupted me. He was on a roll.

"Zander, you are a dim bulb and a liar. And Santucci, you should know better. Really? A dying declaration from my patient that he had wrong site surgery and was paid off? That's beyond low."

I rose. "Two witnesses heard it."

Dr. Pro Se disagreed. "But they are not admissible in a civil hearing you asshole. Only in very selective criminal cases, and even those are often thrown out on appeal."

Dan had told me that we should leave off the wrong site surgery, but I just couldn't let Quincy's declaration go unheard. I decided to pour some gas on the fire.

"The police did find $22,700 in cash in the Quincy home."

Master was unfazed. "So, they didn't trust banks. The police also investigated their unfortunate deaths and have definitively concluded that it was road rage. Were they involved in a drug deal? Who knows? But that money did not come from me."

He then slid another envelope down the table in our direction. I opened this one. It was a nerve conduction study on Mr. Quincy's right arm showing severe carpal tunnel syndrome, including severe sensory and motor involvement.

I wasn't buying it. "Why did we not receive this earlier, and more importantly, why was it not in his chart? What was in the chart was a study of the left arm that was mild compared to this one."

Master was firing on all cylinders. "I sent both. I planned all along to reexamine him prior to the surgery and fix the most appropriate extremity. Your dumb ass outpatient OR staff must have tossed the right arm study out when they saw the notes indicating we were operating on the left. My office notes are very clear."

I didn't recall anyone from the OR staff telling us that they received two nerve conduction studies. I made that clear to the Executive Committee and the defiant Master.

We bantered back and forth over that and other facts when Dan called for order. We had decided to have a written ballot. The bylaws didn't specify that, but Dan thought it might be better if Master did not know who voted with or against him. In the end it didn't matter.

I tabulated the votes and stood. "Dr. Bator, it is the unanimous judgement of the committee that you should be required to relinquish your privileges permanently. A final written decision will be sent to you via certified mail within 48 hrs. Please be notified that according to NJ SB 12.74 at 9 AM tomorrow, this action will be reported to the state. They will inform you of the status of your medical license and other NJ state licenses and detail the steps you will take with them. You have the right to an appeal with the board of directors. The specifics of the timing and rules governing the appeal are in the rules and regulations. Would you like a copy?"

Master screamed. "What I would like is your fucking head on a plate."

He stood and threw his ball at my head. Dan is so short that it sailed over his head. I ducked, but it hit JL in the eye. I Need jumped over the table and tackled Master. I think he really enjoyed doing that. He was good at it, too.

# Chapter 29

### *Emergency Department*
### *Krenshaw Medical Center*

It was red around JL's eye, and she said her vision was very blurry. I took her to the ER and checked her visual acuity. Her sight was 20/200 in the left eye and 20/30 in her right. I then examined her eye using the slit lamp. That's the device that sits on a table or cart in between the doctor and the patient. The patient looks in one side and the doctor in the other. It allows the doctor to see much of the exterior and interior of the eye. During the exam the doctor's and the patient's knees are almost touching. As I focused the lamp, I could have sworn someone was pawing at my crotch.

"Juicy Lucy, what are you doing?"

JL giggled. "Oh, sorry. As a newly blinded person I was just exploring the surroundings using my other senses."

That prompted me to think that I should not be treating her, not because of her wandering hands but because she may have a cause of action against Master. I decided to have her registered as a patient and have Ron Streton see her. Ron was a relatively new hire who very quickly established himself as a powerhouse in the department. He had been nicknamed Streeter.

That was a takeoff from an old ER saying, "Treat em' and street em'." Not too long after his patients came in, they were returned to the street. A lot of ER docs had that talent, but the difference was that Ron's patients were appropriately diagnosed and treated before being streeted!

If I were the treating physician, there is little doubt that Master would allege bias on my part and impugn my exam. Streeter did a CT of her orbit to be sure she did not have a blowout fracture. Fortunately, the CT was normal. He then spoke with Dr. Anita Pepper, our ophthalmologist, and I joined them on the call. Based on his report Anita felt that JL had a grade two hyphema. That was blood in the front chamber of the eye. It was a serious injury, but JL probably would not need a seeing eye dog. Not even half of one. Anita recommended Ron dilate her eye and put her on some steroid drops and some drops to lower her pressure in the eye. He then applied a protective patch.

Streeter explained the discharge instructions. "Lucy, there is no great consensus as to what you can or can't do. Some doctors recommend strict bed rest with the head of the bed elevated. Dr. Pepper thinks it's acceptable for you to be ambulatory, but she doesn't want you performing any strenuous activity."

JL laughed. "No strenuous activity! Good, sex with my husband is ok. Nothing strenuous about that."

I dropped JL off at home. I went in and explained the injury to her husband and the discharge instructions. I left out what JL said about sex. Maybe I am just being paranoid. He looked at me, kind of funny. Do you think he knows about JL's prewedding physical?

I was pondering that dilemma on the way to my truck when Dan called. He filled me in on Master's arrest. I filled him in on JL's eye injury.

"Do you think she should sue him?" I asked.

Dan was quick to respond. "Probably. Let's see if there is any permanent damage and how much her recovery affects her income."

"I can let her stay off a few weeks if it screws that peckerhead."

"ZZ, just do what you normally would do. Don't play this up unnecessarily."

"Yeah, you're right. Will you be able to represent her?"

Dan demurred. "No, obvious conflict of interest, especially now that he is suing us. But this is an open and shut case, and the attorney representing her should get a nice payday for minimal work."

"Who do you recommend?"

"Unless she has someone else in mind, tell her to call Desmond Howard. We kind of owe the kid one."

"We sure do see you tomorrow, Dan."

# Chapter 30

## *Administrative Offices*
## *Krenshaw Medical Center*

Tina moved our meeting from 10 AM to 7 AM I arrived early to brief her on last night's events. She had a meeting in Trenton that she hoped would get us a cash infusion, so she missed the fireworks. I brought a dozen donuts. I didn't trust her to provide brain food so early in the morning.

"Good morning, ZZ. I am so sorry that I didn't get to see the action live last night. How is Lucy's eye?"

I quickly replied. "She should make a full recovery, but any eye injury can be serious. Time will tell."

Dan was silent. He was reading something on his phone. When he finished, he broke his silence. "That bastard Master got out on bail last night. I was hoping they would throw the book at him."

I laughed. "He knows the system now. He probably has a family bail bondsman. He's racking up significant frequent flier points with him. You have to take care of your good customers."

Tina wanted more information. "So, where do we stand with the jerk?"

"He is off staff now and we will report that to the state today. The medical board will probably suspend his license, but he can ask for a stay until his appeal to the board of directors is heard."

"Do you think he will appeal?"

"Very likely. I don't think he is giving up."

Tina nodded in agreement. "What do you think about his lawsuits?"

Dan was quick to answer. "Full of crap and hot air, just like him. But we still must defend them. The suits are probably just bargaining chips that he will drop for the right outcome."

Tina had another question. "What about his assault on Lucy?"

"I am sure he will claim he just lost it. There was no intent on his part to hit Lucy. He just missed ZZ. My guess is that the DA might consider assault and battery charges, but who knows if he will file them. We should be able to get a reasonable settlement for JL once we know the prognosis of her injury."

Tina had laid copies of her plan on the table in front of Dan and me. Luckily, she had extras. I bit into my donut and the cream filling squirted onto her report. In my haste to wipe it off I spilled my coffee. My copy of her masterpiece drowned a horrible death. Six paper towels and ten apologies later we got down to business. Tina stared at me until I put down the replacement donut.

"ZZ, I need more time from you in the Chief Medical Officer role. The hospitalist contract is coming up, and we have a major opportunity to turn some things around."

I responded. "I already know they want more money."

Tina smiled. "What else is new? We may give them some."

Dan interrupted. "I thought we were cutting expenses?"

Tina had our full attention. "They may get more money, but they will earn it. You know our length of stay for inpatients is way out of whack. They are part of the reason for that. When they don't get people discharged soon enough, we run out of beds. That backs admitted patients up in the ER and takes your staff and beds. Then your arriving ER people must wait. They rightfully get angry, and many go elsewhere. We have had to cancel some elective surgeries. Financially that is disastrous. Our patient flow needs an enema."

I was happy to hear an administrator sing my song. "I totally agree with that, but how can I help."

"I need a physician with big balls to take this on. Take over case management. Someone needs to bird dog every admission. When a patient is admitted who only needs a cardiac stress test see if you can convince someone to do it that day or the first thing the next day. You have clout with the medical staff. They will listen to you more than a nurse in utilization review.

A simple change in the hospitalist's workflow could open 10-15 beds by 10 AM daily. You admitted my aunt last week with congestive heart failure. She just adored you! So much for her mental status. Anyway, she was discharged last Thursday at 1:30 PM. But she had no tests or new meds given that day. She sat there all morning waiting to be discharged and tied up a bed. You were holding admitted patients in the ER that could have used her bed. Those patients tied up ER beds that could be used to treat more ER patients. During those five hours eight patients left the ER because they were waiting to be treated. You lost revenue for no good reason."

I couldn't argue with her logic. "You are right of course, but how do we motivate them."

Tina quickly responded. "Metrics and money. Give them the metrics you expect them to meet. For example, 95% of discharges before 11 AM and give them money when they do. Say 2% bonus for each metric met. And don't forget to include patient satisfaction. We want more efficient care, not inferior care. If they meet most of our goals, it will cost us about $200,000. But we will save about $500,000 in expenses and everyone will be happier."

Dan agreed. "ZZ, she is right. I need you more in the Chief Medical Officer roll and Tina laid out why she needs you. Can you turn the ER over to someone else? You will still have input there as the hospital CMO."

I had to think about it. It was like putting my baby up for adoption.

"OK, let me digest this."

Tina was pleased. "Fair enough but now we need to digest this." She held up a copy of her reorganization plan. "Maybe we should coat it in donuts and coffee to make it more palatable. ZZ, you are a genius."

I flipped her a Zander salute. What a great job I have. I can flip my boss off right to her face. Most employees want to do it but can't. Tina expects it.

# Chapter 31

## *Office of the Chief Medical Officer*
## *Krenshaw Medical Center*

I called Angela and asked her to come to my office. Her shift was over at 3 PM  She agreed to stop in afterward. I needed the time to sort out the mess in my office. With JL on injured reserve for a few weeks, I neglected to ask for a replacement. I had twenty phone messages and sixty emails to go through. Believe it or not, none of them were good news to me. Patient complaints, doctors bitching about this or that, and various people biting my ass summed it up well. Fortunately, I was interrupted.

"Anyone home?"

"Come in, Angela. How was it in the pit (slang for ER) today?"

"Pretty good. I don't know where you got those nurses, but they are incredible. Smart, hardworking, wise asses. Perfect ER nurses. How many of them are you diddling?"

I didn't flinch. "Male or female, or do you just want a total?"

She didn't know what to say.

I pounced. "Ha got you. Don't you start too. But smarty pants the answer is zero. I am looking for a committed long-term relationship. Most of those women want a night of ecstasy and nothing more. I am tired of being used like a dildo. I don't know about the men."

Angela stuck her finger down her throat to vomit.

I was forced to explain further. "OK, not buying it huh? I won't date anyone in this facility. Too risky and too much trouble."

She laughed. "More time for Bella. She will like that. What do you need? I have a doctor's appointment at 5 PM ."

"OK, nothing serious, I hope. Just a small favor. I want you to take over the directorship of the emergency department."

She gasped. "Small favor? Are you retiring? Going back to racing full time?"

"I hadn't thought about that. That's actually a good idea but that's not going to happen, yet. I need to free up time. I have so much CMO crap to do."

She thought for a minute. "What about Eric Remmington. He has been itching to move up."

"Well, he's an ok ER doc, but nothing special. I don't think he has what it takes. You do."

She blurted it out. "I also have one in the oven?"

"What are you talking about?"

"Well ZZ, you beat it out of me. Please don't share this with anyone but I am pregnant. I did a home pregnancy test and today I did my own ultrasound. My husband and I agreed that when we started to have children that I would go part time. I intend to honor that agreement."

"But you won't deliver for eight months or so?" I was begging.

"Why don't you think about Streeter? He's an amazing player and both the physician and nursing staffs respect him. You may or may not know this, but in six months or so he will have his MBA."

Wow, that struck me like a lightning bolt. "Can you assume the role on an interim basis until you take your maternity leave? That would give you time to groom Ron and have him ready to go. With the two of you in charge, I can concentrate on the hospital."

Angela was pleased. "Good. You saw the brilliance of my plan. Talk to Streeter. He's on duty now. If he agrees I will assume the director position and he will be my assistant. After my delivery I will happily be his assistant."

**Emergency Department**

I wandered down and grabbed a cup of coffee. The ER had the best coffee in the hospital. I should know; I paid for it. They needed it. I looked at the patient tracking board, and to my delight there were only eight people in the department. There was only one that hadn't been seen. The waiting room was empty for now. I found Ron busy at his desk.

"Streeter, Can I see you for a second?"

"Sure ZZ, who's suing me now?"

"Your girlfriend. She says you're a premature ejaculator, and she's had enough. She's suing you for nonperformance. She said she wanted more from a real man like that ZZ guy."

He laughed. "Take cover, my B.S. meter is reading explode! What do you need ZZ?"

"I hear you are getting an MBA."

Ron nodded. "Yeah. I thought it would open doors for me as I went on. Don't get me wrong, I love the ER, but it's a young doctor's sport. Like being a running back in the NFL."

I agreed. "I hear ya. The older I get, the less I need the constant adrenaline rush. When I was younger, I looked forward to crazy shifts in the ER and wild cases. Now I enjoy a moderate paced day with a little less excitement."

Ron continued. "I plan to work ER until I am 50 or 55, but this won't be my last career."

I sensed my opening and made my pitch. "I'd like to pay for your MBA."

Streeter shook his head no. "I don't have sex with men. Even for that kind of money."

I think he thought I was joking. "You bone head, I'm serious."

I laid out my plans for he and Angela to take over the department. "I will pay for your MBA. When Angela goes to squirt out her kid, you can take over."

"Deal." We shook hands, and it was done.

# Chapter 32

## *Krenshaw Medical Center*

The fall just zoomed on by. The Licensure Board survey was brutal. They had ten people here for a week. Thank God for Joe Crinelli. Two weeks before the survey, he brought a crew in to correct our building deficiencies. They busted their asses. Joe refused to take a dime. I gave each worker a $500 bonus out of my pocket. It was amazing to me how many things they had to correct. Joe was right. We were lucky we never had a fire. The building was a firetrap.

The Licensure Board building inspector was impressed. He still nailed us on a few minor issues, but all in all, he felt our building was safe. The other parts of the survey were another matter. We had tons of minor things. They will be easy to correct, but it will take time.

Our biggest problems were with our Never Episode(s). Officially we had one. That was Buster's retained sponge. Unofficially we had two. We decided to roll the dice and report Master's wrong site surgery.

Things went even better with the Joint Commission crew. It was nice to be able to cancel my colonoscopy next month. Between both of those surveys, I was sure that someone crawled up my ass. Everything had to be ok up there.

We got past them. We were accredited and back in good graces with the Licensure Board. The checks were flowing again.

Master ended up settling with JL for $75,000. Desmond took $15K, but that still left her with a decent payout. Her vision returned to normal, and she should not have any sequelae. That's snotty doctor talk for she shouldn't have any further problems with that eye, provided Master doesn't bean her again.

Speaking of Master, he got community service for the tennis ball incident. You had to like the judge who sentenced him. He got community service all right, but he had to serve it while picking up old eyeglasses for the Knights of Columbus. It was an eye injury, ok. Am I the only one who sees the irony here?

He did not fare any better at the board of directors' final appeal. He delayed that proceeding as long as he could and brought in the highest priced legal talent he could find. Despite that, the outcome was not in his favor. Thaddeus Prinzmetal did his best to impugn mine and Dan's testimony, but the decision was unanimous. Prinzmetal must have sedated Master before the appeal. He did not react in any way when the decision was rendered. He and his attorney stood and walked out to the parking lot. Nothing was said until they were assured of privacy.

"Where do we go from here?" Master asked.

"That's your decision, Roy. I still think it might be better in the long run for you to relocate your practice. I get the feeling that the hospital will not oppose your appeal of this suspension if you agree to leave town."

That brought a quick and very negative reaction from Master. "Why should I leave?"

"Well, sometimes the best resolution requires a different approach."

Master was pissed. He barked at Prinzmetal. "I thought you said we could win."

Prinzmetal was used to physicians' rude behaviors. It came with the territory and his very fat paycheck. "Absolutely we can. We will need to prove that the hospital is a bad hospital. My firm has been successful with several malpractice suits. We will highlight those and the hospital's recent problems with accrediting agencies. That should help to support your contention that you did not follow hospital policies because you thought they endangered your patients."

"Of course, that's why I did it. So, what's this talk of me going elsewhere?"

"I was just pointing out the consequences if you did not win. You could cut your losses and move on with your life."

Master was defiant. "I want to move on with total annihilation of the hospital with emphasis on Zander and Santucci."

"OK, you keep paying our bills, and I'll keep digging."

# Chapter 33

*Master's House*

*Blueberry Fields Estates*

*Krenshaw, NJ*

It can be a good time when old friends get together near Christmas. Master had no illusion that this was going to be a good time, but the economics of the situation dictated that he played the game.

Penelope Bradshaw was the first to arrive. A member of the board of directors of Supreme Medical Center for many years, she had been retained on the Krenshaw board. During my persecution, she did Deuce's bidding, much to my dismay. Attempts by me and I Need to keep her off Krenshaw's board were defeated by other board members who wanted to show transparency. Screw them.

Her chauffer piloted the Rolls into the governor's circle of Master's house and assisted the elderly socialite from the car. She was impeccably dressed as always. She and her older sister were spinsters. But they were filthy rich spinsters. Old money and tons of it. She checked her Rolex for the time as she rang the bell.

Master decided to play the part. He was dressed in a smoking jacket and semi formal attire. He himself answered the door even though he had a butler.

"Penelope, how nice to see you." He proclaimed as he kissed her outstretched hand.

"It's nice to see you, Dr. Bator. Will Dr. Hyman be joining us?"

"He said he would, But he's not so reliable lately. What he says and what he does don't always turn out the same."

Bradshaw let out an eerie laugh. "Tell me about it. He totally blew our bridge game last week. He just wasn't focused."

They were interrupted by Dr. Hyman, who had silently entered the room dressed in a Santa Claus outfit. He staggered slightly. Master figured he had downed a few in route.

Buster joined the conversation. "Who wasn't focused? Who could focus with such a beautiful partner. I was simply distracted." He started to hum Jingle Bells. Penelope gave Master a look that said it all.

"Oh Sam, save it for someone else. You were three sheets to the wind, and you know it. What's up with the Santa Claus routine?"

"Oh, Penelope you might be right about the bridge game, but I am here, and today my mind is clear. I just wanted to show you my Christmas spirit!" No one believed him.

Master led them to the den and closed the door. He fixed them drinks although he thought twice about handing one to Buster. He began his memorized spiel.

"I invited you two here to see if you are interested in extracting a little revenge?"

Bradshaw jumped at the invitation. "Against whom?" Apparently, she was pissed at a lot of folks to want revenge.

Master looked over his glasses at them both. "That prick Zander and Krenshaw Medical Center."

Buster and Old Lady Bradshaw were all ears. Penelope was quick to explain her rationale for joining the group.

"That bastard Zander and his friends exposed my dealings with Thomas Hofecker II. Thomas helped me get out from under a DUI. Since that became public, I have been ostracized from the most prominent social circles. I, Penelope Bradshaw, must work to get invited to cocktail parties. When I do get an invitation, I am not in the top tier anymore. It's disgusting. Can you believe that in the lower tiers they serve inferior liquor? In addition to that, the hoi palloi are all over the place. My social calendar is in the toilet, and someone needs to pay."

Master smiled. "I vow that I will ruin Zander. My goal is to make his life and the life of all around him hell. Regardless of how I make out in the courts, he deserves a royal ass fucking."

"Must you use those terms around me, a lady," protested Bradshaw.

Master made a calculated move. "A lady my ass. You are as vindictive and criminal as I am. Spare me the lady bullshit."

Bradshaw slowly removed her gloves and put them on the table. "Ok Master. Isn't that what Zander named you, Master Bator?"

Master's ears were burning red.

She continued, "I will cut the crap if you two also will."

No one said a word.

Penelope was pleased to have taken control. "Since we have established the ground rules, let's get down to business."

Buster nodded in agreement.

Master went on. "Fair enough. I have a contact that may be able to assist us. This guy or gal, I have no idea, is far from cheap. But he/she is, let's say, very effective. I am positive that for the right economic incentive, they can bury Zander, the hospital, and his friends."

Buster chimed in. "I don't give a damn about his friends. I want to bury Zander and the hospital. If we can stick it to that attorney Santucci, so much the better."

Master waved a document in the air. "We need to also take out the friends. I had a top-notch private eye scope out the Zander kid. Cost me $50,000. He has three friends that call themselves the Dying Was Easy gang. They almost died from heroin addiction in college, and after that incident they all went straight. They have pledged to help each other forever. When Thomas Hofecker II took on Zander, he lost. Not because Zander was so great, but Zander's team was awesome.

We also need to neutralize his family. They are all tight. They work together to support the stable, but they are most involved in The Always Hope School. Any attempt to take out Zander and ruin the hospital must take out his family and other players."

Buster whistled. "That's a whole lot of people to kill."

Master almost lost it for a second, but he remembered his purpose today and controlled himself. "Who says we need to kill anyone?"

Buster wanted another drink, of course. Penelope took the opportunity to adjourn to the living room to make a call in private. Master indulged Buster's addiction for vodka and refreshed his own scotch. He had a question for Penelope when she returned.

"You are still on the board. How is the hospital doing?"

Penelope picked some lint from her blouse. "Unfortunately, much better."

Master was incredulous. "But I thought they were nearly bankrupt. Weren't their bonds downgraded to junk? Aren't they in deep shit with the Licensure Board because 'Putz' here left a sponge in a patient?"

Buster took a few seconds before he realized that he was "Putz."

"Fuck you, Dr. Wrong Site," Buster screamed.

Penelope focused the group. "If you two will shut up, I will fill you in on the hospital. Roy, you obviously called us here for a reason and I suspect you have a plan. I want to hear it when I'm through."

Buster's anger quickly faded as Master filled his drink again. This time it almost overflowed the glass, much to Buster's delight. Master refreshed Penelope's, but more of it had evaporated than she drank. He smiled. The old socialite knew how to do it.

She pulled out a cigarette and held it out. Master obliged her with a light. She took a long puff, exhaled, and she began her report.

"The hospital was on the ropes. It was just as you said Roy. The bond rating agencies threw in the towel. Your fiasco with the Joint

Commission surveyor put them in trouble with the Licensure Board who did an all-out survey. They fined the hospital $50,000 for Sam's sponge left behind. They would have had to spend $250,000 to fix tons of building deficiencies."

Master knew all of this, but he had to feign ignorance.

"Sounds like they were down for the count. How did they get out from under all of that?"

Penelope took a small sip of her drink, just to look the part. She carefully set it down on the cocktail napkin. Her cigarette burned aimlessly in the ashtray. She continued.

"You are so right about Zander's friends and family. Every time that kid falls in shit, they're there to pull him out and clean him up. First on the scene this time was Joe Crinelli. He runs a construction company. He sent a crew in to bring the building back into compliance, at no charge of course. They worked for weeks. Then the COO showed that she is a dog gone good manager. I hadn't been too impressed by her, but I am changing my mind.

She guided the hospital through a brutal Licensure Board survey and a follow-up survey by Joint Commission. There were findings on both, but they were minimal and easily corrected. Her turnaround plan for the hospital is brilliant. She is closing some services that are not profitable or were going to require significant cash infusions. But she is laying off very few staff. She wants to reassign them to other departments to strengthen those service lines."

Buster appeared to have dozed off, but he suddenly spoke up. "They can't keep that up for too long. Penelope how is your big…."His words were too slurred to hear the last word.

Penelope freaked. "My big WHAT Sam????"

Buster realized his unintentional question and worked to appease her. "Your big position on the board of directors?"

She had no idea what the drunk was getting at, so she ignored him.

"True, if nothing changed, they would not be able to continue for too long. But everything is changing. Zander gave up the ER directorship so he can concentrate more on the hospital. He already got the hospitalists to agree to a new contract. He is cutting the length of stay for patients while improving patient satisfaction. All of that helped to get admitted patients out the ER. ER volumes and patient satisfaction are both improving. They opened a pediatric fast track area in the evenings and on weekends. It is staffed by pediatricians, pediatric nurse practitioners and PA's. The entrance wall has a life size picture of Adrian Burns, all pro linebacker for the Giants. Their slogan is 'Faster than a blitzing linebacker.' The turnaround times there are phenomenal, and the community is all abuzz about it.

There was an outcry when the NICU closed and inpatient mental health was shut down. But their partnership with CNJ Children's Hospital to offer clinics has been widely popular. The newspaper just did an article about how much improved outpatient mental health services have become."

Master had enough. "Penny, why don't you put your pom poms down and hear what I have in mind."

# Chapter 34

## *Master's House*

Master retreated to the kitchen and returned with a platter with coffee and tea service. He was followed by the butler, who brought in some cookies and assorted pastries. The butler removed the used glasses, emptied the ashtray, and disappeared. It was time for Master to make his pitch.

"Penelope, I'm sorry if I sounded perturbed. I really appreciate the information you provided us about the hospital turnaround. It wasn't what I wanted to hear, but I needed to hear it. We all want to see Zander and the hospital destroyed. We must anticipate that friends and family that helped him in the past will show up again. So, we allow for that."

Buster now appeared surprisingly lucid, considering how much vodka he had put away. "How?"

"I'm confident that my contact can deliver what we need. The help is far from cheap, but the task is daunting."

Penelope wanted to know. "Who is he?"

Master sat back in his chair. They were nibbling on the hook.

"No, you don't understand. I have a code name for them, but I have no clue who they are. Male, female, white, black, Indian, Scandinavian, I have no idea. I don't know if they work alone or if they have a group. I don't know if are local or from far away. I have only one contact that I know as B4."

Buster was still awake. "Sounds like a number from a bingo game. How does that help us?"

"Let's just say that they were extremely helpful when my wife needed to go away."

Bradshaw smiled. "I thought it was damn convenient for you that she committed suicide. No costly divorce and a big life insurance payout. They staged that?"

Master shook his head no. "Nope. I swear she committed suicide."

Buster, via speech, which was again becoming slurred, claimed not to understand.

Master continued the story. "I was fed up, so I contacted a source that a friend gave me. I told them I wanted my wife gone. I thought I was working with a hit man. In some ways I was; in others, I wasn't. Anyway, they did not kill my wife. She took her own life."

Penelope wasn't impressed. "So, you paid for nothing."

Master pulled back on the line to further embed the hook. "I paid for everything. I remembered something one of my psychiatric professors taught me in med school. 'Suicide is more likely to occur when the pain of living exceeds the fear of dying.' My wife took her own life after months of incidents staged to increase her anxiety. Emails, carefully placed leaflets, and internet pop ups expounded suicide. Medications secretly buried in her prescribed medications increased her depression. Various incidents occurred at night that got her very sleep deprived. They increased her pain of living while decreasing her fear of dying."

Bradshaw thought she understood. "They drove her to suicide."

"Let's just say I got my money's worth. But the contact has very strict rules. All money is paid up front. There are no refunds. After the money is sent, there is no further contact on that job."

Buster found a second wind. "What do you propose?"

Master knew he had scored. "I have been in contact with B4. I have shared appropriate information. I don't think we need to kill anyone although we would all like too. Unfortunately, killing people is much less expensive than what we need to do."

He paused and sipped his coffee.

"For $20 million they will destroy Zander, neutralize his parents, his autistic sister, that Huggins broad, Joe, and let's not forget that freak priest. They will make sure the hospital goes bankrupt or otherwise must close. That will wreck that prick attorney Santucci who is the CEO."

Penelope was excited. She didn't question the price tag. "I want to know exactly what they plan to do. I want to enjoy every bit of the destruction. I want to help plan his demise."

"No Penelope, that's not how it works. We tell them what result we want. They give us a price. If we agree, that is the last we talk. How they carry out the mission is their business. We have no input into how or when things occur, and we have absolutely no advance knowledge. Once we pay the money, we never have contact with them again. Think about it, other than sending money that can't be traced, we are not involved. The caper cannot in any way be tied to us. We just sit back and enjoy the show."

Stoli breath lamented; the price obviously bothered him. "What is $20 million split three ways? Something like seven million, I can't afford that."

Master expected that response. "What can you afford?"

Buster quickly responded. "Three million max. I already blew a ton of money we made on that IUD company. I am now retired so I won't have much income coming in, sorry."

Bradshaw badly wanted this project to go forward. "I can put up my share and my sister can make up for Sam's shortfall."

Master did the math. The Bradshaw's were putting up more than ten million. He was ecstatic but wanted more information. "What is her angle? We all know why we're in this. But what's in this for her?"

Penelope laughed. "Plenty, Elvira has some clandestine investments in thoroughbred horses. She controls a significant amount of stock in Miracle Mile Racetrack and Casino, and she sits on their board. She and two other board members want to dump harness racing there and replace it with thoroughbred racing. To do that they need a license from the state. They can't get one with current contracts, laws, and licenses."

Master couldn't' believe his luck. He smiled as Penelope finished.

"If Krenshaw Medical Center closes, it forces Miracle Mile to cease harness racing. That would allow a reexamination of the law that delineates how casino profits that are paid to the state are distributed. The thoroughbred interests badly want to race at Miracle Mile. They plan to run a quadruple crown for four-year-olds that they think they can build up over time. All four races will be held at Miracle. If they are successful, they make a fortune and thoroughbred racing will quickly banish harness racing to state fairs and other low-class venues."

Master added his summary. "And Elvira cleans up all the way around."

Penelope nodded and asked. "Are we doing half up front and half on completion?"

Master shook his head no. "That's not how this goes. We pay the full 20 up front."

"Roy, we are friends, and I trust you. But I don't put up over ten million without some kind of proof that I will get my money's worth."

Master was getting worried. "Their terms are not negotiable. Either we are in or out." By the look on her face, he could see that he needed to appease the old witch somehow. "I can ask for a demonstration of their work. Would that help convince you?"

Penelope and Buster agreed. She offered to drop Buster off at home. He certainly was in no condition to drive.

Master showed them to the door, sat back down, and poured himself a scotch. He was incredibly pleased with himself. B4 had quoted him a price of twelve million with another million for transfer fees to launder the cash. That was a total of thirteen million.

He got Buster and the Bradshaws to put up over 13 million. He was getting everything he wanted done for nothing. In fact, he made a profit of over $300,000. That more than covered his expenses for the Quincy hit. Sometimes he thought it was unfair how much smarter he was than the people he dealt with.

Within a few days B4 agreed to a demonstration. He demanded two million up front. Master got Penelope and Buster on a conference call.

"Good news. B4 has agreed to provide us with a demonstration."

Buster and Penelope asked in unison, "What is it?"

Master confessed, "I don't know. But I was told that we would recognize it immediately. We must send three million now." (Master almost messed up and said two million. If he had done that it would have been split three ways. He would have had to put up some money. His quick thinking saved him 600k. He got a free ride on the demo too.)

"We have 48 hours after the demo to pay the balance of the cash. If we don't, everyone walks away. If we are in, B4 does its thing in whatever manner they choose. Trust me; they deliver."

# Chapter 35

## *Fired Up Farms*

It was a beautiful day at the farm. The weather was going to be perfect. Maybe a little cool for an outdoor wedding, but the bride wanted an outdoor wedding, and that is what she was going to get.

At 4:30 AM, I found her grooming Fired Up Rio. Rio was standing tall with her head held high. She towered over tiny Stephanie, who was busy combing her tail. Stephanie was combing Rio's tail. Stephanie doesn't have a tail.

"How's the bride?"

"ZZ, you fucking scared shit out of me."

"Sorry." Stephanie must be nervous. In the past few years, she made an amazing transformation. Particularly her speech. Prior to that almost every other word was profanity, and her grammar was poor. With tons of therapy, a few minor medications, and family support, she had significantly improved. If she wasn't nervous, she would have said this:

"ZZ, you scared me."

But this being her wedding day she was allowed to be nervous. Unlike a lot of women, she had not planned this day for a long time. Nevertheless, she wanted it to be perfect.

"Sorry Stephanie, Can I help you do anything?"

Stephanie was happy for the assistance. "Can you finish her tail so I can start working on her flowers."

"Sure. Isn't Azzie coming to help you a little later? How is Rio?" I asked as I took over the tail coiffing.

"Feisty as ever. But since she's been knocked up, she does seem to be calming down a little."

Rio was in foal to Fired Up Frat Boy. They were both horses of the year last year, and both were undefeated in their racing careers. Their bloodlines were made in heaven for a cross. This foal was going to be worth millions when he hit the earth. But we would never know his exact worth because he would never be sold. We were keeping him.

Rio is the maid of honor. Leave it to Stephanie to be creative with her wedding. Rio is a freak of a horse as is her mother, Always Hope. They both are over 17 hands tall. Not a lot of grooms could handle Rio. Dad was worried about having her at the ceremony. Fortunately, I was the best man, so I would walk Rio down the aisle. When we got to the altar, Celeste Maliterna would handle her during the vows.

As I continued the combing task, I thought about how lucky I was to be gaining a brother-in-law like Johnson Stevens, aka Pisscatcher. PC was a great friend and an integral part of the operation that saved The Always Hope School. In the process, he fell in love with my Stephanie. My sister Stephanie deserves the best, and PC is one of the best I know.

Stephanie woke me from my thoughts.

"ZZ, I'm scared."

"Wow Stephanie, I never knew you to be scared of anything."

"What if after we're married, he sees me without makeup, and I look like crap. Or what if he gets disgusted when I start swearing or talking goofy. I'm not good enough for him."

"Stephanie, you know PC better than me. But I think he loves you with his whole heart and soul. Do you love him with your whole heart and soul?"

"Damn right!"

"Great, then you two will be very happy. If you remember why you were attracted to him and wanted to marry him, all will be ok."

I was really thinking, *wait until he stinks up the bathroom, or leaves the toilet seat up*, but I put it aside. Stephanie's time in group and foster homes had to be worse than any guy stuff that PC could pull.

"Steph, it's ok to have the jitters on your wedding day. I have them in big races when you don't. It's nice to know you are human. You will be a beautiful bride and a great wife."

That earned me a big hug. I helped her place the diamonds in Rio's pierced ears. They had become her trademark. Tim Dunstan would put one in each hoof when he arrived later. When we finished Rio was glowing. Always Hope let out a loud whinny, and shook her head up and down in approval as we walked past her paddock.

"ZZ, will God be mad at me for picking Rio as my maid of honor?"

I had no idea where this question came from, but I had to go along with Stephanie. It was her wedding day.

"Why would He be mad about that?"

"Because she's in foal, and she's not married."

I was thinking that a lot of bridesmaids in the world would be sidelined if that was a big part of the criteria, but I held my tongue. Stephanie was worried enough, and I knew she was serious. I had to come up with an answer.

"Who says they are not married? I asked.

"How can they be? Frat boy is humping his brains out with over a hundred other mares."

"That's just his job Stephanie. You know he loves Rio." I had to change the subject.

"Do you remember your vows?"

"Yeah, I promise to let him control the remote, and I will put out anytime he wants. I also vow to drive extra hard when he bets on me."

"Good vows. Don't ever forget them."

Why can't I find a perfect wife like that?

# Chapter 36

## *Fired Up Farms*

Jenny and Mom had a great breakfast on the table at 6 AM. Joe and Azzie were up. We all met at the table.

"Rio is just gorgeous," proclaimed Stephanie. "Azzie, I worked with her all week on throwing the bouquet. I just put it in her mouth, and she throws her head back and lets it fly."

Azzie laughed as did Joe. It was a great breakfast, but at 7 AM Azzie snapped her fingers. "Time to shine folks."

We all knew what we had to do. Azzie took Stephanie upstairs to begin the process to make her beautiful. Stephanie was naturally very attractive, but Azzie took her to another level. Today would be the ultimate level. Stephanie refused to wear a gown. She demanded to get married in her racing colors.

Azzie did manage to convince her to leave off the helmet so her long blond hair could flow. She even convinced her to wear a headpiece. But other than that, she was going to be in her white racing pants, and boots. Stephanie's racing boots were brown, but Azzie got some shiny white ones that Stephanie reluctantly agreed to wear.

Joe, Dad and I went to oversee the setup of the altar. Three large tents had already been erected for the reception. The main one in the center housed the wedding party. The others were at right angles, but still had a great view of the head table. The bishop agreed to perform the wedding, but he refused to sit in Tent Two. He loved the kids and when he was able to be around them, he spent most of his time with them. Who can argue with a bishop? So, he got into Tent Three.

We were expecting about 250 people, including the governor. Father Jonathan would be watching via a live stream. The catering was being managed by a company called Top of the Main Line Catering. Azzie had used them for many functions in the past. Although they were from Philly, they offered more than just cheese steaks. Azzie and Stephanie had selected a great menu. PC was with them, but he just drooled over Stephanie while the girls made their selections.

As Joe and I walked past, all three tents were bustling with activity. Flowers were still being delivered, tables were being set, and catered food was being orchestrated into a fitting wedding meal. At 11:30 a relatively small, bald man, with a handlebar moustache completed his task in Tent One and proceeded to scope out Tent Two. Seeing no one who looked like his twin, he headed for the table containing the salad choices. He waited until all staff had retreated to the kitchen to retrieve other items; then he pounced. He pulled out the spray bottle and let his deadly germs fly onto the potato salad and green bean salad. He smiled as he exited the tent.

B4 was 2/3 of the way finished with his sickening task. As he entered Tent Three, he spied the backside of his twin, the real Donald Lowry. Mr. Lowry was the owner and manager of Top of the Main Line Catering. B4 quickly turned around and walked briskly away from the tents. By the time he arrived at his truck he had removed the mask covering his head and face and discarded the spray bottle.

PC arrived at 11:45. He and I did a shot of Crown Royal with Joe. We had poured one for Billie, but he was MIA.

"Where the hell is Billie?" I asked.

Joe responded, "I haven't seen him since breakfast. He was in charge of getting the rose petals ready for the kids. I hope he didn't screw that up."

I tried to reassure him. "Billie can be a handful, but when he needs to get something done you can count on him."

PC wanted another shot. He was incredibly nervous. I worked hard to allay his fears, but he only got half a shot. We had a long way to go.

Stephanie would never forgive me if I got him tanked before the wedding.

"Of course, you aren't good enough for my sister. She was hoping for someone with a bigger gadoonga."

Joe chuckled while PC just stood there. He didn't laugh at my proclamation. He just stared straight ahead and said, "From the moment she walked down those steps, I was infatuated with her. Every minute we spend together is pure heaven. I know I am not good enough, but sorry for your luck; I ain't letting her go."

We heard the music cue we were waiting for and walked out into the sun. The ceremony started promptly at noon. The first down the aisle were all fifty kids from the school complete with handlers. Azzie had wanted to buy them all gowns and suits, but Stephanie would not hear of it.

"My Army doesn't wear stuff like that!" Stephanie knew that most of them would be terribly uncomfortable dressed up. Azzie quickly gave in, and the kids came however they chose. Some came in long pants, some in short pants and some in their pj's. Their omnipresent handlers were however, dressed to the 9's.

The parade down the aisle took a while. Fifty kids don't go anywhere in a hurry unless there's ice cream involved. We should have thought of that. They were pretty well rehearsed, but they still wandered around like stray cats. They were happy to throw rose petals around as they walked.

It's a good thing that took a while. Billie was late for the post parade down the aisle. Jenny was fit to be tied, and Azzie was boiling mad. Fortunately for Billie he arrived shortly after the last of The Army took their seats.

"Where in the hell have you been?" demanded Jenny with her hands on her hips.

"Sa Sa Sa Sorrrrrrrrry" Billie stammered as he looked down at his feet. "Myyyyy my my zi zi zi zi zi zipper bro bro broke. Wa wa went to houuuuuuuse to chhhhhhaaaaaaange."

Billie's stuttering was back in force. I felt sorry for him. I tried to lighten the moment.

"Well, we wouldn't want the horse getting out of his stall, would we?"

Azzie diffused the situation by turning our attention to the matter at hand.

"Everyone shut up and line up."

The wedding march started. Tim Dunstan took Mom's arm and walked her slowly down the aisle. Mom looked happy. Tired, but happy. She was followed by Jenny escorting Billie. The guy usually escorts the lady, but Jenny had the lead. Billie's fly was secured, and Jenny appeared to have forgotten the incident. At 5' 10" she was a full three inches taller than Billie. I remember when I dated her that it bothered me that she was taller than me. Billie and I are the same size and weight.

Jenny was decked out in a copy of Stephanie's racing colors. White jacket with large gold letters on the back "SZ". They were accentuated by yellow flames protruding from the letters. Jenny had a beautiful headpiece of yellow carnations that matched Stephanie's colors. It was unusual for bridesmaids to almost match the bride but that is what Stephanie wanted. As a contrast, the bridesmaids all wore gold racing pants instead of the white worn by the bride. At least some traditions were respected.

Billie was decked out in his own colors. Brown with yellow lettering. On his back were two small case B's followed by two capital B's. bbBB. Very few people knew what that meant, but I did. In his younger days he called himself "big balls Billie Browner." He had on white racing pants and black boots.

Azzie and Joe were next. Azzie was dressed exactly as Jenny. Stephanie's colors accompanied by gold pants and white boots. Joe was adorned with a black tux and tie.

Then came me and my date. I was in my racing colors, which were like Stephanie's, except my lettering said ZZ. I had on white pants and black boots. My date towered over me. Although I had been with lots of beautiful women in my life, this one was a head turner. From the two carat diamonds that adorned her pierced ears to the roses that were strategically placed on her flowing mane and generous tail, she was dazzling. Her four hoofs shined from a fresh coat of hoof paint that was applied after the other two carat diamonds were placed in each hoof.

She walked slowly down the aisle, casually looking to each side. I had a firm grip on her lead, but she was calm. I was hoping she didn't decide to empty out. We had a plan for that, just in case.

As we approached the altar, she spied The Army. They stood silently, which in and of itself was amazing. On cue they raised their arms high in the air. Rio stopped and slowly stood on her back legs. She let out a loud whinny as her front hoofs paddled in the air. It was an awesome site. She came down to earth, and I slowly walked her to the altar. The bishop blessed her and anointed her with holy water. I then handed her lead to Celeste Maliterna. Rio took her place in the line of bridesmaids.

The music started again, and Stephanie and Dad worked their way down the aisle. Stephanie carried a small bouquet, but she was sporting a beautiful, monster smile. My dad had a tear in his eye, but it was a happy one. His adopted daughter had grown into quite a woman. Azzie about died when Stephanie stopped to high five some of the kids. That wasn't in the plans, and Azzie was all about "The Plan." Azzie calmed down when Stephanie resumed her trek to the altar. They arrived in front of the bishop. Dad kissed Stephanie and handed her off to PC.

It was a great honor to have the bishop perform the ceremony. I would have preferred Father Jonathan, but he was completing his mission in Italy. I knew he was watching via You Tube streaming. I purposely scratched my nose with my middle finger. I could have sworn I heard him laugh clear from Italy. I couldn't help but think. "I miss you friend, good luck and get home soon."

# Chapter 37

## *Fired Up Farms*

The bishop was so elegant in his words and mannerisms. Father Jonathan was down to earth. He was one of us, dressed up like a priest. The bishop was anything but down to earth. He was heavenly. His words were brief but powerful. He acknowledged that this was a big day for Stephanie and PC, (he called him Johnson), but the day ultimately belonged to God. He talked about all of God's creatures great and small. He blessed the kids for the hundredth time and sent some more holy water Rio's way.

Now it was time for the vows. Stephanie went first and had completely shed her nervousness. I had my fingers crossed that the f bomb would not erupt during her vows. The bishop and I were on the same page. He looked a little worried. He had heard Stephanie cut loose before.

"PC, as we leave the starting gate together, I want you to know that we will always be a team. Whether on the engine, first over, or parked the long mile, I will be there for you. When times get tough, we will get tougher. When we think all is lost, we will find that extra gear that all great racehorses have. I can't wait to share my life with you."

The hard asses Azzie and Jenny were bawling. I was a little choked up. Billie was playing with his zipper, which must have broken again. PC took his turn.

"Stephanie, you are an amazing person. Much like your maid of honor you are a champion. But your greatness goes far beyond your performance in any horse race. You are kind, and you are brave. I am honored to spend my life with you. I promise to never let you down and to never bet against you."

Soon thereafter he was kissing my little sister, and we were post parading down the aisle. The track photographer snapped endless photos. We proceeded to the barn area to finish the photos and to get some with Always Hope, as the guests headed for the tents. That was calm compared to the scene that occurred when fifty kids were cut loose from an hour-long ceremony. Chaos, pure chaos.

Damien was a typical boy. Climbing, jumping, wrestling, and now he was bleeding. Nice two inch cut on his forehead. Jenny had applied a dressing, but she knew it needed sutured. His caretaker was beside himself. He only turned his back for a second. No one was upset. These kids were a handful, and accidents like this were common. As long as no one was seriously hurt, it was just a fact of life.

Jenny and I walked Damien to the school just as they began to serve dinner. I was hungry and was looking forward to couple of glasses of champagne, but duty called.

Damien was a trooper until I went to inject him with the local anesthetic. He almost cold cocked me. Jenny intercepted the punch, but he wasn't going to take the suturing lightly. To ease the discomfort from the injection, I applied some topical anesthesia.

We had to let that sit for 30 minutes to be effective. I considered shipping him off to the ER, but Damien was terrified of medical institutions. Three of my ER docs were in the tents and would have gladly sutured him, but Damien freaked out with most doctors. He knew and tolerated me. I had to stay. An hour had passed by the time the topical had kicked in, and I had closed his wound.

We got back to the soiree and dinner was pretty much over. PC and Stephanie wanted to allow Jenny and me to eat, but I said I would eat after the toast. The governor was due to leave soon, and I had to abide by his busy schedule. It was an election year, and he had places he needed to get to. I grabbed a champagne and stood.

"Ladies and gentlemen, it is my honor to propose a toast. Stephanie and PC, you two are some of the best friends I have on this earth. I know that this day will be one that will never be forgotten."

A truer statement had never been made. Before I could finish the toast, I was distracted by a forceful retching sound to my immediate left. I looked down in horror as Stephanie blew her cookies all over the table. That was followed by a loud proclamation of "ahh shit." Then all hell broke loose.

Within minutes in Tents One and Two, fifty or more people were vomiting. Some on the table, others on the floor and a few on their dates. Others were scurrying for the trailers that contained the toilets. Shortly those were filled. A number of unfortunates waiting in line lost it in their drawers.

Jenny dialed 911 and requested ambulance assistance. I dialed Tina and asked for one of our disaster carts be dispatched with extra IV Fluids and a drug Zofran to ease the nausea and vomiting. Jenny ran to the school pharmacy and retrieved as much oral Zofran as we had in stock. With so many people with sudden GI distress, this had to be food poisoning.

We shut down the food lines. Jenny walked around and offered oral Zofran to anyone who wanted it. I took the disaster tags so I could triage people. Green tags were for the walking wounded. They were directed to Tent 1. They would get Zofran and oral fluids. Patients with significant medical problems such as diabetes, heart disease, and anyone immunocompromised got yellow tags if they hadn't vomited more than once. They were sent to Tent Two. They would have blood sugars checked, blood pressures recorded, and be closely monitored. Intake and output charts were started. Red tags were reserved for those with severe diarrhea and vomiting. They would get an IV, intravenous Zofran, and transport to the hospital.

Tent Three for some reason had been spared. A few children in there vomited when they saw people from the other tents upchucking. Kids do that. Considering the number of people in Tent Three to only have a half dozen kids vomit was good news. None of the handlers were sick and the bishop was fine.

I strongly encouraged the bishop to hit the trail back to the chancery. We didn't know for sure yet what had caused the problem. He seemed relieved. I got some very disturbing news about the governor from Jenny. He had suffered profuse vomiting and diarrhea.

"Jenny, you must be kidding me. I know for sure I did not triage him. I just assumed he was well and that his staff evacuated him."

Jenny shook her head. "He was far from well. I did see him evacuate but it wasn't what you are thinking. He was evacuating his bowels behind that oak tree." She pointed to her left.

"His aids and bodyguard were crapping and vomiting all around him. That didn't stop some jerk from snapping a picture of the governor fertilizing the lawn. Once the aids got some Zofran, they whisked him away in his limo. They refused ambulance transport."

"How are Stephanie and PC?"

"Much better now. Both are orally hydrating in Tent One."

It took about two hours to get things under control. All the red tag patients had been taken to the hospital. Ten of the yellow taggers deteriorated and had to go. Everyone else hydrated either orally or IV wise and chilled out.

Once I knew things were stable, I set out to find the culprit. I took culture swabs from each food item in each tent, including the condiments. I had sixty items from each tent. I drove them personally to the hospital.

I met the head of micro in the lab. He had been wise enough to call in another lab tech. They quickly divided each sample into two specimens. Half would be sent for culture and half would be subjected to a gram stain.

A gram stain uses a dye to coat and make bacteria visible. The color of the bacteria and their appearance on the slide are examined. The culture reports would take a few days, but we might be able to make a preliminary determination of the causative agent by examining the gram stains under the microscope. This was assuming the agent was a bacterium. The gram stain was not helpful for viral problems.

They offered me a microscope, but it had been so long since I looked at a gram stain that I felt I would be useless there. I asked them to call me with any results, and I headed back to the farm.

# Chapter 38

## *Fired Up Farms*

By the time I got back to the farm, 90% of the guests had left. Most were doing well and wanted to get home. Many of them needed a change of clothes. Fortunately, we had an adequate supply of scrub suits in the disaster cart. Surprisingly, most of them were more upset for Stephanie and PC than they were at having been made ill.

I finally got myself a glass of champagne and sat down with PC and Stephanie. She was bawling her brains out.

"Oh ZZ, fucking disaster, fucking disaster."

She threw her arms around me, and I hugged her right back. Nothing worse than a ruined wedding. PC took the opportunity to drink my champagne while I was hugging Stephanie.

"I am going to ruin that caterer," PC proclaimed.

"PC, we will have plenty of time later to see how we want to proceed. Why don't you take Stephanie to a hotel near the airport. Where are you flying from?"

"Newark."

"I think things are going to be crazy here for a few more hours. I doubt you will get any rest at the house. Grab your things, and I'll get you a hotel at the airport. In fact, let me get you a limo to take you there. Stephanie will need some time to decompress."

"Thanks, ZZ. Are you sure we won't get sick again later?"

"Nah PC, once this thing settles down you are usually good to go. Clear liquids only tonight. Start out slow with your diet tomorrow. By the time you get to Hawaii you should be good for a luau."

"Hopefully that will sound better tomorrow, but I agree with getting Stephanie out of here. Thanks for everything today. It was a mess, but you and your friends were just amazing."

"Thanks, the Limo driver just texted. He will be at the house in half an hour."

PC turned around as he was helping Stephanie to the house. "Hey ZZ, did someone really get a picture of the governor dropping a deuce behind the oak tree?"

That was slang for going number two. Damn, the whole world knows. I can kiss goodbye any future help from Trenton. I scored another glass of champagne and chugged it before something else happened and somebody drank it for me. I refilled my glass and grabbed a magnum bottle to take with me. I called the ER to check on their status. Angela got on the phone and gave me a rundown.

"We received 28 patients from the wedding. 17 have been discharged. The other 11 are being held for observation. They are doing fine, and it appears that most of them will go home tomorrow."

"How are you doing?"

Angela responded. "I'm fine."

"Where were you sitting?"

"I was in Tent Three."

"Makes sense, the victims came from Tents One and Two. How's the ER? 28 patients on top of a normally busy Saturday afternoon can make for a very bad day." I was worried about the troops.

"They got a couple hours behind. When I got here, I took over the disaster ward. By that time, the patients all had IVs and some meds. I just made rounds and checked labs. Streeter rocked in the department. Like you always taught me, the harder the physician works, the harder the staff works. He set a standard today. I think if you were here, you would say that when you looked at him work, all you saw out of him was an asshole and two elbows."

I had to laugh. My boss in the restaurant where I worked in high school taught me that. "That's good to hear. You two will make a great management team. Please tell him and all staff in the ER tonight that they will be getting triple time pay. The hospital can't afford it, but my family can. We want to express our gratitude."

"That's nice! How is Stephanie?"

"Physically better but emotionally shook. Stephanie does not take things like this well. PC is taking her to Newark tonight. By the time she gets to Hawaii, I think she will be all right."

"Is there really a picture of the governor defecating under the old oak tree?"

Damnit to hell. They might as well put the picture in the paper. I thought. Maybe they did. Everyone seems to know.

"There might be. Any word on the food analysis?"

"I haven't heard anything."

I thanked her again and hung up. I scrolled my phone until I found the listing for micro, and I reached Jeremy.

"Jeremy, any idea what we had?"

"Pretty conclusive proof that it was staph food poisoning. Tons of gram positive cocci in clusters consistent with staph."

That made sense to me. "That sure fits the symptoms and onset times. Where was it discovered?"

"Potato salad and green bean salad."

"Pretty typical."

"Yeah, but there is twist."

"Do tell."

"We only found it in Tents One and Two."

I pondered the information. "That fits with the patient outbreaks. We only had six kids vomit in Tent Three, and no adults. That can easily be explained by hysterical vomiting. I think we can safely say that Tent Three was not infected. But why is there a problem in only two out of three tents? Don't you find it curious that both the potato salad and green bean salad were bad in Tents One and Two but not in Three?"

"That's why you get the big bucks ZZ. I just look at the little suckers under the microscope. Tell me all about it when you figure it out. I need some sleep."

# Chapter 39

## *Fired Up Farms*

I met up with Dan. We wondered over to the catering trucks and found the guy whose ass I was prepared to bite off and chew. Donald Lowry, owner of Top of the Main Line Catering. I dug deep into my brain to come up with an appropriate insult. My ire was interrupted when he held up a glass and requested that I fill it from my champagne bottle. My first thought was to pummel his ass, down the contents of the bottle in one big swig, and bust the empty over his skull. Dan as always prevailed. I proffered no insults, poured the glass of wine, and sat down.

Man, I am so happy that Dan won this one. Donald Lowry was an impressive individual. Not because he was smart, not because he was eloquent, even though he might have both of those things. But Donald Lowry was an honest man. Honesty exuded from his pores and his words.

"Dr. Zander I can say nothing except how sorry I am that this occurred. I pride myself on my food. Apparently, my food infected the guests at Stephanie's wedding. That sickens me to no end. I feel the need to do two things. First, I need to determine how this occurred. Second, I need to do my best to makes things right with you and your family and guests."

How could I smart off to that? I pondered my words as Dan spoke.

"We have some information that may help solve the riddle. I sense you're being forthright, and I want to respond in kind. Can we discuss this matter factually and then talk about reparations off the record? If you are willing, I think I can speak for the Zander family. We would like to avoid legal wranglings."

Don asked for another glass, and I emptied the bottle. I went in search of a replacement and quickly located one. So many guests abandoned the party that champagne was easy to find. Lucky me. I filled all glasses on my return. Dan asked me to explain to Don what we knew.

"Don, I really appreciate your candor. I get the sincere feeling that you do really care."

"I do."

"Good, we know that this was staph food poisoning."

Don took a drink to compose himself. "I knew that minutes after the first people vomited. Very few types of food poisoning occur that fast. But, how did it happen?"

I jumped in. "Not sure about how, but I can help you with where. It was in Tents One and Two. It was found in the potato salad and green beans."

This guy knew his food. "That makes sense with the foods involved. But why only Tents One and Two? Our set ups and equipment were the same in all three units. I personally supervised Tent Three from 11:30 on because of the kids and the bishop. But I was in Tents One and Two multiple times this morning."

I liked this dude, but I still had to believe that someone on his staff screwed up.

"Maybe the personnel or equipment in Tents One and Two were defective. Those foods must be kept a certain temperature."

"Dr. Zander, you're right, but we emphasize that with our staff. They're required to keep a log of food temperatures for every event. Our procedures specify that cold foods must be kept under 40F. Staff are required to take a temperature and log it every 15 minutes, from the time it is placed in the serving area until it goes back in the refrigerated trucks."

He accessed his cell phone and punched a few buttons to access an app. He quickly found the information he wanted.

"The logs for Tents One and Two show no temperature readings higher than 36 degrees. It just doesn't figure."

I finished another glass. I had a nice buzz going. "Maybe the employees fudged the numbers. You know, just filled in some bogus ones to keep you off their backs."

Don thought about it. "I can believe that from one tent, but two tents simultaneously, with the same foods. That doesn't wash."

Maybe they were contaminated during prep?" Dan offered.

"Also, not the answer. We prepared both the beans and potato salad in large batches and then divided them in three. If they were contaminated on creation, all three tents would have been infected."

Dan continued, "Then maybe it was deliberate contamination. This was a high-profile event with many prominent people. Maybe someone did this to create a story."

Don took a big swig of champagne. "Well, they sure got a story if the rumor about the picture of the governor is true. I thought about that when I was interviewing staff. I asked about unknown persons having access to the food. My staff in Tents One and Two swear that no one not affiliated with our firm got behind the barriers we erected. That's standard procedure for us. Many times, florists, security guards, etc., feel inclined to stick their fingers in our food if they think we aren't looking. So, we create barriers and teach our staff to police them. No one in either tent saw anything amiss."

Dan was sorry to have to say, "You realize that we can't pay you for today?" He was somewhat shocked to hear the reply.

"I would never accept it. I will, of course, return your deposit. I have excellent insurance for these kinds of circumstances. Let me talk to them Monday and see what they are willing to cover. We will go from there. I want to do something for every guest, more for those that got sick, and even more for those that had to go to the hospital. I also feel the need to do something for PC and Stephanie. I can never give them back their wedding day, but I can do my best to have them get past it!"

# Chapter 40

*Fired Up Farms*

*The Next Day*

Billie just stared at the computer screen. The wedding disaster turned out even better than he had planned. No one died, but the publicity was awesome, particularly the stories about the governor. His employers had to be happy. Time to check that out.

He clicked on his Cayman's account. That was the last stop for funds that were transferred to him. He was proud of the process that he invented. Sure, it cost him a million of his total take to move the funds in and out of various assets, but he just upped his bid by one million to cover that.

Deposit of $10 million cleared 30 minutes ago. That, coupled with the net of $1.8 million from the wedding, made for a tidy sum. Today's payday was the biggest ever. Business was growing exponentially. Billie was pensive. He was wildly successful for someone who everyone thought driving harness horses was his only gift.

For someone without formal training, Billie had a great understanding of artificial intelligence. He intuitively understood how it worked. Even more importantly, he was able to mastermind the use of AI to complete his nefarious and lucrative arrangements without detection. And who would suspect that he could do that? Everyone thought that he was a dim bulb. A wild and smart ass but not the sharpest tool in the shed. That made him laugh the most. The stuttering was a stroke of brilliance on his part.

He didn't stutter naturally, but he intentionally stuttered in public. He knew that even though people that stutter were often intelligent the stuttering made them sound as if they weren't. The ruse served him well. He initiated the stuttering routine when he was sixteen.

It was then that he found his true calling to a life of crime when he pulled off a triple murder. His parents had given him little over his lifetime. That was until they allowed themselves to be his first victims.

He began to plan their demise after he turned twelve. Prior to that time, he suffered occasional beatings from his father. He often took a week or so off from school until the bruises healed. The beatings stopped right after his twelfth birthday when his parents met up with Sal. His mom and dad liked drugs, and Sal had plenty of them. When they were short of cash, his parents let Sal spend the night with Billie.

He wasn't sure what to think. Mostly, he hated it, but sometimes he looked forward to a visit from Sal. That changed when he was fifteen. Cassie Andrews helped him realize that he wasn't gay, far from it. He spent most of the summer convincing himself. The more time he spent banging Cassie, the more he was repulsed by the sight of Sal. His rage intensified each time his parents arranged for another stay-over date.

That was until the last one. Once his dad told him to take a shower, he knew that Sal would be coming over. Usually, he argued with his dad, but that day he just nodded.

"I need to go downstairs and get some clothes out of the dryer. I'll shower right after that."

His dad said nothing. He was half high on weed and was thinking about what goodies Sal was about to bring. As long as Billie was cleaned up before Sal arrived, he could give a shit what he did.

Billie made it down the rickety steps to the musty basement. He quickly located the tools he had hidden. He had previously loosened and then tightened the connection supplying natural gas to the dryer. It took only a few seconds to manipulate it to leak its contents. He started the small fan, put the tools back in the toolchest, and went back upstairs to the living room.

It was all he could do not to laugh when he saw his mother lighting candles and incense. She and his dad were old hippies. They liked it to smell good when they did their drugs. Little did she know that she was covering up the smell of their eventual demise.

He made it up the steps to the second floor just as the front doorbell rang. Sal, the sex fiend, was here. Billie started the cold water in the shower. After all, Sal wanted him to be clean. He would never forget the time Sal showered him after beating him with his belt because he wasn't clean. Payback is a bitch.

Billie quietly opened the window and glanced at his stopwatch. He removed his clothes and covered himself in a bath towel. By his calculations, he needed another seven minutes. He heard music emanating from a boom box downstairs and smelled more marijuana. The party had begun.

The seven minutes seemed like an eternity. He knew if he made his move too early, he might not get the desired effect. Finally, his watch hit the magic mark. He turned off the cold water and switched on the hot. It ran for about two minutes before the flame from the gas water heater ignited the natural gas that had permeated the basement. The resulting explosion rocked the house.

The first floor immediately collapsed into the basement and was fully engulfed in flames. Billie was tempted to jump out the window, but he decided that he would only do that as a last resort. Shortly, he heard fire whistles followed by fire trucks racing into the driveway. He shouted from the window and waved his towel to attract attention. The house was wobbling, and he feared a total collapse. Fortunately, that didn't happen until he had been rescued and taken to a nearby ambulance for some oxygen.

The oxygen mask concealed the smile that erupted on his face as the roof collapsed. He couldn't wait to identify the crispy remains of his dirtbag parents and the pervert Sal. Compared to the temperatures they were just cooked in, hell might seem more comfortable. Billie hoped not.

The fire marshal was no match for Billie. Billie anticipated his questions and had led him to the only conclusion possible. Billie's dad had disconnected the dryer the month before to repair a problem with the igniter. When he was finished, he failed to adequately reattach the gas supply. Although Billie had told his dad last week that he thought he smelled gas, his dad dismissed it. The leak worsened and gas had built up in the basement. When Billie took his shower and wanted hot water, the hot water tank clicked on its burner to create a fresh supply. That ignited the inferno. Case closed. Billie was fortunate to have been on the second floor.

Shortly after he buried his parents and established a new identity, he almost got caught doing an online scam. He had to bail out of Western Pennsylvania in a hurry and ended up in New Jersey. He had some experience with horses, and he heard that Carl Zander was looking for help at the farm. He needed a legit job as a cover for his other endeavors. Carl hired him. He genuinely liked Carl, and he enjoyed working with the horses. He made enough to survive, but he wanted more.

He couldn't get that from petty online scams. The problem with those was that they took a lot of time to pull off, and very few were successful. The amount of profit was small compared to the time commitment. Good for a bunch of dudes from Ukraine with nothing else to do, but not for him.

His next venture was aided by his growing knowledge of artificial intelligence. All he needed was a good facial recognition picture of his target and their credit card information. With the software he had tweaked, he could make a 3-D mask of the face and a duplicate copy of the credit card. He was then in business. He took a bus to a jewelry store somewhere close to the owner of the credit card. Then, he donned the mask and made a nice purchase. The scheme worked well, but again, he found that the profit margin was small. If he went for a very expensive item, the store owners got hinky. So, he stuck to things around $2500 or less. After the faked purchases, he had to fence them. He quickly learned that he was lucky to get 30 cents on the dollar. Again, a lot of work and risk for little profit.

He was an amazing groom for my dad. Dad spent a lot of time coaching and encouraging Billie. Dad suggested he get his license to race in the fairs, and Billie did quite well. Soon Dad helped him get his provisional race license and then his A racing license. The more he drove, the better he got. He was a natural. The fans loved him. That's how he got his nickname. The fans called him "Billie Cha-Ching Browner." Cha-Ching was the sound of them ringing their cash registers after cashing winning tickets. At first, he drove exclusively for Fired Up Farms, but soon he was getting other offers.

It was around this time that Dad was arrested for homicide by vehicle while DUI, and I returned home to run the family business. Billie had nothing against me; he hardly knew me. That was until he started to race against me. Billie wasn't sure why Dad let him drive when I had been known to be a great driver.

He learned that prior to his arrival, Dad and I had a falling out. I was a world-class driver. But after a serious accident, Dad thought I should concentrate on medicine, which was much safer. He drove me out of the business. I hated Dad for that and left home for good.

That opened the door for Billie, and he took it. That door closed when I returned. I would have to pay for that someday, and I would have to pay for making fun of Billie's stuttering. Even though it was an act, Billie didn't like being mocked. But my day of reckoning would come after Queen Stephanie got her just reward.

Billie was as enraged with her as he had been with his parents. Stephanie didn't pimp him out, but she did something even worse. She rejected him. She was about sixteen when Billie was hired. She was a total head case. Somedays, she talked, and some days she made some sense. Other days, she just grunted.

Her hair was never combed, and often, she smelled. But when she was cleaned up, she was strikingly beautiful. He thought his prospects for scoring with her were good after he copped a good feel in the tack room. But after that day, she had nothing to do with him. He called, he bought her presents, he begged, and she would not give in. He made a vow. "That fucking, retarded, autistic bitch would pay."

Billie poured another scotch and was about half in the bag. He still was amazed about how he found his current occupation. It began as a contract hit, but at the last second, the buyer requested that the victim not die. The buyer instead requested she be otherwise incapacitated. His first thought was to keep the deposit and walk away.

But when he researched the intended victim, he changed his mind. She had a severe underlying anxiety disorder. With his computer knowledge and mask disguises, he gave her hundreds of reasons to be anxious. Threats of bodily harm, rape, and slow death bombarded her from all angles. Her car broke down repeatedly. Every day was filled with disappointments and disasters that drove her wild. Once she was hospitalized in a mental institution, his contact paid him his full amount. He got a sizable bonus when she committed suicide.

That's when he decided to perform limited intentional killing and no more stealing. His business line was now psychiatric ops aided by artificial intelligence. He insisted on full payment up front and no contact after the job had been accepted. He was far too exposed if he kept communications open.

He soon was able to command his price. His reputation spread on the dark web. He had many more offers than he had time. He carefully chose his jobs. The more lucrative ones stood out. He also tended to favor jobs in which he could use his talents to his maximal benefit. The suicide of Veronica Bator put him over the top. He could afford to be very choosey and very expensive.

He switched to coffee and tried to focus on his latest contract. Somehow, he needed to close Krenshaw Medical Center while making my life as miserable as possible. He knew I would not go quietly and that Joe Crinelli, Azzie Huggins, and Father Jonathan would come to my aid. That support, coupled with my family's staunch loyalty, would make the task more difficult. But the difficulty was paying well, particularly with the added support of the thoroughbred interests who wanted to cripple harness racing.

Before he started to mastermind the fall of Krenshaw and yours truly, he wanted to put the final touches on his escape plan. He knew it was likely that his identity would be uncovered during this project. That is why he had planned to fly to Central America when he finished. There, he would have surgery and change his identity.

He would then proceed to a small town in New Zealand that bred and raised harness horses. His plan was to gradually pretend to learn the ropes there and hopefully get back into driving. If he was able to drive successfully, he would use that fame to further establish his new identity. Eventually, he would return to the USA to train, drive, and own harness horses if that sport survived.

Satisfied that his end game was well planned, he got to work. Funny, he thought, to be paid this well for something that he would have done for free. Just then, the scotch caught up with him, and he fell asleep at his computer.

# Chapter 41

## *Fired Up Farms*

It was nice of PC to call, but the shithead failed to correctly factor in the five-hour time difference. He was sipping a beer on the veranda at 10 PM in Hawaii and decided it would be a good time to check-in. The brilliant accountant made a math error. He thought it was 5 PM in New Jersey. Unfortunately, it was 3 AM in Krenshaw. We were five hours ahead of his time, not five hours behind. I was none too happy.

"ZZ, how the hell are you? Everyone done puking and crapping their brains out?"

"PC, you do realize that it is 3 AM here?" I replied in my most seriously pissed-off voice.

"Oh damn, sorry, I got the time zones mixed up. Call me later. Actually, don't do that. By the time you get up, I will be asleep or otherwise entertaining your sister."

Too late. I was up. "Now that I'm awake, how are the honeymooners? Please, no sex stories. That is my sister, you know."

"We are fine. Stephanie was in her shell for the first two days. I wasn't sure what to do, so I just waited it out. This morning, she woke up, and she was better. We did a little surfing and sightseeing today. She seems to be enjoying herself. I just love her to death."

"That's good, you have three whole successful days of marriage under your belt. Keep it going!"

"Will you be visiting me in prison?" PC inquired.

"Who's after your ass, the IRS or track security?"

"No one yet. But help me out with this. Should I hide the gun or just drop it like Micheal did when he killed the two dudes in *The Godfather*?"

"You are starting to talk like Stephanie. WTF are you babbling about?"

"When I kill that asshole caterer, do I drop the gun and casually walk away, or should I ditch it in the ocean?"

"Oh, you should drop your murder plans. You aren't cut out for it, and besides, that caterer is a nice guy."

"He ruined our wedding, poisoned the governor, and generally wrecked the whole day. How's the governor? Even here in Hawaii they are hoping to get to see the picture of him fertilizing your oak tree."

"We found the dude who snapped the picture. Turns out his daughter goes to the Always Hope School on a free ride. That's how he happened to be on the grounds that day. We had the media bozos boxed away in a corner area. They never could have snapped a picture from their location. But as a parent of a student, he was free to roam. Joe remembered that one of the kid's dads was a paparazzi. That evening we combed the files and found his identity. Joe and Azzie paid him a visit. He and Joe didn't hit it off, but he liked Azzie."

PC agreed. "Who doesn't like Azzie? Did she get the picture?"

"That's the trouble with digital photography. It's impossible to prove that no copies exist. She at least got him to agree not to sell it, for now."

"How did she do that? She is so eloquent and so damn smart."

I explained. "She showed him two videos of his daughter. The first video was from two years ago when she was accepted into the school. She was shy with poor verbal skills, terrible coordination, and almost no ability to care for herself. The second video was from the wedding. She was dressed in a gown, and she talked and danced. Once the dude saw those, he broke down. He admitted to taking the picture. He wouldn't sell the rights to us, but he at least agreed not to sell it to anyone until near the election."

PC thought he understood. "He probably figures that the price will only go up."

"He could be right. The governor's opponent pounced on the story. Every opportunity she gets, she says that he crapped on New Jersey. She never references the wedding, but everyone knows what she is talking about. The governor had a sizable lead in the polls, and that has vanished. It is neck and neck now. The governor's pollsters are worried that she will use the picture as an October surprise. They have polling data indicating that the picture could swing a lot of undecided voters. With social media, we have a very visual society. Pictures or videos speak much louder than words. They also discovered that the photographer and his wife are getting divorced. He might become a loose cannon."

PC was sympathetic. "That is worrisome. Right now the picture has no monetary value if not published."

It was still early for me, and I wasn't following. "What does that mean?"

"If I were him, and I was getting divorced, I would not sell the picture yet. Half of the proceeds would go to my wife. I would get divorced first and then sell it. 100% would fall into my pocket."

"Spoken like a true CPA, but that is worrisome. Hopefully, he won't finalize his divorce before the election. Getting back to the caterer. He wants to make amends. He was thinking about a one-year anniversary party with the same guest list."

"Great, the guy blows our wedding, and you want me to pay him for a second chance to screw us? No thanks."

I had left out an important piece of information. "He insists on doing it for free."

PC liked that price, but he was still skeptical. "Wow, that's impressive. He must have royally screwed up to want to offer that much."

"Dan and I don't think so. Because of the location of the outbreak in only two tents we think it was sabotage. We suspect that someone had it in for you guys, or the governor, or the caterer himself. So far, we can prove nothing."

"That's tough to believe bro, but if you and Dan are sure the dude is clean, I will cancel my hit."

"Talk to Stephanie about the anniversary party. It could be a blast. When are you guys' due back?"

"Late next week."

I wanted to impress him with my vast knowledge. "A hui hou!" I proclaimed.

"What? How's your wee wee?" PC replied with a laugh.

"PC, that's Hawaiian for 'until we meet again'. You and my sister need to come up for air and get out of the room every now and then."

"Aloha." Came the reply as he hung up.

# Chapter 42

## *Bella's Apartment*
## *Atlantic City New Jersey*

It took Billie three weeks after the wedding to prepare for the next phase of my destruction. It was a nice day for a ride, and he enjoyed the drive to Atlantic City. Hell, he might even hit the tables when he was through if all went well.

It was a lot of work to make his skinny body resemble Joe's. Joe was not tall, but he was broad. He had a huge neck and tons of muscles on his legs and arms. On arrival, Billie used the reflection in his car window to comb his hair and to check his appearance. "Boom, boom, boom", as Joe would say. He had done it. Now, to get what he needed. He rang the doorbell and looked straight into the camera.

"Hello, what can I do for you?" Bella was careful not to undo the chain securing the door. There had been some recent burglaries in her building.

"Bella, I am Joe Crinelli, a friend of ZZ."

"Where has that little s.o.b. been? I miss him," Bella said as she opened the door to her modest apartment.

"He has been busy cleaning up after that fiasco of a wedding. Did you go?"

"Yeah, a bunch of us from Seaside ER went."

"What tent were you in?"

"We were in tent 1."

"Did you get sick?" Billie feigned concern.

"I didn't, but most of the Seaside staff did. It was awful. I'm an ER nurse, and I see and smell vomit and crap daily. But the sights, sounds, and smells of that wedding are etched in my brain."

"I bet you didn't eat the potato or green bean salad."

"You are right. I don't like either one of those. Is that where the contamination was?"

"Yeah. We can't prove it, but we think it was sabotage." Billie had deliberately asked me all about it so he could speak to Bella accurately. He knew what he had done, but he wanted to tell her what I had told him.

Bella bought it. "That's crazy stuff. Joe, are you doing a follow-up on the guests, or is there something else I can do for you?"

Time for the ruse.

Billie told the tale. "You know that ZZ loves to make jokes and give people nicknames. He also loves to scam his friends."

"Of course, he cons the pants off of me all the time." She laughed.

"Well, ZZ and I have an ongoing battle as to who can create the better spoof. He had me convinced that a grand jury had indicted me on RICO (racketeering) charges. My grandfather may have been connected in the past, and the feds are always looking at me. I am clean, but ZZ concocted search warrants and got friends to act as FBI. They staged a raid on my house. Of course, I fell for it. He laughed his skinny ass off when he showed me how bogus everything was."

Bella enjoyed the story but sensed that something more was coming. "Interesting, but what does that have to do with me?"

"I need your help to one-up him."

"Why would I do that?"

"Let me explain, but first, let me tell you what I can do for you. How about an all-expense paid cruise to Acapulco for two?"

"Serious?"

"Serious."

"Nothing that will hurt him? I mean, a cruise for two is a lot to pay for a joke."

"I promise you nothing that will hurt him. This will be the final joke that will secure me the title. What I am asking you to do may be a little embarrassing, and I want to show my appreciation. The bragging rights this will give me over ZZ is worth the cruise."

"Tell me more."

"Ok. Let's just say that is common knowledge that you and ZZ like to dance with no pants like they say on *The Big Bang Theory*."

"Hey!!!!"

"Hear me out. Everyone knows that when ZZ is in the mood, he often winds up in Atlantic City."

"Go on."

"I want you to get ZZ to wear a condom when he next comes calling."

She shook her head. "He and I have a date for next week, but he knows I am on the pill, and I hate condoms."

Billie had thought this through. "Tell him you are on an antibiotic for a bad tooth and that the pharmacist said it could inactivate the pill."

"Ok, so he uses a rubber."

"When he is done, I want you to get the prophylactic out of the garbage and give it to me."

"That's disgusting!"

"I agree, but that's the key to the con. I will use his semen from the condom as "proof" in an alleged rape. Can you imagine his face when they come to arrest him? I plan to have some friends take him to a fake police substation. I already have Dan Santucci in on the gag. He will arrive after 'booking' and go over the evidence with ZZ. ZZ is obviously familiar with DNA analysis, so we must have a legitimate document to fool him."

Bella was concerned. "I don't know. He and I have a good thing going. I don't want to mess it up."

"Once he finds out how I set this up, you will be in the clear. One thing about ZZ, he's a good sport. He dishes it out, but he also knows how to take it. He will see the brilliance in this caper. But one other thing."

Bella nodded. "And?"

"I know you know not to tell ZZ. But please don't mention this to anyone else. You never know who might spill the beans to ZZ."

"Good thinking, Joe. Without your advice, I might have gone to work later and blabbed. 'Hi everyone. The next time ZZ screws me, I am going to collect his semen for a joke that Joe Crinelli is pulling on him.' "

Billie laughed. "I guess I deserved that sarcastic remark. How about the cruise?"

# Chapter 43

*Emergency Department*
*Krenshaw Medical Center*

It was a quiet morning in the ED. The weather was surprisingly good for the end of March. That may not bode well for the 3-11 shift, but we on the day shift got off to a nice, easy-paced start. Sunday mornings usually were quiet until people started to pass out during long homilies in church. That's something I made up to encourage Father Jonathan to be brief. I think he bought it.

So far this morning, my talents had not been too heavily taxed by our first two contestants. Two patients sustained cuts trying to slice bagels. If everyone bought one of those bagel slicers, I might be unemployed. But for now, I'm good. The nosebleed was a nice change of pace. It was a good teaching case for my resident, who arrived after I finished suturing.

The epistaxis patient was a tough 80-year-old bird who might have weighed 77 pounds. She reported that the nosebleed started five hours before. Her pressure was 80/60, and her pulse was 110. The resident wanted her to lay down flat so he could give her some fluids before he stopped the nosebleed. The medics had wanted her to do the same thing. Granny wasn't buying it. Every time she laid back, the blood filled her throat. She thought she was going to choke to death.

I got into the room as she and the resident were in the midst of a shouting match. I gave the time-out signal to the resident, who backed off. I introduced myself to the patient and told her what I wanted to do. She nodded, then proceeded to cough out a large clot onto my scrub top. I hadn't had time to don my protective gear. Nosebleeds usually were messy. I felt bad for the housekeeping staff, but this was an ER.

"Nice clot," I said as I looked at my scrub top. I liked to encourage my patients. Granny got half a smile on her face.

"I am going to hold your nose while the nurse starts an IV. I hope this isn't too uncomfortable for you, but I must keep good pressure on the nose. She nodded in agreement.

Dawn ran in the fluids and announced that the BP was now 96 and her pulse was 92. I was pleased.

"Run her fluid at 250 an hour. Repeat the vitals every 2 minutes until I get the bleeding stopped."

"Yes, Master Zander," said Dawn as she saluted me.

"Smartass," I replied. That brought another grin from Granny. She was a lot less pale. I turned to the resident.

"You see how I got control of the situation by holding Granny's schnaz? You've heard the expression that bleeding always stops. Well, that can happen for two reasons. The first is that the patient runs out of blood and cashes their chips. Not good. The other is that you stop the bleeding. The most common nosebleeds are anterior bleeds. Almost all can be temporized by holding pressure on the nose. Go ahead. I will let loose, and you do it while I set up my equipment and get on some protective gear."

Within seconds, blood was spurting from the nose, and Granny was looking pale again. The resident was squeezing the bridge of the nose. That's the bony part. Unless he broke her nose, which I hoped he didn't do, he would not be able to stop the bleeding. Where do they find these residents? I have to talk to this dude about a future in another specialty. I may have raised my voice a little.

"Don't squeeze the bony part of her nose, you twit. You won't get any pressure on the bleeder. Grab the cartilaginous (softer) part distal to the nasal bone."

The resident finally grabbed the correct part of the nose, but Granny was still bleeding.

I offered more words of tender encouragement.

"Squeeze damn it, we aren't dabbing on makeup here. Stop that bleeding now!"

That got the desired result. I finished my set up and explained to Granny and the resident the plan.

"The resident will let go of your nose, and I will numb it. Your nose will bleed during that process and some clots may go down your throat. Go ahead and spit them out. Try to hit the bowl, but if you want to decorate my gown again, feel free." Another grin. She liked me.

"Now, this is the important part. Once I get you numb, I want you to blow your nose as hard as you can to get the clots out. I also want you to spit out anything in your throat. Then I will take over. Got it?"

She nodded.

If I or Granny didn't evacuate the clots, the bleeding would not stop. I explained to the resident that the clots had break down products in them that would further anticoagulate the blood in her nose. He looked amazed. He should know this by now. Dah.

On my cue, Dawn fired up the electrocautery, and the offending vein was fried. The bleeding stopped, and it wasn't because the patient died. I then showed the resident how to instill a Vaseline gauze packing laced with an antibiotic into the nostril. I thought about letting him do it, but the department was filling up, and I needed to move on.

The room looked like a bloody battlefield. Granny had good color in her cheeks, and the resident was checking something on his phone. Hopefully, he was searching for open psychiatry residencies.

I peeled off my gear. I was about to expand my education of the resident (Ok, I planned to chew his ass further), when Streeter stuck his head in the room.

"Did you murder the resident? Nice crime scene."

I gave him a Zander salute and asked, "Is it 11 already?"

Ron smiled. "It better be. He, my boss, won't pay me to come in early."

I corrected him. "Angela is a girl!"

"One layer higher, Angela's boss," Ron responded, meaning yours truly.

I joined the joke. "That guy's a prick."

Streeter wasn't done. "A little prick at that."

"OK, who told you? Angela wouldn't know."

Streeter responded. "Nobody in particular. Everyone in the department talks about it all the time. They frequently mention that you have a small endowment."

I laughed even though I tried not to. "I was just about to tell you what a great job you and Angela are doing, but now I won't. So there!" I stuck out my tongue.

We got down to business. "How was your morning ZZ?"

"Pretty good. Steady but far from busy."

We walked to the coffee pot. I took the opportunity to get his opinion.

"What do you think of Jennings?"

"The resident?"

"Yeah."

"Pretty weak. He seems smart enough, but he has little common sense. He frets over minor details while missing big glaring problems. The other day, we had a trauma patient we needed to stabilize. He had severe respiratory distress in addition to a large laceration on his leg that was spurting blood. Jennings ignored the respiratory distress and wanted to explore the wound. I grabbed a medic and had him hold pressure on the wound. Then I got the dude an airway and put a tube in his pneumothorax. What part of the lecture on the ABC's of resuscitation did Jennings miss? I shouldn't have, but I screamed at him. 'A is for airway, B is for breathing, C is for circulation. The order does make a difference.' If he had been alone, that patient was toast. I wonder if he should try another specialty."

My thoughts exactly. "I'll talk with his director. Email me a copy of the trauma patient's chart."

"Where are you taking Bella tonight?" Streeter asked as we walked back into the department.

"How did you know I was taking her out?"

He laughed. "It's posted on the communications board. It says ZZ is going to Atlantic City. Look for him to be in a better mood this week."

Wow, there are no secrets in an ER.

# Chapter 44

## *Bella's Apartment*
## *Atlantic City, NJ*

It was a great time, as usual, in Atlantic City. The more time I spend with Bella, the more I think about settling down. I must be sick. I even called her Sarah last night. I never do that. That's her real name. When I first met her, I called her Sarah. That then morphed into Cerebellum (a part of the brain), and from there, she became, and still is, Bella, except when I screw up.

What began as a pure sexual relationship has evolved over time, similar to her nickname. I felt like I was sinking in quicksand. That's because I was. Bella was wearing me down. She was changing too. She was a little reluctant to tell me about her upcoming cruise. We never talked much about what we did when we weren't together. That worked well for both of us.

I really didn't mind her going on the cruise too much. Although she and Anne Marie were crazy when they were together. Maybe I should mind. Anne Marie won some goofy contest and asked Bella to go. Who can turn down a free cruise? I was thinking way too much about this. On the way home, I decided to call Billie to kill some time. With his stuttering, I could easily get home before we finished the conversation.

"Hello." I'm pretty sharp. Right away, I knew it wasn't Billie. The voice was an octave higher, and there was no stuttering."

"Who is this?"

"ZZ, it's Jenny."

"I was calling Billie."

"I know. I have his phone. He is on his computer in the other room."

I whistled. "Good time to check his phone for calls and texts from other women?"

"Oh, ZZ, you know me better than that."

"Yeah, you've already done that, and now you are scanning emails and looking for porno and lewd pictures."

"OK, busted. You know I don't have the best of luck with men. I don't like surprises. Do you want to talk to him? I can get him. He is studying for his GED."

I was incredulous. "GED?  Gonad Enhancement Day?"

Jenny went on to explain that Billie never graduated from high school. That, and the stuttering, really bothered him. She had been pushing him to get his GED, and he finally agreed. He spends a lot of time on his computer studying when he is home.

"Good for him! Don't bother him, and it was nothing important."

Jenny was half right. Billie was on his computer, but it had nothing to do with a GED. He just finished a tutorial on lasers and had moved on to "Never Episodes", as described by the Licensure Board. He had overheard me talking about them at dinner. He was amazed at how many bad things occurred in hospitals every day, and they were trying to not have them happen. Imagine what could be done if you greased the wheels a little.

I got back home as Stephanie was coming out of the barn.

"Hey Steph, everything OK."

"Yeah ZZ. I was just checking on Rio."

"Anything the matter?"

"No, I just worry with her being in foal and all."

I laughed. "You will have gray hair before that foal drops. Where is PC?"

"I have gray hair now! PC is at the office, as usual. He won't wander home until 10 PM  or so."

"You should have thought of that before you married a CPA. But you only have another week until tax season is over for this year."

"I can't wait! How was Atlantic City? Get lucky?"

"Stephanie!" I was embarrassed. Everyone knows.

# Chapter 45

*Fired Up Farms*
*Krenshaw, NJ*

Azzie was always on time. Sometimes ahead of time but never behind. She firmly believed that the time of her staff, family, and friends was more important than hers. That was why PC and I were in position an hour before her expected arrival. I was going to go alone, but PC offered to come with me. Tax season was over, and he was happy to get out for a ride. My phone rang, but it was the generic ringtone.

"This is Carole Benedict from Seaside ER." She was sobbing.

"Carole, what's the matter?"

"You obviously haven't heard yet."

"Heard what?"

"It's about Sarah Stoner, Bella to you."

"What about her?"

"ZZ, she's dead."

"What, how?" I couldn't believe it.

She explained. "She and Anne Marie Kroskey from respiratory went on a cruise to Acapulco. She told you about that, didn't she?"

"Yeah, I knew all about it."

"Anne Marie says they were pretty wasted. Anne Marie decided to shack up with one of the band players, and Sarah (Bella) went back to their stateroom. She told Ann Marie that she was about to barf, and she wanted to get an emesis bag."

"So, how did she die?"

"On her way to her stateroom, the boat hit some rough seas. She apparently fell off the deck into the water."

I was beyond sick. "Oh, how terrible. They weren't able to save her?"

"No, they followed their protocol for man overboard, and they recovered her body. At least what was left of it."

After about a minute of shrieks and cries, she blurted out, "She had been eaten by sharks. Half of her torso was gone."

I didn't know what to say.

Carol continued. "Her body will be flown back from Acapulco when they finish the identification. There won't be a funeral. Sarah was a different kind of person. Although she was young, she had a will. She once told Anne Marie that she had made one. We found it in her apartment. That will requests no funeral or viewing. She wants cremated, which is good. She wants you to disperse her ashes into the ocean off the pier in AC."

I still was speechless.

"Will you do it?" Carole wanted to know.

"Of course I will. When?"

"Actually, there is no hurry. The ER is in shock, and I think we all could use a little time. As you know, she has no family. We have no idea when her body will be returned. Her birthday is next month. Maybe we can do something then."

"Is Anne Marie ok?"

"Her flight into Newark is arriving as we speak. A bunch of people from the ER are going to pick her up. We'll see."

"OK, I'll get back to you later in the week. We'll pick a time and date for the ash's ceremony, followed by a real Irish wake. No one is driving home. I'll get us all rooms." I hung up.

I was beside myself, and PC sensed it.

"ZZ, that didn't sound good."

I tried to compose myself. It took a few minutes. I then repeated the disastrous news that I was just given.

PC was shaken. "You never know the time or place. I am so sorry, ZZ."

After fifteen minutes of dead air, I broke the silence. "It sure is nice to have a helipad."

He shook his head in agreement. "Much safer all around."

In the past, Azzie's pilots had landed her trademark helicopter right in front of the house. It was a sight to see. Bright pink lips painted on the side of a black helicopter. Above the doors on both sides was her company's name, Exquisite Evolutions, in bright pink cursive.

Her pilots had gotten nervous about landing there. Their trepidation increased when they found out that their flight path took them directly over top of The Always Hope School. Considering that she visited around twice a month, the pilots encouraged her to build a helipad. Mom was getting a little tired of her petunias getting pummeled by the rotor wash, so she was all for it. Azzie finally gave in.

I was relieved to have something to do right now. I really didn't want to think about Bella. That wasn't my style. When I got bad news, I liked to process it while staying busy. PC stayed in the car as I pulled the ATV with the industrial fire extinguisher out of its shed and put it in position about 50 yards from the helipad. Then I lit the landing lights. The windsock was fairly silent. Should be an easy landing.

At the request of the pilots, the landing approach ran parallel to the high-tension lines that crossed the property. They were over 100 yards away from a 500-kilovolt line, but they never had to cross over it. To them, that was a plus.

Billie had been fortunate to catch a first-class upgrade on the flight to Philadelphia. And he was lucky that the flight was on time. His schedule for the evening was tight. He got into position early. Billie knew exactly how the pilot would land. He was situated perfectly. He looked at his watch. He had about 30 minutes to kill. He laughed. That was literal.

He munched on a candy bar and smiled as he thought about his recent successes. He got what he needed from Bella. He was delighted to help her "slip" off the deck. He could still hear her screaming. Music to his sick ass ears. In retrospect, he was happy that he got a picture of one of the crew and impersonated him last night. It was hard to tell where they had cameras on those tubs, and no sense taking chances. His sadistic thoughts were interrupted by lights approaching in the night sky. At the appropriate moment, he lit the laser.

# Chapter 46

*Fired Up Farms*
*Krenshaw, NJ*

The pilot screamed in agony as his retinas burnt into his eye sockets. He instantly lost control of the bird, which veered 90 degrees to the right. Azzie shrieked as they approached the high-tension lines, but the blinded pilot was totally flummoxed. Joe undid his seat belt and rose from his back seat. He had never piloted a helicopter, but he had to try to do something. All he could think was to pull up on the control and hope for the best. To do that, he had to get into the front seat.

From my position, I saw a flash of light going to the chopper, followed by the craft veering eerily toward the high-voltage lines. It was like watching the proverbial train wreck. I knew what was coming, and I was powerless to do a damn thing about it except watch.

The back rotor cut through the first high-voltage line with ease. The remaining three lines caught in the rotor. The craft tilted forward, hanging from the back rotor for a few seconds, and then it plunged to the ground. Flames erupted from the tail section and quickly spread to the main cab.

Out of the corner of my eye, I saw PC speeding in the car to the crash site. I was closer, but he got there first in the car. I screamed and screamed as I drove the ATV furiously.

"Stay away, stay away, high voltage lines down!"

With the noise of the fire and the still crumpling rotors, he never heard me. PC was a great friend and stellar accountant, but he had no training in trauma scene management. He had no idea of the perils involved for first responders.

He reached the helicopter as I continued screaming. I saw him jump from the car as the flames intensified. He grabbed the door handle to the chopper. Tens of thousands of volts of electricity coursed through his body. Every muscle contracted, unfortunately, including the ones gripping the door. His fate was sealed.

It took me another minute to get there. I used the fire extinguisher to beat the flames back from the cab. PC was still gyrating from the voltage coursing through his body. I found a large branch that had been torn from a tree and used that to pry him off the door. Once he was clear of any metal, I pulled him away from the chopper. I checked PC for pulses and found none. Although I wanted to start CPR, I had to check on Azzie and, Joe and the pilot. They had a chance to survive. PC had little to no chance.

I used the branch to pull the wire off the metal cage of the chopper. I spit on the door handle to see if it was still live. I wasn't sure if that was the best way to see if electricity was still flowing. But at this point, I was not thinking very clearly. My training told me to wait for EMS and electrical crews to arrive to make the scene safe. My heart told me otherwise. I lightly touched the door. When I wasn't barbecued, I pulled the door open. Azzie's hair was on fire. I pulled off my shirt and smothered that blaze. I then released her seat belt and pulled her from the chopper.

I saw lights approaching. Dad, Mom, and Stephanie jumped out of Stephanie's truck. I yelled for them to stop in their tracks. They heard me and did as I asked. I pointed out the location of the downed line and the location of PC and Azzie. Unfortunately, Stephanie arrived first at PC's side. I almost stopped her, but she began CPR. It was tough to tell about electrical injuries. Now that we had enough help, it was appropriate to begin CPR. I didn't think it would do much good.

Dad did chest compressions as Stephanie did rescue breaths. The sounds of approaching ambulance and fire trucks got louder. I prayed that Azzie didn't have a spinal injury. In the urgency to get her out of the chopper there was no time for proper spinal stabilization. I knew that I did the best I could to prevent manipulation of her neck. I had to hope that was good enough.

She was moaning and moving all extremities. That was good. The smell of her burnt hair and the burns of her face and entire upper body were another matter. She had a good carotid pulse, so I felt ok leaving her with Mom. There was still a pilot and Joe to be accounted for.

The flames were making their way back toward the cabin. I carefully opened the door and found the pilot strapped in his seat. His head was perched at a very wrong angle to his body. I checked for a pulse, and there was none. His dead head flopped to the side as I did so. He was gone. His neck had been broken.

I saw nothing in the back of the cab, but the smoke was getting thicker. I was looking for a way to access the back when I heard moaning from the field. I followed my ears to one of the most grotesque sites I had ever seen. Joe was lying on his side screaming. Each of his legs bent outward at odd angles. He had been ejected from the craft and either fractured his pelvis or broke both legs. Neither option was great. Those were just the obvious injuries. Who knows how many other injuries he had. He lost consciousness as I attempted to feel his pulse. He was in deep shock. His pulse was about 140 and weak. Joe was fixing to die.

Amos was first on scene. Normally, he would have to rapidly assess all victims and decide who to treat first. But right on his heels were two more medic units, so he went to the first victim. He assessed PC and found no pulse or respirations. Mostly for Stephanie's benefit, he elected to pursue full resuscitation until they got to the hospital. He had a difficult time getting Stephanie to stop doing ventilations. Eventually, she recognized him and relented. Amos intubated PC and got an IV running. He and his crew loaded him into the medic unit and hightailed it to the hospital.

The second unit tended to Azzie. She was now screaming for Joe. She got an IV, morphine, versed, and some sterile blankets to cover her burns. They carefully immobilized her neck. Med command (Dr. Angela) directed them to take her directly to the burn unit. Her ETA there was only about 25 minutes longer than Krenshaw. She needed a burn unit.

The third ambulance on the scene found Joe and me. They rapidly immobilized him while I got an IV in his right arm. Once he was packaged, he was loaded into the unit, and a second IV was started. Fluids were pounded into both veins to combat his going into shock. His pressure rose, and so did his level of consciousness.

He screamed in pain. "Fuck me, fuck me, this hurts."

He got a massive (thanks to me) dose of morphine and settled back down. No medical command physician would have authorized that high of a dose, but they weren't looking at what I was seeing. He needed it.

The last medic unit checked the pilot and confirmed my suspicion. The fire had been put out, so they left him in his seat. They then backed away and set up a perimeter. No one else would be allowed in until the power company and investigators released the crime scene.

I wanted to send Joe to the trauma center via helicopter, but he refused. "Never riding in one of those fuckers again." Fortunately, weather conditions were good and direct ground transport to the trauma center would not delay his arrival by too much. I was really worried his pelvis was crushed. Those injures are very tricky to manage and are best done in a trauma center.

# Chapter 47

*Emergency Department*
*Krenshaw Medical Center*

After Joe and Azzie were safely on their way to different units in the same trauma center, I headed for Krenshaw. I was tempted to call to get an update on PC, but that would just pull staff away from more important duties. Angela was working along with Streeter. If PC had any chance, they would see that he got it.

I found Mom, Dad and Stephanie in the family room. I moved them to my office, which was a bit more comfortable and secluded. Stephanie was wailing. Dad was pacing, and Mom was praying. I quickly emailed Father Jonathan in Rome with the bad news. We needed his prayers and a miracle.

My phone buzzed. It was Angela. She stopped resuscitation on PC and pronounced him dead at 2127. She was on her way back to the office to tell Stephanie and the rest of the family. I knew she called me as a courtesy. She would make the announcement. It was not up to me. I said nothing.

There was a knock on my office door. I opened it expecting Angela. Jenny and Billie were standing there. Billie looked white as a sheet and Jenny was bawling her eyes out. Jenny walked over to Stephanie, and they embraced. I signaled to Jenny to get Stephanie to sit down. Billie wrapped his arms around me and sobbed. Dad begged me to give Stephanie a tranquilizer.

I didn't like to use tranquilizers in grief situations. That just postponed the grief process. But without something, I was worried that Stephanie would totally lose control and possibly hurt herself. I dispatched Jenny to see Angela. She returned with a decent dose of Ativan that Stephanie agreed to take. Angela was right behind Jenny. She walked over to Stephanie and sat in a chair facing her. I had done this a thousand times. It was difficult, to say the least.

Our emergency medicine training had focused on these types of discussions. It was an unfortunate component of the job but an important part. Studies have shown that families recalled words from these conversations years later. The words had to be comforting but realistic. Things were not going to be all right. A loved one had died, and that was going to hurt. Lives would be changed forever from this moment forward.

The best advice that I had been given was to sit or somehow get at eye level with the closest next of kin. There was some debate as to how much discussion you should have before disclosing that the patient had passed on. I never was fond of walking in and introducing myself and saying immediately that their loved one was dead.

For example, "I am Dr. Zander. I am sorry to inform you that your husband has died."

But it was equally wrong to let too much time transpire. Families were waiting for the bad news. If they didn't hear it rather soon, they assumed there was a better outcome, such as in the next scenario.

"I am Dr. Zander. Mr. Smith collapsed at home and was initially treated by the medics at the scene. They first secured an airway by placing a tube in his trachea. Then, they got an intravenous line in and gave him the appropriate drugs. They shocked him numerous times en route to the ER. When he arrived in the ER, we added more drugs and worked diligently to restore a functional heartbeat…."

By now, families were thinking that all was well. After all, why go into all that detail?

My style was to give a little history as to what happened or to recognize the efforts of family or bystanders and then deliver the bad news. I had been one of Angela's attendings, and she had adopted many of my methods.

"Mrs. Stevens", Angela said quietly as she took both of Stephanie's hands into hers. "I am Dr. Angela Morris. I understand that you and your father did CPR on PC." (I had clued her in to call him that, Stephanie called him nothing but that.). "You two gave him the best chance he had at survival. When he got here, our staff gave him drugs and used other methods in an attempt to start his heart. We did all we could, but his injuries were too great. PC passed away at 9:27 PM ."

Stephanie screamed and cried. Even though we all suspected that he had died, we joined in the wailing. Angela didn't cry. But she held Stephanie in a tight hug. After a minute or so, she backed away so the rest of us could hold her. The screaming and crying continued.

Angela waited. She could have walked out, knowing that I would take things from here. But she was a true professional. She knew I was grieving as much as my family. She was there to support all of us, including me. I really appreciated that. When the outcries settled down a little, Angela took up her position beside Stephanie.

"Based upon what I learned about the accident, I am confident that PC lost consciousness immediately. Therefore, I don't think he suffered in any way. I hope in time that will give you some peace." She paused.

"Is there anything that I can do for you, Mrs. Stevens, or any family or friends?"

"I wanna see him." Stephanie blurted out amongst sobs.

Dad was quick to respond. "Stephanie, that may not be a good idea."

I put my hand on Dad's shoulder. "Dad, I appreciate your opinion, but it is Stephanie's call."

Angela took control. "Mr. Zander, I understand your thinking. But we have learned over the years that this is a process. For people who want to begin the process in the ER, we like to accommodate them."

Angela turned to face Stephanie. "Stephanie, we will take you into the resuscitation room. Please know that PC will have tubes and lines in him. We cannot remove those until the coroner gives us permission. As you know, he was badly burned. Be ready for how that is likely to look. I will accompany all of you. But Stephanie, for now, I would like you to go by wheelchair if you don't mind."

I really didn't think it was a good idea, but I knew it was part of the process. I had seen thousands of dead people, but none of them were good friends and my brother-in-law. I put Stephanie in a wheelchair and led the sad procession into Resuscitation Room 2. It was a large room with tons of equipment. It was usually quite noisy, but today, it was eerily silent.

The floor was littered with trash. Empty boxes of resuscitation equipment that had been used in futility were strewn about. Packaging for drugs that had been expended in an attempt to restore a heartbeat covered the floor. Burnt clothing that had been cut from the victim and 15 to 20 feet of EKG rhythm paper sat in a heap at the bottom of the stretcher. I noticed that there was no rhythm on any of it. Pure flatline.

On the gurney lay PC. What was left of him. His body was a charred remnant of a handsome young man. The staff had been able to close his eyelids, concealing the congealed objects that had once been his eyes. The smell of burnt flesh was overwhelming. It dominated the odor control spray that the staff had been kind enough to utilize. There was a sheet over his body that stopped at his neck. An endotracheal tube protruded from his mouth. Hair and eyebrows were black stubble.

Angela stood at the side of the gurney. I wheeled Stephanie there. Angela took PC's hand and placed it in Stephanie's. She got down on one knee in front of Stephanie and held her as Stephanie gripped the burnt remnant of PC's hand.

I surveyed the room. Dad and Mom stood beside Stephanie. They did their best to look away from PC's body. Jenny was visibly upset. She sobbed and looked down at the floor while drying her nose with already soaked Kleenex. Billie had his arm around her. She was at least four inches taller than he was. She was standing in between Billie and me. She partially obscured my view of his face. I noticed that Billie's color had improved remarkably. I also observed that Billie was the only one in the room looking over what was visible of the charred corpse of PC. I moved to get a better look at Billie. I could have sworn that he had a smirk on his face. Nah, couldn't be. Angela's voice brought me back to reality.

"When the coroner is done, he will release PC to your funeral director. Do your best to get as much rest as you can. The next few days will be long and tiresome. But I know you will want to say goodbye in your own way. You have a tremendous family. Don't be afraid to lean on them for support. You also have several therapists. Over time, I want you to pour your heart out to them. I am so sorry for your loss. Is there anything else I can do for you or any of you?"

Stephanie shook her head and said nothing. It would be months before she would utter more than a few words at a time.

Angela stood and addressed me. "ZZ, feel free to stay as long as you like."

I walked over and hugged her. I had a reputation of being hard on my residents. Tonight, I saw a true professional in action, and I was pleased that I may have played a small part in her development. I was thankful that Angela was working tonight. It was the only thing about the night that was good.

# Chapter 48

***Route 28***

***Krenshaw, NJ***

Jenny sobbed most of the way home. Billie worked hard to suppress a grin. What a stroke of brilliance and great luck. PC was out of the game; he was toast. Billie giggled at that thought. Azzie and Joe are on injured reserve and will be useless for some time. Mom and Dad Zander will be busy babysitting that asshole Stephanie. She will be a real basket case for quite a while.

Who would have figured that PC would be so kind as to cash his chips? He was not part of the plan. Sometimes, you get lucky. Bille was almost sorry that he gave Rio the abortion pills. He did that to distract Stephanie. Oh well, she'll get two surprises for the price of one. ZZ got his first taste of things to come with Bella's death. But it was time to turn up the heat on ZZ, Santucci, and Krenshaw Medical Center. Never becomes now.

His attention turned to Jenny. Could she be a valuable partner in crime? The sex had been great, but could she be more useful in the future? After all, she did shoot that guy in Florida right in the nuts. That had to hurt. He never got the whole story, but he knew that she had been having an affair with a guy who she thought was single. He was in Florida for a long work assignment. Billie heard that when Jenny found out that he was married, she got drunk and shot him in a delicate spot. He died. Jenny got off from that murder with some lame story about him abusing her.

Billie knew that she also attempted to kill me with a staged heroin overdose. How I came to forgive her baffled Billie. He chocked it up to me being a wimp. But all things considered, she just might be the perfect woman for him. Except. Except that Billie suspected she still had a thing for me. To bring her fully into his business would allow him to get closer to me than otherwise possible. That could be helpful for Billie. But if Jenny was still wet in the pants for me, she could ruin the whole thing. Billie concluded that it was too risky for now.

### Emergency Department

It took a lot of convincing to get Stephanie to let go of PC's burnt hand. But after an hour, Dad asked me for my opinion. I thought it was time to go. Although I wanted to push her out in the wheelchair, she stood, kissed the blackened forehead of PC, and walked out to the car. I was going to accompany them home, but Mom and Dad felt that there was little that I could do there. They would try to get her to bed. I knew they were right, and I knew that my time was better spent at the trauma center.

As I began the hour's drive there, I tried to make sense of what had just occurred. My thoughts were interrupted by my cell phone singing "On Eagles Wings." Father Jonathan was calling.

"ZZ, I am so sorry to hear that there was an accident. Is PC ok?"

"Father, as we speak, PC is meeting with St Peter and hoping to get his admission ticket to paradise. PC was pronounced dead at 927 PM our time."

Father Jonathan said nothing for 15 seconds. I thought the connection had been lost.

"May God have mercy on his soul. ZZ, what happened?"

I explained to him about the helicopter accident.

"What was the bright light?"

"Can't be sure. Could have been a headlight or something else. The police are looking for evidence that someone used a laser. There were reports of some juveniles playing around with one in the next county."

Father Jonathan sighed. "ZZ that had to be difficult for you to see PC's accident."

"You better believe that. The sight will haunt me forever. I could see what was going to happen, and I was powerless to prevent it. I was able to warn my parents and Stephanie about the downed line, but PC never heard me. He was focused on helping the victims. He died a hero."

"ZZ, I know I need to be there with you and your family, but I can't leave right now."

"Father, that is totally understandable. As you know, there will be no shortage of people to help and offer condolences for the next few weeks. But after that, things die down, and that is when help is the most beneficial. Azzie and Joe will be hospitalized for quite a while. Whenever you can make it home will be fine."

I gave him as much information as I could about Azzie and Joe. We agreed to communicate daily, but he would have to call or email me. He was not permitted anything but emergency calls. He was going to pray, and I continued to the trauma center.

# Chapter 49

## *Mid-State Trauma Center*
## *Youngwood, NJ*

Mid-State Trauma was a level-one facility. It also had a separate burn unit. I had been there for a few in-services and certifications, but I really didn't know my way around.

On arrival, I stopped at the security hut. I explained my purpose and showed my credentials to the guard. He advised me that I would be put through a metal detector at the entrance to the hospital and that weapons of all types were prohibited. He also advised me that I was welcome to park in the physician's lot. That was nice for two reasons. It was closer, and it was better lit. Trauma centers are often located in not-so-great neighborhoods. Nice cars and trucks had a habit of disappearing.

I cleared security and checked in at the burn center. I signed the guest register and handed it back to the volunteer manning the desk. She handed me a few papers detailing the hours of the unit, dress code, and other rules that I was to follow. Normally I would have made some smart-ass remark, but my brain was fresh out of smart-ass. I sat down and read the papers.

Ten minutes later, a nurse appeared. Azzie wanted to see me as soon as possible. The nurse directed me to a dressing room. I applied a gown, cap, face mask, and booties, followed by a very thorough hand washing. One of the biggest risks facing burn patients was infection. I had to do my part not to infect Azzie.

The nurse began her spiel about the unit and burns in general, and then she stopped. "I'm sorry. Ms. Huggins told me you are an ER doc. I didn't mean to talk down to you. I am used to briefing laypeople on their way in."

"No need for an apology. Once I fly burn patients from my ER, I have very little idea how they are handled. Anything you can tell me to make things better or easier for Azzie is fair game.'"

"Azzie, I thought her name was Azquela?"

"It is, but her friends call her Azzie."

"She has been asking a lot about Joe. Are they close?"

"They pretend they aren't, but the whole world can see they are stuck on each other. How is Joe?"

"Technically, I should say nothing. Stupid HIPPA law, but I will tell you what little I know. Being a doc and all, I know you understand. He is in critical condition. He has a badly fractured pelvis, and they are having a difficult time maintaining his blood pressure."

"That makes sense with what I saw at the scene of the accident. Does Azzie have any other injuries?"

"Azzie did put you on her HIPPA list, so I can give you the rundown. But Dr. Scarlotta, the trauma surgeon, is with her now and has agreed to allow you in. I'll be happy to answer any questions you have later, but I don't want to hold him up."

We began our walk to the unit. The nurse was curious.

"What does she do for a living? She asks great questions and appears so organized. Things don't seem to faze her."

"Did you ever hear of Exquisite Evolutions?"

She nodded. "Who hasn't? I just have the hospital direct deposit my paycheck there. They send me back the balance of what I don't spend each month."

"That's funny. Azzie is the CEO of Exquisite Evolutions."

"Oh wow! I have heard her name, but everyone knows her face. Most of her face has been in bandages, so I didn't put two and two together."

I had to ask. "Is her neck ok?"

We arrived at the door to the room before she could answer. When she opened the door, the reality of the situation hit me. There on the bed lay a tall and thin body. A foley catheter was draining yellow urine into a half-full bag. Her neck was immobilized in a hard collar. Her arm was in a splint. But she was a mummy. There had to be hundreds of feet of dressings. She had two slits for eyes, a small opening for the tip of her nose, and a slightly larger opening for her mouth. I didn't mean to, but I had ignored the surgeon standing at her bedside. I finally offered my hand.

"Dr. Scarlotta, I am Zachary Zander.

"You're the guy that sent me the Fournier's gangrene, right?"

I was impressed. I have a hard time remembering the doctors on my own staff. "Yeah, that was a while ago."

He continued. "I was hoping to meet you. You made a great call. The stabilization and immediate medication interventions your staff performed made a huge difference. The patient not only survived but he did very well. It took us three months and five surgeries, but he made it. He is walking and talking thanks in no part to you and your staff."

"You humble me, sir. I appreciate the feedback. What's the story on my good friend Azzie?"

Dr. Scarlotta was happy to explain everything to both Azzie and me. He and I got closer to her head so she could hear better.

"Right now, the biggest threats to life are the pulmonary contusion and infection. As you know lung contusions can go sour quickly. Pneumothorax (Collapsed lung), tension pneumothorax (collapsed lung under pressure), etc. But with our monitoring, we won't get surprised. If she deteriorates, we will do what we must. Regardless, she should recover from that.

The arm fracture will be painful for a while but should heal nicely. She has a fracture of C3. (One of the neck vertebrae.) Despite the fracture, her neck must not have been manipulated too violently. She has a mild spinal cord contusion that should clear itself. She will need surgery to stabilize her neck for the future, but I think she will tolerate that well."

I was relieved. I was worried that I had doomed her to a wheelchair when I pulled her from the wreck.

I had to ask. "What about her burns? Azzie is the CEO of a large cosmetic company. Her facial appearance is critical."

Before he could answer, Azzie spoke up. "Dr. Scarlotta, thank you for saving my life. I am extremely grateful. But as ZZ says."

"ZZ?"

I answered him. "Oh, that's me. Everyone calls me ZZ, and please do the same."

Azzie continued, although her voice was weak. "As ZZ says, I run a large and prosperous company. My appearance has been important to our branding and success. What is the extent of my burns, and what is in store for me?"

"One of the ER nurses told me about your company. Apparently, they all use your products and swear by them."

He sat down beside her bed to better address her. I remained standing as there was only one chair.

"It appears that most of the scalp, neck, and chest are partial thickness burns (second degree), about 27% of your body surface area. We have you on the Parkland formula for fluids, and so far, your blood pressure is stable, and your urine output is acceptable."

I interrupted. "What about her forehead? I only got a quick look, but it appeared to be worse than partial thickness."

"Pretty good for an ER guy. Her forehead and half of her scalp appear to be full thickness (third-degree burns). Very likely, she will need skin grafting. Her hair will never be the same, but the skin grafts on her forehead should do very well. Being tight over bone, they usually don't scar up and contract."

"And???" Azzie was bracing herself for more.

"The partial thickness burns should heal with minimal scarring. We will do our best to keep it minimal. But there will be scarring."

Azzie had tears in her eyes. "Thanks for the information. I now have facts."

I asked, "How long until the extent of all burns is known?"

"About three weeks, it will take about six months for you to see your final appearance. Any other questions?"

He shook both of our hands and left the room. The nurse requested that I stay only a few more minutes. Azzie appeared to have fallen asleep. I kissed her hand and prepared to exit when she woke and spoke.

"ZZ, what happened? I know the helicopter crashed and that Joe and I were brought here, but that is all they have been able to tell me. How is Joe?"

"Azzie, I know as much about Joe as you do. I came to your unit first because I heard that they were still working on Joe, and I might not be able to see him. I know at a minimum that he has a badly broken pelvis and is still in shock."

"And the pilot?"

"He didn't make it."

"God rest his soul. Thank God no one else was injured. We just passed the school."

"Azzie, I have some bad news."

"I thought you said Joe was still alive! Did he die, did everyone lie to me? I can't do without that dumb dago."

"No, Azzie, Joe is in the grease right now but still alive. Do you really think God wants him back yet?"

"Ok, if Joe is here, what else don't I know?"

"PC was the first on scene. When your chopper crashed, it cut a high-voltage power line that came to rest on the metal fuselage. I was on the ATV and screaming for him to avoid the wire, but he never heard me. The fire in the chopper was worsening every second, and he ran to get you victims out. He grabbed the chopper door and was immediately electrocuted. He was taken to the hospital, but he never had a chance. He died."

Azzie gasped and cried. After a few minutes, she said barely audibly. "Poor Stephanie. How will she even cope with this?"

"She won't for a while. No one knows how long. We must get her through the funeral and then see what we can do. Are you in pain?"

"Boom, boom, boom, as Joe would say, but this PCA (patient-controlled analgesia) pump helps a ton. Sometimes, I just want to hold the button down."

"You know it locks out after a certain dose."

"Yeah, spoilsports. My neck is broken, and that is painful, but I know I am lucky to not be paralyzed in some fashion. My chest hurts like hell, and they tell me that is normal for my injuries there. The rest of me feels like someone beat the hell out of me. I can deal with all of that. But ZZ, the burns are another matter."

"You are in one the best burn centers in the country."

"I know, and that is comforting. What is not comforting is that I am likely to be disfigured. I choose to think that I am not vain, but no woman wants to be less than attractive. You know I never go out in public unless I am made up to the nines. That's what Exquisite Evolutions sells, the nines. So, if I end up looking damaged or otherwise imperfect, it will hurt the company. My CFO already called. The stock is likely to be down 15% tomorrow based on my injuries and questions about my appearance."

I had to try to console her. "Your beauty far exceeds your skin depth. Let's take this one step at a time. Let's get our information together, and then we can make our plans."

"OK, for now, ZZ. Please go to Joe. I need that fireplug alive and well. Make sure they don't screw up."

"I thank you for your confidence, but I assure you they know more about what they are doing than I do."

"You know what I mean. You are a dominate force. You don't let bad things happen. Go to Joe. He needs to see that you are on the case. He needs you to tell him that I am ok. He needs to hear that from you. He needs to see you. Just seeing you has helped me get a little stronger and more determined to beat this thing."

I kissed her hand again and made my way to the trauma ICU.

# Chapter 50

*Trauma Unit*

*Mid-State Trauma Center*

After announcing that I wanted to see Joe, I sat in the waiting room for what seemed like an eternity. The sun was coming up. I briefly dosed off but woke up when someone shook my arm.

"Dr. Zander?"

"Yes, sorry I fell asleep."

"No problem. My name is Rex. I am Mr. Crinelli's nurse. Sorry you had to wait so long. He was in surgery for quite a while and recovery for a few hours longer."

"How is he?"

"He is a wise ass."

"That's my boy!" This is a smart nurse. Most of them are, but he appeared to be ahead of the curve.

"Right now, he appears stable. His pressure is around 100. That is the best it has been. He received over 40 units of blood, some plasma, platelets, and clotting factors. He is lucky to be in a hospital that has a massive transfusion protocol. Our pathologist and blood bank people worked through the night to assist."

I had heard about it, but I never worked in a hospital that had a massive transfusion protocol. A lot of doctors and most people think that if you just put in as much blood as comes out, you should be good. Like all of medicine, things are more complicated than that. When people bleed that rapidly, and you replace their blood, things change. Clotting factors and platelets specifically. Trained blood bank pathologists and experts can significantly improve outcomes in those cases.

In sophisticated specialty institutions, they have developed protocols to assist in the resuscitation of patients with severe hemorrhages. The difference is that in these places, the pathologist and other professionals come in and manage each case individually and in real-time. Joe got the ultimate treatment.

The nurse interrupted my thoughts. “His pelvis is badly fractured. As you know, they can bleed terribly. The surgeons did an external fixation on his pelvis, but that did not sufficiently stop the bleeding. They took him back to the OR and did an embolization procedure.”

“I’m an ER doc; you have to help with the fancy procedure jargon. I’ve heard of embolization but not in pelvic trauma.”

“In cases of severe pelvic trauma, and Mr. Crinelli is clearly in that group, the bleeding may be quite severe and difficult to control. In his case, they tried to put wires in his pelvis first to stabilize it. When that didn’t work, they got a catheter into one of his pelvic arteries and injected some gelatin sponges into the artery. It appears that was effective in stopping the bleeding.

My worst fears had come true. “Thank you for the update. I hope to catch up with his surgeons at some point.”

“Well, you are in luck. They are at his bedside. They didn’t want him to have any visitors yet. But he refuses to answer any questions or cooperate with them unless they let you in.”

“Joe can be convincing.”

“And stubborn. Anyway, please wash your hands and follow me.”

Two exhausted-looking surgeons waited at the bedside. As I approached the bed, I first noted empty bags of blood hanging from an IV pole. One of Joe’s arms was in a cast. He flipped me off with his free hand. He had sweat dripping from his brow onto his scarred face.

I was sad to see bilateral black eyes that were moderately swollen. His pelvis was a mass of long metal pins that stuck out from his body at odd angles. They were connected with wires that ran in various directions. He looked more like an antenna than a person. I was attempting to process what I saw when he spoke.

"Boom, boom, boom, my man is here! Can I go home now? Get my clothes. We can catch breakfast on the way back to Krenshaw!"

I had to show Joe that he wasn't the only smartass around. "Joe, can you get ESPN with your wire setup?"

"Screw me, how is Azzie??? These pricks won't tell me anything until she signs some stupid form."

It didn't take long for him to focus on her instead of himself.

"She is stable." I was so tired that I just broke down and cried. Through sobs, I explained everything to Joe.

"She has a broken neck, broken arm, a bad lung contusion, and multiple rib fractures." I paused to get my composure.

"She has burns over 25% of her body. Most are second-degree. But she has some third-degree burns over her scalp and forehead. Those will need skin grafts."

"She will be scarred and disfigured," Joe said as a matter of fact.

"We don't know that for sure."

"ZZ, save your bullshit for your patients. You and I both know I am right."

He addressed the surgeons who, to this point, had just watched and listened.

"OK, gentlemen, what can I do for you?" He asked of the astounded surgeons.

Dr. Gupta, the orthopedic surgeon, went first. "Mr. Crinelli…."

"Call me Joe."

"OK, Joe. You are the newest member of the lucky to be alive club."

"I don't feel so lucky."

"That makes sense. You were in a violent accident and were badly injured. Your pelvis has been destroyed. We fought an all-night battle to stop the bleeding, and it appears (he crossed his fingers) that we might have been successful."

Joe wanted answers. "Ok, so I am not assuming room temperature just yet. Where do we go from here?"

"I would guess that you want the short version?"

"Yeah, I've got a soccer game in 30 minutes, and I have to warm up."

I had to love his sense of humor. I wasn't sure how the tired surgeons would take it. I was surprised.

"Now that is funny. You seem like a guy that wants it straight."

"You bet. If you give me any bullshit, I promise you that I will get up and beat the living hell out of you." Even as incapacitated as he was, Joe was still intimidating.

"Well, let's avoid that. We put external fixators in your pelvis to try to get as much 'normal' as possible back into the alignment. But…"

Joe pounced. "Here the hell it comes, the big but."

Gupta continued, "But it is unlikely that you will walk again."

Joe never flinched. "So, what else?"

Gupta paused for a few seconds and looked at the floor. "You may be impotent."

Joe glanced down at his groin, "My soldier may never be able to salute again?"

(I had to explain what he meant to the surgeons.)

Gupta was honest. "We don't know."

Joe summed it up. “Well, that sucks. No one needs to walk, but everyone needs to get laid.”

I tried to refocus him. “It ain’t over until it’s over. With you, that is never. So how about we sleep on this and see what tomorrow holds?”

I was encouraged but not surprised at his reply. “Boom, boom, boom, Azzie needs me. I have to hang on.”

The surgeons requested that I stay only a few more minutes, and I agreed. They left, and I grabbed Joe’s good hand.

“What is it, what didn’t you tell me about Azzie?” The same accusation she had given me.

“You are up to date on Azzie. But there were two deaths.”

Joe asked. “Two? I heard about the pilot. Poor guy. Who else? Did the chopper hit someone? Not one of the kids!”

“No, the school was fine,” I explained about PC.

Joe said nothing for a full minute. Then I saw something I had never seen before. He bawled like a baby. I hugged what I could of him until he stopped.

“I remember you introducing me to him. I can sum him up in two words ZZ, class act, class act. I was so happy that he and Stephanie hooked up. They were made for each other, and they seemed happy. He died trying to help Azzie and me. What a shame.”

He said nothing more for a full minute.

“How’s my little girl Stephanie?”

“Bad Joe, bad. I fear this will really set her back, perhaps permanently.”

He started to speak, but he only mumbled a few words. Instantly, he was fast asleep. I quietly left the room and headed home. I hadn’t slept in 28 hours, and I was beat.

# Chapter 51

## *Fired Up Farms*

"Hey, Dad, how is Stephanie?"

"Pretty much comatose. Won't speak, and she appears to be sleeping most of the time."

"That's about right for her. When she gets too much bad information, her brain just shuts down and takes her with it."

Dad nodded. He looked just as tired as I was. No one got any sleep since the accident. "How long until we get worried?"

"My guess is that she will get through the funeral and then watch out."

Dad had his head down. "There is another complicating factor."

That's not what I wanted to hear. But I had to.

"What else can go wrong?"

"Rio aborted her colt."

That hit me like a ton of bricks. Not because the colt was estimated to be worth two million when he hit the earth. Not because it was Rio's first foal, and the harness world was anxiously awaiting the foaling. This was another bad blow for Stephanie.

She and Rio were like sisters. Tough to do that when you are from a different species, but they were super tight. She was Stephanie's maid of honor. I am pretty sure that they communicated on another level, not visible to most. Stephanie was ecstatic when Rio got into foal. She had begun to make plans for a "foal shower" for Rio as she got closer to delivery. I wasn't sure if she was inviting people, or horses, or both.

Since her engagement to and subsequent marriage to PC, I worried a lot less about Stephanie. I always knew she was brilliant, but I also knew that she often lacked street smarts. PC filled in her knowledge gaps quite nicely. If I had to let her go, I was happy it was someone like PC who was getting her. He loved her and would cherish her all the days of his life. Those days were now over. Life can be so cruel.

I had so much to do and so little time. But the first thing that had to get my attention was PC's funeral. Dad had asked me to arrange it. Stephanie wasn't capable, and PC had no other living relatives. He had been adopted, and his adoptive parents had both passed away, kind of like Bella.

I phoned Juicy Lucy, and she was sobbing. The whole hospital was in mourning. She had cancelled my meetings for the week and got me off all shifts in the ED. She said she would see me at the funeral and offered to do anything she could to assist. Finally, she asked me to phone Dan at my convenience. My convenience would be about 25 years from now. But since Dan was a good friend, I moved the call up 25 years.

"Hello ZZ, how are you?"

"Tired and flat-out depressed Dan. My life has gone to hell."

"I am so sorry to hear about PC. He was an outstanding person. I was happy to have become his friend. I also am sorry to hear about Azzie and Joe."

"Thanks, Dan, PC was special, and he meant the world to Stephanie."

"How is she?"

"Pretty bad as expected. She won't speak but is still functional. I think she will prop herself up until the funeral is over. There is also another complication. Rio aborted her colt. Stephanie will have a hard time with that, too. I honestly don't know what will happen in the next few weeks."

"Ahh, that is terrible. Can I do anything to help?"

"Dan, there's more. Bella is dead."

Dan was incredulous. "Where, how? Oh, ZZ, I am devastated. I sensed you two were getting closer."

"Thanks, Dan. I am having a hard time getting my head around all of this."

I explained what I knew about Bella's demise.

"How can I help?"

"Will you meet me at Lakeview Funeral Home? I have to make the arrangements for PC. I will fill you in on Joe and Azzie then."

"Sure, what time?"

"11 AM, I am going to grab a few hours' sleep."

"Maybe we can get some lunch after we are done. I hate to, but I really should update you on hospital business."

# Chapter 52

## *Lakeview Funeral Home*
## *Krenshaw, NJ*

The funeral home was light and airy, but it still was a death dungeon to me. The funeral director, Larry, was a friend, and that helped. But friendship only goes so far. As I walked through the casket room, the sheer horror of the reality that I was facing became suddenly apparent. PC, my good friend and brother-in-law, was dead. My sister's life was destroyed. Bella had been eaten by sharks, and two of my best friends were in critical condition.

Dan helped me to focus.

"ZZ, we have to get through this. You gotta do it for Stephanie."

"Ok" was all that I could offer.

Larry took over, speaking slowly and deliberately in a calming tone. "ZZ, I know this is not easy. We need to select a casket, burial vault, and a place for interment for Johnson."

"Please call him PC."

"Sure, we need to make selections for PC's interment. After that we need to plan for the service."

Dan and Larry were looking over some mahogany caskets. I gave them the time-out sign and waved for them to join me in the corner of the room.

"PC was not a pretentious person. Neither is Stephanie. He would want something simple, sturdy, and not pretentious. Mahogany is pretentious."

Larry, being an experienced funeral director, took that in stride. "Maybe something in stainless steel?"

"More like it."

We settled on a blue stainless steel coffin. The burial vault was standard. But where was he to be interred?

"Perpetual Memory is the best choice, as I can see," offered Larry.

I voiced the request that Stephanie had made of me when we were in the treatment room with PC's Body. I had no idea about the legality or steps to take, but I had to ask the question.

"Can he be buried at our farm?"

Larry shook his head. "Not very likely, the rules are incredibly strict."

Dan knew that I wanted to pursue it further. Although he was an attorney, he had no idea about laws on burials. "For the sake of discussion, what would it take to do that?"

Larry sounded very skeptical. "DEP (Department of Environmental Protection), approval. That is almost never granted."

I stepped outside and dialed.

"Governor, sorry to bother you. Also sorry about the wedding. I know I shouldn't ask, but I need a favor." I began to tell him about the accident, but he already knew most of the details.

"Look ZZ. The wedding was a disaster and may cause me to lose an election. But the day I start worrying about that stuff and ignoring what people need will mark my descent into hell. What can I do to help?"

I explained about the burial at the farm. He surprised me.

"There are some regulations. For example, the acreage of the property to house the cemetery has to meet a minimum. I can't recall exactly what that figure is. There can be no zoning issues, and there would be some restrictions on selling the property. I will have the head of my DEP contact your funeral director and guide him through the process. Text me his contact information. But ZZ, if you don't meet the criteria, there is nothing I can do."

"I understand, Governor."

He asked the question of the day. "Anything for Stephanie, how is she?"

"Terrible and about to get worse."

He was sympathetic. "I can imagine. ZZ, I would normally attend the funeral, but I don't think now would be a good time. I hope you understand."

"Of course, governor. I appreciate your help. How are the polls?"

"This goes no further, but our best internal polls show me down four points. Social media will not let go of the incident at Stephanie's wedding, and my opponent takes every opportunity to tell people that I crapped on NJ."

"Well, governor, when I get things straightened out here, I will do all I can to help you. Can my family make a campaign donation?"

The governor gasped. "NOOOO, please don't. At least yet. There is scrutiny of everything I do. If the farm burial is approved, I can just hear the quid pro quos when your family makes a donation."

"Right."

"Have Dan or Tina send me a weekly update on the hospital. There is a lot of behind-the-scenes activity by the thoroughbred people. I hear rumors that they may team up with the teachers' unions. They are banking on the hospital closing. Have you had dealings with MEP Legal Associates?"

"Oh yeah, pricks of misery, all of them. I call them Make Em' Pay."

"I hear that Thaddeus Prinzmetal, the founder of the firm, is itching to have thoroughbreds race at Miracle Mile. Watch your back."

"Yes, sir."

I stepped back into the coffin room.

I explained to Larry that he would hear from the head of DEP.

"OK, if they approve it, I will give you the details and the requirements for the home cemetery. If they don't?"

"In that case, proceed with purchasing plots at Perpetual Memory. If you do that, get four. One for PC, Stephanie, Mom, and Dad."

"What about the viewing? I must insist on a closed casket. I have examined PC, and there is little I can do to make him presentable."

We discussed the details of a video tribute to PC to be used at the gathering. Larry shared with me a template for creating an obituary. He wanted that completed as soon as I could.

He had two final questions. "How many papers do you want it in?"

"Just the Krenshaw Daily. Also, send it to the US Trotting Association. I will get you their contact information."

He made some notes. "Today is Monday. When did you want to have the service?"

I thought for a minute. There was no great hurry. "Friday or Saturday. I will get back to you on that."

I wanted to give the governor time to work his magic. Plus, we needed some time to get Stephanie ready. Also, until Joe and Azzie were out of the woods, I would be making quite a few trips to Mid-State.

Larry made more notes. "I would assume that the closed casket memorial will be here. How about the service?"

"Guess again, Larry!" He looked nervous as I laid out what I had in mind. "I will call you later if I am successful in making those arrangements."

"Oh wow. I have a feeling that this will be one for the record books." Larry gave me a list of things that needed to be decided for the service, clothes to be brought to put on the PC, etc.

"OK, I will have this and the obituary back to you tomorrow."

Dan and I adjourned to The Lamplighter for lunch. I really wanted to have a liquid lunch at the Daily Double, but I needed to keep a clear head.

# Chapter 53

***Lamplighter Restaurant***
***Krenshaw, NJ***

Dan stared across the table. "You look bad."

"I feel like shit. I slept about two out of the last thirty hours, and I feel like I am stuck in a nightmare."

"That's because you are. Your best friend was electrocuted, and although you saw it, there was nothing you could do. Your sister has regressed to a near-vegetative state. Your girlfriend dies tragically. What's the story on Joe and Azzie?" Dan asked as he sipped his coffee.

"Joe nearly died. The trauma team did a heroic job. He will likely survive. Unfortunately, he may never walk again, and he might be impotent."

"Wow, that's terrible."

I gave him a full rundown on Azzie's injuries and likely disfigurement.

Dan took another sip of coffee. "That's a shame. She built that company from scratch. Hopefully, she can recover enough for it not to be an issue."

"Time will tell."

I placed a quick call to Aldo while we waited for our food. I really wasn't hungry.

"Mr. Crinelli, this is ZZ."

"Oh, ZZ, thank you for calling. I have been worried sick about Guiseppe. I called that hospital, but those cocksuckers won't tell me stugots over the phone. I am going out there this afternoon. How is he?"

I recapped Joe's injuries and likely prognosis. I knew Joe would want him to know.

"Make sure he has the best doctors. Expense is no object."

"Mr. Crinelli, I assure you he is in the right place and has the right people taking care of him. The best."

"What can you tell me about the light that was seen going into the helicopter before it crashed?"

Wow, he had good information. I told him what I knew.

"Not much. The last I heard, the police suspected some kids playing with a laser."

"OK my turn to fill you in. The pilot's retinas were burnt with that laser."

I hadn't heard that. Shortly after something like this, opinions are rampant, but facts are few. I replied, "That's a wild speculation."

"Who's gonna win the next Super Bowl is a speculation, what I told you is a fact. I got some juice in the medical examiner's office. They just finished the autopsy."

I was impressed. "That will give the police some incentive to dig."

Aldo was skeptical. "Not that I don't trust the police, but I got two dozen soldiers on the street sifting for information. They have $100,000 to give the persons or person who fingers the prick that did this."

"Will you turn them over to the police?" I knew that was a mistake the second I asked.

"ZZ, you know better than to want specifics. I appreciate what you have done and will do for Guiseppe. What's the deal on his melanzana girlfriend."

I recognized the Italian word for eggplant. In this case, it was a racial slur. I knew Aldo wasn't a racist. But I also knew that he wanted Joe to marry a nice Italian girl and have many pure Italian grandbabies. Anything other than an Italian girl was second best. I filled him in on

Azzie's injuries. He was sympathetic. I knew he liked Azzie even though she wasn't Italian.

"ZZ, I mean this. You call me if there is something that needs to be done that you can't figure out how to do it." That was a convoluted way of saying, "If you need something done that is less than legal, call me."

Aldo was down for the struggle. I would not want to be up against him.

My Reuben sandwich appeared. I took a small bite. I played with more of my french fries than what I ate.

Dan decided to move things along. "Here is where we stand on investigations, surveys and lawsuits."

Tina had made an executive summary that was a work of art. Short and to the point. I digested it along with a couple fries smothered in ketchup. Of course, I got some of the ketchup on my shirt.

Dan handed me his napkin. Mine was on the floor. "ZZ, when we are done here, you need to get some rest. You are too important to everyone. We need you sharp."

"Thanks, Dan. I am beat, but I want to finish the plans."

Dan's mind was made up. "I will take care of those with your parents. You only need to get the permission for the service and do the obituary."

I arrived at the farm just as a Blue Toyota Tundra with a six-horse carrier backed into position to unload. Before I knew it, I was ensnared in a bear hug.

"Hey, Bud. Sorry to hear about PC. How is Stephanie? Joe and Azzie?"

"Timmy Dunstan, what are you doing here?"

A voice from the truck answered, "Someone had to keep me awake."

I turned to see my old friend, Dave Dunstan, getting out of the truck. We struck up a friendship early on in my career. Dave was one of the top drivers at the Meadows. Although I hated seeing him in to drive against me on the racetrack, I enjoyed golfing and hanging out with him away from the track.

Dave was not a large man but an important one. He carried himself with distinction even though he had not one ounce of narcissism in his body. He had the reputation of being the most honest driver and trainer in harness racing. No one else came close. He had on his trademark Dunstan Stable hat. He hadn't shaven but otherwise looked great. He gave me a big hug.

"ZZ, our hearts are broken. We are so sorry for your loss and for Stephanie. As soon as Mom got wind of what had happened, she woke Timmy and me. You know, Mom. No BS. She rattled off what we had to do, and we did it. Here we are."

"That lady is too much," I said. Shirley is the matriarch of the Dunstan family, the kindest, sweetest lady you could ever hope to meet. "So, what are her orders?"

"Timmy and I brought four horses that have special problems we were dealing with. She thought we could work on those out here and maybe race them if we get in. Chris is planning for the rest of our horses to be cared for this week. He and Mom will join us here when they can. We will take care of your horse operation this week. You and your parents have your plates full. We know all too well that no matter what, horses still need to eat and be jogged and trained. We got your back."

I tried hard to keep my composure. "Dave, I don't know what to say."

"Say nothing, Doc, say nothing. And before you get all fired up and try to arrange rooms for us, we are good. One of my owners has a place about ten miles away that is vacant this month. We will be staying there."

I just cried. Too much stuff to process. I lost it. After a few minutes I got myself together, and we went into the house. I gave Mom and Dad a short version of the funeral plans. Mom got up to make some sandwiches for the Dunstans, but Dave waved her off.

"We are fine. Timmy and I need to find out what you need done with the horses here and at the track. Tell me who you want entered to race. I know, Mr. Zander, that you have a training schedule listing all the horses and how fast you were planning on taking them this week. We will make it happen." He pulled out a notepad and sat down at the table.

Everyone demanded that I go to bed. I looked in the mirror, and I was shocked. My scar looked better than the rest of my face. I appeared at least twenty years older than my stated age. I trudged up the steps but did not go to my room.

I knocked softly on the door and went in. Stephanie was rocking on her chair facing the corner of her room. She clutched a fluffy horse that PC had given her for a wedding present. She did not turn around. I knew better than to try to touch her. When she was rocking like that, she would strike at anyone trying to get near her. I got as close to her chair as I safely could, and I started.

"Stephanie, I understand if you don't talk to me or stop rocking. You gotta do what you gotta do. I just want you to know that I made most of the arrangements for PC's memorial and burial."

I laid out the plans that I was trying to bring to fruition.

"I have the governor working on allowing us to have the burial here."

She shocked me when she stopped rocking and, stood up, and turned to me. Her eyes were beyond bloodshot. Fresh tears poured down her face and dripped from her chin. She made no attempt to dry them. She surprised me when she spoke.

"Rio's colt. He bury there too?"

"I will do my best."

She sat back down and started to rock violently.  I turned and headed for my room. I knew for sure that no human being had told her about the colt.

# Chapter 54

## *Fired Up Farms*

When I woke up, I felt more tired than when I had climbed into bed. I slithered into the shower and threw on some clothes. I peered into Stephanie's room, and her chair was still. She was asleep in the chair. I wished she was in bed, but at least she was getting some sleep. I wandered downstairs. Mom had church music on and was busy at the kitchen table sorting out pictures of PC and Stephanie.

"ZZ, why are you up? You only slept four hours. Go back to bed."

"Thanks Mom but I just can't sleep anymore. I feel better. I will feel much better after a coffee." I just lied, of course.

Dad appeared in the kitchen as Mom made coffee and some eggs that I never asked for.

I had to get up to speed. "What's happening?"

Dad sat down to fill me in. "The governor came through. We have permission to develop a home-family cemetery. No more than ten plots, and all interred there must be close relatives. I have a surveyor coming tomorrow to survey the site. Dan will file the necessary documents."

I sipped the coffee; it was great. "Where is it going to be?"

"Your mom and I thought the crash scene would be appropriate. What do you think?"

I liked the idea but doubted we could make it work. "Will the National Transportation Safety Board people be done and release the ground?"

"Yeah, they were reluctant to cooperate. But someone called them, and they decided they could be done in two days."

I suspected I knew who the caller was. "The governor?"

"Nah, Aldo."

I smiled. "Ah, should have known. Stephanie somehow knew about Rio's colt. She wants him buried in the family cemetery."

Dad shook his head. "The DEP was clear that only closely related humans could be buried there. No pets, no horses. How about the infield of the training track, on the far turn across from the school? We can make a nice place for the horses that we chose to bury here."

I thought that was reasonable. "I think Stephanie will be ok with it."

Dad asked further, "What about the rest of the plans?"

"Approved just as you requested. Bishop Carlucci agreed to say the funeral mass. What a great friend he has become. Was I in a fog or are the Dunstans here?"

Dad nodded. "No fog. You know them. Anything for anyone. Tim and Dave got here this morning. They went to the track and took care of the horses there. Chris and Shirely got here two hours ago, and they took care of the horses here. They refused to stay for dinner. They are in Low Plains at a home one of their owners' rents. They are planning on staying here at least this week and maybe longer if we need them."

I was incredulous. They don't make people like that. I wandered into the living room and called to check on Joe and Azzie. I was able to speak with Joe, but I wish I hadn't. He was screaming in pain and "mother-fing" everyone around him. I told him that I would be there in an hour or so. But he said that he didn't want any company. I knew he meant it.

Then I called Azzie's nurse. She reported that Azzie was stable, and her pulmonary problems never worsened. But Azzie demanded to see what she looked like when they changed her bandages. The nurse said that Azzie never said a word. But since that time, she will not take any calls or talk with anyone, including her nurses and doctors. Azzie knew I was going to call, and she asked that I respect her privacy. She did not want to talk to anyone. This was not good.

Maybe we all needed a little time to put things in perspective. I decided to stay home to finish the obituary and the plans. The obituary was difficult. I used the template, but the harsh reality of PC's demise became very real as the words hit the paper. Thank God Anne Marie agreed to write Bella's. I eventually pushed through it and called the track to check on my request.

"ZZ. What you are asking for has never been done."

I didn't want to hear that. "I am not sure that I am asking."

Frederick Vincete was the director of operations for the track. He was a great guy and a solid advocate for harness racing. Unfortunately, he reported to the CEO of the casino.

"My boss isn't sure that we ought to do this. He is worried about setting a precedent. This isn't something we want to do every week."

"Fred, I must respectfully request that you do as I ask. I am busting my ass to save the hospital so that the harness racing operation does not go under. I have never asked you for anything until now."

"But ZZ, you know that certain members of the board of directors want to dump harness racing here."

"Fred, time for you to take a side. Man up."

"OK, have a job ready for me when they fire my ass."

I knew we had plenty of stalls to muck here at the farm.

# Chapter 55

*Office of The Bishop*
*Diocese of Krenshaw*

"Bishop Carlucci, I sincerely appreciate your offering the funeral mass for PC. I know your time is very much in demand."

"Well Dr. Zander (the bishop refused to call me ZZ) I know how crushed you and your family are. If I can be of some service to Stephanie and your family, I am happy to do it. Can we start at 10 AM? I have a number of obligations Saturday."

"No problem your excellency. Can I inquire as to how Father Jonathan is doing with his sabbatical."

"Dr. Zander, you don't need to play games with me. Father Jonathan told me that he told you. He is not on a sabbatical."

"Sorry, Your Excellency. I am just worried about him."

"We all are. I think he has applied himself in the past months, and I hope that he continues to do so."

"I have been praying for him."

"Keep praying. He needs all the help he can get."

He was kind to enough to bless me before I left his office.

My phone buzzed on my way out. It was a text from Fred Vincente. "All good for Friday. Races 3-11 will be the PC Pick Nine Memorial. No takeout. You agreed to seeding $100,000."

If you don't know anything about racing you might think that the track was not allowing any take out food in honor of PC, and that I just bought $100,000 of seeds.  Wrong and wrong. We actually set up a bet to honor PC because he was so fond of betting. To win the bet you had to pick the winner of 9 consecutive races. That is almost impossible.

To make it more exciting, the track agreed not to take any money out of the pool. Say in a normal race, there is a $10000 total bet to win on all of the horses in the race. The track takes 17% of that for their expenses and purses, and the remaining $8300 is distributed to those who selected the winner of the race. For our Pick 9 wager, the track agreed not to take any money out. That means a much bigger payout and usually guarantees more interest on the part of the gamblers.

Our family agreed to add $100,000 to the pool. That will also increase the payout and pique the interest of the fans. All three things together equate to a big jackpot if there is a single winning ticket. PC will be firing it in from above!

I called Dad. "All set for Friday races 3-11. Get a hold of the Dunstans. Between them and us, I would like to have a horse in every race. I plan to win all nine races."

"Good plan, ZZ, but not likely to happen."

"I've won ten before on a card." I was a little indignant that he didn't think I could pull it off.

"I know that, but with us putting up $100,000 it might smell bad if you win enough races that someone cashes a big ticket. No matter who had the ticket, people would think that we fixed things. You can't drive."

"Yeah, I guess you're right. Billie would be the next logical person to drive, but he has that big race in Columbus Friday. That horse is a monster and looks to go far. I don't want to ask Billie to give that up."

"Why don't we put Dave Dunstan in the bike?" Dad asked.

"Think he would do it?"

"I know he would. I already asked him."

I wasn't sure, but I think I was just set up. "Then why let me go through all the BS."

"You had to get it out of your system."

I called JL and dictated to her the changes in the obituary that I wanted to make. I asked her to type it and send it to my email so I could proof it. If it was to appear in tomorrow's paper, it had to be in by noon. Ten minutes later, I opened the file.

Johnson Stevens, affectionately known as PC, age 35, died tragically while attempting to assist in the rescue of the victims of a helicopter crash. PC always put the needs of others above his own.

Born in Scranton, PA, PC lost both biological parents in an automobile accident when he was two. Ursula and Mason Higginbothom adopted and raised PC.

PC was a whiz with numbers. After graduating from Summit High School he attended Rutgers and received his degree in accounting. As a CPA, he founded a very successful accounting firm.

During college Johnson found part time employment at Miracle Mile Racetrack. He collected specimens for drug testing analysis as directed by the track stewards. PC was an ardent race fan and a superb handicapper. He claimed to have fallen in love with world renown harness driver, Stephanie Zander, because of her ability to bring long shots home. PC often said that he cashed the biggest ticket of his life when he married Stephanie. He constantly referred to himself as the luckiest man on this earth.

PC is survived by his wife, Stephanie, and close friends Zachary "ZZ" Zander, Carl and Marcella Zander, Joe Crinelli, Father Jonathan Young, Azquela Huggins, Billie "Cha-ching" Browner, Jenny Rich, and the employees of Miracle Mile Racetrack. He was proceeded in death by his parents and his adopted parents.

A night at the races to celebrate the life of PC will be held at the Miracle Mile Racetrack and Casino this Friday. In honor of his contribution to the track and the Zander family, Miracle Mile Racetrack and The Zander family will underwrite a Pick Nine wager in honor of PC. The track will not take out any funds from the Pick Nine pool. The

Zanders will add $100,000 to the pool. The entire pool will be distributed to the winner(s) of the Pick Nine. A single winning ticket is likely to be worth a million dollars.

A private funeral mass conducted by Bishop Carlucci will be held at the Always Hope School in Krenshaw on Saturday. Interment will be in the Zander family memorial garden.

In lieu of flowers, Stephanie Zander-Stevens requests that donations be made to the Standardbred Retirement Foundation or The Always Hope School.

# Chapter 56

## *Mid-State Trauma Center*
## *Youngwood, NJ*

It was a waste of time and gas, but I went to the trauma center Friday morning. I was planning on seeing Joe first. I ran into Aldo, who was on the way out of Joe's room. He pulled me aside.

"Save your breath, ZZ. Guiseppe is in a very foul mood. He can't stand the pain anymore, and he is convinced that he will never walk or dip the wick again. He is refusing anything except pain medications."

"I have to see him. Maybe I can help him."

"Forget it, ZZ; try another day."

I got a similar reception from the nurse in the burn unit.

"Dr. Zander, Azzie is not accepting visitors. She reluctantly saw her plastic surgeon but refused to be examined by the resident from the trauma team. She will not talk to or answer emails from anyone at her company. She wiped clean her list of approved visitors. I can't let you in."

"How are her burns?"

"I can't tell you. She took you and everyone off the HIPPA list. My lips are sealed."

I called the agent handling the investigation of the crash on the way home. He agreed to talk with me, but the conversation was about as fruitful as my lack of conversations with Joe and Azzie.

"Any updates?"

"No, nothing new. Still looks like pilot error."

"What about the burnt retinas?"

That surprised him. Aldo was more clued in than this guy.

"If the pilot's retinas were burnt, that would give more weight to a laser, causing the loss of control. But we have absolutely no evidence that would lead us to who used the laser and why."

I arrived back at the farm as a large truck of sod pulled into the driveway. Dad and I walked to the site of the family cemetery. The land had been cleared and smoothed. PC's grave had been dug and the burial vault had been lowered into the ground. The sod would make the area into the grassy resting place we had hoped to see. Dad was a wizard with landscaping.

Unfortunately for Dad and me, we had buried Rio's aborted colt at the end of one of the pastures. I remembered to bring masks and Vicks for our noses. We were smart enough to dig the new grave first. Then we dug up the rotting remains of the colt. The smell of death was pungent and horrific. Out of respect for Stephanie, we did not dig up the remains with the backhoe. We dug by hand.

I vomited, and Dad didn't. You might expect a doctor to do better with a death smell, but my defenses were pretty low. Breakfast looked a lot better when I ate it a few hours ago.

We laid the colt to rest for the second time. Dad had ordered a bronze headstone, which was being created as we worked. We sodded both areas with the exception of PC's grave and went back into the house to get ready for a long evening.

# Chapter 57

## *Miracle Mile Racetrack and Casino*

Promptly at 6 PM, the track lights were lit while the grandstand lights were dimmed. Bagpipes played softly in the background. Fired Up Rio slowly exited the paddock, pulling a cart adorned with roses. I sat on the seat of the cart dressed in my racing colors. Stephanie, also in her racing colors, sat beside me. I had a firm grip on the reins. Rio was calm, but she could get feisty in a hurry. In the cart rested the blue coffin carrying PC.

Behind the cart paraded all nine horses that we were racing tonight, each being walked by their groom. Dad, Mom, and Jenny brought up the rear. As we passed in front of the stands, Gabe Vatter, the track announcer, took over. He read PC's obituary as we turned around at the top of the stretch. I pulled the cart to a stop at the winner's circle.

Gabe continued. "Ladies and gentlemen. Tonight, we honor the memory of one of our own. Johnson Stevens, affectionally known as Pisscatcher."

Six members of the Awesome Army assisted by their caretakers carried PC's coffin to the track apron. It was placed on an elevated platform. His picture appeared on the infield tote board. We took up our positions by the casket and began to receive friends who came to say goodbye to PC.

Stephanie stood and hugged or somehow greeted everyone. But she never spoke the whole night. When the call to post was sounded for each race, the line was stopped. We all went to the fence and watched. Stephanie, Mom, Dad and I presented every winning horse and driver with a blanket commemorating the night and PC. Dave Dunstan and his horses collected enough blankets to withstand a blizzard.

I don't remember who won the first two races, but I can tell you all about the PC Pick Nine. It began in race three. Dave Dunstan was driving Fired Up Queen. He got away sixth and was sixth going to the half-mile pole. He started Queenie up just past the half and got in position second over behind Sufferin Succotash. Succotash was unable to get by the top horse and was hanging on the outside as they passed the ¾. Davey went three wide and won by five lengths. At four to one odds, he got a number of patrons a good start on the Pick Nine.

In the fourth Dave was driving Supreme Taco, and in the fifth he had one of his own horses, Scallywag. Neither horse had a ton of gate speed, but each did better on the front. So, Davey had to work something out. The path he chose for both was similar.

In the fourth race The Blue Man rolled Guided Missile out of the gate and easily got the front. Davey left out of the five-hole with Taco but just kind of hung on the outside for the first 1/8th. When he saw Blue Man pull back to rate his horse, he let Taco fly. Track announcer Gabe Vatter made the call.

"That's the Blue Man riding the engine with Guided Missile. Demand Note sits second, with Front Page making no headlines in third. Up on the outside Supreme Taco fires her jet rockets. Dave Dunstan rolls to the front with a quarter in 26:2. Guided Missile pulls to the outside and goes off stride. Dunstan cuts Taco loose, and she opens up four lengths on the field. Supreme Taco an easy winner in the 4th."

The strategy worked so well in fourth that Davey did the same thing in the fifth with Scallywag. What Scallywag lacked in speed, he made up for in guts. If he was in position at the top of the stretch, he dug in for the wire. Tonight was no exception. He got to the front after the ¼ pole and maintained the lead. He battled Shaken Not Stirred the whole way down the stretch, but Scallywag was not to be denied. Many betters had ignored him because he was moving up in class and shipping in from the Meadows. Sorry for their luck. Scally had new shoes courtesy of Tim Dunstan. His left knee was much better after he was scoped and had a few bone chips removed. Chris had entered him aggressively, and Davey drove him like he was the best. Scallywag was a handful tonight. The betters that didn't use him had a handful of tickets that could only be used as confetti.

Stephanie did the same thing each time in the winner's circle. She went to the winning horse's head and looked deep into their eyes. Then she hugged them and went around to put the winning blanket on them. She was positioned for each picture so that PC's photo on the infield tote board was behind her. When the pictures were completed, she walked back to the receiving line and accepted the condolences of family, friends, and hundreds of racing fans.

Race Six was a glitch in Davey's plan to win the entire Pick Nine for Stephanie. He had another one of his horses, Farmer Time, in a claiming race. He was even money odds. In the program he looked to be dominant, but the program left out some valuable information. Farmer Time was a nut. He was a wild man in his stall. He was prone to striking at people, walls, and just about anything when he was in a mood. Chris Dunstan got so frustrated with him that he got him a goat to be his companion. That dog gone goat settled Farmer Time down and made him a better horse to be around.

When they raced at The Meadows, Farmer Time only had to leave his stall and his goat companion about two hours before a race. Because Miracle Mile Racetrack used a detention barn for all races, he had to leave his stall about eight hours before the race. Talk about separation anxiety from that goat!

Farmer Time did not like being detained and goatless. He reared, whinnied, kicked, and bit the wood in his detention stall. When Farmer Time got to the starting gate, he was lathered up and washed out. He got away last and sat last the entire mile. As a heavy favorite he made a ton of recycling from useless tickets.

Dom Giordano won the sixth with Ha Ha U Lose. When he arrived at the winner's circle, he handed his horse's reins to the groom and gave Stephanie a big hug. Dom was one of the good guys. His heart was broken for Stephanie. He handed her a cup on a stick that was PC's personal collecting device. Stephanie gripped it like it was made of gold. To her it was.

Stephanie made her way back to the line which seemed to have gotten longer instead of shorter. Mom told me that Stephanie hadn't eaten and, in fact, had vomited numerous times over the past couple days. I jumped when I heard the screams. I turned around to see Stephanie on the ground.

She was lying on her back, and she was pale and sweaty. But she was still breathing. Her pulse was rapid. After a few minutes she came to. By that time Amos had slipped in an IV and checked her blood sugar. It was only 50, so she got some IV glucose and some badly needed fluid. I wanted to take her to the ER to get some labs and vigorously hydrate her. After all, she still had the funeral to go tomorrow.

She shook her head "NO." When I insisted, she pulled out her IV allowing blood to cover her arm and her racing colors. I put a little pressure on the IV site and decided to cut my loses. She accepted a seat in a chair that someone brought from the grandstand. She motioned for the greeting line to continue.

Shirley Dunstan trusted me as a physician, but she was a nurse by trade. As a nurse she made her own assessments and took her own actions. She wanted Stephanie to have some crackers and orange juice. Good luck getting Stephanie to take them. Once she saw Stephanie in her seat and commencing to greet friends and family Shirley took off in search of her prescriptions.

# Chapter 58

## *Miracle Mile Racetrack and Casino*

Shirley found her way to the Millions Club. She told one of the servers what she needed. While they went off to fetch her requests, she stepped into the ladies' room to see if she could find something wet to refresh Stephanie. She found nothing on the counter, but she spied a supply closet. She quickly found what she needed, but the open package spilled its contents of paper towels on the floor. Several of them went behind the door, so she had to close the closet door from the inside to retrieve them.

As she did so she heard the bathroom door open. She heard a deep gravelly feminine voice apparently talking into her cell phone. The kind of voice you might expect from someone who smoked far too many cigarettes. Shirley picked up her papers and prepared to exit the closet. As she heard the lady speak, she froze in her tracks.

"Just hold a second. Let me make sure I am alone." The voice said. Shirley then heard the woman open and close each stall door. Shirley pressed her eye to the doorframe. She could see the main entrance door for the restroom.

Feeling good about being alone, the voice locked the bathroom door from the inside after posting the barrier that indicated that the room was being cleaned. She lit up a cigarette.

"Ok, Ben? Are you still there? OK good. Listen up, I don't have much time. Starting Monday, I want you to short as much common stock in Miracle Mile Racetrack and Casino that you can without attracting too much attention. Yep, that's right MMR."

Shirley turned her head and pressed her ear to the closet door to hear as much as she could. Unfortunately, she could only hear ½ of the conversation.

“I don’t care what you have to do. Yes, I know I am on the board of directors, and that is not proper. Nor are your fees proper, you weasel.”

There was a brief silence; then the voice continued. “OK Ben, you know that I know people who can make your life short and miserable.” (There was a pause as Elvira listened), “Good. Just so we understand each other. It is looking promising that Miracle may soon be able to dump harness racing for year-round thoroughbred racing. My sister Penelope tells me that although things have improved somewhat at Krenshaw Medical Center they are about to get much worse. If it closes, harness racing at the track is done. The governor is six points down in his race. Without his support harness racing may well lose its casino subsidies. I just got out of a board of directors meeting. If Miracle Millions week turns out to be a flop, the board will vote to dump harness racing. As soon as Wall Street figures out that Miracle Racetrack is in trouble, they will sell off the stock.”

Another pause.

“No, you dumb ass. Please do not keep this quiet, but you must keep my name out of it. Don’t you hold power of attorney over that drunk Hyman’s accounts? You trade in his accounts and other accounts where you can. When we sell out, you can give them 10% of the profit to make it look like you did your fiduciary duty. Use our offshore accounts to route the rest of the money back to me. Of course, you get your 10%. Once you execute my short trades, tell everyone you know. They will drive the stock down further if they pile in on the short side. You will cover when I tell you. At that time, we will publicly go long in my own name and accounts. I will look like a board member who believes in her embattled stock and came to its defense. I should be able to assume control of the board. Then we wait for harness racing to fold its tent at Miracle. When that happens, we announce the thoroughbred racing plan. The stock will skyrocket, and I will have made money on the way down and back up.”

One last brief pause occurred in the conversation.

"I know it's brilliant. I can just see the headlines now. Masterminding diva Elvira Bradshaw saves and takes the reins at Miracle Mile Racetrack and Casino. Just don't mess up your end. I gotta go."

Elvira walked over and unlocked the door. Shirely was shocked to hear Elvira let rip a very large, loud anal emission of intestinal gasses. She then flicked her cigarette into the sink. Elvira unlocked the door and berated the stunned attendant who had been trying to enter the bathroom. "This room needs some attention. Someone created a horrible smell in here. I almost got sick when I walked in. Where have you been?"

Once she was sure that the snotty and smelly socialite had gone, Shirley grabbed her towels. She made her way to the server's station, picked up the juice and crackers and made her way back to the winner's circle.

Davey rolled Curdsandwhey to the front in the 7th and repeated that strategy in the 8th with Fired Up Duck. Curds was 8:1, and Duckie was 5/2, so the number of live tickets was dwindling.

I was a little worried about the 9th race. Davey was piloting Kaboom Kaboom from his own barn. He was moving up in class, but he looked a little spooked in the post-parade. He had never raced away from the Meadows and had mostly raced during the day. The huge crowds and bright lights freaked him out. Somehow, Davey calmed him down and got him a perfect two-hole trip. He won by two lengths when Davey cut him loose. A good drive can help a good horse. Kaboom Kaboom needed some help; tonight he got it.

Stephanie agreed to go to the winner's circle in a wheelchair. She let Shirley wipe her face off with the cool paper towels. She even ate a pack of crackers and drank all the orange juice.

Shirley said to me. "ZZ, we have to talk, but not here."

"No problem. Will you be coming to the house?"

"No, we will be late putting all these horses away. Just make sure I see you tomorrow."

"Sure, thanks for everything and thanks for helping with Stephanie. She looks a lot better after your treatment."

Shirley got closer, whispered in my ear, and went off to tend to the horses. What an asshole I can be! Hot shot ER doc, and I never put two and two together. Stephanie had been vomiting for a few days and had very little oral intake. Then she passed out tonight. I chalked it up to grief and lack of sleep. Shirley wondered if Stephanie was pregnant! It was not certain, but it was certainly possible. I will get the needed testing done somehow.

Gabe Vatter announced that there was only one live ticket in the Pick Nine. If number eight, Fired Up Prince, wins, the ticket was worth $1,126,455.00. If anyone other than number eight wins there will be multiple patrons splitting the large payout.

Fired Up Prince was making his third lifetime start. He was third in his first start. He broke stride two weeks ago in his second race and finished last. I thought there were at least four other horses in the race that were better than what Prince had shown. When we reviewed our strategy before the races, Davey thought he should leave with Prince. I had driven him both starts, and he broke last week when I tried to get him to the front. I told Davey I thought he should race him from behind. But I added that it was ultimately his call, and I would support whatever he did.

The horse felt good in the post parade and Davey thought his best chance was on the front. Other than Stephanie I didn't like to watch too many people drive. But I could learn from Stephanie and Davey. I had my binoculars on him as they approached the gate.

Dave and Chris had decided that they wanted Prince about five feet off the gate. He got him to settle there. About 20 feet to the start, Davey spoke to him. Prince got a running start when the gate folded, and he barreled out of there like a slingshot. He got the front easily and Davey shut him down going to the half. Good thing he did that because Sammy

Molinero rolled his horse first over down the backside and nearly swooped us. Davey kept Prince in front around the last turn, but he earned his keep in the stretch. There was a four horse battle for the wire. At the last second Davey lifted the lines. That put Prince's nose on the wire a millisecond before the other three. Someone made a big score.

Stephanie and I boarded the cart again pulled by Rio after PC's coffin was secured. We slowly made our way past the grandstand to the hearse that had been parked behind the fence near the ¼ pole. PC's last night at the track was spectacular and fitting.

Larry's plan had been to have the hearse take PC back to the funeral home and bring him to the farm tomorrow morning. Plans in our family, and particularly lately, are subject to change. Six members of the Awesome Army arrived at the back of the cart to carry PC's coffin to the hearse. Stephanie let out a scream. Everyone stopped in their tracks. Stephanie ran over to the coffin and two seconds later she had handcuffed herself to one of the rails on the side of the coffin used to lift it.

She looked at Jenny and Jenny back at her. No words were spoken but Jenny knew.

"She wants PC back at the farm tonight along with Rio."

Larry protested. "We can't …" He never got to finish.

Jenny had handcuffed herself to the other side of the coffin.

Larry had to give in, or we were going to be here all night.

Back at the farm the coffin was removed from the hearse. It was carried to the new grave site of Rio's foal. Rio was already there, just standing. No halter, no ties, no fencing. A tent had been set up over the grave site. Jenny took off her handcuffs and Stephanie's. Funny how Jenny found the key when she had no idea where it was when we were at the track. Stephanie removed her colors and put one of PC's blankets on herself, and one on Rio, and one on the ground. Then she and Rio laid down and slept.

# Chapter 59

## *Fired Up farms*

At 5 AM I was in the kitchen making coffee when Shirely Dunstan arrived.

"Shirley, you are here early. Coffee?"

"Tea, if it's no trouble."

"No problem, thanks for coming now. I am not sure we will have much time to talk later."

"Are you sure we don't need to stay. I can leave Timmy and David here for a few more days."

"If we get the horses bedded down after the service, I think we will be fine. Mom, Dad and the kids at the school all need to do some work around the stables to get their minds off PC and Stephanie. You folks have done plenty. I can speak for my family in that we all appreciate what you have done. But after the service you need to get your lives back to normal as we attempt the same thing. Having horses doesn't' give you any time to wallow in your own pity."

"True, but we'll only be a phone call away if you need anything."

"I know, thank you. Now what did you want to speak with me about?"

Shirely went on to relay to me as much as she could remember about Elvira Bradshaw's conversation.

"Are you sure she said Dr. Hoyman?"

"Pretty sure."

"Are you sure it wasn't Hyman?"

"Could have been. I couldn't hear very well in that closet."

I pressed her. "And she said that things at the hospital were about to get worse?"

"She said that her sister Penelope told her that."

I thought. Old Lady Penelope Bradshaw. I wondered how in the hell she knew the hospital was going down the tubes. She was on the hospital board. She would know about Buster and Master's screwups, but she would also know that we cleared our slate with the Licensure Board and Joint Commission. But it was becoming obvious that there were several moving parts here. Apparently, all parts were moving to the detriment of harness racing, the governor, Krenshaw Medical, and yours truly.

I wanted to be sure. "She also said that if this year Million's Week was not a raging success, the racetrack board would vote to dump harness racing?"

"Yes, she did. I heard that part clearly. I didn't understand the financial stuff. What is shorting? It sounded like Elvira Bradshaw was manipulating to take control of the track."

I said nothing as I tried to make some sense of all the information. I then tried to explain shorting.

"When you short a stock, you make money when it goes down. Say you have an ounce of gold, and the price of gold is $2,000 an ounce. I come to you and ask to borrow the gold, and you give it to me. I sell it and get $2,000. Now, sometime later I have to give you back an ounce of gold. If the price of gold goes to say $1500, I buy an ounce and give it to you. I sold yours for $2000, and I replaced it for $1500. You got your gold back, and I am $500 to the good. Pretty slick when it works. Elvira is planning on hurting the stock and then buying it back later. She makes a score on the way down and on the way back up."

Shirley interrupted my thoughts. "I'm riding home with Chris. I'm hoping that we can figure out some way to make Miracle Millions a raging success this year. You concentrate on the hospital. We all must hope the governor gets reelected."

Don't get in Shirley's way when she is on a mission. I looked squarely in the eyes of a very determined lady.

"Thanks, Shirley", was all I could say.

After Shirley left, Jenny arrived to get some coffee.

I was anxious to hear about his race in Ohio. "How did Billie do last night?"

"He won jogging. He said he never started that horse up, and he still took a track record."

"Congratulations. That horse is a monster. I don't look forward to facing him in some of the bigger races later this year. Will Billie be here for the service?"

"Yeah, he got a flight out last night. But it was delayed getting into Newark, so he got a hotel there. I expect him in the next hour."

"Good, it will mean a lot to Stephanie if we are all here. Did you confiscate her handcuffs?"

"Yeah, ZZ, sorry, but she made me do that last night. I didn't see the harm, and without us handcuffing ourselves, I thought you or Larry may veto the idea. I heard that she and Rio slept the whole night. The Awesome Army had a sentry posted that they changed on the hour. Those kids are in a world of hurt for Stephanie, but they have banded together to help her in any way they can."

"Just so we don't have any incidents at the gravesite. People throwing themselves into the vault or jumping on the casket, etc."

"I haven't heard any rumors, but you just never know."

"Jenny, can you find some way to get a urine sample from Stephanie?"

"Sure, I'll ask her, why?"

"She might be pregnant."

"Wow, PC's legacy!"

"Keep that between us until we know." I handed Jenny a urine pregnancy test kit.

"Of course," she said as she pocketed the kit.

# Chapter 60

## *Fired Up Farms*

Stephanie got up when Mom called. Rio stayed on the ground until Stephanie rubbed her head. On cue, she jumped up, and Stephanie carefully applied a head halter and handed her off to the chosen members of The Army and their handlers. They would bathe her, comb her out, and apply her diamonds just as she wore when she won the Million's Mile.

Stephanie walked silently with Jenny and Mom back to the house. They helped her shower and fixed her hair. Jenny obtained the urine sample. Stephanie never asked why it was needed. Jenny stepped into the next room, and a few minutes later, it was known that PC left Stephanie more than a ton of life insurance. Stephanie was pregnant. Jenny texted me and wanted to know if she could tell Stephanie.

I replied, "No." I wanted some time to plan how and when to tell her.

I had thought we would have the mass outside at the finish line of the training track. Bishop Carlucci vetoed that idea. He demanded to set up at the start line. Who was I to argue with the bishop? Start line it was.

The sun was shining, and a slight breeze was blowing. If we weren't here to bury a dear friend, this could have been a perfect day. Billie arrived at 8 AM and quickly got into a suit. I had never seen Billie in anything but racing colors and jeans. He looked uncomfortable but Jenny thought he was handsome and told him so. She wet her fingers and put his cowlick back into place.

Stephanie and I wore our colors as per Stephanie's request. Mom was up late laundering them and making sure they were perfect. Jenny did her best to fix Stephanie's hair. No one could get it right except

Azzie, and she was MIA. She and Joe were still hospitalized, so no one expected them.

But what was unexpected was that neither of them reached out to Stephanie or anyone in our family. If Azzie was herself, she never would have left Stephanie go to this funeral without some token of her love for Stephanie and PC. Likewise, Joe would have figured out some way to show his condolences. Both knew about his demise, but neither one did a thing.

Aldo did send some amazing arrangements with Joe's name on them. But when I asked, he confessed to me that Joe had not requested for him to do so. Both Joe and Azzie were accepting no calls nor any visitors. Joe was in incredible pain, and Azzie was not dealing well with her potential facial scarring. It's the first time since I met either of them that I saw them put their needs, wants, or worries above everyone else's.

I was mad at them at first and then really mad at myself the more I thought about it. I was just as bad as them. I wanted some acknowledgment of grief for Stephanie's sake. But when I put myself in their shoes, I understood why they acted that way. I remembered the very painful adjustment I had to make to my scarred face.

A number of years ago, I woke up in the intensive care unit of The University of Pittsburgh. I had been flown there in a helicopter two weeks before that from the Meadows Racetrack. There was a horrible racing accident at the start of a stakes race. I was thrown onto the limestone track. That caused a number of injuries, but the worst injury happened when a horse stepped on my face. Luckily for me, the lights went out immediately.

I had a severe head injury and was in a coma. My parents were told to prepare for the worst. To spite everyone, and with the help of a stellar trauma team, I woke up. My face was purple and massively swollen. Five surgeries later, it healed with very noticeable scarring. I was happy not to have died but disgusted with my appearance. Over time, I came to view that being alive was far more important than any scar. I prayed that both of my friends would get to that point.

Donald Lowry, owner of Top of the Main Line Catering, handed me a cup of coffee.

"Thank you, Don. I really appreciate your catering our service today. I can't believe you contacted Dan and that you two were able to figure this out."

"ZZ, I owe a great debt to Stephanie and your family. The fiasco at her wedding could have ruined my business. We took a big hit, mind you, but Stephanie and PC's explanation on social media saved me. It's my honor to help you bury your friend with honor and dignity."

Dan came around the corner with his wife. I was gratified to see that most people had followed the dress code. Formal attire was appropriate, but formal shoes were not. Dad was worried that someone wearing heels or fancy shoes with poor traction would slip in the wet grass or trip on the limestone training track. So only boots or tennis shoes were permitted. Dan was decked out in a black suit and his wife in a dark blue dress, but both were sporting high top Vans shoes.

The bishop's vestments prevented any view of his shoes. Silently I wondered if they wore tennis shoes all the time figuring they might get away with it. Silly me. Hey, I need something goofy to keep my mind off the fact that my world was blowing up.

Members of the Awesome Army ushered attendees to their seats as best as they could. When they got off course or distracted, their handlers intervened. Almost every trainer and driver at the track arrived along with tons of casino employees. Those who had racing colors, wore them. I was emotional when I saw how many hospital employees had arrived. JL and her husband found me out before they took their seats. Celeste Maliterna and her husband Adrian arrived shortly later. Most of the ER staff was there.

As we were lining up, I saw several police cars pulling in. Was there a problem? I soon got my answer when the governor's limo arrived. His aids opened the door. He, too, was adorned in a black suit coupled with black tennis shoes. Terry was a good friend.

His aides said that the governor wanted to speak with Stephanie. The Governor had lied. He never spoke to her. He just held her and hugged her and cried. I know Stephanie was touched.

I walked the Governor back to his seat.

"Governor, I can't believe you came today. Don't get me wrong, it means the world to me and my family. But with the controversy that happened at the wedding, we would have understood if you did not come. Arranging the cemetery was enough."

"Well, ZZ, I can tell you that my aides and political strategists were strongly opposed to this. I am down seven points in the latest internal poll. They wanted me to avoid any contact with this farm, harness racing, or your family. They are still worried that the picture of me fertilizing that tree will surface."

"So why are you here?"

"ZZ, if you look at the tote board and you are 7 to 1, and there are four other horses with lower odds than yours, do you give up?"

"Hell no, I just try to figure out how to beat those bastards. I get angry, and I get fired up. If I can get myself to a point where I don't give a rat's ass what happens, I relax and let it fly."

"I hope that explains why I am here. Terry Carrington may lose, but I am not giving up. They will have to beat me. Good luck to them. I am digging in. I fired most of my campaign staff today."

"Whoa, governor. You sound more determined than I have heard you sound in months."

"Feels good. Let's bury your friend."

# Chapter 61

## *Fired Up Farms*

Bishop Carlucci arrived at 0945. He spent 15 minutes praying with Stephanie, our family, and the Dunstans. They weren't Catholic, but that didn't matter to anyone. God is God, no matter what path you take to get to Him. I surveyed the family and friends near me. Jenny was bawling her eyes out but was standing alone. She later told me that Billie had to piddle and headed back to the house.

At 0955, "On Eagles Wings" played on the speakers around the track. All 50 members of The Awesome Army and their handlers walked slowly from their seats to PC's coffin. It was still under the tent covering the grave of Rio's colt. Ten chosen members brought the coffin out from the tent. Chris Dunstan walked Rio out into the sun. She was glistening and glowing. The diamonds in her ears and hoofs sparkled in the sun. When the hymn ended, Rio reared onto her two back legs. Chris just let out more of her lines. Rio paddled both front legs high in the air and let out a whinny that was heard throughout the farm. From the south end of the farm suddenly came an equally forceful and loud whinny. Always Hope was answering back. Stephanie nodded in approval.

Rio came back down on all fours, and Chris led her onto the track. She was followed by The Awesome Army and the pallbearers carrying PC. They slowly paraded to the start line while the 23rd psalm played.

PC's coffin was placed on the stand, and all took their seats. The bishop said a few prayers then Dad and Mom read verses from the Bible. The bishop then took to the podium and explained why we were at the start line instead of the finish.

"Dr. Zander had wanted to hold this service at the finish line. He wanted a fitting way to mark the end of Johnson's life on this earth. I encouraged him to use the start line. If you are a believer, you know that our time on this earth is a very, very tiny portion of our life in eternity. Kind of like a blink of an eye in comparison to eternal life.

Johnson made the best of his life. He was a good friend to all, a great employee at the track, and a highly successful businessman. He was a generous and kind man. But he wasn't complete as a man or a person until he gave his heart and soul to Stephanie. He adored her and was incredibly happy when they married.

But Johnson also gave his heart and soul to God. And for that, he will remain incredibly fulfilled for all of eternity. So, it is fitting that we celebrate the start of his eternal life at the starting line. We should not mourn for him; we should mourn for ourselves. We still have our time on this earth, and we still have time to lose or save our souls. Johnson has completed that task, and I am sure the Lord will smile upon him. May we all be so fortunate, and may the Lord have mercy on his soul."

Billie managed to get back to his seat just as the bishop was concluding his remarks. He tripped on Jenny's shoe and fell flat on his face as the bishop mentioned saving one's soul. I would have found that funny if the whole event wasn't so sad.

We walked to the gravesite, where they placed PC's coffin on the device that would lower it into the ground. The bishop said a few more prayers and blessed the coffin. When he was done, friends and family came one by one to place a rose on the casket. When they all had finished and began their trek to the luncheon, I walked Stephanie to the coffin. She placed a rose on it, and stood as Rio was walked in. Rio rubbed her nose on the coffin and dropped a rose from her mouth onto the coffin.

Chris handed the lead to Stephanie, who walked Rio away. Stephanie did not go to the tent that had been set up for the luncheon. She walked Rio to her colt's gravesite, where Stephanie placed a rose on the grave, and Rio repeated her rose-dropping act. Stephanie removed the halter. Chris had the diamonds. Rio, the horse, laid down on the grave.

I had a wheelchair for Stephanie, but she refused. I held her hand, and we walked toward the house.

"Stephanie," she heard me but did not answer. I continued.

"Stephanie, I want you to know how proud I am of you. What you went through is more than what you should have to endure at your age. I don't have any magic words to say, and now is not the time for a funny story. But I want you to know that I love you more than ever, and I am here for anything you need."

She nodded.

"Thanks for acknowledging me. That means a ton. I have some news for you if you are ready."

She stopped and turned toward me. She made a motion with her hands like she had a big belly and nodded her head. That damn Rio must have told her that she was pregnant. I knew for sure that Jenny and I hadn't.

She wanted to go to her room, which had been my room. My room had a view of both PC's gravesite and the resting place of Rio's colt. Now, it was Stephanie's room. Her bed had been moved near the window. When she arrived in her room, Mom helped her off with her colors and into her PJs. She laid down and was fast asleep in under a minute.

I returned to the tent. The food was magnificent. Billie ran around with a monster-sized bottle of Crown Royal, pouring shots for anyone who wanted to toast PC. I joined him for a few as did most of the people from the track. Billie was getting pretty wasted. Good for him. We all needed a break.

I caught up with the governor as his security staff was preparing for his exit. He was talking with Don Lowry. In fact, he got his picture taken with him. I would have thought that he would avoid him like the plague. Governor Terry had something up his sleeve. That gave me the first smile that I had in weeks.

"Governor, thank you again for coming. It meant the world to our family. And, of course, we appreciate your help with the home cemetery. I hope this doesn't hurt your election chances."

He stopped and pulled out his cell phone to show me a fresh ad from his opponent released a minute ago. It showed the governor getting out of his limo at the farm this morning. The caption read, "The Governor returns to the scene of the slime. He never misses an opportunity to crap on New Jersey."

"That bitch." I said.

In a calm and matter-of-fact voice, the governor replied. "The only way that bitch will see even a toilet in the Governor's mansion is if she comes to clean one."

I smiled. "Were you looking at the tote board?"

"Something like that. Watch your back, ZZ. Things are going to get a little crazy."

I caught up to the bishop as he headed toward his limo.

"Bishop, that was an incredible service and a fitting tribute to a great friend. You helped me put all of this in a little different and better perspective."

"Dr. Zander, death is never pleasant, almost always unwelcome, and occasionally hard to accept. But for those who believe in life everlasting, the grief process should be shorter. I pity those who don't believe. For them, death is final."

"I know that you comforted Stephanie and most of the people here today."

The bishop nodded. "I have been summoned to Rome next month. That usually means that a decision on Father Jonathan will be made then."

"That's a long trip. I hope it goes well, and I hope, of course, all goes well for Father Jonathan".

The bishop grinned. "The trip to Rome will be a little easier. Somehow, I ended up with the only winning ticket on the Pick Nine last night. Of course, 70% of the money went to the diocese. But I did get permission from the cardinal to fly business class to and from Rome. That is after I gave the Vatican the remaining 29%."

"You won the Pick Nine? I didn't know you were a handicapper."

"I'm no handicapper. I bought one ticket using the nine digits of my social security number. The Lord and Dave Dunstan did the rest."

Chris and Shirley Dunstan used the ride home to discuss the problem at hand.

"Well, Mom, Miracle Week has been great for everyone involved. When Stephanie won with Rio, they set new betting records. They were broken last year when ZZ and Stephanie threw down with the two best horses in harness racing. Why shouldn't there be bigger crowds and better races this year?"

"For one, there is still the stink of the horse doping scandal that the Supreme Stables left. The handle at Miracle is down over 10% from its peak. And this year, we don't have two undefeated monsters racing against each other."

Chris was mulling things over. "What did that nasty lady say again?"

"If Miracle Millions Week turns out to be a flop, as most folks think it will, the board will vote to dump harness racing. That is regardless of what goes on at the hospital or with the governor."

"Wow, it seems like we need the big horses," Chris added.

(Big horses were what some trainers called the best horses in their stable.)

"We need a lot of big horses."

# Chapter 62

## *Fired Up Farms*

I woke up at 5 AM I stuck my head in Stephanie's room, and she was awake. She was sitting on her bed, staring out the window at PC's resting place. But this morning, there was little to gain from doing that. The fog was so thick that nothing was visible.

The grief journey for everyone is similar in many respects but very different in others. The stages of grief are the same. But how one deals with each stage and how long each stage lasts varies, depending upon the person and their relationship with the deceased. Let's face it. If Grandma dies after a bitter battle with cancer, the death is often welcomed, and the grief stages move along quickly. The death of a spouse is always problematic. If the passing was unexpected, the difficulties increase exponentially.

Stephanie often used the turtle method to deal with adversity. She withdrew into the shell of her mind and shut the rest of her world out. In the first stage, she was often catatonic. She might be awake or asleep, but she did not interact with her surroundings. This was followed by a period of rocking and chanting. MotherF'er was her most common chant. In either of those stages, she was prone to violence if touched. Once the chanting stopped, it could take days or weeks for her to return to her normal state.

It was sad to watch. I walked over to her bed and said good morning. There was no response. Not a twitch, not a blink of an eye. Her eyes were open, but no one was home. I tried a second time to interact and got the same outcome. I wanted to hold or kiss her on top of the head, but I dared not. She cold-cocked me once during a trance like this, and I learned my lesson. I quietly closed the door and went down to the kitchen.

Mom was busy making breakfast for her and Dad.

"Zachary, what are you doing up? We thought you'd sleep in today."

"Who can sleep?"

She and Dad nodded in agreement.

"Actually, I am pulling a shift in the ED today, 7-3. Angela wanted me to stay home, but I needed to get out of here and get my mind onto other things. Nothing like a day in the barrel to broom other thoughts out of your head."

Carl laughed, "Can I come too? I can empty bedpans or something."

"You two need to stay here with Steph. I just looked in on her, and she was in a trance. Try to get some liquids in her and food if she will take any."

Mom agreed to try. "We will do our best."

"I have some news that may help you try harder. Stephanie is pregnant."

There was a period of silence as Mom and Dad looked at each other. Dad was the first to react. He was obviously pleased.

"Grandpa Zander. Has a good ring to it."

Mom, on the other hand, was worried. "Zachary, how far along is she? Could she still lose this baby?"

"She's early in the first trimester, I think. I can't get a menstrual history from her, and other than a urine pregnancy test, we have no information. I will have Celeste Maliterna visit her this week and bring her ultrasound equipment. But no matter what, her chances of miscarriage go up if she does not eat or drink well."

"Who all knows?" Mom asked.

"Good question, Mom. You two, Shirely, Jenny, and myself. Jenny got Stephanie to give the urine sample."

"Does Stephanie know?"

I nodded. “Yep.”

“Who told her?”

“Rio.”

It was Mom’s turn to shake her head. “Those two have a very powerful and strange bond. They know things about each other that they shouldn’t or couldn’t. I’m not surprised.”

# Chapter 63

*Emergency Department*

*Krenshaw Medical Center*

Streeter had his feet on the desk. He was entertaining the ER staff as usual. As I arrived, he chided the audience.

"Here comes farmer Zander now. Don't make fun of farmers or farms."

Streeter had been to the viewing and had attended the funeral. He and most of the staff present had expressed their condolences numerous times in various ways. This morning it was back to work for everyone. I knew it would help me move on. I also knew he wasn't done when he continued his spiel.

"Hey, ZZ. Do you have any sheep on your farm?"

"Stephanie has four of them. Why do you ask? "

"My girlfriend is out of town. I got some new firemen's boots that I want to try out. You know, if you get those sheep to relax and put their back legs in the boots, it can be a wild time." He barely got the words out before he and the entire night and day shift staff erupted in laughter.

I needed a good laugh, and they all knew it. Friends often know exactly what you need. Streeter was a good friend and a stellar ER physician. The staff loved working with him, and I loved relieving him. He never left a mess. Today was no exception. The entire ER and waiting room were empty. I brought two dozen bagels for the staff. I set them on the counter and helped myself to one.

I asked a question as the staff pounced on the bagel stash. "Who won the AON last night?"

Streeter and the staff were suddenly speechless. AON was a game played in the ER on the night shift. It stood for "Asshole of the Night." Patients, family, and friends over the age of 18 were eligible to be chosen. Each staff member playing contributed $3 to the pool and got to select one asshole. The participating staff voted at 0645. The money was distributed to the person who selected the winning flamer. It was customary for the winner to buy eye-openers at the Daily Double Bar, which seemed to be on the way home for all night shift staff.

They were speechless because I had banned the game. It was shortly after I became the CMO. One morning, by some stroke of bad luck, the ER staff was a little loud at the Daily Double while consuming their eye-openers. Unfortunately for them, the winning asshole was in a booth at the bar and figured out that they were talking about him.

Of course, discussing any patient in public or disclosing confidential information was wrong. Some people thought it was unethical to consider any patient, family, or friend an asshole. But those people never worked in an ER. Especially on night shifts, assholes are real, and they are plentiful.

After I cancelled the AON's bill for the ER, and apologized profusely for the ER staff's bad behavior, I had to take decisive action. I banned the game. OK, I pretended to ban it. What I banned was being stupid about where winners were discussed. It was a type of ban. Tina and Dan were pleased to hear that I put a ban in place. I didn't lie to them, but they might have misconstrued what I said. All right, I lied.

Streeter answered for the group. "ZZ, after your sage advice we all examined our consciouses and souls. We determined that it was beneath our profession to play a game like that. So, we stopped."

"You all are totally full of shit." I laughed, and so did they. I was sure they were still playing, but I really didn't want to know. Plausible deniability, isn't that what it's called?

Streeter asked about Stehanie, and I gave him a full report minus the pregnancy information. Just as he stood to leave, we heard a crash outside. Amos ran out and ran right back in the door and screamed.

"Get some stretchers and some go-kits. We got a head-on at the stop light for the ER entrance."

911 was notified. Amos was at the scene before any other staff. He did a rapid assessment for dangers to rescuers and signaled to the staff that the way was clear. A pickup truck and an SUV had hit head-on. Both drivers had been ejected but were still alive.

Streeter helped Amos with the first victim while Dawn, I, and two aides tended to the second one. He had a fast and very weak pulse. He was breathing rapidly and was unconscious. He appeared to have a severe head injury. His Glasgow Coma was 7. He needed to be intubated. I got a hard collar on his neck. Then we got him onto a backboard and hustled him into the ED. I grabbed my trusty, intubating laryngoscope and secured his airway. Dawn made two unsuccessful attempts at an IV. This dude was fresh out of good veins. From the track marks on his arms, it was obvious that he was a serious addict.

I went to work on a central line. I obtained the blood I needed. I dropped the tubes in my pocket as Dawn pounded in the IV fluid with a pressure infuser. I asked someone to order a trauma panel and asked that I get four units of type-specific uncrossmatched blood stat.

A full type and cross would take 45 minutes or so. In 10 minutes, I could give this guy his same type of blood (like B - or O+), but it would not have a full subtyping done. Yeah, there were still chances of having a mild transfusion reaction, but they were slim. But without blood soon, this dude was toast.

I did a rapid assessment and was pleased that his BP was 70/30. I was happy mine wasn't that low, but 70/30 was good compared to where he started. I ordered a trauma CT scan. The tech handed me the labels for his blood, and I applied them at the bedside like a good doobie. It had been beaten into my head that all specimens should be labeled in the presence of the patient to prevent mix-ups.

I remember that as a third-year med student, I often drew blood from many different patients and then labeled them all at one time. I was lucky I didn't kill someone. I pulled the same stunt as a fourth year.

Fortunately, or unfortunately, my supervising resident saw me do it. After a very thorough ass chewing, I had to throw all the tubes away. Then, I had to go back and apologize to every patient and draw their blood again. The patients were pissed, and I was embarrassed. But it was safe, and it was the right way. As my final punishment I got to present an in-service to my entire class about patient injuries caused by labeling errors. That was after explaining to all 225 what I had done to get me in front of them. An embarrassment like that you don't forget.

I stuck my head into Trauma 2 to see if Streeter needed anything. His patient also needed a central line for blood and fluids. He had drawn the blood for a trauma pack and wanted his patient to have stat blood. The labels were printing on the printer in the room as I entered. I got them off the printer. Streeter handed me the blood, and I labeled them as he pulled off his gloves.

By force of habit, I walked over to the pneumatic tube station that we used to send specimens to the lab. I was pissed when I saw the sign indicating that the tube was down again for maintenance. My anger dissipated when the gentleman in the purple scrubs hurriedly approached me. He had my patient's specimens in a bag, and he wisely sought me out when he heard I had Streeter's tubes. I handed him the specimens, and he took off for the lab.

# Chapter 64

## *Krenshaw Medical Center*

The lab was two floors above the ED, but the purple-scrubbed tech walked up only one flight of steps and found his way to an unoccupied bathroom. He carefully removed the label from each pink top tube used for the type and cross and switched them. He then opened the door and noted that the coast was clear. He continued his journey to the lab and handed the specimens to two awaiting technologists. Both were so focused on the quick work that they were about to do that they paid no attention to the tech who had delivered the specimens. Had they done so, neither one would have recognized him. Unfortunately, he wasn't a new employee that they hadn't yet met.

Streeter and I took turns getting X-rays and CT scans of our patients. We had superb x-ray technologists and staff working. Rapidly, we had great radiographs. Both patients had blood in their bellies and would need surgery. Neither patient had a broken neck. His patient had a skull fracture but no significant brain injury. My patient had a skull full of mush. There was blood and swelling everywhere. He might not survive this. But if he had any chance, I had to keep him alive from his other injuries.

I was happy when I heard Dawn announce that the blood had arrived. My patient's pressure was still 70, so I was impatient about getting the blood going. I asked Dawn to hurry the hell up with the blood, and she flipped me off. She proceeded to do a blind double-check with another RN to be certain they were giving the correct blood to the patient. That was the protocol. It only took another 30 seconds. I waited.

Dawn used a blood warmer and a blood pump to inject the blood as fast as possible. The first unit went in quickly. Dawn screamed as she prepared to hang the second. The patient was covered in hives. I checked his Foley bag, and his previous yellow urine was now red. His blood pressure was not obtainable by machine.

I had only seen one serious transfusion reaction in my career. Two patients had switched beds and identification bracelets because one wanted to be near the window. Staff did not recognize the switch, and one of the patients got the wrong type of blood. That patient died. My patient might join him.

I poured in IV fluid and administered Benadryl and steroids in massive doses. I asked the lab for O Neg blood STAT. Two minutes later, he went into ventricular fibrillation. We couldn't save him.

Streeter's patient did fine. He stabilized and made it to the trauma center. My patient went to the morgue after we drew about 1,000 tubes of blood to figure out what the hell happened.

Someone called Angela, who immediately came in. She relieved me, which was our protocol. This was a sentinel event and had to be fully investigated as soon as possible. Plus, the caregivers involved in the event had to be taken out of service, not as a punishment but as a precaution. It is difficult to be involved in a poor outcome case. Staff needed time to decompress. Continuing to provide patient care was not wise.

We all did our documentation and then reconvened for a root cause analysis to attempt to pinpoint what occurred. What happened was easy to figure out. My patient had an acute hemolytic transfusion reaction. He got the wrong blood! How that occurred was another matter. We were able to determine that my patient had O neg blood. The blood he received was AB+. Streeter's patient just so happened to have AB+ blood.

There were three places where the specimens or blood could have been switched. The switch could have occurred when they were drawn and labeled, when the blood was prepared in the lab, or when the blood was administered. I had watched Dawn do the required double check. We then verified that the blood she administered was the blood that the lab had prepared for my patient. She was off the hook.

The lab was able to test other samples they had on both patients. All my patient's tubes contained O Neg blood except the pink top, which contained AB+. Streeter's patient's tubes contained AB+ except for the pink top that contained Oneg.

That cleared the nursing staff and the lab. The pink top tubes had been mislabeled. That is where the error had to occur. The blood testing also explained why Streeter's patient did ok, and mine died. My patient had O-negative blood. The only blood he could safely receive was O-negative. Anything else was a big, deadly problem. Streeter's patient had AB-positive blood. His type was known as the universal recipient. He could take any type of blood, and he did.

Tina asked, "ZZ, do you recall labeling the blood?"

"Of course."

"Could there have been a mix-up?"

I tried not to get upset, but I wasn't completely successful. "Look, Tina, things happen fast in a situation like that. I swear that I labeled the specimens for each patient in their room. I swear I had completed mine and had them all labeled before I checked on Ron. I handed them both to the new lab tech, who took them to the lab."

Tina flipped out. "What new lab tech? We've had a hiring freeze. The lab is way over budget, and I was planning on laying some lab techs off this week."

I tried to recall the details as clearly as possible. "I handed both sets of blood tubes to a man about my height and weight with brown hair and brown eyes. He was wearing a purple scrub suit with a Krenshaw Medical Center ID badge on."

"Couldn't be," said the head lab tech.

"Why?" Tina and I asked in unison.

"Currently, all techs assigned to the ER are female. I was so hyped up to get your blood to you that I didn't question it. We do have male techs going to some of the floors. I thought one of them might have just tried to help out.

Tina called the head of security. "Please pull as much video as you can of all the activity between the ER and lab from the time of the accident until the transfusion reaction," she said, providing the exact times from her notes.

Dan had said very little to this point. "ZZ, I am so sorry. I will call the malpractice company tomorrow to inform them of a possible claim. Make sure you are available tomorrow. I will meet with the family today along with Tina. I want them to have the opportunity to speak with you tomorrow or Tuesday if they would like. I'd prefer you not talk to them until we get the autopsy report. Was the coroner notified?"

I had called him myself. "I spoke to him immediately after I pronounced the patient."

Tina crossed something off her list. "Dan, we only have three more agencies to report this to."

Dan did not understand. "The family, coroner, and malpractice carrier should do. Who else did you have in mind?"

Tina explained. "How about the police, the Licensure Board, and The Joint Commission? If the person who delivered the blood was not an employee, it had to be an imposter. If he had switched the blood, that would make him a murderer. This is a Licensure Board Never Episode. We are obliged to report this. This is our third this year. The fine will be massive, but it is much more if you don't self-report. Joint Commission requires us to report all sentinel events and do a root cause analysis. At least our RCA is almost done."

Dan nodded. "As usual, Tina, you're right. You take care of the Licensure Board and Joint Commission tomorrow. I'll call the police now."

The police got to the hospital before I left. They, of course, wanted to know about the labeling and the seriousness of a transfusion reaction. In this case, it was fatal, but only the autopsy would be able to show if he would have survived the accident with a good transfusion.

Until they got more information, the police were proceeding with the impression that we had an imposter and a trespasser. They got copies of all relevant tapes and said they would be in touch.

I knew I didn't switch the labels. But we had no solid evidence showing that the imposter did either. It was likely that the malpractice carrier and Licensure Board would take a simple approach. The guy got the wrong blood and died. Hospital at fault, maybe me too. Why in the hell did I decide to do that shift today?

# Chapter 65

## *`Fired Up Farms*

I arrived home just as Celeste Maliterna was walking out to her truck.

"How is she? How is the baby?" I inquired.

"So far, the baby is good. She is about 10 weeks. Ooops, did you want to know the sex? I hope you did."

"I already knew."

"How, did you do an ultrasound too?"

"No, I don't have a machine here. Rio told Stephanie that she was carrying a filly."

Celeste just shook her head. "But ZZ, the baby will not continue to do well unless Stephanie starts to eat and drink. She let me draw some bloodwork on her today. She refused IV fluids. I will call you with the lab results. Do you think she will snap out of this?"

"No way to tell, but my best guess is no. Based upon her previous reactions to upsets in her life and considering the magnitude of this one, I expect a rough road."

Celeste leaned against her truck after putting her equipment away. "When I was at Jefferson, I really came to respect Saul Rosen. He's a psychiatrist. Did you know him?"

"I think he gave a lecture or two to our class, but I may have missed them."

Celeste shook her head in disapproval. "You were probably at the track or jogging a horse. Saul's speciality is postpartum depression, but he also helped pregnant patients with ongoing mental health issues. I think he should see Stephanie. If you want, I will call him and give him some background information."

"That would be great. Are there medications that can help her?"

"ZZ, that is not my field, but I can tell you that most psych meds are worrisome in pregnancy."

"Wow, what does that leave us?"

"I worked with Saul in the past on a significantly depressed mother in her second trimester. We ended up with a feeding tube for nutrition and hydration until the psych treatment took effect."

"What psyche treatment? I thought you were nervous about medications?"

"I am; he used electroconvulsive therapy."

"ECT?" That made me bristle. "That can't be good for a growing fetus."

Celeste gave me a condescending look. "Do you use a lot of ECT in the ER? How do you have an opinion, Dr. I Skipped Psychiatry Lectures in Med School? The ones you skipped were probably about ECT."

She had me there. "Sorry, I really don't know much at all about it. Making someone have a grand mal seizure seems bad in some way, especially a patient with one in the oven."

"Believe it or not, it's safe. I am not sure that is what Saul will recommend but let's get his opinion. The more I think of it, he may be able to do the interview via telemedicine. There isn't much to see with Stephanie that he can't see on a screen. I think he will get enough out of talking with you and your parents. I know he could do it sooner that way, and Stephanie would not need to be moved."

"Wow, that sounds good. I may need some time myself on his couch."

Celeste put her hand on my shoulder. "ZZ, I am so sorry. I heard about the transfusion. If there was an imposter, he must have switched the labels somehow."

"Hey, thanks. I have been beating myself up since it happened. I keep coming back to the premise that the imposter must have been waiting around for an opportunity. But no one could know that we were going to have patients needing blood."

Celeste initially said nothing. When she got into her truck, she rolled down the window. "Maybe he just got lucky. He might have been looking for some specimens to mess with when you guys had the trauma. Did you sound a trauma alert?"

"Sure, we always do."

Celeste continued her thoughts. "If I was an imposter wanting to mix-up some specimens, I would be in the hospital early when most of the morning specimens are collected and processed. If I knew that there were trauma patients being treated in the ER, I just might wander down. Lots of activity and confusion going on. Perfect conditions for accomplishing my goal."

"So, our trauma call may have been an invitation to come and kill one of our patients?"

"Stranger things have happened. Hang in there, buddy. I know you didn't cause the problem. Stay focused on the hospital and Stephanie. I will call you with the labs."

Mom fixed me dinner, but I just wasn't hungry. I opened a beer and never took a swig. I found myself staring out the window. I was learning from Stephanie. My trance was interrupted when my phone buzzed. It was a text from Celeste.

"Bun/Creat up. Creatinine levels are usually low in pregnancy, so an elevated ratio isn't as bad as it looks, but she is still dry. Please get a nasogastric feeding tube into her. I will have a nutritionist send you recommendations for tube feedings and water intake. Call me at any time if you need me. Celeste."

What a friend and a top-notch obstetrician. Within an hour, I was back from the hospital with the tube I needed and the enteral nutrition. The tube was much smaller than the nasogastric tubes we commonly used in the ER. Still, getting any size tube down Stephanie was going to be hell. When she is tranced out, like she is now, she strikes at almost anyone that touches her. Sticking a tube down her nose will amount to a vicious assault.

I took Mom and Dad with me. I explained what I had to do to Stephanie as best I could. I made it as clear as possible that this had to be done for the baby. I got about two feet from her when she swung. Even though she was pregnant, dehydrated, and forty pounds lighter than me, I was still glad she missed me. Two more attempts were equally ineffective. I was seriously considering hog-tying her and giving her a whack of Ativan. With her being dehydrated, I was a little leery of that.

I happened to look out the window, and there stood my answer. Seventeen hands high. Rio had gotten up from her foal's grave and had walked to the yard near the window. It was the first time that I noticed how bad she looked, too. She must have lost 200 pounds. Her normally glowing coat was dull. Her eyes were glazed and not wide awake like usual. Her ears were drooping, and her tail hung very low.

I was shocked by her appearance, but I saw my opportunity. I sent Dad to the barn to get something I needed. When he returned, I opened the ground-floor window, and we moved Stephanie's chair in front of it. As I hoped she would, Rio walked toward the window. She slowly and carefully bent down and stuck her large head in the room. She placed her head on Stephanie's right shoulder. Stephanie never flinched and certainly did not take a swing at her.

Rio lifted her head up as I inserted her NG tube. Once I confirmed the placement, I got some fluid and electrotypes into her, followed by an equine product similar to Jevity. I then greased up Stephanie's tube with some lubricant. I held it in my right hand as I prepared to defend myself with my left. Stephanie never moved a muscle. She rubbed Rio with her left hand as I inserted the tube. Again, after confirmation, I hooked up the enteral feeding.

"Stephanie, that tube needs to stay in until we can get you a little better. I have to pull Rio's, but we will reinsert hers every other day if needed. No response. The only sounds were the slight churning noises of the enteral feeding pumps doing their jobs.

# Chapter 66

## *Krenshaw Medical Center*

I was in my office at 6 AM. I had a ton of emails to read and a mountain of papers on my desk with notes from Juicy Lucy. I dug in and made some progress. JL arrived at 8 AM. She looked disapprovingly at the coffee I was drinking.

"Where did you get that stuff?"

I confessed. "I just heated up what was in the pot. I don't mind yesterday's brew."

"Too bad I wasn't in yesterday. That swill is four days old."

"No wonder I just assumed that Tina was buying cheap coffee for the hospital to save money."

JL nodded. "She is doing that, but I get ours from the ER. They know you pay for their coffee, so they don't mind giving me some. I'll make some fresh. I brought you a cinnamon roll from the cafeteria. They make them every Tuesday, and they are great. You look like shit. When did you last eat?"

"When did I last eat shit?"

She laughed. "You know what I mean. Glad to hear a little of your humor. You are so much more effective when you are jerking people around. I can understand, with what all you have been through, that joking is not easy. But trust me, it helps you."

She was right. The cinnamon roll was out of this world, and the coffee was excellent. Dan and Tina showed up at 11 AM and we took off for the state capital. Master's appellate trial was at 1 PM . After chiding Tina for purchasing substandard coffee beans, I picked Dan's brain.

"So, Dan, how will this go?"

"It will be a little different from other trials in that the judges pretty much run everything. Both attorneys make their brief arguments first, and then the judges each get to ask questions if they want."

"I sure hope there is no way that they can rule for that asshole," I added.

Dan explained, "I will have a better idea after I hear the questions and, more importantly, look at their facial expressions."

Tina was confident. "His theatrics at the hospital hearing and the board appeal can't help him."

"I sure hope I get to introduce them."

"What?" I was under the impression that his antics at those proceedings would be Master's downfall.

Dan laid it out for us. "I will try during my opening statement to allude to his behavior in both meetings and hopefully get out that he pled to assault charges. But since he was accepted into ARD, they may bar those."

Tina was not pleased but accepted Dan's synopsis. "Not much we can do except present our case. I hope this concludes today. By the way, ZZ, the coroner did clear you of the death of the trauma patient. He had severe brain and liver injuries. Neither of which were survivable. The transfusion reaction didn't help, but he had no chance."

"Well, that should help our malpractice case and my insurance!" I smiled.

Dan spoiled my brief happiness. "I think they will still sue you. I would expect Res Ipsit Loquitor."

"I hope that is some type of liquor." My Latin was a little rusty.

Dan shook his head. "It's Legalease for 'the thing speaks for itself.' It's kind of like a retained sponge. Not much defense is possible. A good attorney knows they can get money because your patient got the wrong blood. The amount of damages will be less because he died due to other causes. I think we will be able to settle this out of court if we do get sued."

"Any other good news?" I wanted to change the subject.

"How is Stephanie?" Tina obliged me.

I explained about the ultrasound, bloodwork and feeding tubes. I mentioned a consult with Dr Rosen and possible electroconvulsive therapy.

Tina said softly, "Poor Stephanie. When does it end for that girl?"

**Appellate Division, New Jersey Court System**

Dan's opening was short. The essence of Dan's case was that Master was swimming upstream against all patient safety science by not agreeing to do time outs or site marks. Although we could not prove it, we further suspected and self-reported that he may have done wrong site surgery. He had a hearing and appeal according to the bylaws and his suspension should be upheld. In addition, his actions during and after the hearing and appeal were not consistent with the expected behavior of a physician on our staff.

Thaddeus Prinzmetal rose slowly and fiddled with some papers on his desk. In a clear and somewhat soft voice, he presented his case. I didn't like the prick, but he was a very polished prick.

"I first of all remind counsel for the hospital that under the ARD agreement, Dr. Bator's actions at those meetings were not to be brought up in further proceedings."

One of the justices questioned that statement. "What actions, and why are they not germane to this case?"

Prinzmetal was nervous. "Dr. Bator pleaded guilty to assault charges after both hearings. But as part of the plea bargain, he was granted ARD."

Another justice weighed in. "For the purposes of this hearing I propose that the ARD provisions temporarily be set aside. I wish to hear about the assaults. I would welcome a vote of the justices here on this issue."

A third justice participated. "I propose that any discussion of the assaults be sealed from public discovery. Our purpose in hearing them is to provide context, not to violate an ARD agreement that was entered into in good faith by both parties."

That damn Dan was brilliant. Without mentioning any specifics, he got the dirty laundry into plain sight. Prinzmetal looked a little taken aback. After a small recess, the court returned. They agreed to seal the proceedings with respect to the assaults, but they wanted to know what had happened.

Prinzmetal slowly and reluctantly discussed the gun charge. He left out the fact that Master had pointed the gun at my dick. He was quick to add that the gun was unloaded. Dan said nothing. All he wanted was for the justices to know that Master was a loose cannon. Even a sanitized version of the gun issue was damning.

Prinzmetal then tried to paint a picture of Master throwing a tennis ball in a crowded conference room as an act of frustration. He claimed that Master meant to hurt no one.

Dan had to object. "Dr. Bator threw the tennis ball to hit and injure Dr. Zander. His throw was off, and he struck the medical staff secretary in the eye, causing a serious eye injury."

The justices now wanted to hear more of Dr. Bator's case. Prinzmetal obliged them.

"It is a fact that there is long-standing animosity between Dr. Zander and Dr. Bator. Dr. Bator was the subject of persecution at Krenshaw, meant to ruin his practice and his reputation. Dr. Bator freely admitted that he did not do site marking and time outs before surgery. But Dr. Bator did demonstrate during the hearing and appeal that despite those requirements being in place in most hospitals, wrong site surgery still occurs. Dr. Bator, as the surgeon responsible, did not wish to place his patients in jeopardy by using unproven methods to prevent wrong site surgery. Dr. Bator had never committed wrong site surgery during his 15 years of practice. He felt that his oversight was much more effective than site markings and timeouts. We respectfully request that he be immediately reinstated. We further request that he be awarded damages for loss of income during this witch hunt in addition to compensation for impugning his reputation. He may never be able to recover his image and stature in the medical community.

Dan rose when signaled by the chief justice. "Although it is true that site marking and timeouts are not 100% effective in eliminating wrong site surgery, they are the best tools available. The medical staff of Krenshaw, our accrediting bodies, and just about everyone except Dr. Bator endorses their use. Wrong site or wrong person surgery is a preventable error, and everything possible should be done to lessen its chances. Dr. Bator's lack of acceptance of medical science was the reason he was removed from the staff. His hearing and appeal were handled with meticulous attention to the bylaws. Krenshaw Medical Center firmly denies injuring Dr. Bator's reputation. Dr. Bator himself has tarnished his reputation. We respectfully request that he not be reappointed to the staff, and we vehemently deny that he is owed any compensation."

The justices signaled that they had heard enough and adjourned. We were asked to return in two hours for a preliminary verdict as to any immediate relief for Dr. Bator. We filed out into the hallway. I made a beeline for the restroom. My bladder was about to explode. I have to drink less coffee before these hearings.

# Chapter 67

## *Appellate Division New Jersey Court System*

## *Trenton, NJ*

As I exited the men's room, I saw Master yakking on his cell phone. Dan and Tina, surprisingly, were talking with Prinzmetal. He looked in control, and they looked worried. I elected to let them finish. When they did, I joined Dan and Tina in a conference room that we were permitted to use until the verdict was delivered.

"What did that prick of misery want?" I asked.

Tina was quick to respond. "He is castrating us financially."

"Huh"

Dan added. "He will be filing a motion to have the hospital placed under the financial stewardship of 'The Little Guy Act.'"

"Some midget is going to take financial control of the hospital?" I inquired.

"No ZZ, and by the way, some little people find the term midget to be offensive." (Dan was on the small side, about 5' 2")

"I didn't know that, sorry. But please explain."

"As part of the overhaul of the malpractice system in New Jersey, the legislature passed "The Little Guy Act." Basically, it states that if a hospital has more than four active malpractice claims, any of the plaintiffs may file for "Little Guy Status."

"Clear as mud."

"If you would listen, we might get somewhere." Dan was getting impatient.

"Sorry."

"If a hospital goes under financially, the creditors get paid off first, followed by the bondholders. Any malpractice claims that have not been settled prior to that time are limited to recovering existing insurance coverage. That is sometimes very little or nothing."

I was still trying to get my head around this. "I do feel bad for any patient that was harmed, but I sense there is more to this story."

Dan continued. "' The Little Guy Act' was sold as protecting poor plaintiffs from bad and failing hospitals. But it was really a handout to the trial lawyers. In the past when their clients got stiffed, they got stiffed. It can take hundreds of thousands in costs for a firm to complete a malpractice action. They count on 40% of a large settlement to recover their costs, pay for their boats and a couple of ex-wives, and make large contributions to sympathetic politicians. When 'The Little Guy Act' is invoked, the hospital is required to place an amount equal to the maximum estimated settlement for all current malpractice cases in escrow. That is minus any viable insurance coverage."

I still didn't see how that affected us. "So what?"

Tina answered, "If we are placed on that designation, we will be forced to escrow roughly $10 million that we don't have. Suppliers will demand cash up front for anything we need, including drugs. The bond rating agencies will reduce our bonds to junk status. No one will want them, and if we try to raise any money, we will pay exorbitantly high rates. Even prior to this, we had no buyers interested in purchasing the hospital. This will ensure that none appear. We are financially screwed."

Our discussion was truncated by a call to return to the court.

The Chief Justice gave the verdict. "The court will issue a final ruling in two months on this matter. Today's request for immediate emergency reinstatement of Dr. Bator's privileges to practice at Krenshaw Medical Center is denied."

Master and Prinzmetal did not look phased. They spoke quietly at their table.

"Roy, my best guess is that they will rule against us in their final opinion. Be thinking about what you want to do. To take this to the state Supreme Court will cost you around $250,000.  But if we wait a little, Krenshaw may go under anyway. They are circling the drain, and with the papers I am filing today, we are about to flush their toilet. But they can probably last until we get to the Supreme Court."

A quarter million was a drop in Master's wealth bucket. "I want my name cleared, complete vindication. Understand?"

"OK, I will prepare the needed documents when we get the final ruling from this court."

Dan, Tina, and I piled into Dan's SUV. We were careful to avoid any public discussion. Master had been known to employ private detectives that utilized sophisticated listening equipment.

I slapped him on the back. "Dan, congratulations again. I must believe the information about the assaults cooked his goose."

"Thanks ZZ. It did work out in our favor. But the news about 'The Little Guy Act' is very troubling. I need to get to work on how to fight that. It's hard to do because you look like you are trying to screw an injured patient to help your suppliers and rich bondholders."

Tina further rained on my parade. "ZZ, keep your schedule open this week. I fully well expect Joint Commission and The Licensure Board to come in to look at the transfusion case."

# Chapter 68

## *Krenshaw Medical Center*

I was dog-tired by Friday. As Tina had expected, both The Joint Commission and the Licensure Board surveyors arrived this week. Luckily, we didn't have both at the same time. I was amazed at the difference. The surveyors were both knowledgeable and professional. But the philosophies of their representative organizations could not have been further apart.

The Licensure Board man arrived first. He demanded to see our log of recent blood transfusions and our complaint and grievance logs. He then selected thirty transfusion cases at random and the charts of the two patients involved in our transfusion reaction. He barricaded himself in a conference room and dissected the information.

Four hours later he emerged with numerous violations that he had uncovered. All pretty much were unrelated to transfusions. Things like orders that were not dated and timed and verbal orders not signed within the 48 hours we required in the bylaws. He cited us for histories and physicals that were lacking this or that. Honestly, it was trivial stuff. But the Licensure Board people hate to show up without creating some work for you to do.

Then he dropped the hammer. $200,000 fine for the transfusion reaction. Never Episode number three. He refused to acknowledge that an imposter could have switched the tubes. It was just as Dan said- the malpractice case might go, Res Ipsit Loquitor. The thing speaks for itself. Two patients got the wrong blood. Please pay $200,000 and do not pass go. There was nothing about what he did that made us better any less likely to have a future transfusion reaction. He was out the door by 3:30 PM like a good little bureaucrat.

On Thursday a nurse surveyor from Joint Commission arrived. There was a distinct difference in her approach versus Mr. Licensure Board. She was looking for a root cause. She was looking to make us better. He was looking to collect $200K and hit the bricks.

She asked for no charts to start with. She wanted to talk to the staff. She went to obstetrics, the OR, and the ER. She politely quizzed staff about the collection of specimens and even observed two blood draws. She then went to the lab and looked at the procedures for handling specimens in the lab. Satisfied with that, she then traced the process for blood administration. Unlike Mr. Licensure Board, she was convinced that an imposter must have switched the tubes.

I thought she would finish in one day, as that is what JC had allotted her. But she surprised me. She cleared us on the blood procedures. But she was bent out of shape about an imposter being able to harm a patient. She called JC and got permission to extend the survey until Friday at noon. She then proceeded to take copies of our policies and procedures on employee identification, restricted areas of the hospital, and general hospital safety and security to review that night.

Friday morning, she appeared to be wearing roller skates. We ran all around the hospital. The more things she looked at, the more she found, and the more she wrote us up.

She started her report out at 1 PM and ended at 2 PM We got seven Requirements for Improvement. She required us to improve our procedures for vetting new employees. She found several employee files where we did not complete the criminal background checks that we required. The next area of noncompliance involved security procedures in general. She really was very concerned about our procedures to protect the safety and security of our newborns. She liked the security system but did not like the discharge process.

Unfortunately, the obstetrical nursing staff had gotten into some bad habits. They were very comfortable with deactivating and removing the security bracelet in the morning on the day of discharge. She was right.

Removing the bracelet prior to discharge was an unnecessary risk and defeated the purpose of the system.

She tore apart our employee badge system. She was cataplectic about us using a standard Word program to print our badges. She finished us off with some requirements that we improve the situational awareness of our staff. They had to say something if they saw something.

"Lots of work to do, ZZ," Tina said.

"Yeah, but it's good work. There isn't a thing that she asked us to do that we shouldn't want to do. I am a little embarrassed that we had to be told. We need to do a better job of getting out in front of this stuff."

"True, I'm kicking myself in the ass for not knowing that the pharmacy was still permitting nursing staff to enter the pharmacy at night without pharmacist supervision. That's so basic. I have got to get out of my office more."

"Don't blame yourself. You can't be in two places at once. Your schedule has been a little hectic, No?"

"Oh yeah. ZZ, speaking of schedules, aren't you due to be home by 3 PM ?"

"Oh, crap. Thanks for reminding me."

# Chapter 69

## *Fired Up Farms*

I sped home and arrived with ten minutes to spare. Dad had already registered us for the telemedicine visit. Stephanie was sitting in her chair that Dad had turned away from the window. She just stared straight ahead at the blank computer screen. A bag of parental nutrition and water hung from a pole near her side. The tiny motor powering the pump made a low churning noise as it parsed in the nutrition at the required rate of administration.

At exactly 3 PM, Dr. Rosen appeared on the screen. He introduced himself and asked that we each introduce ourselves. We took turns walking behind Stephanie to greet him. He then asked that we aim the camera at Stephanie but remain close enough to be heard if he asked us questions.

"First of all, Dr. Zander I really appreciate the records that you provided me with on Stephanie. I can see that she is a complex case. You made things much easier for me when you enclosed summaries from her therapists and psychologists. I think I have a good background picture of Stephanie."

I really liked this guy. Not because he was blowing smoke up my ass, but because he didn't act like a lot of psychiatrists I knew. They tended to dawdle around and ask their own questions when most of what they wanted was already in the record. This dude was on point and focused.

Dr. Rosen made three attempts to speak with Stephanie. All were done in a calm tone and were purposely nonjudgemental. Stephanie turtled through his questions. I had to look hard to see if she was still breathing. She was that still.

Dr. Rosen then did not ignore Stephanie. He told her what he was going to do and invited her to join the conversation at any time. But he wanted input from all of us. He asked a lot about PC's death and their relationship. There were many questions about Stephanie's support systems. Then he shocked me. He asked about Fired Up Rio. Celeste Maliterna must have explained their bonding and their uncanny ability to communicate nonverbally. He asked if we had any questions.

"Do you think she needs ECT?" I had to know.

"ZZ, I like to approach these things in a step wise manner. For now, I think Stephanie is safe and stable. True to her form, she has retreated into a protective shell. With the magnitude and suddenness of her loss, that is to be expected. With the tube feedings, I know you are meeting her and her baby's nutritional needs."

Mom interrupted, which was unusual for her. "But can't she see how harmful this could be to her baby. I mean, she is PC's parting gift. I don't understand how Stephanie can ignore her baby's needs."

"Mrs. Zander. I thank you for bringing that up. I would normally answer you later, out of Stephanie's earshot. But I am sure she is processing what we are doing here today, and she needs to hear this. Stephanie is highly intelligent. In fact, she operates at a higher level than most of us. Her psychic trauma is so great that she is not capable of processing new information well, if at all. All circuits are busy. Her brain says, 'please try again later.' She knows she is pregnant, but she is not able to comprehend fully what that means. She is certainly not able to comprehend that her catatonia may be an issue for her baby. It is my job, with your help, to get her to accept the horror of her trauma. Only then will her mind be open to fully understanding her current situation. These things take time, and she is a unique case."

Mom was apologetic. "Dr. Rosen, I'm sorry. I didn't mean to question you."

"I'm glad you did. We must get some of these things out in the open."

"OK, what's the plan?" I asked.

He laughed. "Typical ER doctor. She is stable. She is no danger to herself or others. Therefore, she does not require inpatient treatment.

You are meeting her and her baby's nutritional needs. My experience is that these issues typically subside in 3-4 weeks. Medications can speed that process, but most of the ones I like are not great in pregnancy. I propose that we stay the course for another week. She may come out of it enough that we can make some progress with therapy."

"If she doesn't?" Dad inquired.

"My next recommendation would be that if she remains catatonic, we consider ECT. As you know her physical status is deteriorating daily due to lack of any exercise or movement. I don't like that to extend beyond 21 days. It takes two days of rehab for every day of inactivity. I'm willing to wait a little longer, but not much. Can we get together next week at this time for a telemedicine update?"

We agreed. He said his goodbyes to Stephanie and disconnected. She remained in a trance.

# Chapter 70

## *Fired Up Farms*

Billie sipped his scotch and tried to objectively assess the situation. He was in a good place. The hospital was being crushed under the weight of three "Never Episodes." He still could not believe his luck at being able to create the transfusion reaction. He was hoping to mix-up some specimens from the ER on a day that I was working. But who would believe that I would hand him the tubes of blood? Once he knew that he had the blood specimens for two patients who both needed transfusions, his path was crystal clear.

His AI-designed disguise worked perfectly. I looked right at him and had no idea who he was. Sure, they might have a video of him. But who was him? It sure as hell wasn't Billie Browner. That poor guy working at the Wendy's drive-through in Glenshaw had no idea he was being photographed from about ten angles. He had even less idea that his face would be used to create the mask that Billie wore in the hospital. That dude might have to answer some questions if the cops get that far, but Billie was clean.

The Dying Was Easy gang was on life support. Joe and Azzie were wallowing in their injuries while the monster priest was kissing ass in Rome to save his cassock. Attorney Dan was circling the drain with Krenshaw Medical Center, which was financially moribund.

A couple more "Nevers" and the hospital should fold. It was time to pull the plug on ZZ and get out of Dodge. A quick trip to South America for facial surgery, and then onto New Zealand and a nice long vacation.

Billie knew from Jenny that the Zanders would be in another telemedicine call that afternoon. He wanted to listen in as he did a week ago. Talk about cheap entertainment. Last week he downed a couple of scotches as they discussed that little retard and her catatonia. This week was different, and there was work to be done. He selected a female face from his AI collection and proceeded to create the needed mask. He then applied it, a wig, and the correct scrubs.

Those bastards at Krenshaw had changed their employee ID badges. Making the old ones on Word was so simple. But he found a way to get some blank new ones. When he added the information, he wanted it to look authentic. No one who examined it closely would be fooled, but Billie had no intention of letting anyone examine it closely.

Next, he hacked into the medical record system. It wasn't a true hack. He used the login and password for a triage nurse in the ER. One morning, she failed to notice Billie taping her login keystrokes. He quickly located some perfect victims. Three patients with either dementia or aphasia (inability to speak) from strokes. Vulnerable patients who couldn't tell anyone what really happened to them.

Thirty minutes later, he checked his disguises. Then he walked into the employee entrance. The security officer looked closely at him as he passed by. Billie tried to move down the hall without looking like he was trying to get away.

"Hey, miss, please stop."

Billie was pissed. He turned to face the out-of-breath security guard, who had lumbered down the hallway to confront him.

"Yes." Replied a female voice. Billie had a number of preprogrammed responses that he activated by pressing a button in his pocket. The AI voice patterns were reconstructed from recordings of real people. Billie had learned to lip-sync convincingly.

"Sorry to stop you. But I don't recognize you, and we are required to verify the identity of anyone we don't personally know."

"I am Natalie Wright. I am a new nurse's aide assigned to the seventh floor."

The guard thumbed up an app on his phone and scrolled down to the human resources section. He brought up a list of new employees, and there she was. Just the same as her picture. Natalie Wright. Nurse's aide. Primary floor 7. The information matched what Billie had just told him. It should; Billie entered it just a few hours ago.

"Welcome to Krenshaw, Natalie. Have a good shift." The guard returned to his station, quite satisfied with his spotting a new face and doing his required duty.

Billie made his way to the sixth floor and found the room he wanted. The hallway was empty. It was a change of shift, and both incoming and outgoing personnel were huddled in a conference room, reporting on their patients. Krenshaw had not yet adopted bedside reporting, where report was given on each patient at the bedside.

The first patient Billie had selected was massively obese. Billie about herniated himself, flipping her over onto her side. He took the sandpaper and vigorously abraded her sacral area. Skin breakdown, here we come. He noted that her roommate was equally out to lunch, so he took the opportunity to give her a free dermabrasion of both heels. Those would be nice ulcers in a couple of days.

Satisfied, he peeked out the door. The way to the fire door was clear. He initially encountered no one in the stairway, but as he exited the 7th floor, he passed a physical therapist. Neither one said a word. Billie quickly made his way to room 706. What he found was even better than he expected.

The patient was writhing around on the bed. All four-bed rails were up. The bed was as low and as close to the floor as it could get. There were mats on either side of the bed to cushion her fall in case Ms. 706 pulled a Houdini and got out of bed. It took only thirty seconds to lower all four-bed rails and to raise the bed a full five feet off the ground. He pulled the mats into the bathroom. As he entered the stairwell for his exit, he heard the sweet thud of the patient in 706 hitting the floor. The only question was what was fractured, a hip or a skull. Maybe he would get lucky, and it would be both.

# Chapter 71

## *Fired Up Farms*

Dr. Rosen wasn't surprised that little had changed in a week. He was hoping for better, but hope alone didn't solve many medical problems. Mom asked a lot of questions about the ECT. She wanted to know how it worked, the side effects, and number of treatments needed. Dr. Rosen patiently answered each one. Mom was satisfied.

Dr. Rosen addressed me. "ZZ, can you arrange ambulance transportation for her? Most patients come by car. In her state, I would feel better if she traveled by ambulance."

"Yes, sir. As you might expect, I have several friends in the ambulance service. They will bring her by ambulance, and I will accompany her."

"Good. She needs to be as comfortable as possible. So, barring any unforeseen change, let's plan on ECT at Jefferson Main Hospital in Central City, Philadelphia, next Wednesday. The scheduling unit will call you on Tuesday morning with the time. Any questions?"

"When should I discontinue the tube feeding?" I needed to know.

"Excellent question. Sorry, I did not bring it up. Please give her extra fluid on Tuesday, but discontinue any fluid and food after midnight. Anesthesia would kill me if I forgot to tell you. Thanks!!"

"No problem. Thanks, Dr Rosen."

Dad looked worried as we sat down at the kitchen table.

"Are you sure this is ok, the whole idea of her having a seizure gives me the creeps?"

"That's good, Dad. You keep your mouth shut when the doctor asks if there are any more questions. Then, not more than five minutes later, you quiz me."

"ZZ, you are my son. You won't give me any medical bullshit. I like Dr. Rosen, but he's not my son that I trust with my life and Stephanie's."

"Thanks, Dad." He knew how to shut me up. "I think this is the right thing to do. The quicker we get her up and moving around, the better. It may be a while until she talks, but her inactivity will soon become a medical problem that can threaten the pregnancy."

"That's all I needed to know."

**Krenshaw Medical Center**

The facts that Dan had assembled were difficult to comprehend. I couldn't believe them.

"You mean to tell me that a female nurse's aide walked in the employee entrance and got past one of our better security guards?"

Dan nodded. "He followed procedure and stopped her. When he accessed the human resource files, he was able to confirm that she was an employee and let her go."

Tina chimed in. "The only problem was that she was not an employee. Someone had hacked into our human resources system and created her."

"Holy crap, where all did she go?"

Dan detailed her path. "After she left the guard, she went up the fire escape to the sixth floor. We have good footage of her entering the room where the patients had skin breakdown. From there, she went to the seventh floor and accessed the room of the patient who was later found on the floor."

I interrupted. "How is that patient doing?"

Tina again joined the conversation. "She has a depressed skull fracture, subdural hematomas, and a fractured hip. She has been transferred to the trauma center, but she is not expected to survive."

"Poor old soul. What a way to go." After a pause, I continued my questioning. "Where did the imposter go after she left 706?"

Dan answered, "She went down the fire escape and exited into the parking lot. Before you ask about a license number, she walked through the lot and took the 43C bus. From there, we lost her. The police were unable to determine when or where she got off. She just disappeared."

This was hard to digest. "So, where do we stand with the Licensure Board and Joint Commission?"

Tina scanned her notes, but she already knew the answer. She was just looking for a little delay. "JC is OK, so far. They accept that we have an imposter, and they will leave us alone until they get the police report. We were fortunate that their nurse did such a thorough job.

"The Licensure Board has issued us a 21-day termination notice. That is standard. But considering we are looking at Never Episodes four, five and six, they may not rescind it. Normally, if they fine you and inspect the death out of you, they let the business go on. We can't be sure they will be so generous with us."

Dan looked incredibly tired. "So, where are we financially?"

Tina was dejected. "We have thirty days to escrow $8 million for our malpractice exposure. That, of course, will go up when we get sued for the latest incidents. The Licensure Board will likely fine us $400,000, $800,000 and $1,200,000. We have cash on hand of $735,000. Our bonds are now officially junk, and the suppliers have put us on cash upfront policies. I think I can keep us floating for 3-4 weeks. But we must get out from under the lawsuits and fines. I don't see how we do that."

Dan offered a suggestion. "Let's just chill for the weekend. We have been burning the candle, and it shows. Let's all get out of here and recharge our batteries. No hospital business this weekend. No emails, no phone calls, etc."

The group unanimously agreed.

## Fired Up Farms

I was back home in time to pick up Billie.

Mom quizzed me. I could tell by her tone that she was irritated. "Why are you going to a party in Atlantic City tonight? Don't we have enough to do? Shouldn't you be doing something at the hospital?"

"Mom, It's not really a party. It's an Irish wake. Bella, a nurse I worked with in Atlantic City, died tragically when she fell off a cruise ship. In her will, she asked that the ER staff throw her ashes into the sea off the pier in AC. They asked me to come, and I want to be there to support them. I like those people."

I left out the part where I was porking Bella intermittently for a few years and that she specifically wanted me to distribute her ashes. I also deleted the information about the sharks. I didn't think Mom could process all of that. How kind and convenient of me.

She expressed her concerns. "We have just been having such bad luck lately that I worry about everything. Driving back and forth, and the drinking, etc."

"Well, Mom, there will be some drinking, but Billie is coming with me. Jenny is out of town, and he has nothing to do tonight. I thought he would be good company on the ride down and back. Plus, I got everyone rooms at the casino, so there will be no driving until tomorrow morning. As far as the hospital is concerned, I need a break. Dan, Tina, and I agreed to take a weekend off and hit it hard early Monday."

Talk about bad timing. I just got Mom settled down when the back door flew open.

"There ther there bet bet better be plenty of of o booooooze, aaaannnnndd bbbbbrrroads!" Billie stammered as he entered the back door.

Mom gave me the look. You know, the one that says, "See,

I told you so".

# Chapter 72

## *Bustin Loose Casino and Hotel*

## *Atlantic City, NJ*

Damn it. My freakin' head hurts, and I feel like total shit. I have to give up drinking. I like drinking, but I really hate the next day. I must have had a real snoot full. I remember having a few drinks and adjourning to the pier to distribute Bella's ashes. I recall dinner, which was excellent. Lobster. It was scrumptious. Things get a little fuzzy after dinner. I remember that Billie and I were dancing with Anne Marie Kroskey and Franny Campbell. I know that Bille was pretty wasted. He wanted to hit the sack with Franny, but I don't know how that turned out.

I was a little woozy as I got up to whiz. There was no sign of Billie, so he must have scored. I really hated it when he did that stuff around me. I despised having to lie to Jenny. I know she would quiz me about his behavior. But what could I do? Guys must cover for other guys when their lack of restraint gets them into a scrape.

On the way back from the can, I spied a note on the bedstand.

"ZZ, one of my owners, called early this morning. He wants to see some yearlings in Canada today. I got an Uber to AC airport, where he will pick me up. He will get me back home tonight. I bet your damn head is aching. You were trashed last night. Where in the hell did you go? We came back to the room, and I was half asleep when you snuck out. Lucky bastard. See you later."

I looked down in the direction of my zipper. "Did you do anything last night that I don't remember?" Silence. He never answers when he thinks there might be trouble.

I made a crummy in-room coffee and got my things together. I wanted to go back to sleep but wanted to do that in my own bed. I stopped at the front desk for the bill. $10,000. A lot of money, but Bella was more than a good friend. I am going to miss her.

**Arbitrium Arbor**

**Rome, Italy**

Father Jonathan was placed in a room and told to close his eyes and pray. He was not to open them until he was instructed to do so. If the past few months taught him anything, it was obedience.

"Open your eyes, my son, and your heart."

Father Jonathan opened his eyes. There in front of him sat the pope, the Vicar of Christ. He looked different in jeans and a flannel shirt, but Father Jonathan knew it was him. The terrified priest fell to his knees and reached up to grab the outstretched hand of the pope. He kissed his ring.

"Jonathan, my son, what have you learned since you have been here?"

Father Jonathan thought for a minute. He looked the pope in the eye and bared his soul.

"I learned that I am unimportant. That, and those that place their needs above the needs of others, are evil."

"Very good, Father Jonathan. I see much evil in the world and much good. Our job is to help the good to conquer the evil. You have been chosen by God to do just that. Are you ready?"

"Most Holy Father, I am ready to serve."

The pope blessed him, gave him communion, and left. Bishop Carlucci entered a few minutes after the pope left.

"Welcome back, Father Jonathan. You have passed your test and are restored to your previous position. Your friends are in serious trouble, and you need to help them. But it must be done in a way that respects God and your priesthood."

The bishop gave him the details about PC's funeral, Stephanie's condition, and what he had heard about the hospital. He neglected to mention that he won over a million dollars on the Pick Nine.

The bishop had his own question. "Do you understand what you need to do and how you need to do it?"

"Yes, Your Excellency. I know that I cannot beat evil with evil. Evil can only be defeated with good. After that, it is simple."

"Go forth, my son. Return to your friends and the children of that special school. You have three months until I'll give you a permanent assignment. Until that time, I will assign you to mass duties on the weekends. The rest of the time, you will be free to complete your mission."

The bishop left, and Father Jonathan packed his belongings. The bishop had already made him a reservation on a flight that arrived in Philadelphia at 1 PM Monday.

He texted me. "Arriving PHL at 1 PM Monday. Can you arrange transport to the farm?"

I was shocked to get FJ's text. We had very little contact with him during his time away. He knew about PC, Azzie, and Joe but little else. I stopped the truck to answer him. I pulled back onto the highway, and I was tempted to go to the hospital to catch up on emails and return messages. That's a lie. In the shape I was in, I was only going to the hospital if they would drill a hole in my head. Unfortunately, our neurosurgeon was on suspension, so I headed home.

**Fired Up Farms**

I felt a little better on Sunday. I was hoping to talk with Billy so I could fill in some of the blanks in my memory of Friday night. I did reach Jenny, and she said that Billy was on his way to Australia.

"What the hell is he doing there?"

Jenny laughed. "His main owner, Gerry Saunderson, is on a buying spree. He took Billie to Canada on Saturday, and this morning, they left for Australia. Mr. Saunderson has a line on two trotters there that he wants to buy."

"Long way to go to get a couple trotters."

Jenny agreed. "Yeah, but on Mr. Saunderson's private jet the ride is doggone comfortable. You know Billie. He likes to rub elbows with the filthy rich, hoping some of it will rub off."

"When do you expect him back?"

Jenny sighed. "Who knows? He's been coming and going a lot over the past couple of months. I hardly see him. Do you want me to have him call you when he calls in?"

"Nah, I'll catch him when he gets back."

"Did you give Bella a sendoff with a bang?"

I detected a slight snark in the question. That's the problem about having sex with women. They mark their territory and do their best to defend it forever. They may not want you anymore, but they sure as hell want to know if you are catching any.

"What's that supposed to mean?"

Jenny giggled. "Billie didn't say for sure, but he implied that you might have been on the prowl."

"I hope a kangaroo kicks him in the nuts." I hung up.

# Chapter 73

## *Krenshaw Medical Center*

The best part about a hangover is when it's gone, kind of like an inflamed hemorrhoid of the brain. Saturday was rough, and Sunday was only slightly better, but this morning, I was on the bit.

JL had the coffee ready, and I noticed an ominous number of telephone messages in her hand. I grabbed the coffee and left her holding the messages. I was sure I didn't want them.

"Good morning, ZZ. Did you folks give Bella a good sendoff? The word is that it was a wild time."

"Something like that." See what I mean about women that a guy has slept with? Even though Bella was dead, and JL was married, JL still acted weird when Bella's name came up, especially if there was some chance that I scored, even though it wasn't with Bella.

JL handed me the messages. Before I could dig into the stack, the phone rang. It was Dan.

JL only heard my half of the conversation, but it was enough. "Yes, I heard. No, I don't believe it. We are hosed. Be there in 10 minutes."

Dan and Tina were seated at the conference table in Tina's office. I sat down quietly as Tina was finishing a call.

Tina shuffled the papers in front of her. "ZZ, I know you have to leave for Philly this morning, so we'll try to be brief. That was Prinzmetal on the phone. He is representing the family of the patient who fell. He feels certain that they will be added to group protected by Little Guy Status."

Dan retorted, "He must have some great contacts. That patient died last night, and already he signed up the family."

I agreed. "I am sure he has moles all over town. Some of our nurses live a little beyond their means. Shunting cases to MEP could be a nice income boost."

Tina nodded. "That's a conversation for another day. But the news does add to our financial issues. We need cash, and we need it soon."

I asked, "What would it take for us to buy some breathing room?"

She was ready for the question. "Anything we can raise immediately will be a big help. We are paying cash upfront for supplies, and we can't let them get shut off. So, $500,000 there. We need about another million to be certain we can meet payroll and make up for back taxes that we didn't pay."

I made some notes. "Ok, 1.5 to 2 million now, and how much later?"

"Ten million. Can the governor help in any way?"
I shook my head no. "I will contact the governor. But with our negative news and his reelection in limbo, I have little hope that he can help us. I know that I, my parents, and Stephanie still have most of the money we won on those lottery tickets. We can probably come up with 1- 1.5 million. Stephanie just got her insurance check for PC for $5 million."

Dan objected, "We aren't going to even think about Stephanie contributing. She needs to live off that money. She needs to be able to raise her daughter the way PC intended. Any money that we get is likely to go into a black hole and never be repaid."

I agreed. "I can try a 'Dying Was Easy' alert and see if we can come up with any other ideas. Father Jonathan is returning today. He doesn't have any money, but he can certainly help us try to figure a way out of this mess. I haven't heard from Azzie or Joe, so they may not be able to help us either."

Dan wasn't deterred. "Sound the alarm. Let's see who responds and what they can offer. We need all the help we can get."

I texted Joe and Azzie first and got the same response. Both had blocked me. Wow. Hard to believe that would ever happen, but they both were still struggling in their injury recoveries. When I called the rehab hospital, I was only told that neither one was talking to the other and that both had removed all friends and families from their HIPPA lists.

Dan shook his head when I told him. Tina just kept going over her ledger sheets. She looked at her watch and then excused me.

"ZZ, thanks for coming in today. I think Dan and I can handle things here until you get back tomorrow morning. Go pick up Father Jonathan. Let me know tomorrow how much cash you can raise from friends and family in the short run."

I was happy to get on the road. "Thanks, I'll see what I can do."

I had a little time to spare, so I stopped back at the farm. Not much had changed there. Stephanie and Rio slept outside in a lean-to. In the morning, they walked to PC's grave, where they stayed until 2 PM. Then they got up (with plenty of struggle on both of their parts) and went to the grave of Rio's foal. They stayed there until 10 PM when they wandered back to the lean-to. Each were still receiving fluids and nutrition via feeding tubes. It was a sad sight. It made me look forward to the ECT treatment. Something had to cause a change. I was wondering if I should sign up for a jolt.

I accompanied Dad when he went to change out the tube feeding bags for both. "Dad, the hospital is in real trouble. Do you and Mom have much of the lottery money left?"

"Actually, we have all of it. We didn't feel right about taking it in the first place, but Dan was insistent. Why?"

"I was hoping to borrow some for the hospital. I have $400,000 of mine left. With your $1.2 million, that would be $1.6 million. That would buy us some short-term relief."

"ZZ, you are welcome to it all. We can't let that hospital close before Millions Week."

"You know that, most likely, you will never get it back."

"We don't need it. We are happy to help."

I am barred from telling you about how we all came to get lottery money. That was part of the agreement to save The Always Hope School. After taxes, we each got around $600,000. I wish I could explain but I don't want to spend the rest of my life in a federal lockup. Sorry.

"Thanks, Dad. I knew I could count on you."

"Any word from Azzie or Joe yet?"

"Dad, the news there is not very good. In fact, there is no news. I tried to sound a 'Dying Was Easy' alarm and both had blocked me. Neither one will take texts or phone calls from me."

"Some people have a hard time adjusting to the things they have been through, although those two would have been the last two I would have picked."

I agreed. "Shocked me too. Maybe Father Jonathan will have some ideas."

"Do you want me to go with you to pick him up?"

"Nah. You better stay here and make sure Stephanie and Rio are ok. I'll pick up the Padre. I better hit the road."

# Chapter 74

## *Philadelphia International Airport*

Traffic was surprisingly light. I found the airport cell phone lot and logged into my work email account. So far, no notices of any bureaucrats or surveyors pounding on the door. But have no fear, they will show up.

Father Jonathan walked briskly as he followed the signs towards the Customs desk. It must be his lucky day. The agent at desk four opened for the day and motioned Father Jonathan to come his way. That good fortune probably cut twenty minutes from his stay in line.

He handed his passport and forms to the agent, who carefully perused them. The agent stamped the passport and kept the required forms.

"Do you have anything to declare?"

Father was tempted to declare bankruptcy, but he wasn't sure the agent would appreciate it.

"No, sir."

The agent handed his passport back to him. With a sleight of hand that could make him rich in most casinos, the agent signaled Father Jonathan that there was something under the passport. The mannerism of the agent made it clear that he was not to look at it now. There was no luggage on the belt, so he made his way to the nearest restroom and an empty stall.

He pulled out the passport and found a small envelope attached to the back. Typed on the outside was "ZZ Eyes Only." He put the message back in his pocket and found his way to the baggage area. When he secured his belongings, he texted me. "Meet me outside doorway 28."

I was surprised that he was ready so soon. I made my way to the door, and there he stood. All 6 foot 6 inches, but he looked skinny. I grabbed a spot at the curb right in front of him. I jumped out and gave him a big hug. He had lost weight. I had a great smart-ass line ready when he whispered in my ear. "Code Blue." That meant two things to me. First of all, something big was up and second, we needed to move our asses out of there.

The instant I pulled away from the curb, he handed me the note and told me how he obtained it. I silently read it as I drove.

"Do not enter New Jersey. You will be arrested for suspicion of rape. Disappear for 7-10 days, then call home using safe phone."

We were going north on I-95. I started out of habit to take the exit for the Walt Whitman Bridge. I suddenly realized my error and jumped back out of line for the exit and headed for Center City. I tried to digest the full meaning of the note, but I couldn't get past the rape part. Then I ate the note and the envelope. Maybe I could digest it that way.

My mind was on fire. Rape? Who? When? Where? I didn't remember having sex with anyone since I last visited the dearly departed Bella. But I had no recollection of last Friday night. I didn't, did I? I found my way to 1025 Spruce Street. That housed the Phi Chi medical fraternity, of which I was a member. It was also my former home. I parked the truck. I had no intention of going in to visit the brothers, but I knew the area well.

FJ asked. "What's in the note, and where are we going?"

I deliberately did not answer him. Anyone who knew me well enough would know that I trusted the Padre with my life. But the note was for my eyes only. Someone didn't want him to have to lie about what happened today.

Even though I wasn't sure I had them, I had to take a few minutes to think. Who would be able to deliver a note via a Custom's agent? Who would have advanced knowledge of my being under investigation? The only person who could pull that off was AC, Aldo Crinelli. This was all him.

FJ correctly surmised that he was not getting any more information and sat quietly in the passenger seat. I searched the rear cab and found the briefcase I needed. I told Father Jonathan that I would be right back. I jumped out and ran around the back of the house.

He knew I wasn't coming back, and he had no idea where I had gone. Funny, I had forgotten to take the keys to the truck with me. After an hour of praying, Father Jonathan walked around the truck and got into the driver's seat. After starting the truck, he worked his way to the Ben Franklin Bridge and crossed over into Jersey. Traffic was light as he passed through Cherry Hill on his way to Krenshaw. A few miles outside of Cherry Hill, a police car pulled out behind him and lit his lights. As Father Jonathan pulled to the curb, three other cars arrived in seconds.

A stern voice announced. "Put your hands on the wheel."

He did as he was told.

"Pass the keys out to me."

He complied.

"Now get out of the truck and put your hands on the hood."

In the alley behind Phi Chi, I removed the SIM card and battery from my phone. I used a brick that I found in the alley to smash them to pieces. I grabbed a cab to 30th Street Station. After making sure that the surveillance cameras got good footage of my face and that lovely scar, I boarded the Metroliner for Washington D.C., using my correct identification.

I found my way to a restroom and used some of the props in my briefcase to change my hair, add a beard, and cover the scar. I turned my jacket inside out and applied the baseball cap as a last measure. I kept my head bent low as I exited in Wilmington. Hopefully, they will think Zachary Zander is still on the train.

I made my way slowly to the bus station. I requested a ticket to Hershey. When the agent asked for my identification, I was quick to produce it. I had known they would accept a work ID as long as it had a picture. Dr. Frederick Leasure was as fake as his employer, Premier Rehab Hospital of Lewes, Delaware. The agent never blinked. I wondered if he would have done anything if the ID read "Osama Bin Laden, Terrorist." Probably not.

I was so happy that I had kept that "Go Bag." A few years back, I decided to create one in case my enemies got too close. Deuce and Knuckles were murderers, and they wanted me six feet under. So, I created a bag and an exit strategy, allowing me to hole up for a short period of time if ever needed. I had never used it, but it came in handy today. Twenty thousand dollars, two fake IDs, assorted disguises, and two burner phones were a welcome sight when I opened the briefcase.

I kept the disguises on when I exited the bus in Hershey. I jumped in a cab to my destination. The sign read "Serenity Reincarnations." Their slogan was "We put lives back together." Last Saturday morning, I vowed to quit drinking. That was probably just the hangover talking, but today, I guess I had to do it. When the cabbie left, I removed the disguises and rang the bell.

"Welcome, brother," announced the desk attendant as he opened the door. He continued. "I am Gerald Billings. Whom do I have the pleasure of meeting?"

"Frederick Leasure, Dr. Frederick Leasure, sir." He extended his hand, and I shook it.

"Well, Dr. Leasure, if you came to rid yourself of addiction to drugs or alcohol, you are in the right place. We do put lives back together. Is your problem drugs?" he asked nonjudgmentally.

"No sir, never. But I do have a problem with alcohol that I need help with."

"Are you prepared to sign in?"

"Yes."

He handed me some papers. "Here is a list of our rules. If you aren't prepared to meet them, you might as well head back out the door. We permit no exceptions. We know what works and what doesn't."

I took a few minutes to pretend to read the rules. I knew I wasn't going anywhere, but I needed to convince Gerry here that I was legit and wanted to dry out. I remembered to fidget and look anxious, like anyone else heading into withdrawal. I decided I'd better ask a question to look like I was still debating what to do.

"You require a ten-day stay?"

"Yes, that is the minimum for the inpatient treatment. After you are discharged, we work to find an outpatient program nearer your home. The outpatient programs have no defined time frame."

"What if I elect to leave here before the ten days?"

"Then you forfeit the entire cost of the stay. There are no refunds, period. You put up ten thousand dollars on admission. If you have any insurance coverage, we refund you whatever the insurance pays."

I counted out $10,000 and put it on his desk. "No insurance."

"Fine. Do you wish to have visitors or allow anyone to have contact with you? We find that family members can sometimes be very helpful."

"No, sir. I want total anonymity. No one can know that I am here. I will notify the proper folks at the medical board when and if I am successful. But I need to be clean and sober first. My wife is filing for divorce. She will use any substance abuse treatment against me. I may need my records later to prove that I was here. But while I'm here, I'm not here, if you know what I mean."

"We do anonymity well. Welcome, Mr. Ben Smith."

# Chapter 75

## *Interstate 70 outside of Cherry Hill*

"Dr. Zander. We are placing you under arrest for rape."

The other six officers looked around as Officer Claxton read the Miranda warning.

"Nice day for a false arrest suit," Father Jonathan proclaimed as the officer finished his spiel.

"Do you wish to give up the right to remain silent?" Officer Claxton asked.

"I surely do, my friend."

Claxton was quick to warn. "Anything you say can and will be used against you."

"I sure hope so, and the same goes for you." That got the boys a little confused. Father Jonathan smiled as he continued. "I am not Zachary Zander. If you look in my wallet, you will see that I am Father Jonathan Young. I am a Roman Catholic priest in the Krenshaw Diocese. My attorney is Mr. Dan Santucci. Please have your district attorney and insurance carrier contact Dan. I would prefer to settle the false arrest claim quickly and quietly."

That brought down the house. Cops scurried to their cars. License plates were run again, and copies of driver's licenses were requested on computers. Ten minutes later, Officer Claxton removed the handcuffs.

Claxton was visibly upset. He was in charge of this cluster, and he knew his ass was in hot water. "What are you doing driving Zander's truck?"

Father Jonathan rubbed his wrists. The cuffs were a little tight. "He's a friend. He gave me the keys. Any problems with that?"

"We will have to verify your story."

Father Jonathan had enough. "Look here, folks, unless you charge me with something, I plan to get in that truck right now and head back to Krenshaw."

"There are no charges yet, but we do need to question you about Dr. Zander and his whereabouts."

Father Jonathan spoke truthfully, as he always did lately. "I have no idea where he is. But I will pick up Dan and meet you at the police station at noon. Fair enough?"

The six cops quietly got back into their cars, shut off the flashing lights, and waited until he pulled out.

Father Jonathan phoned Dan, who was at the hospital.

"Father, so good to hear from you. How was your trip?"

Only two words came out of Father Jonathan's mouth. "Code Blue."

Dan quickly responded, "Come to the hospital administrative offices."

The priest parked in the doctor's lot. After all, ZZ had the right decal. He found his way to the administrative suite. JL led him to Dan in the conference room.

Father Jonathan asked quietly, "Is this room safe?"

Dan nodded. "From bugs? Yeah. We check it weekly. It was clean yesterday, and we are very fussy about access to this room. It is only entered when ZZ, Tina, or I are present. Even for maintenance and housekeeping duties we have a chaperone. What's up?"

Father nodded. "ZZ picked me up at the airport. Believe it or not, a Customs agent snuck an envelope in my passport addressed to ZZ. It was for his eyes only. I gave it to ZZ in the truck, and he read it. He was taking the turn for the Whitman Bridge when he suddenly changed course, and we drove into Center City. He got a briefcase from the back seat and disappeared. I waited for an hour, but he never came back. I knew he wasn't coming back."

"Where the hell did he go? What kind of crap is he up to? He pulls these stunts at all the wrong times!"

"Dan, let me finish. I had no idea what he was doing, but it was clear to me that he didn't want me to know. I headed for Krenshaw. On the way I called his cell and got some kind of error message. I never reached him. Just outside of Cherry Hill, I was stopped by a small army of Jersey State Troopers. They thought I was ZZ and arrested me for alleged rape."

"They accused you of raping someone?"

"No, Dan, they accused ZZ of it. They spotted his truck and thought he was driving. They had me cuffed before anyone verified my identity. I voiced my concern about their poor police work, and I might have mentioned a false arrest lawsuit. They let me go, but we need to be at the police station at noon."

"You really don't know where ZZ is?"

"I have no idea, and I have no clue why he took off. But it seems to me that the note must have warned him of his pending apprehension."

"Did you see the note? Where is it now?"

"I never read it, and he ate it."

Dan shook his head. "OK, ZZ has gone underground, and he is being investigated for rape. I had nothing else brewing today."

# Chapter 76

***Serenity Reincarnations***

***Hershey, PA***

"Mr. Smith." Five heads looked up.

"Excuse me, Mr. Ben Smith, let's start with you. What help do you need with alcohol?"

Imagine that? Five guys out of nine in this room are named Smith. I wonder how many of them are hiding out here like I am.

"Mr. Ben Smith. Please let us help you."

"Sorry, mam. I am having a difficult time focusing. My mind and heart are racing, and I am just plain nervous." I got out my well-rehearsed line.

"Yes, unfortunately, that is part of the withdrawal process. Maybe we should take a break and have the nurse do her assessments."

I needed to hit the head. To make my story here believable, I had to look like I was heading into withdrawal. Since I wasn't, I needed a way to look jittery, have a high heart rate, and be anxious. Six cups of black coffee in two hours did the trick. Luckily, no one was monitoring the coffee pot.

The nurse judged me to be in mild to moderate withdrawal, and I was rewarded for my act with 50mg of Librium. Over the next day or two, I would "recover" from the withdrawal symptoms, but for now, I needed them. I didn't want anyone here to get an idea that I was just hiding out or putting in time. I was a little worried that someone might recognize my facial scar, but so far, no one gave it a second look. No harness racing fans here. We took our seats and started the session.

"My name is Ben Smith, and I am a binge drinker." Mild applause.

"Go on, Ben."

"Well, unfortunately, my binges have become more frequent and last longer. I started out drinking most weekends that I was off. Then, I started to leave work early on Friday and come in late Monday to extend my drinking time. The amounts that I was drinking were getting out of control. I was killing a fifth of vodka a day when I drank. The first two days of the week, I was in withdrawal, so my performance at work was poor. Last week, I never made it to work. I called in sick. But I had used all my sick time, and my employer gave me a first written warning. I decided that I had better get my ass some treatment, and here I am. They think I am having a rotator cuff repair this week."

"How are you going to explain coming back to work without a shoulder problem?"

"I will have a shoulder problem. You see, I am a rehab physician, and I know how to fake recovery from rotator cuff surgery. They will never know."

I pretended to be interested as the other Smiths bared their alcohol-soaked souls. I even asked a few stupid questions. But I spent most of the time pondering the rape accusation. It was all I could do not to contact Dan. But in the end, I realized that someone thought the time was needed to aid in my defense. For now, Ben Smith, the binge drinker, tackles his addiction.

### Krenshaw Police Station

Dan and Father Jonathan had some fun with the police. Dan didn't really think Father had a good case for false arrest, but he played it up to gather as much information as he could about the rape allegations. A State Police representative was there in person. The District Attorney for Atlantic City joined via a conference call. They did have some evidence that corroborated the story of the victim. The DA let it slip that the alleged attack happened last Friday night in Atlantic City. He wanted to question me, and he wanted me to submit to DNA testing.

Dan made it clear that he wasn't representing me. He was there as a friend, and he was representing Father Jonathan. The district attorney advised both that if they should have any contact with me, I should be asked to turn myself in. He also demanded that his office be informed of the contact. Dan agreed, of course, knowing that he would not hear from me.

"Where do we go from here?" Father Jonathan asked on the way to the car.

"I am going to 1865 Washington Street after I take you home."

"What's there? I can go with you."

"Not what, who. The who is ZZ's best chance at acquittal. I appreciate your willingness to come, but I think you should rest up. You had a long journey, and I think we're soon going to be quite busy."

Father Jonathan agreed. He was exhausted. "You don't really think he did it?"

Dan thought for a moment. "No, not forcible rape. But let's face it. ZZ likes to drink on occasion. Last Friday, he had the wake for Bella, the girl he was seeing every now and again. We know that ZZ gets in trouble frequently. We have a lot to sort out."

"What happened to Bella?"

"Fell off a cruise ship and was partially eaten by sharks."

Father Jonathan was shaken. "Whoaaaa, that's terrible."

"Yeah, that was a little while ago. In her will she requested ZZ spread her ashes. You know ZZ when he gets things going. He threw a big Irish wake themed party last Friday in Atlantic City."

Father Jonathan was resolute. "He had to be set up, or it was consensual. He's not a rapist."

Dan agreed. "That's the trouble these days. Two adults get schlooned up and have sex. Occasionally, the next day one of them has buyer's remorse and assumes they were raped. If they stick with their story, and there is evidence of a sexual encounter, it is hard for the defendant to prove their innocence. Then, of course, there are many cases of actual rape."

Dan dropped the priest at the farm and returned to the offices of Krenshaw Legal Associates, Jasmine Disimone, JD, managing partner. As soon as he heard about the rape allegations, he requested an appointment with her.

JDJD stood to greet him. "Dan, good to see you. Still battling Dr. Bator?"

"Master?" (I had worn Dan down. He was careful to only call him Dr. Bator so he didn't slip up in court. I won again. The funny part was that JDJD knew right away who Master was. My nicknames were infamous.)

Dan explained. "Yeah, we are. His next move is to the State Supreme Court. His arguments have not impressed any of the appellate courts, so we think our chances are good."

JDJD didn't follow. "Is there something that I need to help you with? It seems like you got him right where you want him."

"As a matter of fact, I need the best defense attorney I can find. I think you are the best, and I need your help."

She blushed and took out a pen and a fresh legal pad.

"Who's the client?"

"ZZ."

Dan went on to lay out the details of the morning and what he knew about the party. He explained what the district attorney had told him about wanting ZZ to submit to testing.

"Where is he?"

"I don't know."

"OK Dan, no B.S. Where is he?"

"JDJD" (as I would say. Dan has been completely coopted to my nicknames.) "I am being totally honest. Someone, and I don't know who, tipped ZZ off. He's gone dark. I suspect that was an effort to buy time. I honestly have no idea where he is and no idea how to contact him."

"That works in our favor. We do need time. But let's get one thing clear. If anyone, and I mean anyone, hears from him, you must inform me immediately. Anyone that aids and abets him could face serious legal jeopardy, and that could also cloud any defense we may present."

Dan agreed. "You got it. You will know the minute he checks in."

"Any idea who the tipster was?" JDJD asked as she finished some notes.

"I have a good guess. Do you want to know, or do you want plausible deniability?"

JDJD thought before she answered. "I'll take plausible deniability for now. But very discretely you might want to reach out to them and see if they have any further information on the case. I specifically need to know what evidence they have and why they suspect ZZ."

Dan stood to leave. "I'll do my best."

# Chapter 77

## *Fired Up Farms*

Dan stopped at the hospital and tackled a mountain of paperwork. Four hours later, he finished. He hoped that Father Jonathan had a good rest because he needed his full attention and cooperation. Mrs. Zander had requested to make dinner, but Dan wanted to start the meeting as soon as possible. He picked up Chick-fil-A for everyone on his way to the farm.

Mom, Dad, and Father Jonathan dug into their food. Dan slowly explained that ZZ was wanted for questioning for a rape that took place in Atlantic City on the night he and Billie were there. He further explained that some kind soul (he suspected Aldo) had gotten word to ZZ before he could be arrested.

Mom wiped her mouth with a paper napkin. "Where is ZZ now?"

Dan took a sip of lemonade and answered, "We don't know, and we don't want to know. I have engaged Jasmine Disimone for his defense. She warned me that if and when ZZ does contact us, that we should call her immediately. When we know his location, we cannot conceal that from the authorities. My guess is that he is somewhere he deems safe and unlikely to be found. That is good for us. JDJD needs more information. The longer ZZ avoids detection, the more likely it is that we will get the information we need.

Dad was disturbed. "What information do we need? Obviously, ZZ did nothing of the sort."

Dan was sympathetic. "I agree with you, but we still have to convince the legal system. JDJD needs to know what kind of evidence led them to ZZ and how reliable it is."

Father Jonathan asked a question as he bit into his third helping of curly fries. He was making up for lost time. "Can Aldo Crinelli help out?"

Dan shook his head. "I already tried, but he doesn't have any great contacts in Atlantic City or with the State Police. He didn't tell me, of course, but I suspect he got the information about the impending arrest from inside the Krenshaw Police Department."

Father Jonathan sipped his soda. "Then let's get Joe on the case. I know he has a lot of pull-in AC. I will call a Dying Was Easy."

Dad deflated everyone's balloon. "ZZ called one before he disappeared, and no one responded. They both have him blocked."

Father Jonathan was incredulous. "I can't believe that."

Dad explained that both Joe and Azzie were in a physical rehab hospital. Even though they were in the same facility, they had no contact with each other. He further relayed that they are refusing to allow anyone to visit, and they are taking no calls. ZZ was pretty sure they weren't even talking to each other. Joe was in 304, and she was in 204.

Father Jonathan was still skeptical.

Dad continued. "The rumors are that Joe is in terrible pain from his destroyed pelvis. Azzie is having a hard time dealing with scarring from her burns. Exquisite Evolutions stock is down 45% since the accident."

Father Jonathan dug in. "Well, if there ever was a time to get everyone together, now is it."

Father Jonathan sent the text. He soon found out that he was blocked. He called the rehab hospital and was told that neither patient was taking any calls. They would give him no further information.

Father Jonathan stood. "I am going out there. I need to reach them. Not just for ZZ's sake but for theirs as well. For them to retreat into a shell is evidence of severe issues for both of them."

Dad offered to join him, but Father Jonathan felt he should go alone.

**Next Steps Rehabilitation Center**

The weather quickly turned sour as he turned into the rehab hospital. The only thing more sour than the weather was the puss on the nasty soul at the reception desk. Father had wisely donned his black shirt and white collar. He very kindly asked permission to see Azzie. The witch was quick to respond. "That patient is not accepting any visitors."

"But I am her priest!"

"NO VISITORS!"

"How about Joe Crinelli?"

"Same deal. No visitors, no priests, no rabbis, no Buddhist Monks." She thought she was funny. His middle finger started to quiver, but suddenly it stopped. The image of the pope in a flannel shirt filled his mind and all was well.

Father Jonathan walked outside into the pouring rain. He grabbed an umbrella from the car and proceeded to walk around the outside of the hospital. He was quickly joined by a security guard.

"Where are you going?" asked the guard.

"Around this side of the hospital." Father Jonathan said as he continued walking.

"Sir, you cannot walk there. The only place visitors are permitted is the parking lot and in the facility. Please go back to your car."

"Or what?"

"Or I call the police and have you arrested for trespassing."

Father Jonathan was about to cut loose with a string of expletives when he caught himself. Again, the pope's message echoed in his head. At the same time, he noticed where he needed to go and what he needed to do.

"Sorry, officer. I am just so worried about my friends. But you have your rules, and I will respect them."

"Thanks for your understanding, sir. Please return to your car."

The average-size rent-a-cop was relieved that he didn't have to tangle with a 6'6" dude. Even one that lost a bunch of weight.

Father Jonathan drove to the office building next door to the hospital. In the grass that separated the office building parking lot from the hospital, he located the tree he saw earlier. His slimmed-down body made the task of climbing that tree much easier, but the pouring rain did not. He carefully climbed until he was dead even and about fifteen feet from the window of room 204. He knew it was 204 because the hospital had room numbers on the windows in case of a fire or a need to evacuate. The room numbers made it easier for firemen to know what rooms they were heading to.

He took out a flashlight and held it under his chin as he began to throw acorns at the window with his free hand. It took about five minutes to get a response. Suddenly, the curtains in the room parted, and Richard Nixon looked out. Father Jonathan was shocked at first but realized that Azzie had been in hiding and was using masks to cover her face. He kept throwing acorns at the window until it opened.

"Go away, whoever you are, go away." That was Azzie's voice coming from the Tricky Dick face."

He screamed the magic words. "Dying Was Easy."

"GO AWAY!"

"Azzie, this is Father Jonathan. Please talk to me."

"Leave me alone. Do you want me to call security?"

"Our father who art in heaven hallowed be thy name" was the reply. He just kept praying. The window closed, and the curtains were pulled. Three rosaries later, the window opened.

"You can stay there all-night Father, but I am not talking to you."

He couldn't help but laugh. Dah, you are talking to me right now he thought, but he said nothing.

"Go home." She pleaded in a slightly reduced volume.

"Azzie, we need you. ZZ needs you."

"Boom, boom, boom, everybody needs something. Hit the road" Came a gruff reply from the third floor.

"Joe, nice to hear from you."

"Fuck you, padre."

"Hail Mary full of grace, the Lord is with thee….."

Both windows closed, and both curtains were pulled. The thoroughly soaked priest continued to pray.

**Fired Up Farms**

Back at the house, Dan, Mom, and Dad sat at the kitchen table and tried to be calm. There was a knock at the door. Mom opened it and screamed.

"Stephanie, how did you get here?"

She grabbed Stephanie as she began to collapse and put her in a chair. Dad rushed over, and Dan got her a cold drink before he realized that she wasn't drinking.

Stephanie looked up and said, "ZZ needs us. Rio and I want to help."

Those were the first words she uttered since the funeral. The three of them were shocked. Standing in the doorway was Rio. She looked as bad as Stephanie.

Stephanie pulled out her NG tube and said. "Can Rio and I get some food? We can't take any more of this shit, and we need our energy."

Mom quickly made some eggs and toast. Stephanie forced herself to eat. It would take a while to get back her appetite. Carl led Rio back to her paddock and got her some mash, which she reluctantly ate. Stephanie asked a few questions but seemed to be clued into most of the facts.

"Where is Father Jonathan?" Stephanie asked as she laid down her fork.

Mom answered. She was happy to hear Stephanie speak. "At the rehab hospital. He is trying to get through to Azzie and Joe so we can all help ZZ."

"Call him."

Father Jonathan put down the flashlight and rosary and answered the phone. He was hoping for Azzie's or Joe's voice, but it was Stephanie's.

"How you making out?"

He answered, "I talked with them, but they don't seem interested in helping. I am appealing to a higher authority." He went on to explain his perch in the tree and his plan to continue praying until they came out to talk with him, no matter how long that took.

Stephanie said simply, "Hang on, we come."

She closed the phone, handed it to Dan, and addressed the group.

"ZZ needs us, we go, we all go!"

# Chapter 78

## *Next Steps Rehabilitation Center*

When Stephanie said we all go, she meant it. Dan, Mom, and Dad had to hook up the horse trailer for Rio. While they were doing that, all fifty members of the Autistic Army donned rain gear and climbed into their buses with their handlers.

The entourage arrived in the parking lot where Father Jonathan had parked his car. They unloaded Rio. Stephanie walked her to a spot at the base of the tree. They both kind of stumbled because they hadn't walked much in weeks. Then, The Army lined up. They had umbrellas to protect them, but Rio and Stephanie refused any. Everyone joined Father Jonathan in a new Rosary. He was on number twelve. It took fifteen minutes, but Azzie's window opened first, followed by Joe's. Nothing was said. The crowd continued to pray. The rosary was interrupted by two Krenshaw police cars that simultaneously arrived in the parking lot. Through a bullhorn, they announced, "This is an unlawful assembly. Please return to your vehicles and depart the area, or you will be arrested."

The group kept praying as the same announcement was made for a second time. A shout emanated from the third floor of the hospital.

"Hit the trail, pal. Go arrest some drug dealers or some real criminals. This is Joe Crinelli talking." Joe's voice was clear as a bell.

"Mr Crinelli, it was you that called us."

Joe stood by the window with the aid of crutches.

"Well, I am uncalling you. My friends and I are praying the rosary. You can join in or hit the trail."

Azzie followed that up. "Thank you, officers, but we have this under control. We had a misunderstanding that is now crystal clear."

The police left, and the group finished another rosary. Father Jonathan was invited in. He climbed down the tree and accepted a towel from Dad.

Father Jonathan dried his bald head. "Carl, I think we got what we came for. Why don't you take everyone back home and I will join you later. I know they will be very fussy about visitors.

Stephnie demanded, "I go too!"

It was always difficult to say no to Stephanie. Father Jonathan was eventually successful in getting her to accept the fact that Rio would not be allowed into the facility. Secretly, he really wanted to see Sourpuss's face when big Rio stood at her desk. But the more he thought about it, Stephanie might be just the tool he needed. He relented.

"Ok, but let me get a wheelchair in the lobby. Your gait is worse than some of the crippled trotters that I bet on in years gone by."

The witch at the desk didn't know what to say. It's a good thing she said very little. Father Jonathan was still in his be nice mode, but he didn't need much to help him fall off the wagon. Stephanie was not on a wagon. She had a ton of pent-up F-bombs that were looking for a target.

Father Jonathan called Azzie, and they decided that it might be easier for everyone to meet in Joe's room. Father Jonathan pushed Stephanie to Azzie's room and knocked on the door. When the door opened, there stood a 120-pound Tricky Dick Nixon. He had a white face with black arms and legs.

Stephanie jumped out of the chair and hugged the former president. No one said anything for a few minutes. Stephanie stepped back a half step, took Azzie's hand into hers, and put both hands on her belly. It wasn't much, but she was showing. As skinny as Stephanie was, it didn't take much for that to occur.

Tricky Dick bawled. Stephanie got a little wobbly and sat back down. Mr. Nixon looked at Father Jonathan for an explanation.

"Yes, Stephanie is pregnant. She is about 18 weeks now. To the best of our knowledge, she and the baby are doing well."

Nixon wanted more information. "What's up with the wheelchair? Why can't she walk?"

"What's up with the mask?" Stephanie blurted out. "The Azzie I know doesn't hide behind anything or anybody."

Father Jonathan suggested that the three of them go to Joe's room and bring everyone up to date. No one said a word in the elevator. Joe's door was already open when they arrived. Joe was sitting in a bedside chair. He had lost 25 pounds, and his skin was sallow. His voice was a little weak.

"Boom, boom, boom. Welcome to hell."

Tricky Dick stayed at the door while Father Jonathan wheeled Stephanie to Joe's side. A river of tears ran down both cheeks as he watched her wobble when she stood. She kissed him and sat back down in her chair.

Father Jonathan grinned. 'Hey, fireplug, do you notice anything about our sweetheart Stephanie?"

"Yeah, she looks like hell, but she put on a few pounds."

"Can't fool you, Einstein. She is pregnant. She's got a filly in the oven, and she's about 18 weeks."

Joe's tear production doubled. He reached out and grabbed Stephanie's hand. Father Jonathan pulled up two chairs and motioned for Tricky Dick to take one. Azzie started to mumble, but he cut her off.

"Before we go any further, can we say a small prayer of thanks?" Everyone agreed.

Father Jonathan then stood. "We have to catch up on everything, and I would like to go first. I wasn't in Rome for a sabbatical. I was in Rome because they thought I was a bad priest." He let that sink in and told them about Decision Tree.

"I took stock of myself there, and I didn't like what I saw. So, I worked. On the last day, I met a man in a flannel shirt and jeans that changed my life forever." He went on to explain that the pope didn't need vestments, crowns, or hats.

"That dude had it all together. He opened my eyes and strengthened my heart. But he didn't send me to a mission in Guyana or give me another assignment. He told me that he saw evil around me and that I was to conquer it. Well, I tell you now, I am like the Native American guy in *One Flew Over the Cuckoo's Nest.* I am ready to do what I need to do to see that right and order are preserved. Whatever it takes, but this time, I will respect what God wants in the process."

No one spoke for a few seconds. Then, the silence was broken by a window shattering. Joe's bedside lamp had penetrated the window.

Joe spoke in his previous forceful tone. "Whatever it takes, Dying Was Easy. I am such a weak asshole. I am so ashamed. When I woke up after nearly dying, I didn't care too much. But when I couldn't walk or wipe my own ass, I was uber-pissed. When my trusty friend failed to salute the sunrise, I lost it. Father, how much time in hell do you get for telling God to go F himself? Before you answer you need to know that I did it more than 1000 times."

Father Jonathan was calm. "Christ can take that and 10,000,000 times more. After all, he died on the cross. What are some insults from a crazy Italian compared to that?"

Azzie jumped in. "I, too, have doubted God's love for me. Although I have prospered greatly, I have worked very hard to give back to everyone, especially the school. I don't understand how he could have disfigured me."

Joe grabbed his crutches and stumbled his way to Azzie. He hugged her. After a few minutes, he carefully tried to remove the Richard Nixon mask. She initially grabbed his hands to stop him, but then she helped him remove it.

Joe smiled. "Boom, boom, boom, the Azzie I love is beautiful. But what she may not know is that I love what is inside of her more than what is outside."

They kissed and held until Azzie giggled. "Joe, there is something coming up between us!"

Joe laughed. "Boom, boom, boom."

Stephanie had enough. "I hate to interrupt, but ZZ needs our help."

The next couple of hours were spent with Azzie and Joe explaining their experiences. Father Jonathan filled them in on the funeral and what had been going on with Stephanie. She just sat there as if they were talking about someone else. He mentioned the problems at the hospital and how a hospital closure could affect the track.

Azzie hung on every word. "There's a definite domino effect here. If the hospital goes down, the track will likely stop harness racing. Those precious kids at that school are dependent on harness horse racing. It's a vital link to a world that autism has tried to lock them out of. I am not sitting by and letting someone destroy what we all have worked so hard to build."

Joe nodded his head and then changed the subject. "Stephanie mentioned something about ZZ needing our help. What's up with that?"

Father Jonathan recapped his arrival in Philadelphia and ZZ's disappearance. He mentioned the note, although he did not know what it said.

Joe interrupted, "That had to be a gift from Grandpa. That showed some style, finesse, and clout."

Father Jonathan then told them about his arrest and the fact that ZZ was suspected of raping someone in Atlantic City.

Joe flung a bottle of pills out his broken window. "Padre, get me out of here. We got work to do, and it isn't getting done while I am here and quaffing down pain pills like Pez candy."

Azzie was ready to leave, too. "I can do what I need to do as an outpatient. They do wonderful things here, but Joe is right. We have work to do, and we need to get out of here to get it done."

Father Jonathan, Joe, and Azzie discussed where they wanted to stay and how they would get there. Father Jonathan called Dad, who agreed to make things happen.

Father Jonathan hung up. "All set. Plenty of room at the house. Joe, you will get a bedroom downstairs that will be handicap accessible. Azzie, you will be upstairs. Mrs. Zander will arrange for a physical therapy evaluation for all three of you tomorrow."

Azzie interrupted. "Three?"

He answered. "You, Joe, and Stephanie. We need all three of you strong and ready to help. We have some of the best therapists at the school. They will work with you while we bail out ZZ and the hospital."

Father Jonathan pushed Stephanie's wheelchair to the door. He turned to say goodbye, but no one was paying attention. Joe and Azzie were sucking each other's faces off. He pushed the wheelchair into the hall and quietly pulled the door closed. As he did, he clearly heard Joe proclaim. "Sweet cheeks, stand back. I don't know how big this thing is going to get."

Father Jonathan could have sworn that Stephanie had a smirk on her face. If true, that was a very welcome change.

# Chapter 79

## *Fired Up Farms*

"Stephanie, please eat a little more of those waffles."

Mom pleaded, but she knew that Stephanie was doing the best she could. Dad and Father Jonathan spent a large part of the night making Joe's bathroom handicap accessible. Not having much time, they just ripped down the wall containing the door, yanked out a couple 2x4's, and put up a curtain on a rod. Ugly but effective. Joe and Azzie arrived by wheelchair van at 8:45. Azzie was ambulatory, but she wanted to ride with Joe.

Father Jonathan walked out to the van. "Welcome home, you two. Anyone want breakfast?"

Joe declined. "Nah, I goofed up and ate the powdered eggs at rehab. My guts are churning already."

Azzie also declined. Dad invited everyone into the living room as Mom brought in coffee and donuts. She heard Joe say he wasn't hungry, but you didn't arrive at Mom's house without some food being shoved in your direction. Joe insisted on walking. He begrudgingly accepted a wheelchair ride into the house to appease the ambulance attendant. He stood with great difficulty and balanced on metal crutches attached to his wrists. Father Jonathan tried to assist him, but Joe waved him off with a middle finger.

"Do you need a pain pill?" Mom asked.

"No, Thanks, Mom. Those damn things are just like heroin. You feel good when you take them, but they wear off. And you need more and more of them. I threw what I had out the window last night, and I am not going back down that road. Let's get to work. I need something to take my mind off me."

"Azzie, would you feel more comfortable in a mask? It's ok," Father Jonathan asked.

"Thanks, Father, but I feel so much better as myself. I can't believe I was so vain to think that my appearance was so damn important. I am working on some enhancements to my appearance, but at least when we are together, you will have to tolerate me as is."

"You, as is, are a ton better than most others with a lot of help," Joe added. She smiled and patted his hand.

Dan arrived, and everyone sat down.

The session began with Azzie in the lead, of course. "I spent the night reviewing and planning. Here is where we are. ZZ is accused of rape. He is in an undisclosed location, and no one has heard from him. JDJD will defend him and manage his turning himself in when the time comes. She has been told that the police have a video of ZZ entering the victim's room at the time of the alleged rape. They have a rape kit in process. JDJD is planning a consensual sex defense, but she really wants to see those tapes.

The hospital has been plagued with Never Episodes. They have had five in the past three months, which is unheard of. There may have been imposters at work, but the tapes are inconclusive. There was one of a male lab tech and another of a female nurse's aide. So, if there are imposters, we are dealing with multiple players. The episodes have caused lawsuits, bond downgrading, and supplier constraints. Without a cash infusion, the hospital will likely close in 21 days when their Licensure Board participation is likely to be terminated.

It is suspected, but not proven, that there is an effort to ruin harness racing. The governor has been a staunch ally of harness racing, but he is down 8 points in the latest polls. If he loses, or if the Miracle Millions does not exceed expectations, it is likely that the harness racing subsidy from the casinos will be cut, and harness racing will die. Should the hospital close before Millions Week, the Million's Races would be cancelled.

The Dunstans have arranged a Millions Week, which, if pulled off, will surpass anything done in racing. Thoroughbred, harness, cars, dogs, any kind of racing. I met Tim last year. I can't wait to meet the rest of them. I could use their ideas in my future marketing efforts."

After a few questions and a bathroom break, Azzie explained the teams that she proposed and their goals. "ZZ defense. We all need to help where we can, but Dan, you will lead. Joe, we must find a way to get those tapes. Stephanie, please assist them.

Hospital financial. I will take that on. I have some ideas that may buy us some time. I will work with Tina.

It would be helpful to find out who is masterminding the Never Episodes and the destruction of harness racing. We know that Elvira Bradshaw is shorting the casino stock and has designs on taking over the casino and racetrack to run thoroughbreds. Father Jonathan, can you try to see who is behind this and why?

If the hospital is still open, we need to pull off a Million's Week that exceeds anyone's expectations. What the Dunstans have planned will require a lot of massaging and coordination. Dad and Mom, can you work with them?"

In the past, Mom was called Mom, but Dad was always referred to as Carl. I wasn't getting along with Dad when I met up with my friends, so they called him Carl, as I did then. After Dad and I mended fences, they still called him Carl. Today, he was Dad. He got a little choked up when he heard it.

Mom answered for both. "We would be glad to. Azzie, Joe, and Stephanie, please remember that you have physical and occupational therapy from 12-2 daily."

"Maybe in a few weeks." Azzie and Joe shook their heads no in unison.

Mom dug in. "Think about the team. You three know that we have a lot of work to do and a long way to go. We need you to be as healthy and functional as possible. Please do your part."

Mom didn't ask much, so it was almost impossible to refuse her. There was a knock at the door. Dad opened it and greeted Billie.

"Billie, thanks for coming."

"Uuuuuuu bbbbbeeetttttt." Stammered Billie

Joe spoke first, "Billie, I want to go over the night of the alleged rape. Do you have time?"

"IIIIII dooooo FLFLFLFLight leaves at noon."

Billie was driving in some Ohio Sires Stakes races in Columbus. With his speech impediments, the story took about three times longer than it should have. But Billie was forthcoming. He and I rode down to Atlantic City together to Bella's Irish Wake at The Bustin Loose Casino and Hotel on the boardwalk.

As soon as Bille mentioned the specific casino, Joe smiled. Dan noticed it, but the rest of the group was focused on Billie. Billie continued to explain that the wake attendees met and had a few drinks. They then accompanied me as I spread Bella's ashes into the ocean off the pier.

Mom was surprised to hear that I spread the ashes. Somehow, she got the mistaken impression that I was just going to support the staff. She made a note to quiz me after I got out of trouble.

Billie recalled that we next went in and had dinner. Billie admitted that everyone was pretty wasted. He saw me dancing with Anne Marie. But around 1 AM, I made Billie go back to the room with me. Billie said we both were wobbly, but we made it. Billie collapsed on his bed, and I went to the bathroom.

Billie said he woke up 30 minutes later, and I was gone. Billie figured I went to score with Anne Marie, and he went back to sleep. Around 3 AM, he got an urgent call from his principal owner. Billie explained that this owner was filthy rich but very demanding. He also didn't sleep much. He wanted Billie at Atlantic City airport at 5 AM, so they could fly to Canada to look at some yearlings. It wasn't unusual for him to get calls like this. He jumped in the shower. When he came out of the bathroom, he found me fast asleep. He wrote me a note and left.

After a few more questions and long, painful, stuttering answers, Billie left for Philadelphia.

Dan looked at Joe. "When he mentioned the Bustin Loose, you got a smile on your face. What's up?"

Joe nodded. "We may have caught a huge break. I've got some juice there. We need more information. We know that ZZ left the room and returned in a timeframe that would fit the crime parameters. But we don't know where he went and what he did, if anything. So, as of now, we know shit. I hope to change that."

# Chapter 80

## *Bustin Loose Casino and Hotel*

## *Atlantic City, NJ*

Dan had to ask. "Joe, can't you just call? I mean, for you to go to Atlantic City has got to be painful."

"Some things must be done in person. Can someone drive me?"

Mom agreed. "I will, after you three go to therapy."

Joe slept most of the way to Atlantic City. When they arrived, they were met at the front door of The Bustin Loose by Alphonse Millessi, the general manager.

"Joseph, so good to see you." He kissed Joe on the cheek and helped him into a wheelchair that Joe had been wise enough to request.

Joe introduced Mom. "Alphonse, please meet Mom Zander. ZZ's mother."

"Nice to meet you, Mom."

Joe asked, "Alphonse, you crazy dago, how the hell are you?"

Alphonse pushed Joe in the wheelchair. Even though he had tons of staff, he could have pressed into service. He stopped at the entrance to the casino and pulled five black chips from his pocket. They were worth $100 each. He handed them to Mom.

"Mrs. Zander, feel free to try your hand at blackjack or any game you like. Joe and I have some business."

Mom opened her mouth to object, but Joe had told her this was likely to occur. She spied an open craps table and made her way there. Alphonse wheeled Joe to his office on the top floor of the casino. It had a breathtaking view of the ocean.

"Joe, can I get you a drink, some food?"

"No, Al. What I need is your help."

"If it's about Dr. Zander, I can't help you. The cops have been all over me. The DA, who is an ignorant baboon's ass, threatened me if I am caught helping him."

"With what?"

"You know, the typical stuff. He, of course, didn't say any of this, but the message was clear. They will sneak some minors into the casino and then bust me for letting minors in. They will coerce someone on the banned list to somehow gain entry and gamble. They will have daily fire inspections. Then they will fine the shit out of us. We are doing ok now. But I still have a lot of debt to work off from the bad five years prior. I don't need any aggravation."

Joe dug deeper. "Why does this DA have a hard-on for Dr. Zander?"

Alphonse thought for a minute. "It is an election year. He is up for reelection. Dr. Zander is well known in the state, and he is a known friend of the governor. This DA is not of the same political persuasion as the governor. DA's love to bring down famous people particularly when they can be tied to a big shot from the other party."

Joe nodded. "But his leaning on you that hard smells of more than election tactics. The governor is already down in the polls. Does this DA have any outside interests?"

Alphonse laughed. "Like porn, little boys? Not that I know."

Joe was serious. "I mean, who is he connected to? Whose bidding might he be doing?"

"I got no proof, but I have heard a few rumors that might be germane to our discussion."

That got Joe animated. "Boom, boom, boom. I like rumors. Go on."

Alphonse sighed. "I hear that he is the shadow owner of some pretty nice thoroughbreds. A little too nice for what a DA pulls in."

Joe kept digging. "Who's the owner named on the papers?"

Alphonse thought. "Pissmetal or something like that."

Joe quickly replied, "Prinzmetal, Thaddeus Prinzmetal?"

"That's the dude!! He and the DA were in law school together."

Joe thought about that as he looked out the window. That might be helpful in the long run, but it didn't help ZZ.

"I hate like hell to call in favors, but I have no choice. If I didn't grease the skids with the casino commission, you might be parking cars here instead of farting in this big office. And let's not mention the money that was made available to you when you needed it most."

Alphonse was stuck in the middle. "Ok, we won't mention it. But you must understand that I am in a hell of a spot."

Joe sensed Al weakening. "All I know is that a dear friend of mine is having his nuts squeezed. I want to know who is squeezing and what they are using. As you know, I can be very discreet, but I need some stuff."

"Like what?"

"Everything you can tell me about what Dr. Zander did that night. Any tapes you can pull together of him. Especially any tapes that the police took. You did make copies?"

"Dah, I didn't think of that." Alphonse slapped himself on the forehead, and then he flipped Joe the bird. He reached into his desk and held up a flash drive.

Joe spiked the football. "I'll take that drink now. Scotch, neat."

**Fired Up Farms**

Azzie looked at the stock price for Exquisite Evolutions. It was down another 5% today. 50% from its all-time high. The shorts were killing the stock. Up to this point she had done nothing but watch her fortune get cut in half. Her net worth was still $400,000,000. The money didn't mean as much as the fact that someone was trying to destroy what she had built from the ground up.

On the way up the ladder, she crushed those who underestimated her. Those were often the same folks who alleged that she was just a black female figurehead who took credit for things she never did. Maybe it was time to climb again and kick some scumbags off the rungs along the way.

She used the small glue-on-masks that she invented to soften the appearance of some of the scars. She then applied a small amount of makeup and picked out an appropriate wig. She walked down to Joe's room and knocked on the door.

"Come in? Oh my God," Joe exclaimed.

He looked her over for a minute before continuing. "Azzie, you are stunning. You have some scars, but they are hardly noticeable. But you didn't bury them in makeup. What did you do?"

Azzie explained as they headed to therapy. They stopped by Stephanie's room to pick her up.

"Azzie, you beautiful again!"

"Thank you, Stephanie. You are, too."

After therapy, Azzie sat down with Tina. Tina couldn't believe what she heard.

"Do you think $15 million will get you through?" Azzie said while she sipped her coffee.

"That would get us through, but you don't need to. It is very unlikely that you will get the money back."

"I'm not worried about that. Not only will I get my money back, I'll get all my previous wealth back. Some short sellers are about to get slaughtered."

# Chapter 81

## *Serenity Reincarnations*

I was getting tired of sitting through therapy sessions with the pickled liver club. It was hard because I had to make up a bunch of stuff to sound real. Then I had to remember what I told them yesterday so I didn't contradict myself. Most of them probably paid as little attention to me as I did to them, but the counselors may get wise.

I was glad to get back to my room for an hour off before lunch. I turned on Fox Business and was shocked at what I saw. The banner read, "Exquisite Evolutions halted for news pending." Wow, I hoped it was good news. The stock could also be halted if there was bad news. I wanted to call Azzie or Dan, but I still couldn't. So, I watched and waited for Stu Varney to get the news.

Stu eventually looked into the camera and did his thing. "Azquela Huggins, CEO of Exquisite Evolutions today announced the formation of Perfect Imperfections. It will be a subsidiary of Exquisite Evolutions that will help patients with scars and disfigurements to perfect their total appearance. Azquela, tell us all about it."

"Thank you, Stuart, please call me Azzie. I'm delighted to tell you about this new venture. My friend Joe Crinelli and I were critically injured in a helicopter accident that claimed the life of my pilot Hank Bivens. I was severely burned. I have not made any statements or public appearances since the accident until today.

"In addition to painful surgeries and debilitating injuries, I have had to endure short sellers attempting to wreck my company. Today that all ends. There is an enormous market for people who are scarred or disfigured to improve their appearance. Perfect Imperfections is set up to do just that. And not just for those who can afford it. We will make our products affordable to all and cover the expenses of those that can't through one of our many charitable foundations."

Stuart nodded approvingly. "That's very generous."

Azzie continued. "Thank you. There is more. In addition to the formation of Perfect Imperfections, I am pleased to announce the acquisition of a controlling interest in Krenshaw Medical Center. I plan to construct a new wing dedicated to the research and treatment of disfigurement of all causes. Birth, trauma, and surgeries, there is no limit to what we will tackle. I plan to staff 'The Stevens Institute for Perfect Imperfections with the best talent the world has to offer. The Institute will be named after Johnson Stevens, a dear friend who perished while trying to save us from the helicopter crash."

I noticed on the ticker that EE had resumed trading. It was at 75 up 15 points. Azzie was crushing the short sellers. Then she went for the throat.

"I am further announcing a Dutch auction to purchase 20 million shares of Exquisite Evolutions for between 100 and 120. That will give me a 58% controlling interest in the stock."

As Joe would say, "boom, boom, boom". The stock rose to 95. After Azzie signed off, Stu reported that Going Down Partners was short 10,000,000 shares. They specialized in short selling. They drove many companies into the ground. Not EE, not Azzie Huggins, not today. Going Down was going down. They lost $250 million in less than ½ hour.

Sometimes, when you mess with the bull, you get the horn. I so much wanted to phone home, but I went to lunch instead. I would make my call to Dan tomorrow during the field trip.

### Fired Up Farms

Father Jonathan wasn't having any luck figuring out who might be behind this mess. Dan asked him to return a call to Angela. He explained to Father Jonathan that Angela was a physician friend of mine who was currently running the Krenshaw emergency department.

"Hello Angela, this is Father Jonathan."

"Father, thanks for returning my call. ZZ speaks so highly of you. It's hard to believe a deadbeat like him would pal around with a priest."

Father Jonathan chuckled. "With the trouble he gets into, he needs the pope."

This was Angela's turn to chuckle. Then, she got down to business. "I don't know if this means anything, and please be careful how you use the information. I should not be sharing, if you know what I mean."

Father Jonathan reassured her, "I think we wrote the book careful."

"Good. Buster Hyman, I mean Dr. Hyman, just passed away. As you may know, he was a profound alcoholic. He went into cardiac arrest during treatment for delirium tremens (DT's), and I couldn't save him. I was reading his chart before I entered my code note, and I saw that he was admitted yesterday. He was in full-blown DTs with both visual and auditory hallucinations. He was picking bugs off the wall, etc. But in between hallucinations, he would come out with a sentence or two that was close to coherent. He kept talking about Penelope Bradshaw's vagina."

"Her vagina?"

"Yes, and how it was as big as her big mouth."

"That's odd, any idea what he meant?"

"No, I have no idea what the significance was. He was a gynecologist, but it still didn't make sense. Anyway, he also said, 'Before wrecking the hospital and Zander,' and then he laughed that 'Penelope would spill the beans.'"

Father Jonathan asked a few more questions.

Angela answered as best as she could. "No, nothing else makes any sense, as if that does? That is what the ICU nurse wrote on night shift. I thought you should know."

"Thank you, Angela. We will put it in the brain trust blender and see what we come up with."

"Please get ZZ acquitted. We need him!"

JDJD, Dan, and Joe reviewed the information that Alphonse had sent via courier. The news was not good. I checked everyone in and took two keycards for each. I was to distribute them at dinner. Most of the attendees were placed in twos in each room. Anne Marie, the alleged victim, had her own room. There were an odd number of attendees, so someone had to be alone. But it was still suspicious that she drew the short straw.

Most of the tapes that Alphonse had were from the casino, and from dinner. They didn't show much. I was easy to spot. I was wearing a bright blue Hawaiian shirt. I did seem to dance a little longer and little closer with Anne Marie than some of the other women. But we were far from appearing like we had hooked up.

The most damming tapes were from the hallway outside of my and Billie's room. The first thing that was obvious was that Billie and I were shit-faced. We both stumbled as we went down the hall. Eventually, we made it to our room. I struggled to use the keycard to get into the room, but I finally got access. We staggered into the room, and the door closed.

A few minutes later Anne Marie appeared on the video. She, too, was in bad shape. She was practically being carried down the hall by two ER nurses. They deposited her into her room and went across the hall to their own room.

Thirty minutes later, just as Billie said, I, wearing the same blue Hawaiian shirt, exited my room and wobbled down the hall. I pulled out a room key and let myself into Anne Marie's room. I exited 25 minutes later and returned to my room.

JDJD shook her head. Those tapes fit exactly with what Anne Marie and Billie told the police. Anne Marie had almost no recall of going back to her room. She did not say that she knew for sure that I had raped her. She couldn't even say with any certainty that I was even in her room. She said she woke up with no pants or underwear on, and her bra was opened with her shirt but not off.

The nurses confirmed that they did not remove any of her clothes, and they did not feel that she could have removed them. Anne Marie reported that she felt "wet and sticky down there", meaning her vaginal area. So, she went to the ER and asked for a rape kit. It did confirm the presence of semen.

Dan responded, "OK, maybe ZZ did have sex with her. There is no evidence that it was not consensual."

JDJD replied, "No irrefutable evidence, but there is some evidence."

Dan was impatient. "Go on."

"The nurses told the police that ZZ came on to Anne Marie in the lounge before the party broke up."

Dan was in defense mode. "Still nothing there to suggest she didn't consent."

"True, but Anne Marie told one of the nurses about it. Apparently, Anne Marie always had a thing for ZZ, but out of respect for her friend Bella, she kept her distance. So, she turned ZZ down."

"That's pretty thin."

"Yes, Dan, thin. But we can't find anyone to say that she invited ZZ in, came on to him, or otherwise encouraged him. She wakes up mostly naked with semen in her vagina. There is visual evidence that ZZ entered her room with his own key. Juries have convicted on less."

# Chapter 82

## *The Giraffe Says*

## *Hershey, PA*

I always liked field trips in high school. A day out of class, and sometimes they were even fun. On the seventh day at Serenity Reincarnations, the class goes to The Giraffe Says. It's a bar built around bar jokes. In their case, the cocktail napkins say it all. It shows a giraffe at the bar addressing his animal friends. "The high balls are on me."

Now, this field trip was a little different. We were in a bar at happy hour, but we were not supposed to drink. We had to spend two hours there with all the temptations possible. Beer nuts, pretzels, sports shows, pinball machines, cornhole, and cheap drinks were readily available from scantily clad waitresses. The second hour was even more difficult because all drinks were free.

Two of the weaker members of the class bellied up to the bar shortly after arrival. No attempt was made to stop them. It was felt that if they were still weak after seven days of therapy, they were not likely to succeed. That smelled to me for two reasons. First, if they washed out, they forfeited their $10,000. That was a nice way to add to the bottom line for Serenity Reincarnations. Second, by letting some of the most likely to fail residents leave before completing the program, Serenity increased their success rate. A success rate that was advertised heavily but was based only on those who completed the ten-day program. What a scam. It was a good thing I wasn't really trying to beat an alcohol problem.

Being in the bar didn't faze me because I was faking my addiction. I did use the time out of the program to my best advantage. I brought my burner phone and made my way to the men's restroom. I knew I could get the privacy I needed there. I turned on the water in case there were ears near the door.

Dan answered on the third ring. "ZZ, are you OK?"

"I'm fine. I got a message to go dark, and I did. What's up?"

"I am going to put you on speaker. I am here with Father Jonathan and JDJD."

That was ominous. "Oh wow, I must be in deep shit if JDJD is on the case. Before you give me the good news, Father Jonathan I am sorry to have split on you."

Father Jonathan accepted the apology. "I totally understand. Given what I know now, I think it was the right move."

JDJD took over. "ZZ, you are right. You are suspected of having raped Anne Marie last week in Atlantic City."

JDJD just jumped right in, didn't she? No "how are you" or other small talk. Just bang! At least I knew what the hullaballoo was about.

I had to confess. "I wish I could tell you that I didn't do it. I know I wouldn't force a woman to have sex with me, but I remember very little about that night. After dinner, the next thing I remember clearly was finding Billie's note."

JDJD dug in. "I need to ask you about the note that Father Jonathan gave to you. I don't want to know what it said, but I take it that the note advised you to go dark."

"Something like that."

JDJD kept peeling the onion. "Where are you?"

"Should I say?"

JDJD explained that we had bought the time that we needed. In her opinion I should come home and turn myself in. She felt that any further delay in my appearance might be detrimental to our case.

I agreed. "I'm in Hershey, PA, at an alcohol abuse program. I demanded anonymity, and I'm pretty sure I got it."

JDJD was impressed. "Great place to drop out of sight! Plus, we can use that in our defense. You voluntarily sought help for an alcohol problem. I can use that. Head for home. I will arrange for you to turn yourself in tomorrow for DNA testing."

I exited the bathroom and headed to the bar. I had two beers, tipped the bartender $5 and waved goodbye to the shocked counselors. I had to leave, and why not get a couple of free beers to celebrate. I rented a car and was safely home in three hours.

**Fired Up Farms**

The following morning, JDJD and Dan ran down the charges and discussed the evidence. JDJD was adamant. Under no circumstances do I say or imply that I ever saw the tapes.

I didn't remember that I had visited her room, but the tape was clear. I did. Or someone that looked like me did. That was a pleasant thought while it lasted. But whoever returned to my room after I did or didn't do the deed looked up in the direction of the camera. The scar was unmistakable. I had gone out for a walk, and I might have just walked myself into prison!

We took a break from the evidence rundown for a group meeting that had been planned. Father Jonathan asked the group what they thought about Dr. Hyman's delirium rantings.

Joe laughed. "I am having a hard time getting past Penelope Bradshaw having a big mouth and vagina."

I added, "He probably heard an echo during a pelvic exam."

Azzie shook her head. "You might have thirty years to figure out the riddle. For now, can you boys grow up, so we get past Penelope Bradshaw's cavernous vagina?"

Joe accepted the dressing down and continued his analysis. "Before wrecking the hospital and Zander." So, what happened in the hospital before that started to happen? No one had a clue.

He continued, "Penelope would spill the beans." That tells me that Hyman knew that Penelope had some information, information that might help us.

Everyone nodded, and then Stephanie jumped into the discussion.

"Let's grab that big twatted bitch and see what she has to say."

Joe laughed. "Something like that Stephanie. Something like that."

# Chapter 83

## *Aldo's Office*

## *Krenshaw, NJ*

"Hey, Grandpa."

"Guiseppe, how the hell are you?"

"I'm doing ok. Walking a little better every day, and the employee I have down south has returned to full duty." Aldo laughed when he figured out what that meant.

Aldo was pleased. "Good Guiseppe, good. How's Azzie doing? I made a nice score on her stock when it shot up. Thanks for the tip!"

"Don't mention it. I mean that literally; don't mention it. The Securities and Exchange Commission is nosing around."

Aldo laughed. "Yeah, they already called me. But over the years, I have been in and out of that stock more times than you have been in and out of Azzie's pants. They had no case, and they walked away."

Joe whistled. "I should have known better. Thanks for getting word to ZZ to go dark; that really helped him. Can I ask one more favor?"

"Sure."

"We have someone that may have valuable information for us. She is unlikely to want to cooperate. Can you swing a South American organ donation?"

Aldo laughed. "Name, address and what do you want to know?"

"Penelope Bradshaw......."

## Ajax Trucking Storage Facility

### Carnation, NJ

Not a single photon penetrated the room. That's why it was so special now. Penelope Bradshaw sat handcuffed to a chair. Her eyes were bandaged shut. Aldo's men knew exactly what to say in heavy South American accents.

"Ha, ha, society bitch. We gonna remove those cuffs. Then you gonna pull down those dressings. And guess what? You will see what you do now. Nada, nothing." They both laughed.

Penelope gasped but did not speak. They continued.

"You see, Mrs. Bradshaw, you are a generous woman. You have donated your eyes to people who need them."

They then removed the cuffs. Penelope quickly pulled off the bandages and saw exactly nothing. She started to cry.

"Yes, we removed your eyes. We put some silicon balls in there for effect, but what you are rubbing sees nothing. You can still cry, though. Many people get along well blind. So will you. But you may not get along so well without your kidneys."

She whimpered.

"Oh yes. They are next. Both of them. Then, a few days after that, your heart, lungs, and liver. Your tissue type is in great demand."

"What about me?" Penelope sobbed.

"Chu lose, gringa bitch! You will die. Asshole, we are harvesting your organs. Do you not want to be harvested? Think of the lives you will save."

"I don't want to die."

"Then talk."

She screamed, "What? Anything you want!"

"What do you know about the bad things happening at Krenshaw Medical Center?"

Penelope couldn't talk fast enough. "Roy Bator and Sam Hyman talked me into joining them to wreck the hospital. My sister Elvira chipped in because she wanted to ruin harness racing."

One of the men sat down in front of her. Of course, she could not see him in the pitch-black room.

"How would they do this?"

Penelope continued her verbal diarrhea. "All I know is Roy Bator said a guy called Before could help us. That's his name, Before. Roy had used him to get his wife to commit suicide."

"What was Mr. Before to do?"

"We didn't know any specifics. Before was to ruin the hospital and Dr. Zander. And he was to make sure that Zander's friends and family didn't help him out. But we had no idea as to how or when."

They got no more useful information from her. She was drugged, taken to the city square and handcuffed naked to a flagpole.

The news broadcaster had to fight off a giggle.

"In a bizarre turn of events, socialite Penelope Bradshaw was found naked, handcuffed to the Krenshaw flagpole today. Neither she nor the Krenshaw police would comment.

**Fired Up Farms**

Father Jonathan decided to be inventive. Searches for Before were coming up empty. That's all Aldo's boys gave him. The dude's name was Before. They had not thought to ask Penelope how it was spelled. He tried every iteration of the spelling that he could think of. No luck.

He moved to the dark web and started again. He tried Bee Four, Be four, Bee Fore, and Bea four no luck. He sat and stared at his computer.

Then out of desperation he typed B4 like a number in a bingo game. Bingo, it was.

"B4 can do clandestine psyche ops to get the desired result."

# Chapter 84

## *Atlantic City Police Station*

I turned myself in right on time. They fingerprinted me and collected saliva samples for DNA. They must not have found any foreign pubic hair on Anne Marie, or they would have combed and plucked some of mine. I had to surrender my passport and promise not to leave Jersey, but otherwise, I was free.

We proceeded immediately to arraignment where I plead not guilty. We weren't permitted to present much of a defense today. But we were able to get a timely preliminary in three weeks.

JDJD probed me on the way back to Krenshaw. "If that's not your DNA in Anne Marie's hoo-ha, you are off the hook. Will it be yours?"

"I hope not."

"That's not very encouraging. If it is yours, how could it have gotten there?"

"I guess we must have had sex."

"Can I get a little thought out of your sorry ass? If you didn't put it there, how could it have gotten there?"

"I don't know."

"Think. Who else have you screwed in the past few months?"

I wanted to give her a big list, but it was small. "Bella, Juicy Lucy and maybe Anne Marie."

"How often did you connect with Bella? I guess actually Sarah?"

I blushed. "C'mon JDJD, this is personal."

"Not half as personal as what you are going to get asked in court and one-tenth as personal as when Bubba decides you are his butt muffin for the next twenty years. Talk to me."

"Ok, about every six weeks or so."

"What birth control did she use?"

"She was on the pill."

"Did you use any other birth control?"

"JDJD, I am embarrassed to talk about it."

She wasn't backing down. "Embarrassed is good. Your being bare-assed in a jail cell is not. Go on."

"Most of the time, no. But now that you mention it, the last time I had sex with her, she made me use a condom. She said she had a tooth infection and was on an antibiotic that her pharmacist said could inactivate her pills. She made me glove up."

"Where did you discard the used device?"

"In her bathroom waste can."

"So, you left it there?"

"Why not? Was I supposed to take it with me?" That seemed like a dumb question to me.

"Hmmmmmmmmmmmmmmm!!!!" was all she said in reply.

**Fired Up Farms**

I wasn't too surprised to learn that Buster and Old Lady Penelope Bradshaw had teamed up again. They had previously tried to wreck my career. It was also not too surprising that Master was calling the shots. That guy truly despised me. Maybe I shouldn't have made that crack about his diplomas. Some people just can't take a joke.

Father Jonathan wondered if Aldo could find some way to question Master, but Dan was not so sure that would accomplish much.

"He is not a simpleton like Hyman and Bradshaw. He might have paid for someone to create hell here, but I'm 99% certain he didn't do anything more than provide funding. If he's questioned and that's somehow linked to us, it would bolster his lawsuits. Unless we tie him to one of the Never Episodes, we should stay clear.

Azzie reviewed the data. "We have six episodes. Buster and Master caused the first two. Either ZZ mislabeled specimens, or the imposter lab tech caused the transfusion reaction. The last three, two skin breakdown issues and the death after a fall from the bed, were either caused by nursing negligence or a female nurse's aide imposter."

I was dejected as I gave my report. "We've had zero luck trying to locate the imposters. Security went over the tapes for a full month before the incident and for a few weeks after. Each imposter appeared on tape only on the day of the Never Episode. Not before and never again after."

Father Jonathan speculated, "Probably brought in from out of town and then sent packing."

Dan agreed. "That's possible."

Azzie continued, "With my investment, the hospital is financially stable for now. But these fines are astronomical. Security has to account for all employees they encounter. We need to restrict entrance and exit for all employees to one door. We need security there, and we need facial recognition software."

Joe politely challenged her. "Sweet cheeks, does that stuff really work? I know it does for my phone, but is it really that good?"

"Actually, Joe, that is the basis for Perfect Imperfections. A friend of mine is really into this. I asked her to modify a program for me. The software she made me magnifies a small section of a scar 100 times. We then use that to make a reverse template of the scar. With that we use a 3d printer to make a small layover for the area. We can make most scars much less noticeable."

"Even mine?" I asked.

"Even yours. But I am not so sure you want to. That scar is your trademark."

Joe added, "Forget it, ZZ. That scar is an improvement on your face."

I flipped him a Zander salute. Everyone laughed. Then it hit me.

"What if I was an imposter?"

"Meaning?" asked Azzie.

"What if someone made to look like me went into Anne Marie's room?"

Joe quickly replied, "Impossible!"

"Why?"

"There is only one Hawaiian shirt that ugly, and you had it on in the room."

# Chapter 85

## *Fired Up Farms*

JDJD watched the tapes, and watched the tapes, and watched the tapes from the hotel. Joe watched the tapes, and watched the tapes, and watched the tapes from the hotel. But they were focusing on the faces that they saw.

In a stroke of genius, Father Jonathan stumbled onto something, gait recognition. There was mounting evidence that people could alter their appearances, but most gaits were specific. Some experts felt that it might be superior to fingerprints. Father Jonathan made a few calls and was able to get a beta test of a gait recognition program. He ran it and nearly filled his drawers.

Both imposters at the hospital had the same gait. His heart was pounding as he hit the keystrokes necessary to analyze the hotel video. There was a 99.5% chance that the person in the hall at the hotel was the same as the imposters. Before he shared this with the group, he ran another comparison to a tape he had of me walking. There was a 0.1% chance that I was one of the imposters at the hospital or the person seen entering and exiting Anne Marie's room.

We all sat spellbound as we reviewed the tapes, with Father Jonathan's added analysis. The evidence was stunning.

I was convinced and relieved. "Well, that should get me off."

JDJD rained on my parade. "Don't get your hopes up."

I couldn't believe it. "What, that stuff is pretty conclusive!"

JDJD deflated my balloon. "But the science is still in its infancy. There is a good chance that the judge won't accept it."

Azzie shocked the group. "Then let's make sure she is as convinced as we are!" She shared her thoughts with the group. JDJD said nothing but made a ton of notes on her pad. I really hoped we could pull this off.

The next morning, no one ate much for breakfast. Mom was up early and cooked her brains out, but no one had much of an appetite. Stephanie interrupted the silence.

"ZZ, ok if I don't go today? Not feeling so good."

I kissed her on top of her head.

"No problem, Stephanie." I took her hand and put it on my head like a Vulcan Mind Meld. "I know you will be with me every step."

I then rubbed her belly and said, "You rest up and take care of my niece-to-be! Billie is still sleeping. He didn't get back from Ohio until 4 AM. He will be here if you need anything."

We piled into the van and started our trip. The hearing was to start at 9 AM. About an hour from the farm, I noticed Stephanie's phone in the console.

Stephanie cleaned up the kitchen and was on her way to her room to lie down. Father Jonathan's computer was still on. He had looped the videos he had, and they were still playing. He mentioned at breakfast that he was up all night getting ready for the hearing today.

Stephanie intuitively understood how gait recognition worked. She had done it for years. She could tell any horse that she had seen before by its gait on the track. It didn't matter what equipment they had on or who was driving them. She knew who it was.

That's what caused her to enter Father Jonathan's room. She thought she recognized the gait of a person in the video. She sat in front of the large screen and studied for a few moments. She knew who the lab imposter was. A few keystrokes later, she verified that the same person had impersonated me in Atlantic City.

She screamed, "fucking Billie, fucking Billie!"

She reached for her cell phone. She was shocked that it wasn't in her back pocket. She had to get word to the gang as soon as possible. She ran down the steps to get to the school; they had landlines there that she could use.

# Chapter 86

## *Municipal Courtroom 8*

## *Atlantic City, NJ*

There in the front spectator row of the courtroom, sat the asshole in a bright green bowtie. Master was in his glory. He would have paid a million to get here. Actually, his friends paid $15 million.

To start the proceedings, the state presented their evidence. That took about two hours. The tapes from the hotel were played numerous times. The prosecutor admitted that Anne Marie had no knowledge about what had occurred in her hotel room. She only remembered waking up almost naked and feeling wet and sticky in her vagina. He had statements from the nurses who took her to her room that they had laid her down on the bed, and she was fully clothed when they left.

The rape kit evidence showed semen in her vagina. The DNA analysis was 99.99999% certain that the little swimmers found there had come from me.

JDJD asked appropriate questions but, in the end, accepted most of the evidence. When she was able to mount a defense, she presented the information about gait analysis. The prosecutor, of course, objected. After some back and forth in the courtroom, the Judge called for a brief adjournment and ordered prosecution and defense teams into her chambers. A full-scale war erupted. In the end, the judge said that she would not bar the use of that information at the trial. However, she admonished JDJD that she had better line up some great expert witnesses to corroborate the validity of the gait analysis. The prosecutor licked her chops as they headed back to the courtroom.

When the hearing resumed, JDJD shocked everyone when she called me to the stand. Most defense attorneys don't have their clients testify, and certainly not at a preliminary hearing. She asked me a lot of background questions about how I knew Anne Marie. I had to testify about how often I saw her at the hospital and if I had ever made any advances toward her prior to the night in question. She asked me about that night. I did my best to answer her truthfully, but I had to admit that I didn't remember much because of the alcohol.

Although she had told me that she would ask me, I was shocked when the words came out of her mouth.

"Did you rape Anne Marie?"

"I did not rape her, but I may have had sex with her."

"May? May," she asked in a tone a prosecutor might use.

"How else would you explain the presence of your semen in her vagina?"

I had no answer.

The judge interrupted. She would not say it, but she was thinking that she had to stop JDJD. The judge felt that JDJD was burying me. She had seen defense attorneys deliberately blow cases in the past. It was an attempt to allow clients to claim poor representation and get a new trial if the first one went against them. This wasn't this judge's first rodeo.

"Does the counsel for the defense wish to offer any further testimony or object to evidence? If so, how long will it take."

JDJD slowly replied. "Yes, your honor. I will need another hour."

The judge nodded. "In that case, I am going to adjourn for lunch. Everyone, please be back at 1:30. Ms. Disimone, I want to see you in chambers."

The judge read JDJD the riot act. "I'm telling you now that I will fight like hell any attempt to have a new trial later based upon poor defense. You are burying your client, and I think you know it."

"Judge, I understand your concern. I'm sure that I will be able to clear up any misconceptions after lunch. I'm confident that you'll see that I'm vigorously defending my client."

Joe had rented a room at the Hampton Inn across from the restaurant. I left the restaurant first and hung out in the room. Azzie came in ten minutes later and went to work. I sat in the corner of the room and waited. JDJD was adamant. I was to be in the courtroom at 1:45, not one second earlier. I was to leave the room at 1:40. At 1:20, everyone else returned to the courtroom. Seconds seemed like hours as I waited.

**Fired Up Farms**

Stephanie pulled the front door open. The board made a sickening thud when it impacted her skull. That aroused Billie, who had swung the board. What a great day it was going to be. Stephanie almost ruined things. Fortunately, he was awake when she passed his room. He observed her watching the tapes on Father Jonathan's computer. She was so engrossed that she did not notice him.

Stephanie had amazed him over the years with her ability to identify horses by their gate. It was a natural extension to think she could do it with humans. When she screamed, he knew that he was busted, and it was time for his exit. He had just one score to settle. He then would don a fresh mask and put his plan into effect. That included taking an untraceable path to Central America. After some surgery there to alter his appearance for good, he would disappear to New Zealand and enjoy his $14 million.

He took the unconscious Stephanie out to the paddock that Rio normally occupied. It was empty because Stephanie planned on cutting it today. Rio was in the paddock next door. Bille looked in the direction of the school and the barn and luckily, he saw no one out.

He carried Stephanie to the picnic table, where he removed her clothes. Then he tied her arms to the top of the table and positioned her kneeling on the bench. He then secured her legs. Satisfied with his work, he splashed cold water on her face. It took two buckets, but she finally woke up. She fought her restraints but could not loosen them. He taunted her.

"Hey, you damn retard, are you awake yet? I ain't got all day." His stuttering had been miraculously cured.

She slowly turned her head around. "Billie, go fuck yourself. Let me loose!"

"Now listen here, you little slut. You know all along you wanted me. Why did you refuse me years ago? Then you insulted me when you hooked up with that black asshole, PC. That never made any sense to me. But it did make it a lot more fun when I watched him die when I wrecked that chopper."

Stephanie whimpered.

"Too bad he never got to appear on Dancing with the Stars. He would have easily won. I can still see him dancing around after he came into contact with a couple thousand volts. Talk about moves!"

Stephanie screamed at the top of her lungs. Billie got close to her head and yelled in her ear. He wanted her to know what was coming.

"Look, I am going to have my way with you. You owe me that. Wise up and don't resist. You will hurt a lot less, and I have a plane to catch. And to show you what a nice guy I am, I will not bother your baby. I'm approaching this mission from the back side, if you know what I mean."

Then he let out a hideous laugh. Loud and long. Just long enough and loud enough that he didn't hear hoofbeats approaching. Rio ran full steam at the fence. She had never jumped anything but shadows, but she cleared the four-foot fence with ease.

Billie had removed his shirt and dropped his pants. He was preparing to mount Stephanie when he heard a powerful snort. Startled, he turned around. Rio was right behind him. She reared up on her back legs and then came immediately back to earth. Her right front hoof slashed Billie's abdominal wall. It happened so fast that he felt no pain.

That was until he coughed. When he did, his intestines spurted out of his open abdomen. The pain and reality hit him at the same time. He tried in vain to stuff them back in, but the more he stuffed, the more they spilled. He screamed in pure agony.

Rio got into position and planted her feet. With all the speed and strength she could muster, she let her back left leg fly. That same leg had powered her to win millions of dollars and allowed her to set world trotting records. Her aim was true. Billie stopped screaming the second his head was detached from his disemboweled body. Blood spurted from his torso as it crumpled to the ground. His head flew at 50 mph into the barn wall. It banked off the wall and landed in the manure bin.

# Chapter 87

## *Municipal Courtroom 8*

## *Atlantic City, NJ*

At 1:30 PM, the judge reminded me that I was still under oath. I nodded and then continued to answer JDJD's questions. At exactly 1:40 PM, I exited the hotel and made my way to the courtroom. I entered the courtroom at 1:45 PM, right on cue. I walked over to the defense table and stood with JDJD and the other ZZ. The judge went apoplectic.

"What the hell is going on here?" she screamed as she pounded her gavel.

The courtroom erupted in shouts and screams. It took a full ten minutes to restore order.

"Ms. Disimone, you are in contempt. Explain yourself before they cart you off for a richly deserved night in jail."

JDJD said nothing. All eyes in the courtroom were focused on her and the two ZZs standing on either side of her. They were identical except for their height. Even with the lifts I had on, the other ZZ was still taller than me. The taller one on the left slowly removed her mask and then the ultra-thin white skin gloves covering her black hands. Azzie never looked more beautiful to me. With Azzie on JDJD's left and me on her right, the three of us faced a seriously pissed-off judge.

"I demand an explanation!" she screamed.

JDJD went on to explain that we had used artificial intelligence to make a double for me. We used AI of my voice patterns to allow Azzie to trigger responses to questions that JDJD had asked. Everyone in the courtroom thought that the person on the stand was me. But it wasn't me; the real me was still in the hotel at that time.

The judge then wanted to know who I was. "Zachary Zander," I said.

She made me approach the bench. She picked at the skin on my face. When she drew blood, she was satisfied that I wasn't a fake. After another ten minutes of bedlam, she cleared the courtroom except for the prosecutor, JDJD, me, and Azzie.

She allowed JDJD to present videos of Azzie and me entering the courthouse—Azzie at 1:25 PM and me at 1:40 PM We looked the same, and AI said it was 90% certain it was the same person. She then used the gait analyzer. It quickly surmised with 99.7% accuracy that the first ZZ had an exact match for the gait of Azzie Huggins. The second ZZ had a gait match for Zachary Zander.

The judge acquitted me without prejudice. The prosecutor was free to bring charges if they could explain why the artificial intelligence information couldn't be trusted. But believe me, everyone in that courtroom got a demonstration that they would never forget.

**Central Ave.**

**Atlantic City**

Master waited in the hallway until he heard the outcome of the hearing. He wanted to shout and scream in disgust, but he slowly and quietly made his way to his car. He sat there for quite a while, pondering his next move. He could just drive away and go somewhere else in the country to resume his life. But that would mean that he lost and that asshole Zander won. That was an outcome he could not tolerate.

Master watched as the impromptu news conference two blocks ahead on the courthouse steps broke up. The group headed down the sidewalk toward the van they had arrived in a few hours ago.

*Beautiful*, he thought as he peered through the binoculars. Zander is in front with his giant priest friend, followed by that Huggins bitch pushing the crippled Italian. The two attorneys and the Zander parents brought up the rear.

He carefully pulled the pin on the grenade but held the clip in place. He started up his lime green Corvette, which matched his bowtie. Father Jonathan and I reached the van first. He opened the passenger door, and the rest of the group lined up to help Joe into the van.

Master floored the Corvette and headed for the van. He knew the clip would detach from the grenade on impact. Anyone that survived the initial crash would be killed when the grenade went off. Adios scumbags.

The first bullet flattened the front left tire instantly, causing the vette to veer. The second bullet hit Master in the chest. He dropped the grenade as the vette hit the parked postal van. Three seconds later, his car was in thousands of small pieces as Master began his descent into hell.

I and the rest of the entourage ducked small chunks of fiberglass that rained down. I was shocked to see Father Jonathan standing in a shooting position. He had a gun aimed in the direction of the blast. Once the roll was taken and all were safe and accounted for, he lowered the weapon. Our trip home would be delayed for hours while the police evaluated this new crime scene. But at least everyone was ok.

"How did you know?" I asked Father Jonathan how he knew to grab the gun.

"I heard the Corvette whining and knew that it was too many revs for a city street. I also saw that prick Master get out of that Corvette this morning. I don't know how or why I put it together, but something told me to start shooting. I knew the gun was in the glove compartment."

I patted him on the back. "Thank God you did. He was coming right for us. What did you hit to explode the car? Those vette gas tanks are in the rear, aren't they?"

"I hit the tire, and I got one into the driver's side. I have no idea why the car exploded like it did."

# Chapter 88

## *Always Hope School*

Jenny signed off her computer at the school. She was late leaving, but she had finished her investigation. She was 4/4, and Billie was 0/4. He supposedly was out of town on four separate dates driving horses in stakes races. He had told her he won three and finished second in one. Pretty good. Except today, when she accessed the US Trotting website to verify his winnings, she saw that on all four occasions, Sammy Molinero was the driver of the horses that Billie usually drove. Billie "Cha-ching" Browner hadn't driven at any of the four tracks on the nights she checked.

Jenny was uber pissed. She was angry that we made her give up her gun. She wanted so badly to shoot Billie in the balls just like she did that liar Vuckovich in Florida. She located her tear gas spray in her purse and began the short walk to the house.

On her way, she pondered her past. Why did she have such bad luck with men? Why? Vuckovich was married, but he never told her. Billie was up to no good, and now she had the proof. The only guy who ever treated her well and with respect was ZZ, and she tried to kill him. Maybe she deserved her bad luck. There will be plenty of time to analyze this later after she makes Billie into a gelding.

She carefully entered the house and found her way to Billie's room. It was empty. She would search it thoroughly later. Maybe she could find out who he was cheating with. That bitch deserved a little grief. But first, she had to find Billie.

When she saw that his truck was parked outside, she figured he was likely in the barn. She made her way to the barn and found no one in there but hungry horses. It must have been near feeding time as ten heads sequentially appeared at stall doors as she traversed the barn.

When she arrived in the yard on the opposite side of the barn, she could not believe her eyes. Rio was standing guard in front of a naked woman on her knees tied to a picnic table. At Rio's feet was the headless, bloody torso of a disemboweled human body. Even though she had seen plenty of gore in the ER, she was close to vomiting. She stopped in her tracks and looked up as Stephanie shouted. "Jenny, Jenny!"

Rio stepped aside as Jenny quickly untied Stephanie. She spied a cooling blanket on the washing line and retrieved it to cover Stephanie.

Jenny was perplexed. "What the hell happened here? And who was that?" Jenny pointed at what was left of the corpse on the ground.

Stephanie sat on the picnic bench. Rio came over and nudged her. Stephanie rubbed Rio's head for a few seconds without saying a word. Jenny then noted a laceration on the back of Stephanie's head and examined it. By this time, the blood had clotted, but there was still considerable swelling around the wound.

"Stephanie, are you ok? How did your head get injured?"

"That crap on the ground is what's left of Billie. I am ok. I saw the tapes in Father Jonathan's room. I knew right away that Billie was the imposter by the way he walked. I couldn't find my cellphone and left the house to go to the school. I needed to call ZZ.

"Billie must have hit me on the head in the house. I woke up here naked, tied to the table. Billie told me he was going to butt hump me. He dropped his drawers as Rio jumped the fence. When Billie turned around, she reared and one of her front hoofs cut open his belly. His guts spewed out into the dirt. Then Rio lined up and kicked his fucking head off. It's over there in the shit bin."

Jenny walked over and there it was. Billie's head, with a stunned look in his dead eyes, sitting on a pile of manure. Jenny only wished that she had done it.

Stephanie refused to go to the hospital. Jenny first called the police, and then she called Celeste Maliterna. She was calling me as our van pulled in. I was terrified to see four Krenshaw police cars with their lights flashing.

I asked JDJD, “Are they here to arrest me again? The judge changed her mind pretty fast if that’s the case!”

We were directed to avoid the crime scene. I was thrilled that they weren’t there for me, so we adjourned to the house. We were filled in on the bizarre events that occurred while I put a few staples in Stephanie’s scalp laceration. She had taken a severe blow to the head. But other than the laceration, her exam was normal.

She refused to go to the hospital for a CT scan, which was par for the course. But she was speaking in mostly full sentences, and that was a very welcome change. When I finished, Celeste did her thing. She proclaimed the baby to be fine. What a day! What a day!

# Chapter 89

## *Fired Up Farms*

It took about two weeks for us to get our heads around what had occurred. Once the police got a hold of Billie's computer, things started to fall into place. I was really pissed when I found out that Billie's name on the dark web was B4.

"What an asshole I am!" I proclaimed to the group.

Joe added, "That's what Master always said." Everyone laughed.

"Ha ha." I continued. "I knew that Billie had called himself the Four B's. That was short for big balls Billie Browner. He must have modified that to B4."

Dan had something he wanted to show us. He asked, "ZZ and Azzie, did you know that Joe visited Bella?"

"Joe!" Azzie and I screamed at the same time.

Dan laughed. "Well, don't believe it, but here's the tape of Billie impersonating Joe visiting Bella. Sure, looks like Joe. But gait recognition software confirmed it was Billie. The police suspect that he conned Bella into having you wear a condom so he could get DNA evidence to use against you later.

"ZZ was told that Anne Marie won a cruise for two to Acapulco. The cruise was in Bella's (Sarah's) name. The police suspect that when Billie impersonated Joe, he convinced Bella to cooperate in return for the cruise. They also are pretty sure that they identified Billie impersonating a crew member on the cruise ship where Bella was killed. It is likely he murdered Bella to shut down any trace of a frame.

"Billie had a ton of information on his computer about the use of lasers in military situations, and the police found a receipt for some

RU486 that he had ordered. They feel strongly that he caused the helicopter crash and gave Rio the drug that caused her to abort.

"He was the lab imposter, and he was also the nurse's aide. Gait recognition of the person entering Anne Marie's room confirmed that it was Billie. The police suspect that he had ZZ's DNA in a syringe that he injected into Anne Marie's vagina. If he hadn't taken the time to try to pay Stephanie back for what he felt was a slight a few years ago, he might have gotten away with it all."

Joe proclaimed, "I always knew he was a shithead. It was a fitting final resting place in that manure bin."

Jenny shocked no one. "I would have found the bastard even if it took the rest of my life."

We all laughed a sigh of relief.

# Chapter 90

## *Miracle Mile Racetrack and Casino*

Millions week was a tremendous success. Every prominent name in harness racing was there. The top trainers, drivers, owners, and horses in the world showed up. The Dunstans had explained to everyone in the sport that harness racing was in danger. They convinced every harness track in the world to close for the week and for their best horses to come to Miracle Mile Racetrack and Casino. The biggest of the big harness horses were on display.

They raced 15 races a day, all week. In the evening they held yearling sales and racehorse auctions. In the last four days they had run the harness racing equivalent to the World Cup. Teams of four drivers from each country competed against each other. The racing was intense, and it was heavily bet. Wagering records were shattered. In addition to competition for trainers, drivers, and horses, there was also an announcer competition. Thirty prominent announcers from around the world went head-to-head. The winning announcer would announce the World Cup Trot in addition to pocketing $250,000. It was the last race of the meet. The purse was $25 million. Unheard of. Plus, the winner would likely determine the winner of the world cup.

The weather was perfect. Preston Tucker took his place at the announcer's window. "The Gold Caller", as he was known, eked out a win over a stellar performance by the announcer from Harrah's Philly, and a spirited effort by a Norwegian announcer. Preston held the program in both hands. The bottom of the program rested on numerous gold chains that hung from his neck. They were his trademark.

"Ladies and gentlemen. On behalf of Miracle Mile Racetrack and Casino and the world's greatest harness horsemen, drivers, and horses, I welcome you to our final race of an historic Millions Week. Five new world records were set, seven track records were shattered. Finally, a track handle that eclipsed all hopes and dreams marked this incredible week.

"Let us first take our hats off to the Dunstan Family for getting the ball rolling. And thanks to all our sponsors for their support. This week has clearly shown that harness racing can attract numerous new fans while reinventing the experience of older patrons.

It is my honor to call this race. An honor that I will never forget. This race is likely a race that will never be forgotten. In addition to the great horses, this race will decide the winning team in our World Harness Cup competition. Sweden and the United States are the last teams standing. Good luck to all."

I was a little nervous but not much. I was more nervous about the ad, and how it would be accepted, than about the race. The race was important, but I had been in hundreds of important races. I wanted to win, and I wanted my team to win, but I was worried that none of that would make a difference if the governor lost his race next week. Preston interrupted my thoughts.

"Here's the rundown for the big race. Team Sweden has the 1,3,5,7 holes. Team USA has the even number positions. Team Sweden is captained by Nils Swensen, a legend in the sport. Team USA is captained by Dave Dunstan of Hickory, PA. Davey and I go way back to our careers at the Meadows. He has had an amazing week."

Preston ran down the field. One of his best talents throughout his career had been to make even the most boring race of less than talented horses sound like the Hambletonian. He would have no need for that talent today. This race was plenty exciting. With all the hype, exotic wagering, and gambling interest throughout the world, it was likely that wagering of $50 million or more would get his best effort.

I felt like I was an Amish kid taking an old horse for a stroll on a deserted road. I had not a care in the world. After all, I just escaped a rape sentence, Stephanie was ok after her attack, and her baby was fine.

The Dying Was Easy gang was back in full swing. It was time to sit back and enjoy the sport I loved best.

Davey, who was normally talkative, was quiet. The man was focused, and that was great. Our team had spent hours planning our strategy. But that's the funny thing about racing. The plan might be great, but 75% of them never get put into action. Horses and people sometimes don't do what you expect them to do.

We turned to head to the starting gate. Fired Up Atom was a little excited. When he saw The Awesome Army at their customary position at the top of the stretch, I had to grab a little leather. I hope he reacts that way at the top of the stretch in the race.

Preston ran down the field for the last time. "The best trotters in the world are on their way to the starting line. From the rail out:

Hedda's Dream, piloted by Lykke Zetterberg.

Vortex is in the very capable hands of Sammy "The Hammy" Molinerno.

Sphincter of Oddi driven by Team Sweden captain, Nils Svenson.

You Are A Duster with Team USA captain David Dunstan in the sulky.

Sumptuous has the services of Isak Fredlund.

Number six is Berry Picker, driven today by Drew Kettering.

Exothermic is being guided by veteran champion Theodor Kjellberg.

On the outside looking in is Fired Up Atom with Zachary "ZZ" Zander at the helm.

"They round the turn and head for the start line. It's post time, and yabba dabba do; they are off and trotting. Sphincter Of Oddi blasts out of the three hole and easily grabs the front. Vortex also left smartly and falls into the two-hole. Hedda's Dream is third at the pylons, two lengths behind Vortex. Drew Kettering, who was hung on the outside with Berry Picker, picks his spot and slides into the three-hole in front of Hedda's Dream. Exothermic is hung 4th on the outside with no place to hide or duck. Sumptuous is trotting 6th. You Are A Duster is eating plenty of dust at 7th. Fired Up Atom races 8th."

I had no intention of leaving the gate. Atom had great closing speed but couldn't leave worth a lick. I really thought Davey would put Duster on the engine, but when I saw how easily and quickly Sphincter got out of there, I knew why he didn't. I had a fleeting thought of pulling the earplugs on Atom and sending him to the front for all he was worth. That was a bold move that had won me many races. Not today. Those Swedes came to race, and when they did that there was no pulling back. I knew that Svenson would be rolling Sphincter without looking back. Going to the front now would be racing suicide.

The Gold Caller's announcing again grabbed my attention.

"They are in single file as they pass the ¼ pole. First quarter in 25.3. These trotters are stepping. They are in straight alignment down the stretch. No one has yet to make a move on Sphincter."

I figured to sit tight until the half and then try to work something out. Dave Dunstan had different plans as called by Preston.

"Team Captain Dave Dunstan pulls aggressively from the seven hole, and Duster gets into gear."

I knew I had to follow him. That wasn't our original plan, but he was rolling, and I was going with him, for better or worse.

"Duster is followed by Fired Up Atom. This backfield is in motion. They reach the half in 51.2, the second quarter in 25.4. They are smokin'!" Preston was going nuts.

"That's Sphincter of Oddi on the engine. Vortex is second and getting the trip of his life. Drew Kettering makes an aggressive move as they race down the backside. He is first up and now in second. Hedda's Dream stays at the pylons. Sumptuous is second over behind Berry Picker."

There was one hell of a traffic jam in front of us. Luckily, I was following Davey, and he had to figure things out. Davey surveyed what was ahead of him. No guts, no glory. He veered to the outside, pulled the plugs on Duster and sent him flying. I did not expect that so I might have been a little slow to react, but I woke up in time to get Atom to follow Davey to the outside.

The Gold Caller was in overdrive. "Three wide and firing on all cylinders are You Are A Duster and Dave Dunstan. Tied to his helmet is Fired Up Atom with ZZ Zander, also three wide. Three quarters in 118.3. That's a world record on any track. That's Sphincter of Oddi leading, Vortex on his helmet, Berry Picker first over, and Hedda's Dream second over. You Are A Duster is gaining three wide. Fired up, Atom is right on Davey's helmet. Farther back are Sumptous and Exothermic but well within striking distance."

I had a good feeling. I had a ton of horse in front of me, and he loved the stretch.

"And here they all come. Move The Army and clubhouse. They are coming six wide!" Preston was animated.

I fanned out to get a clear run down the lane. Atom looked to the outside at the cataplectic Army, and he broke stride.

"That's Fired Up Atom off stride" screamed Preston. "Sphincter of Oddi with a narrow lead. Vortex slides into the lightning lane. You Are A Duster is rolling on the outside. Sphincter tires, Vortex and Duster, are battling down the lane. Their legs are flying faster than all the rest. This is history in the making!.

Here's the wire. I can't tell them apart. Look at the timer! Mile in 144.4. A new all-world record for trotters. Hold all tickets. We have a photo finish."

I got Atom back on the trot, but we finished last. I had no idea who had won, but I knew that Davey was in it. I turned Atom around to the paddock entrance as I heard Preston announce.

"Ladies and Gentlemen, while the judges sort this one out, we have a final word from one of our sponsors."

The screen in the infield, all tv screens at the track and at home went dark. With no sound, the following message was typed on the screen in bright pink ink on a black background:

"Azzie Huggins, CEO of Exquisite Evolutions and Perfect Imperfections, proudly presents the following."

I knew what was coming, but it still shocked me. It was the picture. The one of the governor defecating on my lawn. His face was clear, and his position was what one would have to assume to do the deed. His private parts were tastefully blurred. In large, bold, bright pink lettering, characteristic of Exquisite Evolutions, were the words:

"VOTE FOR TERRY. HE GIVES A SHIT!" Then his voice added with a laugh. "This is Terry Carrington, and I approve this message."

That Azzie was too much. Maybe she was too much. What a bold move. "The picture" that everyone said would bury Terry was right in front of me. Nothing like a good offense.

Davey won the race with You Are A Duster in a world record time. We narrowly won the driving championship, but harness racing won everything.

# Epilogue

## *News 7 Krenshaw*

The analysts were incredulous. "In one of the most contentious and unusual elections of the century, our statisticians are prepared to declare that Governor Terry Carrington has won reelection in New Jersey. Initial indications are that he will prevail in a landslide and may capture both houses of the New Jersey legislature.

At the start of this campaign, the governor had good approval ratings. His opponent capitalized on the governor's development of diarrhea caused by food poisoning at a wedding. She led in the polls until a week ago. One of her main campaign promises was to shift casino subsidies for harness racing to fund education. She also vowed to allow the state to expand thoroughbred racing.

There is little doubt that the election was won with a late ad paid for by the CEO of Exquisite Evolutions. The ad was a little unorthodox but incredibly effective. It ran only once as a paid ad. But it got so much social media attention that it was viewed millions of times. Then we in the media covered it extensively, giving it even more exposure.

That ad, coupled with the incredible success of Millions Week, swayed many voters to back the governor for reelection and, with him, harness racing.

On a sad note, Socialite and financial wizard Elvira Bradshaw committed suicide tonight. According to preliminary reports, she jumped from her 50$^{th}$-story apartment to her death. It was well-known that she had recently made a large, short investment in Miracle Mile Racetrack and Casino that backfired when the stock exploded to the upside today. "Elvira Bradshaw dead at the age of 67."

## Fired Up Farms

Celeste was pleased when Dr. Rosen had discharged Stephanie. He felt that the trauma at the barn likely evoked enough of a response that she came out of her trance. She was eating normally and speaking reasonably well. He still wanted her to have ongoing counseling, but he did not feel he needed to see her further. And to everyone's delight, he felt that she no longer needed ECT.

Celeste was happy not to have to deliver a patient who was catatonic. But that didn't mean she was ecstatic with the latest turn of events. I had never known Celeste Maliterna to be frazzled during a delivery, but she was for this one. Maybe because this delivery was quite different from the thousands that she had performed, I clearly heard her proclaim, "I must be out of my damn mind for agreeing to this."

Stephanie pawed the straw in the stall as she danced around. On more than one occasion, her external fetal monitor came off. Celeste decided to place an internal one. She needed good tracings to feel just half comfortable with this nutty scheme. I did my best not to laugh. I had been dealing with Stephanie for a long time and had gotten used to her quirks. Celeste was just getting started. She wasn't thrilled when Stephanie wanted a home delivery, but she relented.

She protested vigorously when Stephanie proclaimed that she was delivering in the birthing barn where our broodmares delivered their foals. Celeste did protestith, and Celeste did loseith, and here we are.

Celeste and I tried to cut our losses and to prepare for most eventualities. The feed room at the end of the barn had been set up for delivery, resuscitation, or both. Out of Stephanie's sight, Amos and his crew were idling in their ambulance in case anyone needed a means of emergency transport.

The world's biggest doula, Rio, stood at Stephanie's head and licked the perspiration off her face. Mom held her hand. Father Jonathan, Dad, Joe, Azzie, and Jenny prayed silently in the courtyard. The entire Awesome Army sat quietly in the grass. At 11:42 PM, their silence was interrupted by a sharp cry when Pea Sea Rio Zander-Stevens entered the world.

www.ingramcontent.com/pod-product-compliance
Lightning Source LLC
Chambersburg PA
CBHW070642310726
48982CB00001B/384

* 9 7 9 8 9 9 1 5 1 5 7 5 7 *